Farrisford

by S.T. Fielder

*Dedicated to the memory of **Tony Herbert**, **Barbara Montgomery** and their son **James Herbert**, who, aged 25, suffered a heart attack after being detained 11 minutes by a Police Community Support Officer who enlisted men from a pub to put him in a police van. James was never seen alive again. He had offered no resistance nor committed a crime.*

Chapter 1

ON A BRIGHT April Sunday, Farrisford wakes. Dawn rises on misty fields, farms stir, rooks caw, crocuses line the banks of the Brate through woods by the Yenton council estate. The river emerges fast by The Lugworm, where upstairs, Annette sits up in bed, giddy. Stuart snores like a stretched-out hog beside her.

Annette reaches for her phone – yes!! a message: *Sorry for delay, darling, here they are.* She clicks Download All, waits for photographs, reads:

Dear darling, I miss you so. Here are new pictures of Morris. I love you with all my heart. Dewy

24 pictures! 1. Morris on the lawn in sunshine. Aww! 2. Near the tupelo tree, paw raised, sniffing the air. *Ahh!* 3. On the sofa, look! With his cushion!!

Morris, a Boston Terrier, hardy and independent, will be nine soon. 14 dogs attend his birthday parties. Morris is home in Massachusetts. Annette's in Devon, England, pining.

Annette has a Civil Engineering doctorate. She is Dr Annette Stephens. Few people know, for Annette talks mostly about how wonderful and curious the world is, smiling as she speaks. Asperger's recurs in a side of her family. Annette maybe has a form of it, but most people think she's on drugs. She teaches part-time at Exeter University, researches climate-change technology there and works in The Lugworm's kitchen for free lodging.

Stuart snores louder and scratches himself. He is argumentative, 20 stone, locally-raised and likes computer war games. In the pub-restaurant's kitchen he wears a baseball cap backwards and a T-shirt saying Vagitarian. He drags bins outside, crashes pans into sinks for Annette to clean and operates a plate-wash machine that clattered and flooded for years until Annette fixed it.

Annette's unsure why Stuart's in her bed again, fifth time in six months, third man she's ever had sex with (to Dewy's 12 men and at least 60 women). Staff drinks late Saturday nights continue upstairs, where Stuart latches onto Annette because she never dislikes anyone. She doesn't know how to.

But gazing now on Stuart's gurgling head, Annette decides no more experimentation with men.

"Dewy's right, Booboo," she whispers to the Morris screensaver: "She and I prefer girls and always did. I don't want a man, I want *her*. I wish me and Dewy were close again."

Annette is pregnant. She doesn't know.

7AM'S LIKE NOON, the sun's so strong. Marlon Wright and his foster dad John are up at the coast already, 28 miles away. Six foot two at 19, Marlon trains by walking fast on shoreline sand towards the sun. Alone in blinding rays, the sun retreats as it watches him, like Dave the physio does.

74-year-old Mr Wright surveys the pale, still sea. Marlon had said: "Use my smartphone, Dad". John will look up the Mail On Sunday in a bit. Farrisford Tattler too, if not too many pop-up ads.

Marlon slows his pace. He breathes deeply. *Every day, in every way, I'm getting better.* He breathes in, nervous. Tuesday week is on his mind…

IN THE TOWN, Tesco Metro and Caffe Nero are early-open, while Spillet's newsagent opens pre-dawn, seven days.

Near Cressy Bridge, John Talbot beeps a wall-pad to de-alarm Asda. It will open at nine, as does Farrisford Organics, whose staff are in glum and early for Sunday stock-take.

Leading off The Swainway is Green Street. Along from the Post Office, a shop, Kitchens Now, occupies old, traditional premises on the corner with Wolf's Lane. In its marble, recessed doorway, Annie Cameron lies in a sleeping-bag. Her first night in Farrisford was safe. She sleeps in peace, warm at last.

Released from a two-year sentence for house-breaking, Ayrshire-born Annie, 24, walked south for weeks. She'd forgotten people often pointed at her red curls and bawled "Orphan Annie". In Exeter, Romani women showed cash earned fruit-picking: "*Farrisford.*" Annie can't read, but knew *Fa* meant F. She'd head to where the women pointed until a town beginning F.

Early sun on Wolf's Lane windows, a row of gold mirrors. Annie wakes, packs her rucksack, heads to the centre, sees a dark-sandstone, large hotel in Market Street, yellow sign, three stars. "Ask for kitchen work. Ask everywhere, gottae be casual work? Even a live-in? A *bedroom…*"

LUGWORM MANAGER DOUGLAS Fent is first downstairs. Balding, lean, tattooed and tall, he flings back doors open, switches ovens on, bangs metal bins, chucks cutlery into steel troughs, drops a cup (or throws it?) *kplshh!*

The landline shrieks in the empty main bar. Fent eventually answers:

"Yeah? Speaking… *Yup*. Yup. Cool. Bring it on. Yup. Ciao."

Delivery company call. Brewery, butcher, farm or fishmonger. The Lugworm has daily deliveries, dry rot, old equipment, cask beers running out, rising prices, clueless area managers and a rain-pond with a plimsoll in it on the flat kitchen roof. Fent monitors this pond from "where that stoned American girl kips". Meaning he goes in Annette's room at will.

The Lugworm: Douglas Fent, 35, commander. Under him, in order:

Head Chef: Beverley Dawes, 40, from Worcester, England.

Chef: Tommy Rourke, 38, London.

Sous Chef: TBA (Adam Marshall quit last week).

Trainee Sous (Tue-Thu) Martin Davidson, 16, Loddleford.

Kitchen Assistant: Stuart Bunkle, 24, Farrisford.

Kitchen Assistant (Fri-Sun) Dr Annette Stephens, 26, near Newburyport, Massachusetts, USA, via University of Exeter.

Bar managers: Bernadette Dodds, 46, Farrisford, Douglas Fent, 35, "Been around, lived all over. I'm about journeys, not places."

Bar/restaurant rota: Kate Tcatz 24, Jon King, 21, Karen Lilly, 20, Millie Zena, 18, all Farrisford, except Karen Lilly, Cressy.

Mr Fent is in love with Beverley Dawes.

Beverley Dawes is in love with Annette.

Mr Fent can't show or declare his love and is privately unhappy.

No one knows Beverley likes women, loves Annette, and how the Stuart Bunkle-Annette affair has nearly destroyed her.

Breaking news, 11am: Stuart Bunkle has quit. No explanation. No farewells. Gone. The remaining Kitchen Assistant will struggle. Yesterday was The Lugworm's busiest day for years. The weather forecast says today's hotter. Annette arrives in the kitchen to work, cheerful but pale.

"Be early, it'll be rammed in this weather," tweet Lugworm Sunday lunch regulars. Beer-garden and bars are crowded already. Douglas Fent barges outside to gather coffee cups. A stack on a table falls and smashes. Fent marches out to Keeley Lane, to be alone a moment. It's sunny and deserted but for a drifter girl with red curls approaching in heat-haze. Fent doesn't really see her until she stops at the pub and says:

"Excuse me, d'ye work here?"

"Why?" barks Fent.

"Is it possible to see the manager, please?"

"Why?"

"I'll discuss that wi' the manager."

"I *am* the manager."

"Got any kitchen work, please?"

"No. Uh… *No*. Worked in a kitchen before?"

"Aye, I've an NVQ practical in food prep, and –"

"No. Actually *yeah*, hurry up." Fent leads her to the kitchen, gives her a form to fill in and vanishes. Annie leans on a work-surface to slowly write her name.

A dreaming, handsome girl with bunches softly halves a lettuce. Seeing Annie, she beautifully smiles: "How lovely your curls are!" says a healing, American voice. "Oh, you're *so* lovely to see."

"Er. Cheers." Annie blushes.

Beverley, harangued by Tommy, rushes to Annette: "How you getting on?"

"I love the crunch of a knife through wet lettuce-core!" beams Annette.

"Okaay, thanks for making a start on that one, love," says Beverley: "Would you mind washing-up again?"

"Of course," nods Annette. "Nice to meet you, Annie."

Beverley starts chopping lettuces fast. Annie says:

"Let me do that? I'll go wash my hands."

Soon, Beverley and Tommy approve of Annie. On

finishing a task, she helps Annette briskly, until called to make gravy, stir sauces or drain boiling pans. An ex-police officer, Beverley instantly read Annie's old Converse and floppy cardigan over T-shirt with holes: homeless. She hoped Annie might be offered a live-in, but Douglas Fent had crammed old furniture to the ceiling of the last spare bedroom.

Annie's back at the sinks, drying slippery floor with a dish-towel under her foot where Annette stands. Her instinct to protect Annette wins Beverley over more. Suddenly Beverley runs: "All right, love?"

Annette, held by Annie, is sick into a bin.

"Drinka watter?" says Annie. She turns up a tap, lets it run, fills a cup fast.

"Go lie down, Annette?" says Beverley. "We're OK here, now that we've got…" She turns to Annie: "Sorry, don't know your name? I'm Beverley."

Annie and Beverley eye each other.

She's a cop says a voice in Annie's head.

You've got previous, haven't you? says one in Beverley's.

CATHERINE WREN STOPS on the *Tattler* stairs, holds the banister, catches her breath. Sundays alone in the office are her choice. In peace she can lay out 64 pages, write headlines, sub-edit copy and e-mail updates to Geoff Carruthers, Malcolm Zane and photo editor Stephen Ellis. Catherine is the only woman to work full-time in the paper's 224 years.

Editor Geoff Carruthers keeps overlooking Catherine is now nine months pregnant. She reminds him each day to find maternity cover. Has he amnesia?

But in the office the paper is everything. This week's front page: the bankrupt Bettle to Moresby bypass works. An open letter to the local MP from Bettle Parish Council will fill most of page three. Catherine sighs. Sure enough, in her in-tray, a thick envelope:

From Bettle (Prsh Council) For: G. Carruthers
URGENT

Has no one in Bettle heard of e-mailing letters? Catherine must now type up the handwritten copy. Next week a longer, worse letter from Moresby will likely arrive: *Why does Bettle believe themselves the only bypass-afflicted village?*

A lurching sensation, a clunklet.

"Whoa!" smiles Catherine, deep-breathing. "Big kick!"

The baby kicks again. Catherine gasps fondly:

"We're the only ones getting our kicks from the Bettle to Moresby bypass."

ANNETTE WOKE AT 4pm desperately missing Dewy. Back home was 11am, the time Dewy was allowed to visit on Sundays to bathe Morris. Annette dialled. She loved the steady purrs of US phones on overseas echo and felt homesick.

"Yes?"

"Mom?"

"*Hi*," said Joanna Stephens, riding instructor to Boston's North Shore.

"Is this a good time to ring, Mom?"

"Not exactly, a lot happening. Dewy!? ...*DEWY!?*" Her voice returned to the phone: "Out with your dog someplace. Was it her you wanted?"

"Uh, y-*yeah*. And, um, to say 'hi'? And 'hi' to Dad?"

"OK."

"Any of the boys home on leave?"

"Jack."

"Oh, that's good! Will you say 'hi'? Say 'hi' to ~"

"Yup. OK, take care over there? We'll see you in a couple –"

"Mom? Can I, uh, please call Dewy on your landline?"

"*She's* not sticking around. We've people coming."

"Please? We won't be long."

The call ended. Annette dialled the landline. At last:

"Yes?"

"Mom?"

"Chrissakes! Why our *landline*? Where's *her* phone?"

"Its contract ended, and they said ~"

The receiver clunked. Footsteps receded. Annette's heart rose at: "It's Annette. Don't be long," then Dewy's faraway: "Thank-you, Mrs Stephens."

Seconds later, smooth and clear:

"Honey?"

"*Darrling*," Annette began to cry but stopped herself. "H-how's Morris?"

"He's wonderful. How are you, angel?"

"Not great."

"You're tired? Is it late-afternoon in Britain?"

"Yah. It's real hot."

"Really? Here's cold. Spring's late this year."

Annette asked about Morris's meals, moods, sleep pattern, weight, appearance, bowels and daily activities. Dewy said Consuela reported all fine.

A pause.

"Hon?" said Dewy, "What's up?"

"I-I keep vomiting and… I haven't carried Roo for three months?"

"Oh, lamb. And you had something going with that man? Might you be having a baby, darling?"

"*Oh…!*"

"Would you like it I came over?"

"Wouldn't I not?" cried Annette. "*Could* you come? Really?"

"Of course. In a week?" said Dewy, wondering how. She had 15 dollars and two years' rent arrears. "Realistically 10 days?

Chapter 2

NINE DAYS LATER, the 605 Exeter to Penzance roared into Farrisford's outdoor bus station. The engine ran loud, the door *ptshhh'd* open, a man in shirt-sleeves stomped out to open the luggage compartment.

A straight-backed woman with long black hair and a sea-green cashmere coat stepped barefoot from the bus, carrying stilettos.

"Is this case *yours*?" bawled the driver. While the woman still approached, the man heaved a pink, huge case out. *Boomph!* it landed.

"Mine's the smaller, dark-blue case, sir?" said the woman.

"What's *this* then?" said the man, kicking the bright pink one.

"The heart of darkness?" said Dewy.

The man swished Dewy's case out with a pole and dumped it by her. She thanked him. He kicked the pink case again:

"If you'd *said* this wasn't yours, I wouldn't've got it out?"

"Oh." said Dewy, unsure why she was to blame. "Well… thank-you again, sir. Good-bye."

"Hff! *Americans!*" said the man, watching her go. "Fuckin' *ridiculous*. She's a looker, mind."

The bus station led out to the Specsavers corner of Church Street. Directly across, Market Street stretched away. Men in lemon-lime hi-vis occupied the road there. Orange plastic barriers surrounded dumper-trucks, bulldozers, cranes, cement mixers, generators, large machinery, Portaloos and men in orange boiler suits, an elder tribe, who did nothing. Those who *did* work drilled, hammered, dug, revved, or sawed kerbstones with a stubby machine like a monster screaming itself to death.

Dewy paused before this hundred metre scene of male rage. Through bonfire-smoke, tall equipment, dust clouds and Portakabins, she saw the Grand Hotel span the far end of the street. Dewy crossed Church Street's gridlock of grey cars and muddy Land Rovers into Market Street and headed for the hotel.

Shops to the right shared an old, ornate canopy high over the pavement. After British Heart Foundation and two shut-down shops were Greggs, Farrisford Vapes, Cash Converters, Superdrug and an open-doored games arcade, where unemployed young men gathered outside. They wore puffa jackets and grey sweatpants, heads shaved with a wet-gelled pelt on top. They smoked or vaped, spat, scarcely talked and sometimes nodded to a passer-by. Roadworks aside, the street was busy: shoppers, browsers, older people in raincoats, mothers with buggies stopping to talk.

Dewy approached the canopied side, but a welder's sparks crossed the pavement. She crossed to the other, where afternoon sun flooded The 99p Shop, Sue Ryder, Bargain Booze, a key-cutting/shoe-repair booth then four boarded-up shops. Dewy padded along a pavement covered by long wooden boards that gave under footsteps. To her right, a machine sawed into a stone block: tsh**rvVV** *VVVV***GRRRRRVVRRRR RRVVVVARRRRRVVV** *VVV***RRRVVVRRRVVVVRRGRRRVVVRRRRRRGGHH!!** went the machine. Another began but was stalled by shouts and whistles. Both machines stopped.

Dewy sensed they went quiet because men watched her. They did. No one who saw Marcia van der Zee's and

Todd Durant's daughter ever forgot her. As Dewy walked on, the road fell quiet by sections. A workman or two wolf-whistled. At last a machine restarted way back, then others, rising up Market Street one at a time.

Outdoor noise fell away in the Grand's empty, oak-panelled lobby. Dewy crossed a black and white marble floor to a rosewood reception counter, enjoying cool marble on her soles.

Permanently barefoot since 15, what began as "a need to defy petrol machines by being opposite as possible" was instantly so comfortable and liberating after lace-ups and four years of ballet pointes, there was no going back. Never cold, injured or sore, being barefoot was far better than footwear, even in New England winters.

12 years on, aged 27, Dewy might carry shoes if alone in a place where she must meet strangers, so to seem a "normal" person who'd removed tight shoes. For if not carrying shoes, alone somewhere new, she risked the one _and only one_ difficulty of living barefoot: it can make other people aggressive. Dealing with sudden: "*Where's your SHOES?*" (or the despising: "Aren't your *feet* cold? You'll *cut* yourself won't you? What do you do in *winter*?") was difficult, and Dewy never replied. *By silence I defy you, coward. The next person you treat like this might be nine years old. Or 90. Know now your power doesn't always work.* And cowards they were, for Dewy was only confronted if alone. Bullies target the lone. Cowards, always.

She pressed an old, brass counter-bell. A minute passed. She rang it again. Three minutes and several rings later, a fleshy blond man in a tuxedo bounded from a back-office: "Afternooon! Welcome to the Grand Hotel Farrisford! My name's Damian, how can I be of helping you today?"

"Good afternoon, sir," said Dewy. "Have you a room, please?"

"Should do!" said the man, crinkling his nose as he

smiled. "Let me see if there's an offer on. Wait." He returned to the back office awhile.

Dewy's poise and perfect posture hid a spinning mind. Her 20 hour journey played before her. Incredibly, the Millards had offered to drive her to Boston on their way to Connecticut. After a hung-over 80 minutes in their airless car, Dewy flew to London, took a train to Paddington, then Exeter, where it rained, but Dewy felt happy. An hour on, the 605 sped through ancient, rugged country bursting with greenness, new flowers and bluebells. Swifts and swallows raced over lakes. Miles of old lanes passed valleys, forests, tors, farms, heathery moors and standing-stones. Hills rose to thatched-cottage hamlets of sorbet-pink blossoms. Ouzels and larks paused on weathervanes, lambs and ewes on village greens.

Damian loomed:

"Sorry, love. Offer was *last* month, 10 per cent off two nights or more."

"I'd still like a room, please," said Dewy.

"*Loving* the accent by the way!" said the man, pointing at her. "HA-ha-HA-ha-ha-*HA*!!"

His phone rang, a ringtone of belching noises. "Lemme take this call, love," he said, half-closing the mirror-strips office door behind him.

He was gone seven minutes. Dewy surveyed the high foyer's beautiful chandelier and ebony staircase's red plush carpet. She sensed a glamorous past here, and felt the hotel mildly haunted. She would have stayed, but not with service like this. As Dewy readied to leave, the man returned: "That was my uncle, wants car insurance advice". He frowned: "Minefield, car insurance is."

Dewy handed him her bank card: "Two nights, double en-suite, please?"

"Yeahyeah," said Damian. Faintly singing *zabadaba-dooo! zabadaba-deee!* he rode a castor-wheeled chair to a computer he tapped at awhile.

In reception 16 minutes now, Dewy felt her mood change. *Don't be rude, or you'll hate yourself. Don't be rude, or you'll...* She'd try very hard not to be.

"Now, you're in room *one-eight*," said the man, meaningfully, as if Dewy knew this room. He slung the key along the counter and produced a printed form.

"Thank-you, sir," sighed Dewy, taking the key, gathering to go.

"Annnd, just *this*," said the man, tapping the form. "At the top... Miss? Ms, Mrs?"

"Whatever you like," said Dewy, voice tightening.

"'Miss'? That do?"

"Sir, what is this form?"

"Just a procedure," said the man cheerily. "Name, address..."

Dewy gave answers. The man wrote them down. When she said Ipswich Road, he leered: "Woah! We *have* come far! Other side of the country!" But Ipswich Road, Massachusetts perplexed him ("Is that *real*?")

The next question asked Dewy's occupation.

"I'd rather not say," said Dewy.

"Oh." said the man. He stared at her eyes for three seconds, then:

"Annnd... zabadabadoo ...last question: 'Purpose Of Visit'? Basically – why are you here? Business? Holiday?"

"Excuse me?" said Dewy.

"Purpose of visit?"

"To wash my tits. Good day, sir."

ANNETTE COULDN'T CONCENTRATE. Her text book swam before her eyes. The bedroom was hot, airless, knee-deep in clutter, had three buzzing flies. The window had no hinges, could never open.

At least the night was over, the loneliest, most ill of her life. Nauseous lying or sitting, Annette had paced the landing outside her room, for going downstairs would trigger night alarms. In cold, very long hours, of creaking sounds, and cries of owls and foxes, terrible thoughts and feelings had arisen.

Annette could never cry for herself, but at 4am, gazing at Morris on her phone, she'd wept: "I'm f-*frightened*, BooBoo." Perhaps Morris was with her, but really no one was, except a child inside her, whose father had gone.

Near dawn she'd looked from her window: "Dewy, where are you, darling? I see Cassiopeia, our constellation. Didn't we used to say: 'Ask her to point where you are and I'll come?' Oh, Cassie, tell Dewy I'm here, please?"

Recalling the night made its strangeness return. Annette slowly stood. The Angler's Bar was empty on weekdays, she could read there.

As she carefully stepped downstairs, book in hand, she heard Bernadette:

"As if *you* care, Millie! You're up to something, girl!"

"I'm not!" said Millie Zena: "I only want someone to come Homebase."

The pair faced each other in a dark hall of colourful bottle crates, where paths to bars and kitchen met.

Bernie turned, saw Annette: "A'right, love?"

"Hello, Bernie!" said Annette, delighted. "Hello, Millie! How nice to *see* you both! Millie, you look so *pretty*. Your hair!"

"Thanx," said Millie, bashful.

"She's all got-up for *some* reason," said Bernie, plucking tonic bottles from a crate, "No good I expect."

"Mmm, nice perfume," smiled Annette.

"Oh, er, I always wears it," said Millie. "Will you come Homebase with me?"

"*She* don't wanna go!" said Bernie. "And *you* shouldn't be here, Millie, y'ain't working til tomorrow. Scoot! If Douglas sees you?"

"Ooh, Douglas! Like, I'll poo my paants!" pouted

Millie, leaving through the Angler's Bar. Annette followed.

"Sorry I can't come, Millie," she said. "Kinda busy for school, and no sleep."

"No sleep me neither," sighed Millie. "I *hate* this pub. *You're* OK, but *they're* all tosserrs." She crashed out the door. Annette sat in the empty, grey bar by a wall with crossed fishing rods and paintings of fish. She gazed at the door, tried to read, but sat thinking.

TODAY WAS BEVERLEY'S day off. She and Annie returned from a river-walk and kissed awhile, then Annie went downstairs to work.

Beverley reflected. No one knew she and Annie shared a bed. Her first-floor room above the pub's front doors led to an attic over the restaurant. The day Annie arrived, Beverley asked Fent if Annie could live there. Fent said no, but Beverley took the bold step of welcoming Annie anyway.

She reflected again. These days had been messy. Her old behaviours had surfaced: too loving, maternal, over-affectionate. They'd properly kissed on the third night, to Roxy Music's "Avalon". Annie was lovely to kiss. They'd slept together from the first night, neither naked yet, Beverley moving closer in the nights, Annie lying still, back turned.

Where was this new situation going? It wasn't even Beverley's main worry. *That* was Annette, pregnant by that idiot Stuart, who'd vanished.

At least Beverley's six months' unrequited love for Annette had finally shifted. But that painful feeling returned at the news Dewy – a "girlfriend" she'd heard much about – might be coming to Farrisford.

"Maybe just an old friend?" said Jonty last week. He ran "The Bibby" [The Bibendum, Crendlesham's LGBTQ pub]. "American women refer to all female friends as 'girlfriends'."

"But her eyes light up about this 'Dewy'," said Beverley. "Inseparable since childhood. The girl moved into their house aged 10. Last week Annette said: 'My parents are quite strict Protestants. They never bothered Dewy and I shared a bed for years, but were uneasy at us always kissing as we got older."

Beverley's friends regularly told her to give up on Annette. But Annette was helpless without her. Beverley woke Annette early Tuesdays to Thursdays, cleaned and ran the bath for her, cooked a US-style breakfast, coaxed her to bathe, then drove her to Exeter. On Tuesdays Annette taught a module on statics, another on hydraulics. Wednesdays she spent in the materials lab or the library. On Thursdays she tutored three students an hour or more each.

On Beverley's Tuesday off, she'd meet Annette out of university. They'd drive to the coast, where Annette loved the birds and knew all the kinds there were. They'd go to any of the Michelin-starred restaurants out in the countryside – warm evenings now, driving roof-down under the stars.

Beverley brought Annette flowers, washed her clothes, hung curtains for her, bought a rug, new bedding, a standing lamp. She paid Snappy Snaps in Crendlesham to print 60 photos of Morris for Annette's wall. But Annette's self-care was erratic, her room a chaos of bags, toolboxes, luggage, books, lab-equipment and a vague path to the window.

On this Tuesday afternoon, Beverley examined herself in her full-length mirror. A man's two-piece pinstripe suit, white sneakers and vintage Blondie T-shirt, name in pink above a photo of the group. Beverley wore it because she loved the band. She shook out her long, dark-brown hair, wished she wasn't so tired-looking and suddenly fought tears. Again she ached for Annette, but that was being cruel to Annie, who, she sensed, *did* feel something back. Trust was taking time.

Leaving the pub by the Angler's Bar, Beverley saw Annette reading. She sat, took Annette's hands, rubbed them.

"Beverley?" said Annette. "Do you know where Stuart is?"

"Douglas said something about him starting A-levels at Swole College."

"*College?*" smiled Annette. "Oh, he'll do so *well* there! Stuart's kinda bright."

Beverley said nothing. She went to the kitchen to bring Annette home-baked blueberry cornbread and a pot of tea. When Annette smiled and thanked her, Beverley's heart filled with happiness and despair. "I'm going to the Bibby now," she said, to no one. Annette rarely listened, lost in trances. As an afterthought, Beverley asked:

"Any news from your friend, love?"

"Dewy, yes! Um, she's coming... *soon*! Today? Tomorrow?"

"Oh." said Beverley. Aware her tone had dropped, she faked: "Good. Sounds positive!"

"Oh, Dewy's the most positive person *ever*," said Annette warmly. "She has *no faults.*"

IN ROOM ONE-EIGHT, Dewy wrote e-mails to each of three Hispanic children she taught English to in Roxbury, then felt obliged to write her blog Sweet And Bitter, or SAB. Days ago, desperate to fly to Annette, Dewy hopelessly tried a crowd-funding appeal, mentioned it in SAB, and to her shock received $5,640 from 308 readers. One woman sent $500.

SAB began in 2010 as Tanager, a birdwatching blog which often digressed onto Dewy's precarious life. Until last week, she never knew anyone even read SAB. Now she did. She posted:

> Thank-you from Britain, I'm here now! Hotel wi-fi, plus confusing new phone, so can't get Whatsapp. {To SAB-only readers: excuse please while I answer two WhatsApp friends who read this blog: Mrs J, Iowa, I agree re Tim Buckley. He and Hank W – the only men I'd do anything for. Both passed awful young. Ms Blixa of Kansas thank-you so much for the $$, and I agree about Lemmy. I'm glad someone else also dances naked to this (and the Girlschool one)! No, hadn't heard of Stacia until you told me and, *girl*, am I blown away? I wish she was my sister. Good luck on Friday, Ms B. Xx}

> Thank-you for your patience, SAB readers. Back to here: check-in at this hotel takes long, tormenting minutes. Eventually I swore {a side of myself I don't like} at a friendly-rude receptionist called Damian.

> Can't open padlocked case, key lost years ago. Should have gotten rid of the padlock, but clicked it shut yesterday, distracted, as I faced Wal Millard, first time since the gun incident.

> "Hello, Waldo, thank-you for the ride to Boston," I said, shutting the lock to look busy. He climbed into his huge vehicle ignoring me. A blessing, for a ton of water I'd drunk for a hangover gushed like an oil-strike. I dashed behind the car to throw up the lot in two seconds, best sleight-of-barf since at Tallulah L's wedding.

> On the journey, Vacua eased tension chattering about a trip to Maine with her watercolor group. She then asked how long I'd be in Britain. The question was obviously planned. "Five days," I lied. {Saying: "A few weeks" would be Wal's green light. He'd go to the cabin, remove my things, e-mail Notice to Quit and a cold request for the 29 months' rent arrears.}

> As long-term readers know, there's always a Mil-

lard moment. The latest:

"Andrea? How do I open the window back here?"

"Oh, we don't want windows open, Dewy, just wanna get you there."

I'm overthinking Damian & padlocks. It's time to find my girl. She told me her address: "A pub. One of those, like, British ones?" I'll find it. Ahh-de-o. Xx

After posting this, Dewy fell on the bed face-down. *I hate what I write. Who is that cheery fuckwit?*

But how can I be my true, vile self to people who donated money and wished me love for rushing to my pregnant girl's aid?

Washing-powder scent from sheet over bedspread made Dewy roll onto her side. A sash window showed a different Market Street, no shops, only a row of centuries-old buildings above them. Sun brightened their colours and textures, reflected in small, highest windows.

Sure, I love Annette, thought Dewy. *But we're so apart and different now. Christmas was lovely, her return home for three weeks, she, me and Morris slept together like old days but... ...we're utterly the past.*

The room was lonely. Dewy hugged herself.

Sometimes Annette's company annoys the crap out of me. She talks at two miles an hour, watches films of her dog, her idea of music is Donald Fagen's "Ruby Baby", she never gets drunk or dirty, she has no political anger. She's so... fucking WHOLESOME.

The room was cold, pillows heavy. A stranger's yellow hair lay across one.

Annette's pregnant. She's having a child! Who with? A man who's vanished. Am I the surrogate parent? Is that what this is? Who else is here to look after Annette and the baby but me? I'm being selfish, but... what IS this?

Chapter 3

MILLIE CHECKED HER reflection in the car-wash dark glass wall. Short white denim jacket, red tropical shirt-top, brand new, dark, boot-cut jeans. Her white mum always told her she didn't need make-up, as Millie's light, smooth, mixed-race complexion was perfect. But Millie had gone for it around the eyes, and burgundy lipstick. Her grown-out corkscrew curls had a daub of blonde tint at the front. Millie took out her compact again, checked no lipstick on her teeth, stepped carefully in high-heels across a foot-high rounded wall dividing the car-wash from Homebase car park, and walked towards, but not straight to the store. She wanted to seem to have driven there, or arrived by taxi, not walked the path that came out by the car-wash.

Millie needn't have worried. Marlon wasn't outside pushing trolleys. Maybe he was inside. If not, he was off today. Millie had been here twice this week, pretending to browse. Marlon never appeared. Would her third visit be lucky?

She breathed deeply. Main doors neared. It felt she was motionless and the entrance moved around her. *There he is!* Stacking anti-freeze!

"Hello!" said Millie, voice too high. She cleared her throat. "I wonder if I could ask your help? Oh it's *you*! Didn't realise!"

Marlon nodded. Millie smiled. Marlon glanced away.

"Marlon, isn't it?" she gasped.

"Yeah. You Bobby's daughter?"

"Yeah! That's right! Yes! Um… *yeah*! Dad said you play for the Town now?"

"Reserves. But I got a injury."

"*Oh.* You shouldn't be crouching if you're injured!" Millie bent to quickly fill low spaces with bottles from the box. Suddenly she worried if this annoyed Marlon. Again her mother's voice: "Don't do stuff for people what ain't asked. They don't like it."

Marlon was oblivious, looking at the highest shelf. He reached to open a box on his trolley, but stopped.

"Sorry, madam. What was it you wanted?"

"Madam! Ha-*ha-ha-HA!!*" Millie covered her mouth guiltily. Everyone said her laugh was too loud. She bit her lip, breathed in, balanced herself: "I'm… I'm *here* on behalf of… of who I work for, actually. They asked me to source ideas, though actually, er, I'm the manager? So it's like I was *consulted*, not asked?"

Shit, thought Millie, *why did I say that crap?*

"It's a pub, see? I mean a *restaurant*. A-a restaurant with a little pub."

She waited for Marlon to ask "Which one?", or say anything.

"Er… um…" Millie tried to speak low: "I'd like to see some paints, please?"

"Aisle five," said Marlon.

"Ah…" Millie turned, vaguely pointing to the middle of the store. "Aisle five… *Thanks.* I'll-I'll, um, *actually*, could you come with me? Help choose?"

"Gotta finish this."

"Of course," said Millie, smiling, hunching her shoulders, palms frantically rubbing each other. "Well… I'll… I'll be over *there*. Bye, Marlon."

"Bye," said Marlon, lifting bottles of autolube, not looking at Millie.

Millie gazed at him. How tense he was, a tension in him always.

84-YEAR-OLD FATHER ENTRETON opened French doors to his garden and stepped out to a favourite journey, through gold-red roses and laurel bushes, to a hidden clearing by an old stone wall. The retired priest's bungalow, high on Calls Hill, has a 40 mile view on days like this.

Father Entreton is happy to see what he sees, happy to feel what he feels. He survived lung cancer in 2012, an all-clear again last year. But his greatest contentment is young Father Alan, eight years in the town and at last a perceptive, articulate priest. At this thought, Father Entreton murmurs: "He still has a bit to go. But don't we all?"

He looks over Farrisford's buildings and roofs glowing warm in late sun. Market Street, straight as a rod to the Grand Hotel, those separate slate roofs the Grand has, unseen from street level, triangles tweaked up so the sides curve in. Beyond the hotel are plane trees and poplars then, over the river, a small retail park. Hidden by Homebase are: Matalan, Argos, Lidl, PC World, Sports Direct and a closed-down carpet superstore.

Father Entreton remembers the red-stone Victorian railway station where the retail park is now. Its carvings and turrets, friezes of graces and muses, arches to platforms under long glass canopies were all demolished in '63. The railway had been closed by the government's Beeching Cuts. For 90 years the line ran from Exeter straight to the Grand Hotel.

The hotel's chalk-blue ballroom opens to a terrace of weeds now. It hosts maybe a wedding a year. Farrisford's largest employer – Alpha Staplers – had staff Christmas parties there until 2008. Father Entreton saw many ballroom wedding receptions since arriving from County Cork in 1957. One wall has signed photos of people who'd stayed at the Grand many years ago: film stars, radio personalities, sportsmen, big-bands, aviators, light entertainers. The photos are still there. No one would take them down, would they?

The priest surveys the town, silent from up here. St Botolph's chimes the hour. The ancient church's deep bell is said to contain melted shot from Waterloo. Farrisford (population 14,670, last census) was busy in the Middle Ages. Remains of Roman villas have been found, but this wasn't a spa town, the Brate's too fast. Crendlesham, 11 miles off, *was* a Roman town and spa, but Farrisford's older. Remains of an Iron Age fort were found in 1901 near the Grand Hotel. River bridges have stood since prehistoric times where Cressy Road Bridge, by Asda, is now.

Father Entreton returns to the house. "Time for a pot of Farrisford Organics' loose tea, and their fresh vegan paté on toasted bread from Willow's…"

The *Farrisford Tattler* has published a new poem by Father Entreton, without fail, every other issue since 1958. Editors retired, saying to the next: "And Father Entreton's verse? Will that stand?" The reply: "Of course," a keystone of trust, a relief for the departing editor. "The soul of the paper," he'd wryly say, as once was said to him.

DEWY PADDED FAST downstairs and out. Workmen stopped drilling to watch her descend the Grand's wide steps. She turned left, towards an alley leading to High Street. Her spirits rose, a floating feeling of jet-lag, no-sleep and thrill to be overseas. She thought with clarity, felt confident, even decided to look for a job – *why not? Take charge of this situation, start NOW…*

In Pilgrim's Lane, a pale green sign: JobCentrePlus.

Is that French? thought Dewy, *No, 'center' is spelt 'centre' here. Could 'job' 'centre' be a labour exchange?*

An hour on, Dewy sat at a chunky communal table in Farrisford Organics's cafe. She'd bought the *Farrisford Tattler* and wrote in her blog:

If I stay in this town and look after my girl (and her

baby soon), I must work. Farrisford is rural (maybe 15,000 people?) near the middle of a south-west county called Devon. I visited the labor exchange here.

Three yards in, a security guard stared me down while a hard-faced man in shirt-sleeves walked at me: "Got an appointment?"

"No, sir, enquiring."

"Why you here?" he said.

"I hope to find employment."

"Uh?"

"I'd like to see the employment noticeboards, please?"

"Where's your *shoes*?"

"Sir, is this a place where people find work?"

The other man, "Security", leaned in, wearing Britain's most popular modern male garment – a lemon-lime neon waistcoat. {They call it 'hi-vis'. I call it Hell on Earth. The most aggressive, unrestful color ever.}

"Looking for work?" said Hi-Vis Man. "Is that why it's you're here for?"

By now, five men – one very drunk – had passed us unhindered. The drunk roared: "*I'm a fuckin' fighterr pilot!!*" then shrieked like a hyena. I said to the pair:

"You've let these men in, but not *me*?"

"They come and go, them," snapped *Homo Hi-Visicus*.

"Sirs, may I see the noticeboards before the drunk guy smashes them for firewood?"

Anyway… a maternity vacancy at the *Farrisford Tattler*! I like this newspaper, good-enough reporting, copperplate title like the *Boston Globe*. A lot about farming – the paper serves miles of country. An overworked, kind woman at the labor exchange

**called the paper to fix me an interview, day after
tomorrow, with a Mr Carruthers. Please, *please* can I
not screw it up?! Ah-de-o. Xx**

HOME AFTER WORK, Marlon lay on his bed watching an
extended i-Player news item on refugees. A tear rolled
down his cheek.

"What the –? I'm being *daft*, crying, man. Get a grip.
But... it's *bad*. They're dying in the sea in boats that don't
work, kids and everything. Feels like this isn't a modern
world no more? Ancient times again."

He moved to the kitchen. John was making an early
meal for them both:

"Just salad, as you've got training tonight."

"Great. Thanks," said Marlon.

"Are you OK?" said John lightly. He knew Marlon was
shaken.

"Yeahyeah, Dad, looking forward to training, see if I
can play soon. Then, er, come home, we can watch a DVD,
something funny?"

"Can do," said John. He saw Marlon, in the sitting
room now, at the sideboard, looking at a photo of himself,
aged eight, Tottenham, London, where Marlon had lived
in a children's home.

Marlon turned, holding the photograph. The smiling,
perplexed child, big front teeth, thick Afro hair, looked
odd against the tall young man in trim navy Adidas,
cropped hair, unhappy countenance:

"200 years ago, Dad, this boy would've been a slave.
They'd've put him in a boat, if it sank – too bad. Now it's
happening again. These ain't modern times."

DEWY GUESSED EXETER University's Farrisford annexe
might be on the outskirts, Annette's pub on the way. She

headed along a road out of town. Beyond a launderette and a tanning salon, terraced houses faced a wide park of sports pitches, surrounded by woods. A drop in the land before these was maybe a river. A petrol station lay ahead. "Hell, I need a beer," thought Dewy.

Two minutes on she emerged, newly informed: a) British garages don't sell alcohol. b) The staff don't care the misunderstanding was because alcohol's sold in US ones. c) British people stare furiously at someone barefoot. d) the answer to: "Where's the town's university campus, please?" can be either: "You need a mental hospital, love, not a uni" or: "Why don't you go home and ask Donald Trump?"

Dewy walked on, trying to be strong. Pattering rain became a cloudburst. She half-sat on a thin red ledge in a bus stop, leaning against rainy glass. A bird sang clearly in Spring evening rain, no other sounds.

The river was powerful, hypnotic to watch from a bridge spanning park to woods. A sign with a map showed Nature trails and pictures of birds. Nine were European species Dewy hadn't seen or heard.

She saw from the map she'd get lost in the wood and must follow a road dividing it. But on hearing her first ever curlew Dewy ran to the trees. The bird's strong call repeated. Dewy danced, pirouetted, did jetés and jumps, took her clothes off, lay on moss surrounded by bluebells, glimpsed sky through high beeches and oaks. Occasional raindrops and pollen motes fell on her. She saw whinchats, jays, watched a chalk-blue nuthatch pick bugs on an oak. The woods resounded with warblers and woodcocks. As she dressed, Dewy heard the far cuckoo and returned to the tree-lined, empty road in a trance.

Council housing appeared, 1930s semi-detacheds with trapezium roofs and messy, or very neat, gardens. Dewy saw a small shop called Spar. Youths on mountain bikes watched her go in. They exchanged glances and frowned.

Dewy emerged two minutes later to a chorus of: "Where's your SHOES?" A boy rode his bike alongside her. "Ain't you cold, miss? That not hurt your feet?" Dewy's eyes briefly smiled at him as she walked. Her power, beauty and what he'd call *class* overwhelmed him. "Take care, love," he gasped, stopping.

From an ancient bridge Dewy watched the river gush over wet black rocks. A distant grey tower peered over woods to the right, a word, Asda, in neon green. Dewy wandered the wood, to an outcrop of boulders under open sky, river below. She'd bought red wine in Spar and settled to drink and read the *Tattler* more closely. A robin hopped and watched her.

Twilight thickened. Dewy had drunk half the wine. She hugged herself warm and continued through the wood, soft underfoot, but darker, the river-roar louder. At last she stepped onto a silent road. Opposite, interwar houses again, similar streets rising behind. Dewy walked along the low road. Woods on the right fell away, river curving off towards a gap in far banks of poplars.

Rain returned. A pub lay ahead, painted grey. It looked dismal in rain. Dewy believed the 2010s' grey bias in décor, vehicles and clothes a form of tyranny. SAB often declared: **Colors nourish hearts and souls. Erasing colors for gray is spiritual murder, a sign of fascism** plus Dewy's regular vow to avoid: **...anyplace repainted gray: bars, offices, stores. Therefore 90%.**

The pub's shape was dark against dusk, left side jutting to the road, a meeting hall once, now a restaurant by a courtyard of grey-painted picnic tables. The restaurant wasn't open yet.

"No way do I enter this Stalinist dump," muttered Dewy. But to go back meant wandering a dark wood. The pub would at least have a taxi number to ring. She approached and pushed a dove-grey door into a hall of turpentine-grey. Ahead were open doors to a main bar, where a tall man in a grey T-shirt poured beer with his back to her. Dewy walked as far as the doors, saw a spacious, near-empty room of leather sofas, plants and a conservatory with wicker chairs. Walls, woodwork, fabrics, even lampshades' tassels, were pumice-stone grey. The treacle-dark, old wooden floor was spared.

Dewy retreated, muttering, noticing a smaller bar opposite the restaurant. She pushed a door into a low-lit, intimate room of framed old prints and shut grey velvet curtains, empty but for someone vanishing through a doorway behind the bar. Dewy saw the person's back one-tenth of a second, and bolted through a hatch to the bar and doorway. Annette was slowly climbing a dark staircase.

"Darling?" said Dewy.

Chapter 4

7PM, GARTON ROAD, home of semi-professional Farris-ford Town FC. Floodlights on emerald grass, red road-cones, players training, shouts echoing, mainly from manager Alan Woods and assistant Lisa Tarek. Two long whistle blasts, players to divide, firsts v reserves, firsts in royal blue, reserves cherry-red, all with **ALPHA STA-PLERS** in white across the chest.

In a changing-room under the ground's small, only stand, Robert Obogo unbuttons a Fiorucci shirt:

"Whassup, Marlon?" he says, noting Marlon is rarely relaxed.

"Alan said 'wait here'," replies Marlon. "Dave's coming for me."

Studded boots heard. Physiotherapist David Yates appears at the open doorway, black tracksuit, anorak. "Wanna come through, Marlon?"

Yates sees Robert Obogo: "Hello, Lord Lucan, what time d'you call this?"

"The boring bit before the pub," says Robert.

"They're out there training without yer! Standing here in your pants?"

"Mr Dave," smiles Obogo. "These are not 'pants', they are brand new, forest green, Egyptian cotton, boxer shorts. And let us also clarify: Robert Obogo, five years the rock of midfield, cause of ever-increasing female attendance at games, scorer of 15 goals this season, is allowed latecoming leeway."

"He isn't. C'mon, Marlon."

Marlon's tendon was "coming along, but not there yet". Marlon felt it inevitable he'd be dropped from the club at season end, six weeks away.

"The healing process needs three months' absolute rest," said Yates. "No more fast-walking on beaches, careful even up and down stairs."

"We live in a bungalow," said Marlon.

"What about work?" said Dave. "Still part-time?"

"Couple of days, here, there, y'know?"

"Sounds good for *this*. Follow the regime, you'll be good for next season. OK: come out and watch, still be part of this, don't do what Bobby Zena's done, staying away. We want you around, even if injured."

Marlon hadn't played since January. Watching when sidelined was an agony of frustration. Football was one of few things that made Marlon *feel*. Others included the news, or going for drives with Mr Wright: to the coast, to museums, castles, tourist attractions, walks on Dartmoor. John and Eleanor Wright had taken Marlon for drives most weekends after fostering him at 11. At 12 he began to speak. At 15 they legally adopted him. On Sundays John and Marlon take flowers to Eleanor's grave.

Robert Obogo joined the match and scored, always modest when he did, though off the field, as everyone knew, his bragging was endless. Marlon readied to leave. He needed to say cheerio and thank David Yates. He hoped Alan Woods might notice him, say words of encouragement. Yates and Big Al were talking to 45-year-old Bobby Zena, who, absent a year injured, was 10 years the reserves team captain. Woods put an arm round Marlon's shoulders, the other over Bobby's: "I want you pair back ASAP!"

As Marlon departed, Bobby Zena stared hard at him, not returning his nod.

Have I offended him? thought Marlon. *What'd I do?*

THE ANGLER'S BAR was unstaffed and empty except two women in a far corner, hugging. Annette nuzzled Dewy's left ear: "You smell *gorgeous*! Your *hair*!" She disappeared into Dewy's thick, glossy hair to sniff deeply: "Oh I smell *home*, the woods, the cabin! That New England wooden-house smell!"

"Yeah, I stink," said Dewy, taking a swig from her emptying wine bottle and reaching to hug Annette close. More kissing began. Dewy's heart felt relieved. She *did* want to be with Annette after all. How could she not? Beautiful, trusting, unworldly Annette, who blushed as she talked, and loved everyone? Dewy felt ashamed of her earlier thoughts and for being absent from Annette in recent years, needing freedom and wild lovers, not a steady, intimate girlfriend.

"Oh, darlingnessest!" wept Annette. "You look amazing!"

"Oh, hon," said Dewy. She kissed Annette's face softly all over.

"Your beautiful ears!" said Annette. "Please may I give them a *snoo*?"

"Of course, darling."

Annette placed her nostrils over Dewy's right ear and sniffed deeply.

"Aww*ahhh!!*" she groaned, exhaling. "The *pungencies* of your ears! Like Christmas cake, hon! And *ginger root*! Beautiful scents!"

"Oh, darling," murmured Dewy into Annette's hair-line. "Let me look at you?"

"I'm having a baby, hon,"

"I won't leave you."

After Morris had been discussed, Annette said:

"Thank-you for coming, darling."

"Is this a liveable place?" said Dewy. "Do you feel happy here?"

"Plenty birds, hon! Plovers, grebes, kittiwakes, dozens more. But my room faces the back, not the woods or river.

I asked to put a bird-house near the parking-lot, but Mr Fent said no. I hear the birds sing high at dawn, and longer evenings now?"

They kissed. Annette took Dewy's hand, laid it gently over the bump on her tummy and rested her hand on Dewy's.

"We'll be brave?" she whispered.

"Of course," said Dewy. She lightly stroked Annette's belly. "And so will little ~?"

"Bachelor," said Annette, smiling at her emerging bump.

"Oh. You... found out he's a boy?" said Dewy.

"No. Gonna wait see. I want the surprise?"

"So... if a girl, she'll be called...?"

"Bachelor."

"Oh. Boy *or* girl... Bachelor?"

"Yah," smiled Annette, snuggling into Dewy and closing her eyes. Dewy kissed along Annette's hairline. After a time she said:

"Did you... have other names in mind?"

"No."

"Oh." said Dewy.

"You don't seem very..."

"I... can't help thinking it might sound a little *strange*, in some situations?"

"Really?" said Annette: "What would *you* name the child?"

"Sylvia," said Dewy. "Hiram if a boy."

"Oh, *yes*," said Annette. "Sylvia Bachelor Stephens. I *like* that. Hiram Bachelor Stephens.

"I love you," said Dewy, kissing.

Douglas Fent entered. He reared to see some long-haired boy and a woman in a cyan cashmere coat, kissing like teenagers. He cleared his throat, expecting they'd jump. They didn't.

"Hey!" he barked. "*Excuse me!*"

The two slowly parted and looked round. It wasn't a

boy, it was the American washer-up woman, and… *what in the world…???*

"Hello, Mr Fent!" smiled Annette, "This is my friend from the States."

"Oh, *right*," said Fent, approaching. "Hey. Cool to meet. I'm Douglas."

He resembled a vulture. Dewy disliked his interruption and the manner of it. For Annette's sake she nodded graciously but avoided his gaze.

Fent stood over them, very focused on Dewy.

"Long flight?" he snapped. "Leave your shoes on the plane?"

Annette felt Dewy's handclasp soften as she relaxed into a Dewy silence. Dewy often gazed, faintly friendly, like a 100-year-old, until a questioner went away. She wasn't looking at the questioner's eyes but the area between them, to avoid the stare. Her eyes blanked out that area, replacing it with trees she knew, birds she loved, the ocean…

Fent persisted until Annette said: "She's kinda tired." He left, but hadn't given up. "Drink, girls?" he said, behind the bar. "On the house."

"A bottle of Merlot, please," said Annette.

"Er, *hello*?" said Fent, "I meant *a* drink, not a whole…"

"We're buying," said Annette, holding up £20 Dewy had slipped into her hand. She turned to Dewy: "Honey, you must be thirsty, I'll getcha couple bottles of water, big British pint glass with ice?"

"You've not enough," snapped Fent, opening wine. "Merlot's 18.95. Have to be tap-water."

"Sure," said Annette, taking wine glasses and bottle to the table. From a low sink Fent scooshed water into a pint glass, banged it on the bar and left the room.

Annette lay back in Dewy's arms. She asked where Dewy was staying. Dewy tensed slightly. Annette knew the story without a word. Dewy always fell out with hotels.

"Stay here!" said Annette. "I'll smuggle you upstairs."

They kissed awhile. Dewy waited for talk to begin about Annette and her child. Who, where was the father? What was Annette's and the child's future?

But Annette wanted to talk about anything else. She held Dewy's hands and continued about work she was doing, her colleagues at Exeter, students she mentored and her ongoing delight at being chosen from 180 applicants, for a role mixing post-doctorate research and part-time teaching.

"Have you seen many people out?" said Annette, changing the subject – oddly, Dewy thought, for Annette had no interest in Massachusetts social matters. "Did you go to the Paleys' for their daughter's party?"

"I'd not be invited there," said Dewy. "Everyone said it was amazing."

"Ivanka Trump was meant to be there with Jared?" said Annette. "Mom says she doesn't think they made it. Dad said they did."

"Yeah, what on *Earth—*"

"Old network, Oscar Paley's side. A lot of DC there, Mom said. And New York, of course."

Annette, I have never heard you like this.

"Roberta Paley's surely a Democrat?" said Dewy. "In the '70s her Mom was a policy adviser to ~"

"Families and friends are divided now," sighed Annette. "A strange time. We gotta say no to being divided. Even if it's total differences, we must build bridges, be together."

"I wonder," said Dewy.

Annette began to cry.

"Oh, honey," said Dewy. She held Annette.

"I-I'm sorry," trembled Annette, "You've come all this way and I'm…"

"Don't apologise? We're in a situation. It's scary, but exciting. We'll be OK. We've been through *everything* together? We'll get through this, hon."

Dewy knew now she and Annette were exclusive again, first time in years.

She felt ready in her heart to accept this.

Or is it because I've had a drink? When booze kicks in, ANYTHING feels right.

MILLIE WAS ECSTATIC. House empty! Evening to herself, first time in… *when*? She ran to the kitchen to dance to Beyoncé and put sweet-potato chips in the fryer.

She made a perfect omelette, fresh tomatoes on the side and a heap of chips, drank tea and felt bliss with strawberry cheesecake. And it's o*nly 7.30!*

She tried to remember when her father was last at football training. What time did he return? *LATE!! Yes!!* The players went for a drink after.

Millie took her tiny, powerful music speaker upstairs, placed it on a cork-topped storage tub, ran a bath, put Ariana Grande, Lioness, Aretha Franklin, AB6IX and Skepta on shuffle, ran to her room, danced, shook her hair out, waved her arms, sang, danced to the window to close the curtains so she could undress.

NO!!!

Her father's square-faced hulk of a van was pulling into the drive.

Millie switched her music off. Bobby Zena entered the house, switched the TV system on. European football boomed. A beer-can was *tsch!*'d open.

Millie leaned over the banister. "Back early?"

"Only went for a talk. Gonna be one of the training staff next season. You having a bath? Let me in first, use toilet?"

He leapt upstairs. "Whassa matter, girl? Face like a slapped arse! Cheer up!"

Right that's IT!! thought Millie. *Me and Marlon'll get a*

flat together and be a couple. I'll make it happen. Within
WEEKS...

ANNETTE DRIED HER eyes and spoke of her recent life.

"Beverley's so good to me. It's her night off. She asked if I'd like to go down Crendle-sham, but I had to study? As well I stayed! My girl would've walked in here, seen it empty, gone back out into the night, her lovely eyes so sad, and her bare footies."

Annette always said 'footies' with no hard 't', nor much 'oo', nearly 'fiddies'.

"Was it Beverley took you to the midwife?" said Dewy.

"No, that was Annie. She's new here. She's Scotch, kinda shy, has the beautifulest red curls. Annie tidied and cleaned my room all good for the health visitor coming. It's sure gotten back to messy though."

Later, Dewy returned from the wc.

"Tampax machine's empty. Nearly no tissue, either."

"I've nothing, not needed them. I'll ask Beverley, or..."

Annie arrived behind the bar to fetch something. Annette called: "Hi, Annie!"

Annie turned. She'd thought the warm-lit bar empty. In a far corner were Annette and the most beautiful woman Annie had ever seen.

"This is Dewy," smiled Annette. "Wanna meet her? Or you busy?"

"Busy," whispered Dewy, half-drunk now.

Annie approached. "That *hair*," murmured Dewy. "Ronald McD v Louis Fourteenth."

"H-hello," said Annie nervously. "Nice t'meet ye."

"Can she get some water?" said Dewy.

"There's some that Douglas poured," said Annette. "Let me get it."

"Ah'll get it, darlin'," said Annie, pacing to the bar.

"So kind and thoughtful," whispered Annette. Dewy

curled her lip.

Annie carefully carried the pint glass. The top of the water wobbled.

"Stagnant," said Dewy. "Even has surface tension."

"It *does*! There's a meniscus!" said Annette, leaning to peer. The water surface wobbled but remained still around the glass in a sharp line.

"Keep it like that," said Dewy to Annie. "Put it down gently. *Gently.*"

Annie did so while Dewy stared at her. The water didn't alter.

Annette spoke delightedly about surface tension then left for the wc.

Annie stood. Dewy sat. Neither looked at the other. Eventually:

"Is there a reason you're here?" said Dewy.

"Sorry?"

"A reason why you're *here*?" said Dewy.

Annie slightly relaxed.

"Well, ah've a new job here," she began. "Just getting settled intae it…"

"No, I meant: a reason why you're standing *here* at this moment?"

"Sorry?"

"Is there a reas – ah *Christ*, it's a simple proposition – is there a reason for you being here? If not, can you *go away*?"

"Er…" Annie's tone darkened: "Wait a minute…"

"*Another* minute? No. I'd like you to *go*. Or provide a reason to stay. I've offered that option *four times*. But can we work on the idea of you *going*?"

"Uh?" Annie couldn't suppress a brief, mortified laugh.

Pink patches arose on Dewy's cheeks. She placed an outspread hand on her chestbone, breathing hard. Annette returned, rushed over: "Darling?"

"Ahh," groaned Dewy, mouth quivering. "Anything I say to British people today, they say: '*Uh?*'. I repeat myself, they say '*Uh?*', yet I've to pretend I'm enjoying the exchange! Now I'm being *Uh?*'d by someone outta Stephen King."

"Darling, calm down?" said Annette, clutching Dewy. "Your poor heart. Take breaths! Oxygen to the heart, darling. Oh, your arms are cold!" Dewy's coat had slipped off, she wore a black camisole dress. Annette rubbed Dewy's bare arms and shoulders and lifted Dewy's feet one at a time to rest on a chair.

Annie couldn't stop an appalled glance at Dewy's feet. First noticed as glowing and smooth, neat nails painted deep red, Annie saw only the soles now, hard, leathery and dark. Ancient, tiny creases and cracks lay in random places. Insteps and toes' undersides were dirty white. Annie looked away. This lovely, offensive friend of Annette's was filthy.

Douglas Fent entered, annoyed with Annie.

"Why's the kitchen still open?" he barked. "Finish off! Wanna lock up."

Annie walked away. Fent saw Dewy: "Mind getting your *feet* off there?"

"I do mind," said Dewy.

"*Excuse* me? It *doesn't look good* if ~"

"No one's here."

"I'm *just asking* ~"

"You needn't explain you're asking."

Overhearing, Annie felt reluctant, faint liking for Dewy. From the doorway, she saw Annette approach hand in hand with her.

"She's not going upstairs!" snapped Fent.

"I'm her guest, sir," said Dewy. "Are live-in staff not allowed guests?"

"You planning to stay the night?"

"No."

"Staying somewhere else?"

Dewy turned to Annette: "Lead the way, darling."

"*Excuse me?!*" exploded Fent. "This is *my pub.*"

"It's not, it's the brewery's," said Dewy. "And you've let their Tampax machine run out. Before you see to that, here's 20 pounds, another bottle of Merlot?"

"Uh, I *don't ~*"

"Do you want this empty bar's income up 20 pounds?"

"*OK,* ONE bottle." He pushed past Annette and exited, ordering Annie to: "Get those… *girls* a bottle of Merlot, make sure they pay."

Annette and Dewy climbed narrow stairs. They entered a bare-floored, small, messy room, single bed on the left. A metal vent-pipe outside blocked half the window. The room smelt in various ways, a note of mouse under floorboards or in boarded-up fireplace. West-facing, the room would get hot late day. Annette gazed trustingly at Dewy: "Welcome to my home." Dewy nearly cried.

Stuck to the wall by the bed were rows of Morris photographs. His old collar and one of his half-chewed toys – an eye-missing small teddy bear – lay by the pillow. Dewy noticed one or two photographs weren't Morris, but his beloved Boston Terrier predecessor Bachelor, 1995-2009, Annette's first dog. Bachelor's old, tooth-marked, blue rubber ball was by the pillow too.

Dewy and Annette sat on the bed. In a single movement they swayed, pulled their legs up and lay entwined.

Annette told Dewy no one knew of her pregnancy, only Annie and Beverley.

"I'll stay in Farrisford until my child's birth in September."

"I will too," said Dewy.

Annette cried softly, saying she daren't go home in July as planned. She couldn't face her parents pregnant ("and," thought Dewy, "with no sign of the father"). But by September she'd be eight months separated from

Morris. Annette heaved with sobs as she said this.

The subject of Stuart was too much to face. Annette seemed to deny realising he'd abandoned her. Dewy hoped they might discuss this, but Annette looked tearful and lost.

"Let's go wash our feet in the bath," whispered Dewy. "Is there one?"

"Next room to this. Five of us share it. No hot water except mornings."

A moment later, other side of the wall, sounds of peeing, a wc flushed then old pipes screeched and groaned.

"You need a new place," said Dewy. "Quiet and clean. I'll get a job, find us an apartment real soon, maybe in this street, near people you know?"

"Oh, Dewy. Do you think we could do that?"

"Of course we will, darling." Dewy saw a plastic washing-up basin. "How about I bathe your feet in here instead of the bath? Make 'em feel nice?"

Annette's foot-washing lasted an hour, Dewy kneeling on a pillow on the floor. Cycles of soapings and rinses meant frequent visits to the bathroom to empty the basin, half fill it with cold water and fill Annette's travel-kettle.

Dewy was horrified by the Lugworm staff's purple, yellow, mint-green, brown, white and peach bathroom. She vowed never to use it. A pink WC with a cracked black seat faced the door. A murky, lime, Garfield window-blind towered over a sill crammed with aerosols and stiff face-cloths. Two dust-clogged, high-up vents started growling for 10 minutes whenever the light was switched on, heard in Annette's room. A tan basin had dislodged from crumbled woodchip. An occasional pubic hair skulked on brown-white, sticky lino.

Back in the bedroom, a last kettle-boil warmed a towel nestled round it. As Dewy warm-towelled Annette's feet, the deep bell of St Botolph's struck midnight a mile off.

Each chime from the ancient stone tower rang pure in the still night. Dewy loved such a British sound.

Annette lay on the bed, feet in space above Dewy's lap. After delicately drying between Annette's toes, Dewy massaged them slowly one at a time, then all of Annette's feet for an hour, pausing to drink wine. When Annette was asleep, Dewy left to empty the basin, returned, put it in a small alcove, peed in it, then crept downstairs. She'd drunk 2.9 bottles of wine in six hours. To not set alarms off, she tried the kitchen, guessing chilled vodka was stored there.

At 4am Annette sleepwalked to the bathroom. She returned to hear sobs.

"Darling?" said Annette, peering into dark: "Wha' happen? You OK?"

"It's-it's, *ahh*," wept Dewy, lying on the floor, sobbing. She blew her nose into her hair – *hfffghrfffHFF!!*

Annette reached, found and kissed Dewy's shaking shoulders. Fumes of vodka filled the space. Dewy swigged from a bottle, blew her nose into her hair again, wept, said: "I… I s-*sold*… I…" then drawled words of no sense.

"You've maybe had a bit to drink, hon?" said Annette.

AT FIRST LIGHT Beverley was woken by a window breaking somewhere in the building. Annie, beside her, slept on. Beverley went out to the landing. A terrible noise arose from Annette's room – a woman who couldn't sing yelling music with all her strength.

Beverley slightly opened the door and peered in. Up at the window a long, naked woman, back turned, was dancing, swinging a pair of knickers above her head, roaring: *Ah got the loook! I belawwng t'you! Do anythahh tha-you wah me to!*

"God in heaven," gasped Beverley. She couldn't help noting the woman a beguiling, effortless dancer, lovely to watch, nudity irrelevant, long black hair shoogling and bouncing as she leapt.

Dewy's hiccups were notoriously loud. She hiccupped now: *Heeeek!!*, fell against the alcove and collapsed a part at a time, a dying swan.

Cold air blew across the room from a window-pane Dewy had punched through with the base of a vodka bottle Beverley noticed was taken from the kitchen fridge.

When Annette got up at 7am, Dewy lay naked on the floor. Annette rushed to assist her upright, led her to the bed, pulled blankets over her. "Oh! Your poor body," said Annette, hugging her warm. "Please be well?"

Arms flapping in a sheet, Dewy struggled upwards like a deranged, pretty heron. She zig-zagged to the alcove to be sick in the basin. The kitchen vent-pipe belched brown steam.

On the other side of the bedroom wall, Beverley began the 20 minute running of Annette's bath then went downstairs, returning with coffee and Danish pastries for Annette and Annie. Annette rushed from her doorway.

"Beverley? Could you please help me lift my poor friend?"

"Sure," said Beverley, ready to meet this "friend", whose few hours in the building had caused problems. She entered the room. The "friend" lay unconscious in a dire position over a mound of bags and clothes.

"I put her coat over her," said Annette, clambering over mess.

"Careful with your feet, love," said Beverley. "There's broken glass."

"I think it's from the window?" said Annette. "It's broken. I don't know how that happened."

Beverley straightened Dewy's lower legs: "Cold. Legs all mottled."

"She's nothing on under the coat," said Annette. "Can we try keep it on?"

First-Aid trained, Beverley raised Dewy deftly and lay her on the bed.

"Oh!" said Annette, kneeling to warm Dewy's ankles with her hands.

Beverley retreated, surveying the room, watching Annette exhale warm air over Dewy's toes.

"Nice feet," said Beverley, blank tone hinting they were no saving grace.

"Oh, she has the beautifulest footies in the *world*," cried Annette, "but they never smell."

"Lovely-looking girl," sighed Beverley. "I don't understand why she's…"

Beverley fell silent.

In the car to Exeter, Beverley asked Annette: "Does your friend have a drink problem?"

"Uh… no," said Annette. "To some people yes, but she says not. She *was* alcoholic in her teens but not now, for, as she put it: 'I can go without booze and still be a person'. She's no way as bad as in the past, but drinks four, five days if she's been down. She rarely feels down when she is, it hits later."

Annette continued: "She was sent back from Africa once, an assignment with a New York documentary team she was to write about for Marie Claire. Or was it Harper's? No, she says she never messed up with Harper's. Anyway, Dewy couldn't stand the documentary people, and stopped attending things they did. One day she woke naked on the floor to find them all in her room. Three were men. They yelled what a drunken let-down she was. Dewy wee-wee'd on a towel then attacked them with it. The hotel made her leave. Oh…"

"You OK?" said Beverley, slowing the car.

"Yeah, I… ah… yes, thank-you…" Beverley stopped in a layby. Annette opened the door for air. "Dizzy… this happens a lot… *ah*…"

"Oh, love. Shall we go back? You can have our, er, my

room for the day."

"I'll be fine in a minute," said Annette, head back, eyes closed.

When they drove on. Annette continued: "So Dewy wandered bar to bar in Johannesburg... unaware she was in a huge, dangerous city at night, a riot going on a street away. A man who worked the last bar was concerned and called his sister, who took Dewy to a religious retreat for the night, US consulate next morning. They rearranged her flight to that day. This was four, five years ago. She doesn't work for magazines much now. Right now I'm glad. It means she can be with me. No one's as focused and capable as Dewy."

Beverley said nothing.

Chapter 5

AT MIDDAY, FENT barged into Annette's room, expecting her absent. But the other American woman lay asleep, back and shoulders naked, sheet to her ankles. Fent stared aghast at her black soles, then saw her arm hugged a vodka bottle.

Beverley had warned him about the broken window. Fent kicked his way through cases, books, bottles, plates and mess to examine it and look out at the kitchen roof. Today was sunny, some roof-water would evaporate. Fent turned to leave, but saw a washing-up tub of dark liquid and bathroom tissue in the alcove. He glanced at the woman, and only held off shouting her awake.

Fent would exact full cost of the vodka and evict both women. The Annette girl was dispensable, could be sacked today. Fent took the vodka bottle and left.

At 5pm, Dewy woke, cold, nauseous, head pounding, womb aching. "In England," she mumbled. "Annette's at school, I guess." She searched for her dress and coat, wondered how the window got broken and reread Annette's:

> *Darlingestness, Plse keep warm all day. How about a*
> *<u>disgusting</u> evening? <u>Please</u> can we be disgusting tonight?!!*
> *Xxxx*

Dewy's headache boomed, she bled and had lunking chest pains. Aspirin, Tampax, water and a sugary snack were urgently needed.

She put Angela Foster's Oscar de la Renta dress back on, hugged Mrs Hall's cashmere coat around her and padded downstairs. Eight steps down, the stairs double-turned. Dewy rounded them to see Beverley and Annie staring up. Dewy held her nerve. "*Hi.*"

Both stepped back. Dewy breathed "Thank-you", and darted into The Angler's Bar: "I'll go out this way."

"You do that," Annie muttered.

Beverley and Annie resumed their war-meeting. Annette's friend must *go*. Her vandalism, drunkenness, stealing, all-day sleeping and making that room more squalid risked Annette and the baby. Meanwhile Fent was so enraged that Beverley and Annie resolved they – not he – would eject Dewy. Their priority was to protect Annette, even Dewy, from Fent's violence.

Now Dewy wandered in open air, breathing deep. She wasn't well, yet alive to novelty and beauty. She heard and saw blackbirds, a thrush, a chaffinch. Passing faces looked at her. Only one snarled: "Where's your *shoes*?" Four or five children began to follow her. Dewy thought them sweet. She liked the area. Its scruffy, dull-brick semi-detacheds felt homely. The children caught up with her.

"Why aren't you wearing shoes?"

"I don't want to," said Dewy.

"Why do you talk loik tha-at?"

Dewy looked down at the children kindly.

"Like what, honey?" she said.

"Americanish?"

"Because I am."

The children found her astonishing.

"Why are you here?" asked one.

"Visiting a friend."

"Shall I ask my mum to give you some shoes?" said a small girl.

"*Aww,*" said Dewy. "No thank-you, I'm fine. But is there a store someplace?"

"A what?"

"A store, er… a shop?"

"Down the hill then left," said the children.

Londis in the Yenton estate was staffed by Barbara and Derek, both 63, red-cheeked and watchful. They shared a high-counter halfway up one of two aisles. A jagged piece of card said: *We do 'Not' accep £50s note's.*

Middle-aged friends stood around the counter half the day, a community hub. All gaped at the arrival of Dewy, who didn't see, for the door's electronic *beep-boop!* distracted her. She gazed above as she padded left, then right, into the other aisle.

Stocky, half-bald Derek rolled up grey acrylic sleeves, stepped down the counter's one stair and stomped after her. All heard his footsteps in the other aisle. When these stopped, the shop fell silent. Derek cleared his throat and spoke his hardest tone:

"Y'*allroyt*?"

"Yes thank-you, sir," said a calm voice (an *American* voice!)

"Hmph" grunted Derek. "Anything here what it is you're looking for, is ut?"

"Red wine, sir," said the woman. "I've found it, thank-you."

"Wine's there, yuh," said Derek, backing away. "Just there, where you found."

He returned, wide-eyed, to the counter, closed the hatch and took position.

Dewy's sweeping, soundless entrance, clutching three Blossom Hill bottles to her chest, surprised everyone.

"Put them here, you'll drop 'em," snapped bowl-haired, glaring Barbara.

"Sure," said Dewy, padding to the counter. As she placed the bottles, everyone saw her in close-up, realising, moment by moment, an exceptional sight, whose coal-black hair defined her head's outline and fell elegantly, but whose lily-white face was grubby, hair beside it stuck together.

Beep-boop! went the door. A lean man in a white England shirt and brown leather jacket entered, – the eighth amazed watcher of a barefoot woman in a blue-green, expensive coat, placing Tampax and Caramacs next to bottles of wine.

It was all too much for a bulky man. "Where's your **SHOES**?!" he roared, approaching Dewy. "Why ain't you got *shoes*? Where's your *SHOES*!"

"I don't wear shoes," said Dewy, gaze blurring the area between his eyes.

Purchase over, she walked through glaring people, struggled out the door and pirouetted, to see children watching her. They parted in silence to make a path. "Thank-you, darlings," said Dewy shakily. "Thank-you so much."

ANNETTE EMERGED FROM the bathroom. Annie, passing, saw she'd been crying.

"Back from college, aye?" said Annie. "Whit's up? You OK?"

"Y-yes thank-you," said Annette, trying to smile. She entered her room, left the door ajar. Annie lingered, saw the broken window and more mess than ever. She'd have to intervene soon. The health visitor was due again.

Annette said: "Come in, if you'd like to? Please shut the door?"

Annie did, leaned against a wall, arms folded. "Something upset ye?"

Annie hoped Dewy was the cause. Maybe Annette wanted Dewy gone too. If so, eviction would be easy. This keen hope died when Dewy burst in, put a bag down, flung herself around Annette: "You've been crying, hon? What's wrong?"

Dewy turned. Annie looked at her steadily.

"Hey," said Dewy to Annie. "Why the wrong face?"

She returned to Annette and hugged her: "What happened?"

"Douglas. He burst in again. I was ~"

"*What?*" said Dewy and Annie.

"H-he *knocked*, but came in. He... knocked as the door opened. That's how it happens."

"'Happen*s*'? said Dewy.

"He needs to, um, check the roof?" said Annette. "I'd returned from Exeter, was lying down. Douglas went to the window, looked out, went crazy about the broken window again – he'd yelled about that when I arrived earlier. Now he saw the... the basin in the alcove? He said: 'What's this red liquid'? I said 'Oh *that*? It's OK.' Then he... *changed*. He got *really* uh... *close*, looming over me. He... he was yelling... I... *I can't remember.*"

She buried herself in Dewy, who held her close.

"What was in the basin?" said Annie.

A brief pause. Dewy primly looked away, Annette fell quiet.

Annie stared at Dewy: "What was in that basin?"

Dewy tutted. "Only piss, vomited wine and~"

"*Could you no' have emptied that?*" roared Annie. "Ye just *left* it?"

Heavy steps, male voices. A single knock, the door flung open, Fent marched in, then a man with a toolbox. Dewy stood and blocked Fent's way:

"Sir, don't come in this room without permission."

Fent recoiled, wide-eyed.

"Get out my pub," he growled.

"It's not yours, we've been through that. Enter like that again I'll report you for harassment of staff."

She looked around Fent to the other man.

"Who are you, sir?"

"Glazier."

"Please step outside? We're not ready?"

The man left. Fent changed colour, eyes insane. Dewy looked at him:

"Go out, close the door. Knock, *wait* 'til you hear 'Come in'. Do that *always*."

Fent snarled. Dewy said:

"What's asked of you isn't difficult. It's how *you'd* expect to be treated."

"*VRGGH!*" roared Fent. He left, slammed the door.

"You can go too," said Dewy to Annie. She opened the door half a foot, pushed Annie out and shut the door. Fent began knocking loudly.

"Better open it?" shook Annette. "Douglas and the glazier need in I guess."

"Fuck 'em," said Dewy. "Before we let Ryan Gosling and Errol Flynn in, do you need anything hidden or tidied?"

"Just to hug and kiss you, darling?" said Annette, still trembling.

They kissed. Knocking got violent. "Shall we let 'em in?"

"No," said Dewy, kissing again. Knocking turned to ramming. Kissing fell apart as they nervously laughed. Dewy whispered: "One, two, three," both yelled: "*Come in!!*"

Fent stormed in. He'd no reason to be there and stood in the glazier's way. He left, telling the glazier "this black-haired one here" was paying.

Later, glazier paid and gone, Dewy lay on the bed near-asleep: "I feel *strange*."

"You scarcely ate all week, hon," said Annette, kissing her. "You're hungry."

"Nah's not that."

"It *is*. C'mon, let's go downstairs, be *disgusting*."

Through an arch in the main bar was a candlelit dining room, preferred by those-in-the-know to the main restaurant. Dewy and Annette chose a banquette by a small oak table and began kissing.

Trainee sous-chef Martin Davidson arrived, serving so Karen Lilly could run the main restaurant. Chubby, perspiring, shy and pink, he recited the specials:

"Cous-cous with—"

"*Never* cous-cous." said Dewy, "Wall-insulation, that stuff."

"It's desiccated wheat semolina," said Annette.

"I don't care if it's wheat semolina's Mom," said Dewy, "Meat-eaters think vegetarians *like* cous-cous. No wonder they think we're ridiculous. Mice don't touch that stuff. Even Communists didn't."

"N-next," quaked Davidson: "Home-made vegetinarian s-sausages."

"*Yes!*" yelled Dewy and Annette, posture high, hands clasped.

"W-with mashed potater and a choice of cabbage. Or… or kale?"

"*KALE!!*" bellowed Dewy.

"*Disgusting*!" cried Annette, dancing as she sat.

"We'll *puke* it!" cried Dewy. "Oh, Goddess!"

After ordering, Dewy and Annette kissed, shared Merlot and sat as always, in each other's arms, heads touching, dreaming. Dinner was served. Annette cried with happiness when Dewy, using knife and fork, British-style, would cut or fold kale, fork it on some sausage, pat a lather of mash and gravy over, then gracefully raise fork to mouth.

Dewy always chewed thoroughly, mouth pouting and closed, head lightly bobbing, gaze faraway. Annette loved to rest her fingertips on Dewy's cheeks to feel food inside, or place her ear against a cheek to hear Dewy chew.

Dewy forked a piece of sausage, put it between her teeth and leaned to Annette. Startled by the Disgusting's sudden start, Annette quickly leaned forward, placed her mouth over Dewy's and received the food. As she chewed and swallowed, both returned upright. They leaned forward to kiss, then upright once more. Now Annette forked a kale-leaf into her mouth and leaned to transfer it to Dewy's.

A Disgusting was something no onlooker forgot or

believed. Dewy wrote "How to Disgusting" in SAB after she and Annette were asked to leave a diner in Vermont for practising the ritual in 2010. While a Disgusting is simple – leaning to transfer food to another's mouth, the art is intricate:

> Disguster and Disgustee lean to each other until mouths connect. After Disguster transfers food to Disgustee, both lean back. <u>Neither hovers before the other's face, ever</u>. Gentle, steady lean-in, pass food {or kiss}, return upright. When food's been swallowed, Disguster and Disgustee kiss and swap roles.
>
> *Hiccups, coughs or sneezes.* Beware these. One of us {OK, me} sneezed mid-transference once. An explosion of food sprayed our faces, necks, hair and chests. We licked each other clean fast, stopping for briefest kisses.
>
> *Warning:* dark green leafy vegetables – cabbage, kale, greens – cause frenzy. These lawless plants hold more gravy than you'd believe. And their toughness means *you can have a mouth to mouth tug-of-war with them!* Forget rules with these boss-leafed foods. Succumb to the mess and plaster your darling's gravied mouth and chin with kisses.
>
> Meat-eaters perhaps have the best Disgusting deal? Their carcass chunks are firm and absorb gravy. Chicken-breast may even be the ultimate Disgusting, or anything carcassarians eat: dead cows, sheep, pigs, ducks {How can you eat *ducks*? Beautiful ducks! Good-natured, peaceful, funny – aren't they not a blessing to this world? How graceful they glide! That gentle, earnest quacking, doesn't it break your heart? Their lovely, strange, orange feet! If anyone kills a duck again I'll throw me under a train.}
>
> Happy Disgustinging, darlings. Damn any fascist bullies harassing you for it like they did my girl and me in Vermont last night. Slurp's up!! Drool power!!

Disgust on!! Ahh-de-o. Xx

The Lugworm was unprepared. People peered in from the main bar. When only kale was left, the women tug-of-war'd it with their mouths. Whoever won a tug-of-war would *pfth*! the kale-mesh out into the room with a toss of her head, grab more and lean to pass it to the other's mouth. They knelt on the banquette facing each other, kale-fibre collapsed like a rope-bridge between them, gasping, gravy-smeared, kissing. Douglas Fent entered.

"*What the hell's going on!!?*"

Dewy turned:

"We are *dining*, sir! What does it look like?"

"A fucking *ZOO!!*" said Fent, shocked by spat-out, latticed kale everywhere.

"Calm, sir!" said Dewy, "You're cursing and yelling at customers."

"This is a *restaurant*!!"

"We're paying for this meal, and won't be harassed."

"*Look at the mess!*" shrieked Fent. "And once and for *all* do you mind—"

"I *do* mind."

"*I haven't finished my sentence –*"

"We haven't finished our meal. Leave us alone!"

Fent stormed out. Dewy shook her head: "Kale on the menu, what does he *expect*?"

MARLON OPENED THE kitchen door. By the dining table at the back of the sitting-room John Wright was absorbed in a 2,000-piece Tower of London jigsaw. TV boomed by the front window, gold curtains closed. Marlon was flustered.

"Dad, sorry this cake's taking ages. I started it two hours ago!"

"Don't worry, son, smells nice," said Mr Wright.

"I wanted us to have cake with tea before bed, y'know?

Might have to be tea and biscuits, this ain't gonna be ready."

A sound. Both froze and stared. Fast-rising car engine, end of the road. Tyres screeched. A vehicle roared through the crescent, hand-brake-turned.

"No, Marlon!" cried John. "Don't go to the window. That's what the police said: *'never* go to the window'."

The vehicle stayed, revving loud. Sometimes there were two, it was hard to tell. Mr Wright and Marlon looked at the curtains. Stones hit the Plexiglass, two sharp clacks. The car roared off. Marlon strained to hear the top of the road. If the car went left it would return, fast circuiting the crescent several times. It went right, receding to quiet.

With a jolt Mr Wright saw his jigsaw piece: he Blood. He pressed it into its rightful place to complete The Bloody Tower.

"Just one car these days," he said calmly. "Past month anyway."

Marlon wasn't listening, flinging the oven-glove hard into the kitchen, following it, closing the door behind, ashamed of his rage.

AT 4AM DEWY finished her third wine bottle and stopped crying about years-old events. Rising from the floor, she half-upended Annette's midnight foot-bath basin. Dewy had since peed in it and needed to again. "Gonna *empty* the bastard first."

She carried the basin to the moonlit door and left. Edging along a wall in pitch-dark, Dewy then reached high to the clean part of the bathroom light-switch, pulled it *cl'tunk!* and flitted into the too-bright, hellish bathroom.

Glancing away as she emptied the basin, her gaze met heavy-lidded eyes of the cartoon cat on the window-blind: **Wake me at dinnertime!**

"*Fuck*," panicked Dewy, dashing from the room, tugging the light-cord. As it clucked off, the hall light clicked on. Dewy turned.

Annie charged forward and shoved Dewy backwards into the dark bathroom.

"What kindae friend are you tae *hur*?" growled Annie. "Ye pish and puke in her room, smash a windae, sleep a' day. *Get the fuck oot of here!*"

"I g-get your point," said Dewy. "Now go away."

"*We* thought you'd *look after* Annette." whispered Annie into Dewy's face. "Instead, ye've *shat* on her. Some fuckin' friend! If ye're here the mornin', I'm *throwing* you out."

"Annette'd be upset. If *you* upset…"

"*You* – in a pregnant gurril's room, smashed oot yur brain, boaking and pishing in a bucket, smashing windaes – telling *me* no' tae upset her?"

"If Annette wants me, I *stay*."

Annie's silhouette receded, backlit by the hall: "You're here the morrow, ah'll *kill* ye."

She left, snapping out the hall light. Dewy stumbled through darkness, climbed carefully into bed and lay awake.

"OH, *DARRLING*," PURRED Annette at dawn. "How lovely to wake in your arms. Your hands are clenched? Oh, but you're lovely and warm."

"So are you, bae," said Dewy.

"Please may I give your ears a snoo?"

"Of course, darling," said Dewy, rubbing Annette's back.

Annette deeply sniffed Dewy's right ear. "*Ohhahh* the morning pungencies! Honeycomb, malt, *soot!*" She shuddered with joy, pressed her lips on Dewy's bosoms, cuddled into her: "What's my girl thinking?"

"I'm drunken bullshit," said Dewy. "People want me out of here."

"They *don't*, hon," said Annette from under the sheet. "They're probably glad someone dependable's with me." She continued kissing Dewy's chest.

"You can't teach college *and* work in a kitchen?" said Dewy. "I'll find a job, rent us an apartment. Meantime, I'll pay rent to Dr Death, meals included for you, no kitchen-work."

"But I like working downstairs, darling."

"Friday through Monday, nine hours a day?"

"Mm, gets kinda long. But I get meals, this room and £30."

"30 a day? Way under minimum."

"No, 30 all four," said Annette, reappearing.

"*What*? Under a pound an hour??"

"I do get tired, I guess."

"I'll offer rent to Skeletor, set your hours to 10 a week, never all one day. I've £200 here, and one thousand in… *darn!*… my case is in that hotel. I'm to check out today. If I don't, they'll throw the case away. And the Louboutins."

"You have *shoes*, hon?"

"They're Angela Foster's. Not quite loaned, but she knows I have them."

Dewy sat up. "I'll go downtown, get my case."

Suddenly, fear: *my newspaper interview's in two hours!*

Chapter 6

THE NUMBER 12: **TOWN CENTRE** VIA YENTON AND SORRELL PARK swung around a corner. Elderly, anorak'd people stirred at the bus stop. Dewy boarded last. Her beauty astonished the driver. Her polite, American tones requesting a fare perplexed him. Why's someone like *her* on the bus? Must be a reason. He felt entitled to ask. When she got off he'd say something.

A fingerless-leather-gloved hand pulled the gearstick. The bus roared forward. At Londis, other sedate, older people boarded. Hard acceleration flung them painfully back into seats while they tried to sit.

For 10 minutes, fast-changing forces meant older people were swung side to side, bounced and jolted. Soft hands tried to grip seat-rails. Shopping bags whacked across the aisle. The bus raged through a new housing estate towards a dual carriageway.

Lights changed. The driver braked. Dewy padded up the aisle.

"Sir? Excuse me?"

Behind rattling plastic, the man turned.

"Can you please not drive so fast?" said Dewy. "There are senior people here?"

"You come to our country to tell people how to do their jobs?" said the man.

"Sir, if…"

"I've got to get to the *destination*!"

"So have they, sir. Safely."

"*Sit down!!*" bawled the driver. He swung the bus into the carriageway and hard-accelerated. Dewy fell backwards, grabbed a pole in time.

"Sir, *please* slow this bus!?" she cried. "You leave me no option but to report you. An option I fucking hate."

"You've sworn at me! A *criminal offence!*"

The bus charged into a lay-by and braked hard. Dewy was flung to the front window. The door *pshhhh'd* open.

"*Off the bus!*" screamed the man.

"What is your name?" trembled Dewy.

"I don't give my name to *abusive passengers!*" he yelled, leaning to make the whole bus hear. Voices rose, a woman with no shoes trying to rob the driver. A high scream – "Get her off!" – from the back.

Dewy left the bus. The man's door crashed open. He pursued, filming Dewy on a phone: "*HOY!! Excuse me!* Turn around for me, please? I need your photograph. You're going to be *prosecuted!* We take *full actionising* of persons doing abuse to our job. *TURN AROUND!*"

Dewy walked into a verge of weeds and grasses. The man stopped.

"You ain't getting away!" he screamed. "You've *no right* to buses in our country if we don't want!! *And where's yer SHOES!!!*"

DEWY'S FEELINGS FOR Britain were mixed. Some people's depth of rage at her being harmlessly barefoot alarmed her. She'd experienced more menace in four days than a year in the US. But it was lovely to be in the UK, abroad for the first time in years, new sights, new air, new birds, buildings, people, accents. Novelty flooded her senses and mind, the sky was beautiful and varying, rain a healing replenishment. The downpour as she'd walked the grass verge felt like rapture, a cleansing of her soul – and her soles, for after rain-grass, her feet shone. She raised a foot behind her to look, a peaches-and-cream sole, outstandingly clean for once.

Early and nervous, Dewy strolled up pedestrianised Bridge Street, no sign of centuries past in its building societies, phone shops, Boots, Costa, Accessorize, Pizza Express. At the far end, a lane between offices narrowed to an alley into Market Street. Dewy returned along Bridge Street towards the Tattler office, gazing at it all the way.

She arrived at an ancient clearing where paths from Farr's Lane and Groats met Bridge Street by a compact 17th-century building nestling against East Lane Park's leafy oaks: the Tattler office, beamed and whitewashed, a woozy relic from a fairy-tale, partly a storey off the ground, propped by thick old timber posts. Colourful fruit and vegetable stalls thrived beneath.

Antique doors opened to steep stairs of blue industrial carpet. Dewy climbed these to a 50-foot office, windows on one side and the far end. Desks lay empty until near a 1900s wood and frosted-glass editor's office in a corner. Men aged 25-40 worked at these desks. Most wore an open-neck shirt under V-neck sweater and blazer. Dewy approached. The men looked up. One went: "Pff!". Another laughed. Everyone watched the following:

A dignified, fatherly man of 50 – tidy beard, dull suit – emerging from the editor's office, reading his phone.

"Mr Carruthers?" said Dewy.

Geoff Carruthers glanced up. He took in Dewy's appearance: "No *shoes*?"

Dewy looked him up and down back: "No *clitoris*?"

MILLIE, LATE, SAW Bernadette glare across outside tables, dragging the big, hinged picture-board with *Thank Fish It's Friday!* above a happy fish wearing a bib.

"You're late!" snapped Bernie.

"I'm early! I starts 12.30."

"*You*, hold on a minute ~"

The same weekly row, the same Fent roar: "Girls! *Shut it!* We're behind with setting up! The anglers are *coming now!*"

Millie knew no fishermen arrived until past 1pm, but she must pretend the same urgency as Bernie and kitchen staff, who, wrongly told by Fent anglers were imminent, must prepare a buffet (besides the restaurant menu) and clear space for the frying or grilling of fish caught by the anglers.

Millie put crisp tablecloths onto tables, secured them with clips, prepared hotplates, wrapped cutlery in napkins. The worst part was helping Fent carry a glass-cased fish up from the cellar, a grotesque, five-foot, yellow and black thing, some kind of pike caught long ago, displayed only when the anglers' club came in. Any landlord not honouring that tradition was threatened with boycott by the "Brate Fliers" as they termed themselves.

"Horrible old twats," was how Millie Zena termed them. When groped in her second week, she'd dealt with it in her usual way by punching the man, only to see, as his dentures fell, he was 75. Fent had instantly sacked her, but stupidly said: "You must work your shift first." Millie walked out. Fent followed, pleading: "The bar can't be unstaffed!!" When Millie stomped back, flung her coat off, re-entered the bar, Fent took pride in his management skills, only to hear: "*RIGHT*, shuddup a second! If *any* of youse touches me, looks at me wrong, makes fun of my colour, my accent or being a girl I'll smash that old fish and stuff bits down yer fuckin' throats. I *MEAN* it!"

I've grown up a lot since then thought Millie now, pulling one end of the glass case up the cellar steps. *And none of them old bollockses has groped me or said "You from umba-wumba land?" since.*

An hour on, anglers chattered, ate and drank. Many had pink faces and white facial hair. All wore tweed

Trilbies with colourful fishing-flies in the hat-bands. Millie quite liked these hats.

She earned £7.60 an hour at the Lugworm for 12 hours a week, but was paid for 11, as Fent excluded clearing-up time after shifts. Millie gave Bobby £30, spent 30 and saved for clothes and driving lessons, though hadn't had a lesson yet. "But I *will* learn!" she thought. "I want to be someone Marlon wants. I want to go to college and learn to be… *professional*. But at what?"

Her father's: *What you good for? You've no thoughts except weed and trainers* had hurt badly, though he'd said it two years ago, "when I was a different person ago," Millie thought. "Today I want a future. I want an office. I'll live in Crendlesham and London. When Marlon retires from football, playing for England, we'll have kids. He'll be 34, I'll be 33. That's the plan, I'm feeling this happening, it's early stages, but I'm realistic?"

DEWY FOLLOWED GEOFF Carruthers. They walked in silence through the empty half of the office to the door. Dewy's mind reeled: *I've fucked this totally. WHY am I such a shitbag?*

Carruthers was less uneasy. His "OK, quick chat, follow me," was his brisk reply to this woman, who he'd escort quickly out before she could speak again. He'd briefly treat her as an interview candidate, then say they were fully-staffed. (A pained lie, Catherine leaving any day now, mostly working from home.)

Carruthers secretly gave interviewees points. Good candidates reached 850, even 900. He once started one on *minus 500* for saying: "Basically I want your job in three years and I'll get it in two."

They stopped by the door. Carruthers took in the woman before him: a mindless, "easy on the eye", American show-off who'd humiliated him in a cheap way.

She wants an interview? Fine. She starts on *minus 1000 points.*

Dewy faced the door. When she or Carruthers spoke, her upper body neatly turned to him. Years of ballet made Dewy ever precise, light and graceful.

"So," said Carruthers: "*Seriously* looking for work on this paper? Sure it's your thing? (*minus 1000pts*)

"I hope so, sir." (*-980pts*)

"Worked on a paper before?"

"Six months on a local daily, magazines a couple years." (*-680pts*)

"Local – in America, was this?"

"Yes, sir. Medford. Near Boston."

"Magazines? Women's magazines?"

"I guess. I've been to Elle and back, I'd go again," said Dewy. Disliking what she'd said, she added quickly: "This is a good paper. I don't want to waste your time." (*-630pts*)

"Why 'a good paper'?"

"I like the news coverage. Not a wasted word. I counted 48 items this week. Longer ones had incisive quotes from a range of viewpoints. Feature articles were strong, community-rooted. The piece about the school play was real good, the rehearsal diary? I liked *all* the paper. It's... uh... it's good! I hope not to m-make a patronising overview, sir, but the paper seems very much at the heart of this town. And the town feels that." (*-280pts*)

"Letters pages? See them?"

"I did, I read them all. (*-80pts*) A real community forum. I like you have two pages of letters, (*-30 pts*) even two and a half? (*0 pts*) Contributors know they can write in without awkwardness, they're among others." (*+70pts*)

"The poem? See it?"

"I did! I thought it was lovely. (*270pts*) Kinda like, um, Edward Thomas? I-I'm not over-familiar with poets. But... I liked it. Father... uh... Entreton, is that right? (*370pts*) Is that how it's pronounced?" (*400pts*)

"Enntriton, yeah. Quite a long letters page this week. Lucky to get his poem in actually, he sends 'em regular. If you were asked to *edit* the letters page, and we got loads as usual, what about the poem? Hold it over to next week?"

"No, sir, I'd run it there and then."   (*Uh-oh. **700pts***)

"Cut the poem down, maybe?" said Carruthers: "Get rid of a *bit*, surely?"

"N-no, sir, every word stays. I'd… find a way. I-I don't know how, but I *would*. Without losing any readers' letters."   (*She's aced it. As no one before. **1000pts***)

FENT WAS INSTRUCTING Annie by the kitchen when Dewy burst in, bedraggled, with a vast plastic bag of washing-up basins, another with wine-bottle outlines amid other bulgings, and tugging a navy-blue case.

"*Do you think you're fucking living here!?*" roared Fent.

"Must you yell?" said Dewy.

"*Can I have a WORD please!?*"

Bernie dashed in from the main bar: "*Douglas!* Stop being a wazzock! They can hear you out here. *Shut up!*"

Millie Zena peered from The Angler's Bar. Pointing at Dewy, Fent bawled at Millie: "Why did you let *this* in through your bar?"

"Whatd'ya mean '*this*'?" said Millie. "She's an *her*. And a nice 'un."

"Why did you let '*her*' behind the bar and in *here*?"

"Don't shout at *me*. I weren't there, I went toilet."

"Why?"

"You asking me why I went *toilet*? For *real*?"

"*GOD'S SAKE!!*" roared Fent, throwing up his hands: "Speak to me like that again, *you're sacked!*"

"Shaddup," said Millie. She turned to Dewy: "You the new America girl?"

"Yeah. Hi," said Dewy, quietly.

"I'm Millie. Int your feet cold?"

"No, hon."

"*Get in that bar!!*" bawled Fent.

Millie pulled a face and left. Fent glared at Dewy, who said: "I'd like to talk to *you*, sir."

"What about?"

"Cash."

ANNETTE WOKE, RED and damp. Dewy bustled in, bags everywhere: "I'll get water, you're way hot." She dashed downstairs, returning with Perrier and ice.

Annette sat up to drink with both hands around the glass. She wore her old white pyjama top covered in tiny cartoon Boston Terriers in different poses. Dewy tugged wine-bottles and Louboutins from the carrier bag then upended it: "Gotcha some things". Out tumbled face-cloths, vitamin B6, baggy white T-shirts, Floradix, Crunchies, underwear and a plastic fan.

Dewy unpacked the fan from its box: "The town has a covered market! Stalls full of tiger-print cushions, yellow shampoo, mirrors with the Manhattan cityscape. I got you no-brand cotton knicks, thin T-shirts and ~" She plugged the fan in: "…*this!*" It whirred fast.

Annette changed her pyjama top for a new T-shirt. Dewy kissed her, noting her eyes were glazed. Annette leaned on Dewy, whispering:

"Where else did you get to, hon?"

"'Ovah heah, ovah theah,'" said Dewy, nuzzling Annette's hair.

"Were people nice?" said Annette.

"Plenty nice."

"Did they ask about your footies?"

"Not that I recall."

"Oh, honey," said Annette. She turned her face to Dewy and snuggled close. "Will you stay with me?"

"Of course, darling. I live here now – it's official! I

spoke to Dr Death, gave him £800 rent for the next month. Your meals are included, kitchen hours 10 a week over three days. He'll hire someone new to work the rest."

"Oh," smiled Annette, still dizzy. "And *your* meals?"

"I'll eat at work, hon."

"You've a job?"

"Short term. They said: 'we'll still advertise it'. Start Sunday, Farrisford Tattler."

Part Two

Chapter 1

IN A TREES-HIDDEN house in Pegasus Lane, Tessa England looks in the mirror.

"Happy birthday, old girl. Keep going!"

Beezer bursts in, tail walloping, leaps on the bed, "*Get off!*" roars Tessa England. The two-year-old Doberman jumps to the oak floor, whimpering with joy. The *scents* out there in Sunday morning mists! Foxes! Badgers! Rabbits!

"WUFF!"

"Shut *up*, Beeze! We go in two minutes!"

Tessa England, 68, views her nude reflection, as every birthday. *Not bad. Everything working, thank God.*

Gentle old Alsatian, Rudyard, wanders in. Beezer lies back, softly paws him.

Sunrays flood the room. Tessa England's blonde hair shines. New warmth caresses her. She faintly smiles.

"'When I grow old I'll wear purple,'" she murmurs, half-remembering a poem.

She reaches for navy blue clothes, but again sees the mirror.

"When *I* grow old, I'll wear *nothing*," she muses. "Days like this, out with the dogs, naked in the woods. 'Morning, Tessa! In the buff again?' 'Yup!'"

She frowns: "Why 'when I grow old'? Why not **now**?"

She sighs: "Better not…"

Tessa England has been MP for Farrisford and Crendlesham 15 years, a Conservative.

THE 1830S GRANDFATHER clock in Father Entreton's dark green sitting-room softly clucks the seconds. After praying, the priest slowly stands, stretches, opens the doors to his garden. He sees the day's brightness and heads out.

Early morning birdsong peaks, a spirited, busy market. Father Entreton closes his eyes to listen. Hot weather has returned. Every bird in miles sings and yells, greeting these hopeful days.

Mists haze far country, but Farrisford's streets begin to bake. Windscreens dazzle white in watery mirages. The town looks vibrant in strengthening sun. Father Entreton looks to where distant Cressy Road vanishes into low hills. Halfway along, below the road, silvery structures gleam – the floodlights of Farrisford Town FC. "The Blues" twice reached the second round of the FA Cup, in the '60s and '80s. The club's other achievement is natural to remember on a hot day of blue sky like today. On a hotter day one July, 10 or more years ago, Farrisford Town played a friendly match against reserve and youth players of an Italian team, on an off-season tour, called Juventus.

Garton Road was capacity-filled, 86 degrees. Sun-hatted children lay stupefied in mothers' arms. Many women and girls hadn't been to a football match before. Most were astonished by the passion and madness of local men. Never had so many been seen. Dads, brothers, cousins, teachers, Mr Bolt from the Grammar, years-known faces from shops, the market, schools, pubs, churches – all shouting, singing and emotional. Glamorous, perfect Juventus players running around made it all the more odd.

The day wound down, three minutes left, Juventus winning 9-0, though Farrisford had played well (defenders Gary Sheekey, Ali Hassein, Keith Miller and Steve-somebody prevented far worse damage). But 1200 sober-now, sunburnt men were sad. They'd wanted a thousand wives and daughters to see one home goal, feel the joy, see *why we blokes come to these things.* The sun fell under the stand, shadow over a fourth of the pitch. Singing stopped. People were leaving.

Then Billy Nevin scored. The roar crossed fields to the faraway sea. Sunbathers in county gardens squinted at a sound they couldn't place.

Picnickers on Crendlesham's hills stopped mid-word: "What was *that*?" "I didn't hear anything." "Must have been me." It wasn't.

But that ball going in let Billy Nevin's demons out. Front page star of next week's *Tattler*, unslept and growling with happiness, Antrim-born Nevin, then 35, was soon sacked from his forklift job at Alpha Staplers. Drinking around the clock up and down The Swainway, he didn't turn up to work for days, then did. He hit a manager and roared abuse at the CEO. Over years he was arrested often: drunk and disorderly, theft, affray, criminal damage, grievous bodily harm. Eventually a fed-up judge gave him six years.

Nothing's been seen of Nevin since. He's not missed. A few spoke of brief likeability, and a unique singing talent (if made-up songs in a military rhythm about violence done by himself is a talent.) But Nevin's demons aren't funny at all. Everyone says the town's better without him. Terrible to say, but true.

The countryside shimmers in sun. Radiant gold fields, lines of trees and green hills stretch miles to far, blue-faded hills. A southern edge of Crendlesham gleams mid-distance, the rest hidden by the Tassens – a ridge of hills skirted by ancient woods. Crendlesham locals call the hills Bess, Mary, Anne, Victoria and Lizzie. Bess on Guy Fawkes Night has a bonfire so big its wood-stack beforehand can be seen from here, 11 miles.

Father Entreton looks north, to hills of dense woods, how cool and aromatic they must be. He sees the Brate curve, and curve again, through an oxbow's separated jigsaw pieces, gathering speed towards Sherrier's Waterfall, a lovely spot. It's said most of Farrisford was conceived there over the centuries.

Father Entreton returns to his house to get ready for Mass. Had he bided a minute more, he might have heard faraway singing by a man banging time with a stick on a beer-can:

My name is Billy Nevin!

They sent me down from Heaven!

And I'll deck any man who feckin ar-gues.

In Farrisford's east edge, person after person froze. They knew who it was.

I'll string him from the rafters,

That'll learn the feckin' bastard

Then I'll kick his feckin' rump

Like I did to Donald Trump!

ALPHA STAPLERS IS silent. The sun heats used air and carpet tiles. On weekdays the 100-foot office resounds with phones and meetings. A knocked-through wall leads to a larger, all-white space, of abstract art, sofas, vast plants and **LOVE AND THINK** stencilled across the ceiling. The 1950s block backs onto Alpha's warehouse and dark Victorian factory building, soon to be apartments.

Two miles away, Alpha Staplers' 48-year-old Head of Design, David Bennett, is in his greenhouse, on the phone to his partner, John Talbot:

"I'm going back to bed."

"Don't be daft," says John, who's from Yorkshire.

"Can't stop thinking about work."

"Forget 'em. They're idiots. Real ones."

"I don't know what to do," says David, inspecting a reddening tomato.

"You're gonna resign," says John. "Have a year off, start painting again."

"The company's being crushed by new managers, brand consultants, HR, merchandisers. No industry experience, yet they make senior decisions…"

"I know," says John gently "But you'll resign soon, we agreed. Come over, Davie? I'll sign you in as a guest. Have tea and one of our superb muffins."

"Better not. I've masses to do."

"David! Missing out on stewed tea in the Asda manager's office!?"

After the call, David returns to the house. He opens his 1960s satchel briefcase, removes a thick envelope. An HR intern gave these out after last week's Integral Management Cadency-Triage.

After a year of fortnightly meetings of that name, David still has no idea what Integral Management Cadency-Triage means, or why the nursing term Triage is used. He suspects no one else knows either, but he daren't ask.

Printed on the middle of the envelope: *Don't open this til chill-out time. Go for the run, have a shower, get into yer comfies, _eat_ (don't forget!!) get yerself proper relaxed then open this!! :-)*

The envelope contains a 45-page questionnaire requesting information and assessments of any six members of staff – *your choice!!* – who he deals with daily:

This exercise is much as anything about seeing what it takes to interact & sharpen apreciative awareness of other's immediatley around in order to give feedback at ground atmospherics level that improve everybody's performance and the teams "as a whole".

David reads the first question: *In _your_ own word's, describe this colleague's attitude, input, commitment and*

*achievement's, then list FIVE positive qaulities in him/her
and TWO negatives/neutrals ones."*

"What's this got to do with the manufacture of staplers?" sighs David.

MORESBY VILLAGE HAS been spared the noise of bypass works since government contractors Scrippa went into administration. Jade Tyler is woken instead by a phone-in downstairs on the kitchen's lisping radio. She drifts back to sleep, but another worked-up radio voice wakes her, a caller hissing 'Syrians' a lot.

Jade, 14, sits up, films herself, saying to camera: "I get up, I'm OK for *one minute,* then a weight lands on my big tummy. School. Exams. Homework. So much to do…! And…. *and…"* Jade can never speak when she needs to most.

Downstairs the radio spurts:*"NO, I'm not ssaying it'ss the Syrians' fault their country's got dilemmass. But what kind of people puts their kidss in lorries with no windowss? What kind of parentin' is that? What kinda VALUES is that?"*

Jade lifts the curtain by her bed. Gold rays flood over her. She feels peace for one second, then her father booms up the stairs:

"Danii?"

"She can't hear you, you idiot," muttered Jade.

"Danii? Can you hear me?"

"*Unna ett uff ina minnid!"* faintly from Jade's mother's shut bedroom.

"You should listen to this, Danii! It's a lotta sense. They reckon them Syrians is coming into our country far more a lot than what it is that was being thought!"

His voice receded: "And coming round here! At least Romanians or what-are-they's work in the fields. Syrians don't wanna work, it ain't their culture."

CATHERINE WREN LIKED Dewy instantly and was grateful for her arm as they climbed the *Tattler* stairs. Dewy was concerned about her, but wouldn't say. Instead, she'd try to save Catherine work by doing all she could while Catherine watched.

The empty Sunday office was perfect for concentration. Dewy was slow on page lay-out after six years off, but Catherine was glad Dewy could tactfully rewrite articles and quickly sub-edit, invent headlines, standfirsts and picture-captions, and keep a list of facts, names and spellings to be checked.

She enjoyed inducting Dewy into the paper and its world. By noon they'd completed nine pages, including a controversial **Approval For 35 Homes In Balaton** article, a photo-spread of the 76th Lairsdale Young Farmer's Club Annual Show, its 30-person tug-of-war, *Frozen* bouncy-castle, and children bottle-feeding goats. Brock Hill Primary School's Spring Fair filled page 8. On page 11, Farrisford Fire Station launched its Be Moor Aware campaign, advising safety and fire rules in open country, especially south-west of Farrisford. Page 12 saw a preview of the Moresby May, featuring opera groups, vintage tractors and a folk band.

Apart from: **Rise In Jobless 'Was Expected'**, **Car Chase Man Jailed** and **Burglaries Rise In Warm Weather**, this week's Tattler seemed a pageant of local people, all ages, in beautiful weather, often pictured with an animal. "May and June are easy," said Catherine. "A million fun-runs, village fêtes, school proms, farm-shows, prize-givings, Crendlesham open-air theatre, and all those lovely, rural Readers' Photos. I think we'll get a four-pager out of this week's Readers' pics. *But…*" continued Catherine, with a sigh: "There's grit in this part of the world too. Far too much, If anything."

"What is DWP?" said Dewy, still on **Rise In Jobless 'Was Expected'**.

"Department of Work and Pensions," said Catherine. "Or 'of Whopping Porkies' some say, as unemployment figures are manipulated to look less. Porkies is British rhyming slang. Pork pies – lies."

"What is this 'Universal Credit'?" said Dewy, squinting at the computer.

"Ah," sighed Catherine. "You'll be coming across that a *lot*."

Dewy read out: "'Higher unemployment numbers were expected because Universal Credit has been factored in, which replaces other benefits.' This is all to do with Welfare, right? Welfare's known as Benefits over here?"

"Yes," said Catherine, filling a kettle. "If we Google Universal Credit, I'll try to explain it, but it's stupidly complicated, harsh, and plunges people into destitution for one wrong or misinterpreted answer. Even the DWP doesn't understand it. Brush up on your Kafka, basically."

Dewy made Catherine rosehip tea with honey and asked if she'd like to eat. Catherine requested a sandwich from Farrisford Organics. Dewy obliged, but dreaded another visit to the grey-décored shop and cafe whose joyless, middle-class staff were rude.

Thankfully the man she'd retaliated to last time wasn't there today, nor was "Went barefoot with no shoes on in Goa but *why here*?" man, but Aggressive Tattooedess was, frothing cappuccino milk for a young woman and man. Dewy waited in line behind them. Both wore black running tights and grey-hoodies. The man's hood was held down by rucksack straps to expose a **CARPE DIEM** tattoo around the back of his neck. The couple slowly debated if swimming burned more calories than a gym work-out. Milk-frothing roared.

Dewy felt air waver on her neck. She turned to see a post-run, panting, drenched, midlife man in a sports body-stocking five inches behind her. Violated, Dewy left the shop. The man went inches behind the couple. Dewy glanced back at Farrisford Organics: "*Never again.*" She'd said this before.

Catherine was grateful for water, fruit and a sandwich from Tesco Metro.

She wondered how to tell Dewy the Tattler often felt like feminism hadn't happened.

"Did Geoff mention money?" said Catherine.

"400 a week officially, or 260 unofficially," said Dewy. "I said I'd prefer officially. He said: 'That'll mean emergency tax'."

"He's a sod," said Caroline. "Trying to pay out as little as possible. I'm on 600 a week pre-tax. That's what *you* should get."

Catherine asked if Carruthers mentioned a women's page. Dewy nodded:

"He said: 'You're probably good for women's stuff.' I said nothing. I feel *totally bad* for not saying: '"What in fuck – '…sorry, Catherine, my language is bad."

"Worry not."

"But I just *stood* there, stunned he'd hired me on the spot at an interview I thought I'd blown."

"Geoff'll ask you to create a double women's page each week," said Catherine. "He'll say: 'You know: fashion, beauty, recipes…'"

"Ah, Christ."

"I'm glad you said that. Perhaps we feel alike about that rubbish?"

"I saw something about make-up in last week's," said Dewy, "a couple recipes and 'Look Good For Spring' dresses."

"Geoff buys that stuff from press agencies, but wants in-house to save money. I wrote it for six months, couldn't stand it."

"Shall we put a recipe in this week?" said Dewy. "I got one."

"Er…?"

"Peanuts and lettuce, dab of mayo? Gives you real firm

shits. 'Geoff, here's the women's page: "Girls! Does hubby spatter the bowl with beer-and-pizza shits? Firm him up with delicious peanuts and le~"'

"Don't make me laugh," wheezed Catherine, seriously.

IN EAST LANE Park Billy Nevin finished a can of cider, rested his square head on a hold-all and fell asleep. Weeks unshaven in camouflage jacket, filthy jeans and army boots, he'd been placid lately, even earned £90 fruit-picking out at Trone. His dark pink, street-drinker's face is flat-nosed and yellow-eyed, but Nevin's physique is lean for a man in late-40s. He plans to find farm-work where few know his reputation for robbery and sudden fights. "I never attack a man," he insists, "I'm Billy Nevin." One of these claims is true.

Like anyone returning to Farrisford he saw changes, or rather closures. "Feckin' Kwik-Save, man! Shut down!" In the town centre he saw dark, empty shops and To Let signs. Gone: Home Depot, Hallmark Cards, Pastie La Vista, William Hill, John Wilde Outfitters, Lloyds Bank, Farrisford Travel, Lucia's, In For A Penny, Lycett's, Phones 4U, Aladdin's Cave, Citizen's Advice Bureau.

And Farrisford Library. Seeing the library boarded up baffled Nevin: refuge on many a cold day, things to read too.

He remembered Lycett's (where he stole toasters and kettles to sell, even a microwave once) and William Hill, Lloyds (Edwardian windows metal-boarded now) and Lucia's womenswear, as everyone does. Many have special memories of Lucia's separate bridal shop through a hidden door in the side alley. Lucia's, John Wilde, Farrisford Travel and Aladdin's Cave were decades-old local institutions.

On his way to the park, Nevin cautiously toured The Swainway, going in no pubs. He was startled to see the town's biggest pub The Bull, boarded up and abandoned. So too The Barley Mow, The Weathervane and two pubs with names Nevin had forgotten despite years shouting in them.

"But that dump The Fusilier's still going?! Makes no sense."

DEWY RETURNED TO The Lugworm at 9pm to find Annette still working in the kitchen. Annette cried out and ran to her. Annie, Beverley and Tommy looked on, like anyone who ever saw the pair. Even half a day apart meant euphoric hugging, cries and kisses.

In the bedroom, Annette undressed and lay on the bed. Dewy switched the fan on, removed her dress: "Did you eat, hon?"

"Through the day," said Annette. "Two apple crumbles. Tommy makes *amazing* desserts. Did you eat, darling?"

"Plenty ate, hon."

(Dewy hadn't eaten since the Disgusting, which caused a minor bowel movement before her interview next day. She'd emerged from the Farrisford Organics cafe wc to: "Hey! *Don't* go in there without shoes!" from a male staff member in grey hoodie and wooden beads.

"Back off," Dewy'd said. The cafe's few customers looked up. All wore grey hoodies too. "Now you've woken the greyful dead," Dewy told the man.

With The Lugworm and Farrisford Organics wc's now out of bounds, Dewy had purchased a trowel from the covered market. She'd go for dumps in the woods and bury them, but hadn't needed to yet.)

Dewy and Annette fell into bed. Dewy carefully climbed over to lie by the wall.

"Going that side, dear?" said Annette.

"So you have the fan on you, bae," said Dewy, already asleep.

An hour later they woke in each other's arms.

"It's nice," breathed Annette. She buried her face between Dewy's bosoms. "Oh, darrling. I love your boo's so."

Annette often kissed Dewy's bosoms, loved to place her hands over them, spread her fingers and breathe out warm air through the gaps. She softly did now.

"Mmmm's nice," said Dewy, in sleep. "I love you."

"Your boo's are perfect."

"Li'l small," murmured Dewy.

Annette kissed Dewy's mouth unstoppably.

"Sorry," said Annette. "I should go brush my tooths."

"I don't care," said Dewy, waking enough to kiss her. "Taste of apple crumble." She fell back asleep, but Annette lay awake. A time later, Dewy woke: "Wsup, darr-ing?"

"I'm gonna be a *mom*," whispered Annette.

"It'll be good, hon," said Dewy, waking, smacking her lips, stretching til she juddered. She reached for Annette's hands and clasped them to her chest. "I'll look after you' an' baby," she whispered. "I'll quit drinking too."

"I'm gonna *give birth*," whispered Annette.

"I'll be there, sweet."

"Will you?"

"Darn right."

"How will I tell Mom? How'm I –"

"Don't worry 'bout that now."

"My family will disown me!" cried Annette.

"They never would, darling. Robert loves you, your brothers adore you."

"They'll be angry. They'll ask why I didn't tell them."

"You didn't want a scene, it'd risk the pregnancy."

"They'll wanna meet Stuart, or certainly know who he is."

"Darling? Hear me? A new Stephens will take all the limelight. Robert Jnr's children will have a new cousin, so will Clifton's son. Morris will be a dogfather. *You'll* be forgotten in the rush to welcome a new Stephens. Joanna's nuts about grandchildren, her guard drops. She'll love and accept you at last."

"Morris, yes. A godfather. Did you say 'dogfather'?"

"I meant 'godfather', sorry."

"Do you think Morris is sleeping OK these nights?"

"Snoring like a grampus."

"Oh, his snores! I miss his snores! *Awww*. They *do* get kinda loud though."

"Hmm," said Dewy.

"Louder than Bachelor was. Bachelor sure snored too."

"He did."

"In a *lovely* way," said Annette. She snuggled into Dewy's arms. After reflecting awhile, Annette continued:

"Bachelor knew his own mind. He understood who he *was*. But Booboo… Booboo's *experimenting*. He… he *searches*. He's very… Are you awake, hon?"

"Yuhhh."

"Remember that documentary about ancient Greece? Like, Apollo? And that other fellow, Dionysius? *He* was BooBoo *totally*. And Bachelor was Apollo!"

"uhh… …"

THE MORNING SCHOOL bus bumped and swung through country lanes. After Balaton, it stopped at villages east of Farrisford: Loddleford, Brinton, Volcombe Basset, Moresby, Case and Bettle. Then to Farrisford's schools: Farley Wood High and Sir John Wyce Grammar.

Jade sat alone near the back. Across the aisle, an older boy, a "Wysee", sat glued to his smartphone.

Jade dreaded Sir John Wyce school. She'd only now got used to Farley Wood after three years, but must start at Wyce in September. Everyone said: "The drongos stay on at Farley, the clever ones go to Wysee," but that was no consolation. Older Farls were nasty to younger Wysees on the bus. Jade, already targeted for her weight, wasn't even a Wysee yet.

The bus reached the summit of Brinton Hill. Its pano-ramic view made motorists stop, awestruck, but had no effect on the raucous school bus. Only Jade looked out, inspired by distances, possibilities... *escape*. She peered to where sky and land blurred and wondered if Somerset began there.

Her brother Warren roared, fought and laughed at the front of the bus. His and Jade's older half-sibling, Brandon, hadn't been quite so loud at school. Jade reflected on how different the two were, Brandon a tall, tattoo'd, sharp-faced, bearded man at 19, black hair grown out in a Rod Stewart cut. He was a shop security guard. Warren *ugh!* – he was *Warren*: same builder's build as his father (though taller), hair a two-inch-high rust morass around a big face with whey-grey teeth. Vacantly cheerful, he bullied in the guise of humour.

Jade worried he and Brandon would increase their mockery in September when she'd wear a Wyce uniform. Suddenly a feeling struck Jade they wouldn't. She'd no idea why.

THAT MONDAY WAS Dewy's official first day at the Tattler. As the number 12 bus was no option to her now, she walked.

The week's editorial meeting was in a 10th solemn minute when Dewy swept in, earth-soled and rosy. Geoff Carruthers stopped talking. Malcolm Zane, Colin Hendry, Stuart Dean, Michael Fenwick, Ian Balloch, Ryan Palmer, Tim West and David Cartwright looked Dewy up and down, stopping at down.

"Aren't your *feet* cold?" said Michael Fenwick.

"No," said Dewy. "Don't yours sweat?"

"Did you walk through *fields* to get here?" said Mal-colm Zane.

"Did you sit in a tailback burning petrol?" said Dewy.

"You're late," said Geoff Carruthers.

"So what? I was here til gone eight last night."

"Weekly meeting, Monday 9.30," said Carruthers. "Be on time, please."

He addressed the men: "Everybody? You *probably* remember this woman – Dewy – from Friday?"

A rumble of male chuckling. Carruthers added: "Taking Catherine's role a couple weeks until we get someone."

"I wanna talk to you about that, Mr Carruthers," said Dewy.

"Geoff. We're all first names."

"Dewy sorted the whole paper yesterday and saved a lot of work," said Catherine, appearing at last, heavily moving across from a far door where a wc flushed. She dried her washed hands on her trouser-thighs and sat awkwardly on a cheap, fold-out, wooden chair. Yesterday she'd told Dewy the orthopaedic chair she'd had delivered was entirely adopted by Stuart Dean. He sat in it now.

"Why don't you get off her chair?" said Dewy to Stuart Dean. "Catherine has to perch on a picnic seat?"

"Why don't you put some shoes on?" said Stuart Dean.

Dewy replied: "Why are you in that chair while a pregnant woman sits on slats, with no low back support?"

Catherine looked at him, with a hint of banter: "Yes, Stuart. Why are you?"

"You *want* this chair?" he said.

"Yes please, seeing as I paid for it."

"How was I meant to know that?"

"Me telling you 60 times?"

"Hff, have the chair, then. *I* didn't know."

Six foot four, never friendly, he stared lazily as Catherine brought him a seat and dragged her own heavy chair back. As she sat, sighing: "*That's* better," Stuart Dean glared at Dewy. Other men looked fixedly at her too, some with frowns and slightly bared teeth. Dewy ignored them, sat upright, crossing an elegant leg over the other. In one effortless move, she leaned, flicked a soil-dot from a cherry-red toenail and returned upright.

Silence.

Staff reporter Colin Hendry stood up, booming. "I's'd better go t'the court!" Stocky, pink and 65, he wore a Trilby and pale raincoat like reporters in old films. "Inquest's continuing, 10.30."

"Right y'arr," said Geoff Carruthers. "If concluded, it's front page. What else you got, Colin? Tell us quick?"

"Gotta go, Geoff. All's on *moy* page plaan. I hoyloyted ut. Go through ut, you'll see."

"Yup, no botherr," said Carruthers, who went very local if talking to Colin Hendry, who was so local he was hard to understand. For all his "gotta go", Hendry took time to smooth out his raincoat, put a laptop into an ancient satchel, check his pockets, count pens, transfer things from pockets to satchel and vice versa. He called to Dewy:

"That's is a good strong page lay-out, noice and clearr."

"Thank-you, sir, it was mainly Catherine."

"D'you walk around like thaat in wintirr?"

"Excuse me?"

"Like thaat in wintirr d'ye go? I bets she dunt."

"I don't wear shoes, sir."

"In *wintirr*?"

"No."

Lanky 23-year-old David Cartwright leaned in. Unattractive, honest-eyed, Topman stylish, he winced at Dewy's feet.

"What about *snow*?" he blurted. "Do you have *snow* in the States?"

"Like, that white stuff?" said Dewy. "We don't have that."

"What, not in America?"

"No. That's Antarctica."

"R-right," nodded Cartwright, slightly frowning. "Well, I tell you *what…*"

His hair, a gelled fin, he now straightened by clamping his palms each side of it and pulling upwards, saying: "It snows *here* in Devon, right? And I tell you, if it does, you'll need shoes."

"Will I?"

"*Ohh* yeah. When it comes to the snow time."

"What's wrong with the phrase: 'when it snows'?" said Dewy. "Why: 'when it comes to the snow time'?"

David Cartwright seemed half-likeable. The other men made Dewy uneasy.

Chapter 2

DAVID BENNETT WALKED to work, showed ID to a man in hi-vis he'd known 10 years and crossed a marble foyer. Two billboards from Alpha Staplers' ad campaign filled opposite walls, black and white, but anything red, very red. One photo was a toned man lying in profile. What at first seemed an erection was an eight-inch stapler emerging from his red underwear. Across the top of the picture: **alpha male**.

On the other wall a woman faced the camera, red bra under a man's black blazer. Her fingers caressed a red-pink stapler as she gazed amused at the viewer. A blazer lapel had been stapled a dozen times. **alpha female**

David's desk, for years at a window, was now in a windowless office named Clash City Rockers. He shared it with his four staff: Sarita Sumal, 25, from London, Toby Fanshaw, 28, Surrey, Selina Morel, 25, Manchester, and Sahid Vahouzian, 30, from Brighton. Sahid's Fashion and Textiles degree doubled Alpha Staplers' designers qualified in any design field to two, the other David.

Toby Fanshaw, jet-lagged from visiting factories in China, rolled up a sleeve of his grey T-shirt. A sore-looking, new tattoo **RAW POWER** needed air.

"*Oh* BONDING *up yours!!*" bawled a man's voice, 30 yards off. Everyone rose and left, as in a fire drill. Out in the central whitewashed space (named Something Better Change) sat CEO Pip Runcolm, Alison Brett and Paresh Patel. The 60-strong office workforce quickly arrived:

Merchandising, Marketing, Accounts, Sales, Influencers, Product and last, least, Design.

"Come in, guys, the water's fine!" smiled 32-year-old Pip Runcolm.

"Why a bonding meeting, you ask?" called Paresh Patel.

"Coz we got shit to kick, guys!" grinned Alison Brett, waving her arms high.

"But first!" said Pip Runcolm. "Round the group, in a tweet: 'My weekend was…'" He pointed to Selina Morecombe: "Go!"

"A 9k challenge that made me stronger," she said.

"Nice one," said Runcolm. "Next?"

"Jet-lagged body, mind in rhythm," said Toby Fanshawe.

"Loving it," said Alison Brett. "How *was* China?"

"Good, proactive, cool."

"Liking the order you said these words," said Runcolm. Toby Fanshawe's posture straightened. Runcolm pointed to David: "Next!"

David froze and blushed.

"Don't ask 'what's a tweet?" said Pip Runcolm. Everyone strongly laughed.

"Well?" persisted Runcolm. "Your weekend…?"

"Uh… it was very nice," said David, trying to sound light-hearted "Just… fine, really." Any who heard him tutted and curled a lip.

After the tweet session, Runcolm made a long speech. It concluded:

"Hopefully you've made solid progress after the consumer segmentation study. As we approach compass deadline we'll align on verbiage? Then fly low to supplant last year's compass points… which were?"

Many chanted: "Inspirited! Tribe! Expressive! Tastemaker!"

David gulped. Before Christmas he'd been made to write four reports on each of these words – words he didn't understand in relation to Alpha Staplers, or to anything. He now fell into a December memory: crying at

5.20am, up all night trying to write 200 words for each of four headings per word: *Your Personal Vision of...* **Tribe**, *Design Team's Vision of...***Tribe**, *Design Team's Application of...* **Tribe**, *Process Follow-Up on...* **Tribe**. Next night, all these again for each of **Expressive**, **Inspirited** then **Tastemaker**.

Runcolm moved to the nearest white wall, clucking a can of spray-paint.

"And *here* are *this* year's compass points!"

He sprayed a compass cross, then, attempting graffiti script, wrote *Millennial* at west, Gen-Z north, *Millennial Parent* east, Gen-Y south.

"Please action these descriptives in *all* your dialogues?" said Runcolm.

He spread his arm wide: "OK let's upgrade the reach-out? More of a circle please, wanna see *everyone*. Move."

Some seconds' group shuffling later, Runcolm began:

"A motorway, a freeway, but *we* go off-road, explore *different* routes. What lies before us..."

His gaze scanned the group, eye contact with all.

"Think a *mountain path*. A *new* path. Of philosropy, and giving."

He announced Alpha was donating 4,000 staplers and hole-punchers to African schools. The room erupted in clapping and cheering.

Runcolm beamed: "Myself, our social media and press teams, and *two of you*, we'll announce who soon – will fly out, check the products in at a port, drive trans-Africa with an education charity, hand out staplers and our other desk products in classrooms."

"Can we spare the product?" yelled Runcolm over ecstatic applause and chatter: "12k's-worth *given away*? Yes we can! The items are all Alpha Basic, nothing glam, it'll free up warehouse space *and* we can offset it against tax! The travel's half-paid by the education charity. *Most* importantly, press will be huge, social media'll rocket."

Huge applause. After a minute, Runcolm patted air to bid everyone quiet.

"You see… philosropy is *so in* right now?" he said. "Cool companies are peak-spending on a philosropic side. Like how, in olden days, big business established philosropic foundations?"

"Do you mean 'philanthropic'?" said Sahid Verhouzian.

Runcolm's posture changed, eyes violent. Other senior managers glared at Sahid. The room fell silent.

"Philosropy…" said Runcolm, recovering authority, "is *basically* the philosophy of giving? Philosophy's something that started out being all about giving. Giving *is* philosophy, basically. And the new, or new-old, way to say that, is *philosropy*."

"Hence why *this*," he said holding up a bulky A4, glossy pamphlet, *Alpha Philosropry*. "HR spent a lot on this. Oh, and David? Can you make sure it's triaged with Design? To ensure unity leverage?"

THE TATTLER WAS busy, phones ringing, staff writing or rushing about. Local radio played in the background. Receptionist Jane Townsend came to introduce herself to Dewy from her desk by the door, greeting couriers and visits from the public, most weekdays 11 til 2. Many townsfolk preferred to deliver classifieds in person. David Cartwright told Dewy a woman in her 80s often arrived to insist Jane show staff her items for sale in case they'd like to buy first. "'Grapefruit-squeezer, bowl only'," said Cartwright, "'2010 Yellow Pages, unused'." He hoped Dewy would laugh, but she looked concerned and asked: "Is she poor?" Cartwright became concerned too: "*That* I wouldn't know. I could get Jane to ask her?"

Catherine and Dewy sat together, sharing a computer at one of two desks to the left of the editor's office. To their right, past Carruthers' doorway, was a low, latticed window overlooking all of Bridge Street. Behind them, the men's desks, other side of a middle pathway through the office.

Dewy was unfazed by the Farmer's Bulletin Notice-board, to Catherine's delight: "You're the first person *ever* to not mind reading that weekly hell of 5,000 words then trying to fit them on one page in tiny script! You've ~"

Carruthers appeared:

"He can't do it. Can you?"

"Who can't do what?" said Catherine.

"No time, Catherine. Can you do it?"

"Do *what*?!"

Gregor Finniston had rung, "legally advised *not* to" submit his **All Right Then, I'll Say It** column. He'd written about the Council again. They'd sued last time and lost, which hadn't helped. Could someone quickly write a replacement column? Finniston, 74, wore tweeds, drank a hip-flask and did nothing short-notice, so wouldn't rewrite.

"Fine," muttered Catherine.

The replacement **All Right Then, I'll Say It** was ready 16 minutes later, subject: *Why Is Pregnancy Overlooked In The Workplace?*

While Catherine wrote, Dewy looked through "An Eventful Life", a book by one of the town's oldest residents, Mary Winters, sent in for review.

Carruthers re-appeared.

"How you getting on, girls?"

"Why are you interrupting us, *boy*?" said Dewy, not looking up. She felt Catherine's body suppress a giggle.

"I wasn't *interrupting*," pleaded Carruthers. "At least… not meaning to."

"Thereby admitting you *did*?" sighed Dewy.

Carruthers moved an in-tray so he could half-sit on the desk.

"How's the 'Eventful Life' book?" he said.

"Why is your butt on our desk?" said Dewy.

"I'll ignore that."

"I wish we'd that option."

"What's the book like? Eventful?"

"Um…" Dewy held up the cover. "If it *is*, she conceals it well."

"Example?"

"Like: watching her father wallpaper a room's the only mention of her father, or pretty much all her childhood. In the war, age 19, she was a Land Girl. She doesn't discuss the Land Girl movement, or what they did, beyond the fact she was one, and her friend Doris drove her each day to a farm. When Doris got 'suddenly pregnant' – by who, or to what destiny, we aren't told – rides to the farm stopped, so Mary's aunt lent her a bicycle. That's it for World War Two. Next page, she's working in a dry-cleaner's."

"Someone else should review it," sighed Carruthers, reaching for the book. Dewy swiped it from him: "Get off! I'll do a lovely review, make her heart happy. She's 97, look at her, she's beautiful, I'd rather die than hurt her. My review will *glow*. Sales will soar. Where's it sold anyhow? Better mention that."

She glanced to the press release: "Spillet's in Farris-ford, News Stop in Crendlesham, and Crendlesham Library. No library in Farrisford?"

"Not now," said Catherine bleakly.

"You mean there *was*?"

"Closed in 2016," said Carruthers. "Government cuts. *Anyway*… I wanna talk about the women's page."

"You close *libraries* in this country?" said Dewy, "For real? Who closed it?"

"County Council," said Carruthers. "No money from central government to run it."

"No *money*? But everyplace I go has building renovations, sidewalks replaced, roadworks. 'No money'? Every 10 yards, a hi-vis man's doing something insane with a machine. In Crendlesham, from the bus, I saw avenues of trees, all branches chainsawed off. Stark trunks, pale circles around the top. Happens everywhere now. Didn't before."

"Anyway," said Carruthers. "The women's page…"

"Geoff, we're not chimpanzees!" said Dewy. "We needn't be in a cage, fed articles about make-up and casseroles."

"I'm not arguing!" said Carruthers.

"Can't we not do something else?" said Dewy. "Why not a 'memory lane' page, old photos of the town, readers send *their* photos too, and write us their memories?"

"Good idea," said Carruthers. "Wanna set it up? Get us a page for Tuesday week. But I want a new women's page too, no more syndicated stuff."

"And do I clean the floor?" said Dewy, as Carruthers walked away.

MILLIE KNEW THE times Marlon left work. Sometimes he wore a sleek black trackie with electric blue trainers, or the *really* nice, deep red Adidas Firebird over black trackie bottoms. Everything he wore was brand new, or looked it. Millie was ashamed she knew Marlon's route home after hiding in Homebase car-park several times to follow him.

But that was *then*, before she'd the courage to approach him. Nowadays she felt proud she'd moved beyond "saddo level", but sometimes found herself following Marlon home again, like today. She knew what obsession was: "but he's my addiction, yeah?"

At 1pm Marlon left Homebase. Soon he walked up Bridge Street, sports bag over a broad shoulder, back straight and V-shaped, *awwh! Look at the people, gazing up at him, they've seen him before, barely a dozen of us in this town. If they see me as well, this'll be their first two black people in the same minute.*

Millie watched Marlon walk along Farr's Lane to East Lane Park's gates. She saw him cross the small park to Knight Street, where he'd cross over, go left at the dentist, into long, wide Trant Road – 1930s semi-detacheds under big, sullen sky. Two minutes later, left into Arkwright Crescent, where Millie dared not go, all bungalows, one side lower than the pavement. Any new person would be seen – by Marlon too, he lived on the higher side.

Millie caught her breath outside Michael Wade Dental Surgeon. She peered round its corner, saw the length of Trant Road. There was Marlon. These were the last two minutes she'd see him for days, unless using another "innocent Homebase visit" token. But she was saving these until she passed her driving test, could hire a car: *Fancy a lift home, Marlon?* even: *Come for a drive?*

A black car with black windows and booming bass screeched to a stop beside Marlon. Marlon walked faster, looking straight ahead. The car went at his pace, shouts and jeers from the passenger side. Millie heard a man scream at him.

"I know that car," she thought, breaking into a run: "Tyson Bradley. Dickhead. He'll be with them scuzzers whose dads Dad fought off years ago."

The car revved hard and roared off into the distance.

Millie cried Marlon's name. He didn't hear. She speeded up. "Marlon?"

He turned, flung his bag down, sat on a low wall, eyes blazing. Millie touched his wood-hard shoulder. Marlon did not look at her. He trembled.

"Don't worry about *them*, Marlon? I know for a fact they're dead sad."

Marlon drew breath. He didn't like the word 'dead'.

"Haters have nothing about them," said Millie.

Marlon beat his thigh with his fist five times, stood, kicked his bag, picked it up, paced away. Millie ran to keep up. Marlon didn't slow.

They approached 23 Arkwright Crescent. The bungalow's green garage door had random daubs of greener
green painted over. Millie sensed they covered racist
graffiti.

"Bye then, Marlon."

"Bye."

Millie watched him walk the short front path. She
knew he wouldn't look round. But he did, a slight nod as
he closed the door. Millie smiled and waved.

She'd lie awake worrying her smile and wave were
inappropriate, and if handing him her number on a bus
ticket was too. Did he think her shallow? She couldn't
know until next time they met. When would that be?

DEWY RETURNED FROM her first working day at 7pm.
Annette stirred awake. Dewy rushed to embrace her: "Oh,
hon, been here all day?"

"Worked in the kitchen. Beverley made me a big
lunch. Did you eat, hon?"

"I'm OK, darling, thought I'd go out, see if I can't get
some wine. Wanna come?"

They walked arm in arm, a warm May evening. The
Yenton estate's hill of streets rose to the right, buttercup-
dotted river-meadow left, field poppies and bluebells too,
anglers' green tents at intervals along the riverbank to the
furthest curve. Thrushes and blackbirds' songs enchanted
Annette and Dewy. They stopped, rested against each
other, listening. Dewy felt sad Annette hadn't walked here
since her first night in Farrisford last year, lost. (Beverley
had driven past, seen Annette smile up at the street-lamps
all coming on at the same moment. Later, returning from
Asda, Beverley saw she was still there and stopped the car.)

Past the river, birdsong was keener, absorbing Annette, while Dewy looked high to the right. Somewhere up
there was Stuart's family, even Stuart himself. What if he

appeared? Dewy was angry. Stuart had violated, impregnated, abandoned Annette, leaving her alone, frightened, above all confused.

Despite outstanding academic prowess (predicted only by Dewy, two of Annette's brothers, and a few alert teachers) Annette seemed often a child. To treat her as Stuart had done to her was an outrage. Dewy stopped, put her arms around Annette, held her close for a long time.

Keeley Lane thereon was woods left, houses right. After the houses was one end of a rusty-goaled football pitch, then a playground Dewy and Annette cut across, diagonally upslope to Londis.

Annette liked it there. She put Crunchies, Oreos, dry-roasted peanuts, kitchen-rolls, Ryvita, shoelaces, Philadelphia cheese, shower-gel, Best-In custard creams and Ribena in a basket then stood at a pet-food section. The range of pet toys was small, but a red, rubber figure-of-8 for tug-of-war delighted her. "Something else to take back to him! Five gifts now!"

Dewy took one bottle of Merlot, five Caramacs and mineral water to the till.

"You gotta try these Hula Hoop things, hon," smiled Annette, reaching for a packet. "Wear 'em on your fingertips, eat them off one by one." She leaned up and kissed Dewy passionately, to audible gasps from Londis regulars.

On a bench midway in the playpark they ate Hula Hoops, dreamed and talked. Annette lay her head against Dewy. Children appeared in ones and twos. A youngest child crouched to pat Dewy's right foot, which rested two inches above the ground from sitting leg crossed over the other. "Ow!" smile-frowned Dewy as patting got louder.

"Oh! Don't make princess-angel cry?" said Annette. The child hugged Dewy's foot to her chest.

"*Is* she a princess?" asked a boy.

"Of course!" said Annette. "Isn't she not beautiful?

Don't you think?"

Some children nodded. A girl said: "Can I put these scrunchies in you hair?"

For half an hour Dewy's hair was tied, bunched, pleated, piled on her head, let fall, finger-combed out then dotted with dandelions and bluebells. A boy of three stood on her thighs, held her shoulder, sang a song with no words then asked her where her mummy was. "She's gone to a place where everyone's happy," said Dewy. Girls surrounded her, trying to get flowers to stay in her hair, putting dandelions on one side, bluebells the other, then reverting to all at random. An older girl and boy knelt by her feet making a daisy ankle-bracelet and headband.

Dewy sat dreamily, holding Annette's hand. When the daisy headband was placed on her, everyone gasped. Annette hugged her: "Wanna cookie?"

Oreos were shared around. The children were impressed Dewy and Annette easily levered Oreo discs clean off with their teeth, leaving spotless white filling on the other disc, to be gnawed. Most of the children were veterans of Oreos eaten this way, but few got one whole disc off first go.

"We must leave now, dears," said Annette, standing heavily.

"Awww!! Can we finish her hair? We nearly finished! Please?"

Five minutes later Dewy was released in a necklace of bluebells and dandelions. Amid flowers in her hair, was a mid-high, subtle pony-tail tied with the Oreos wrapper the children had made into a bow. Dewy would keep it forever.

"WATCHING, JADE? *CONCENTRATE.* Soy sauce, add it near the end."

Dave Tyler shook the bottle and poured. The wok hissed.

Danii and Brandon arrived through the back door from work, tired.

"Whaa! Like a Chinese takeaway in here!" said Danii, grimacing. She wore a belted, tan raincoat and carried department-store bags.

"Stir-fry," said Dave Tyler. "Summin' different. Bought more clothes?"

"On my staff card," said Danii, leaving.

"Don't blow your money for Dubai!"

Tall, black-uniformed Brandon leaned over Jade: "Not eating tha-at!"

"Out my space, Bran! I've a sharp knife."

"*Foof*, keffs in here," said Brandon. "Probably through the house." He left the room: "Stinks like a foreign country."

"Well it *ain't*," said Dave Tyler.

Half an hour on, the family stared at their phones and ate. At the head of the table, Tyler sat back and opened a bottle of lager. A scaffolder until a fall, he'd retrained as a plumber and started a business. Danii's divorce money from her first husband had paid the deposit for a fine 18th century house with courtyard in Moresby village. Tyler had it demolished and replaced by a concrete and smoked-glass house that stared like a skull. The Tylers had lived there 12 years.

"Jadey?" said Danii. "When you're down to 11 stone, you come with me, I'll show you to the girls, get that hair done, get you waxed, yeah?"

"I don't *want* to go to your work! Don't want them waxing me!"

"Not want brows like mine? Summing wrong with my eyebrows?"

She turned to Tyler. "*Is* there summin wrong with 'em?"

"They're all right."

"'All *right*'? It's my brows, not a set of spanners!"

"Taking *Jade* to the salon?" mumbled Warren, "Might as well take a fish!"

Brandon rocked his head back, laughing quiet, nasal *hagh-hagh* sounds.

"Anyone can be special if she works it," said Danii, pushing her plate away. She lit a Dunhill International.

"But her underbite, whatever it's called," smirked Warren. "That lower lip."

"She'll get that fixed when she's older!" said Danii. "Her 18th from us innit?"

"Thought we's getting her a car?" said Dave Tyler, opening more lager.

"Warren we're getting a car for. *She's* getting her lip done."

"Jade's got a good heart, 'aven't you, love?" said Tyler.

"She's got a fat arse," said Danii, tapping ash onto her plate.

"She's the bright one," said Tyler. "University, this'n will."

"Uni's a bunch of losers," said Warren. "Wanna get out, *earn* my livin'."

"Will you even *go* to them GC-whatever exams?" said Danii to Warren.

"Don't need 'em for Swole College, doing tree surgery…"

"You will if you're doing *surgery*!?" said Danii.

"Nah, it's chainsaws and stuff," said Warren. "We still *gettin'* chainsaws, Dad?"

"Too right. Back garden – half of it's trees and bushes. Bloody disgrace."

Warren grinned, yelling: "*Vrremmm!! Vvvrremmm!!*", pretending his arm was a chainsaw.

Dave Tyler stood and gathered plates: "Right. Dessert? Is Jade allowed ~"

"She's having *nuthin'* else!" snapped Danii. "Don't want her droolin' over everyone's desserts neither! Take the dog out, Jade."

"I don't care about dessert!" cried Jade. "And *you* has chocolate cake *every night* with coffee, so *shut-up!*"

"*ENOUGH!*" roared Dave Tyler. All fell quiet.

"C'mon, Ocean, walky-walks!" said Jade shakily. "He won't go, wants chicken scraps."

"*OCEAN!!* **OUT!!**" roared Tyler. The 10-year-old white Bull Terrier scampered from under the table.

In Church Lane Jade let Ocean off the leash. He ran slowly, panting. The Domesday church chimed eight. Jade liked both the sound and full-leaf May trees sheltering the small church.

As the bell thinned Jade heard a drone. She climbed a stile into a field sloping down. The drone's gnawing whine intensified, operated by Rory and Gareth Woods.

"Whooo! Jade Tylahhh!" yelled Rory, a year younger than Jade.

"Eatin' doughn-u-uuts!" bawled his brother in a high voice. He began steering the drone at her.

"Don't! Stop it!"

The boys laughed. The machine soared towards a hill until out of sight.

"They're in them trees!" screamed Gareth, 15. "I bet they are! Put it higher!"

"We've looked there!" said Rory.

"But they'd've hid when they heard the drone. Now it's high they won't hear."

"Who won't?" said Jade.

"*Syrians,*" said Gareth and Rory Woods, faces like masks, utter strangers.

Chapter 3

ON DEWY'S SECOND day at the paper, she tried to make sense of Britain's political situation.

Catherine: "No idea, they're all idiots."

Geoff Carruthers: "Ask Tessa England. What do you mean: 'Who's Tessa England'? You'd better get sharp on *this* stuff, working here."

Stuart Dean: "Is this an ad-related enquiry? Then don't bother me."

David Cartwright: "Do you know what a MP is? Well, Tessa England – her's the one here. She's not spoke to this paper in years, far as I know."

Dewy replied: "What are these 'Parliamentary votes' Selena May keeps losing?"

"*Theresa* May," said Cartwright. "I don't know. But I tell you what? My mate Wool, Steve Wooler, he's put a four-to-one bet on her not being Prime Minister end of June."

"Really?" said Dewy. "So who'll be your prime minister?"

"Wool's gonna win good if May goes."

"Amazing, but I'm trivial, so I'll ask again: who'll lead your country?"

"I don't think you're trivia!! You're actually *all right*, like, for an American pers… er, er, I mean, you *look good*, and er…"

"Who will be your Prime Minister?"

"Er…"

"No one knows," said Stuart Hendry, joining them.

"But I reckon a General Election before year's out. That Labour man Clissenden's gearing up for one. Keen to be our next MP."

The team behind local Labour Party candidate Matt Clissenden sent daily press releases and hourly social media to the newsdesk. Fit, balding Clissenden, 34, was in several photographs per Tattler, smiling so broadly his lower teeth were visible as the upper. On page 5 last week, he and Team Labour smiled in Lycra, warming up for the Bettle to Hollenby half-marathon. Page 12 saw his visits to John Wyce School, then to a farm, one of six men in hi-vis and orange hats looking up at silos, Clissenden smiling. When the plentiful, faintly beige teeth had slipped from memory, they returned on page 32, a Town Hall reception for visitors from Farrisford's twin-town, Jørskjeyn.

Dewy was fed-up with these teeth. Press releases, bulletins, leaflets from Team Labour lay teeth-up on every in-tray and full-up bin. Breeze from open windows made them fly off and swing side to side to the floor. One of Matt Clissenden's teeth, top left, was a dagger.

But in this week's issue, Clissenden did not smile, outside Farrisford's Polish shop on Knight Street with its owners, the windows boarded-up, smashed by people who'd sprayed sloppy, thin swastikas on door and walls. Dewy at last identified with Matt Clissenden, but, though glad someone important in the town stood in solidarity with Mr and Mrs Wiszniewski, Dewy couldn't help thinking he'd leapt in to publicise himself. She nonetheless asked if the photo might be a top-front-page "See inside" lead. She was answered by near-applause and "definitely!"s from some of the office. "Help get rid of Tessa," said Carruthers, to grunts of assent. The photo went upper front page left: **Shop Attack Condemned – page 4**.

The office dislike and tang of chauvinism towards Tessa England made Dewy wonder more about her. Why was she scarcely visible, and what were her policies?

Wikipedia said Tessa Boyd-Brown was born in Nairobi in 1951. Her family returned to Farrisford in 1956, mother a vet, father a Liberal town councillor. She studied medicine in Edinburgh, was a haematologist in London, and divorced Sunday Times and Spectator journalist Peter England in 1994. He passed away in 2000, they'd no children. 15 years an MP, she'd voted for Britain to remain in Europe, against the town's 58 per cent vote to leave.

"She doesn't seem an idiot," thought Dewy. "So why is she a Conservative? Does she *support* that party's 10-year assault on education, community services and free healthcare while hundreds of billions are spent on private infrastructure companies? While unchecked developer and landlord greed bankrupts businesses, stores and their workers? I want to meet this Tessa England."

The week's copy deadline was 5pm, advertisements noon next day. Catherine warned Dewy deadlines were disobeyed, plus a weekly struggle "to get Stuart Dean off his backside to confirm which ads are in, and have artwork."

After "Chairgate" as Catherine (seated always in her chair now) named it, Dewy predicted Dean would make her wait until print-run. "Advertiser still hasn't sent it," couldn't be disproved. Dewy vowed to never show the stress and rage he planned to reduce her to by withholding ads. She'd never nag him. Let Carruthers do that.

Late afternoon, Catherine said the paper was so well laid out, she and Dewy could go early. All was in except Colin Hendry's cover story about the inquest, to be edited tomorrow. He'd requested the headline: **Lessons Must Be Learned**, sub-heading: Farrisford Man 'Legal Highs' Death Open Verdict.

Tomorrow would also see photographer Stephen Ellis in for his "sports session", supplying captions and names for every personal and team photo in nine pages of local: football, cricket, rugby, netball, darts, lacrosse, hockey and softball leagues, show-jumping, eventing, school-sports and the back-page sagas of Farrisford Town (who, from 2-0 up, drew 2-2 away at Storringham).

Dewy wandered through drizzle exploring the medieval town. She liked The Swainway's ramshackle buildings and road lower than the pavement, two, sometimes three kerbs rising as steps beside a shallow, pure stream along one side of the street in a smooth stone groove. Green thin mosses waved here and there in the quick current. Dewy stood in the stream, water deliciously cold and healing over her feet and ankles.

A pub called The Bear had a weathered thatched roof and latticed bay windows. Inside was thrillingly dark and haphazard, a floor of black beams, a cave of a fireplace, ancient tables with smudged studs. England untouched for hundreds of years.

Dewy sat in a window nook with a pint of Wennoxford's Scrumpy, a dense, flat cider like dishwater. She watched British people walk past after work, slightly frowning into drizzle, alone in thoughts. Bald men in overalls, middle-aged women in work-shirts under North Face fleeces, dark red-purple rinse in their hair, searching a bag for a car key. Each face had a character and an innocence, passing the window like a soul from birth to death through the world. Dewy felt intense love for Britain and its people. She bought a second pint.

Later, when a flashing fruit-machine went *bzrrrnk!! Pamp-pamp-pamp* as men fed coins to it, Dewy tried The Nor' Gate across the road. Within oak-panelled walls and ceiling of beer-labels, Dewy discovered a scrumpy called Rattock's.

Again she sat looking out. Modernity had spared The Swainway, few cars passing, none parked. The street had five pubs, a kebab shop, a small Co-op, old empty buildings, extinct shops and boarded-up pubs, including the vast Bull, forlorn in its deserted car-park, bright yellow signs threatening wheel-clamps and fines.

Down at the town end, The Swainway met traffic-jammed Hallam Road, where Kennedy's stretched around a corner, once a car showroom, now a bar with plate glass windows, thumping music and orange signs for Happy Hour and vodka shots. The pavement outside it was stained and covered in cigarette butts. Above Kennedy's, rounding the corner, was **Galaxies Nitespot**, windows replaced by black wooden boards, no images of stars, galaxies, anything. Owned by Kennedy's, the club, closed since February, was believed to be reopening soon as a late-night "Health and Massage Spa".

Up at the far end, not long before The Bull, was The Swainway's last occupied building, The Fusilier. Few dared this narrow, run-down tavern, windowless but for two rows of glass cubes in a mortar front wall. The pub's propped-open door was up a thin side-alley, bar facing the door. Dewy paused in the doorway, saw the server was female and entered. Six peaceful, wrecked men stood off to the right, drinking. "Yeah, love?" said the young server.

"Hello," said Dewy, "Have you Rattock's, please?"

Half an hour later, Dewy sat in a far corner by the non-windows, blogging:

> **This is cider country. British cider is strong, even psychoactive. Class A is *scrumpy*, which I'm drinking now. A brewery nearby makes a brand called Rattock's. With a name like that, you know it's the Devil's own. I'm on my third pint of it. I earlier two of another scrumpy had also.**
>
> **Excitement and warmth fill my chest, my soul has woken and I feel like a genius. That's alcohol all right.**
>
> **I went to The Bear then The Nor'Gate, now The Fusilier. I've had *no hassle in these pubs* yet I'm a shoeless young woman with fairly nice hair and – as I'm not responsible for the pedi, I can say without**

boasting – beautifully painted toenails (thank-you, Mrs A) plus I'm on my own, wearing a dress. Sometimes you grasp the nettle, go to the roughest dive in town, *that's* where you get a relaxed, unmolested drink. Provided one, any, woman is there, and she's conscious, you'll be fine. Go through the door, think nothing but: "Where's the woman?" If none, quick-turn, get out, don't linger or look back.

Often in the scuzziest dives in town, where no one gives a screw about décor, customer profiling, branding or any corporate fuckology, there's *no sexist shit at all* and women are *liked*. These places have humility. People broken in by life, no pretensions. They know the score and leave you alone. They'll help you if you need help. They have conversation if you want it, *good* conversation. They sit and drink, sit and talk, sit and drink, go to the john, or to smoke, or smoke in the john, return to sit and drink. *They relax deeply*. That's what drinking is *about*!

Rattock's may cause blackouts, psychosis, lock-jaw, but it's the champagne of drinks. I have some lot of it had. Better get back to work now. *Arrr*-de-o Xx

MARLON'S PHONE RANG, 9pm, Robert O.

"Yeah?"

"What kind of a way's *that* to answer?" laughed Obogo. "Where you?"

"Home. What's up?"

"Driving! I'm on your road, go to the door?"

Robert stopped the car, leapt out, jogged up the path, arms spread: "Get here, give us a hug!"

Marlon nearly smiled. "I don't hug guys."

"*Gimme a hug!*"

Marlon stepped down to half-embrace Obogo, who hugged him yelling, "Ha-*HAA!* Not seen you in ages,

Marlon. How you feeling?"

"Feeling?"

"Er, tendon, you know? Getting out and about?"

Marlon shrugged.

"Come for a drink?" said Robert. "Just finished training. Paul and Craig have gone to the King's, I said, 'Let me get my friend, see if he'll join us?'"

"Nah. Staying in. Thanks though."

"We don't have to be with them, you can sit and listen to *me*. I have much to tell!"

"Kinda settled. By the way, don't ring if you're driving? That's ~"

"Hands-free, mate. No phone in my hand."

"Ah, I see."

"Come for a drink sometime? Listen – Saturday? Come along? Wyll Albion at home. They won't beat us this time. Come watch?"

A minute later, driving away, Robert rang Bobby Zena back:

"Bobby? Can you hear me?"

"You with the young man?"

"He didn't wanna go out."

"Uh?"

"Bobby? *Turn it down*, I can only hear football."

"Wait a second…" barked Zena. He turned his TV down 10 per cent. "Is he coming the game Saturday?".

"He said 'maybe'."

"Boy's a cabbage."

"Come on, Bobby? Your daughter told you he's going through it. And he is. He's frightened. Can't walk down the street."

"Hmmm," sighed Bobby Zena.

A pause. Football noise from Zena's sitting room reverberated the car.

"And we've been there…" said Robert.

"*Hmmm.*"

THOUGH CATHERINE HAD OK'd going home hours before, Dewy's scrumpied mind thought she was required in the office. She returned at 9pm. Only Colin Hendry and two youngest reporters were there.

"Ahh! You back?" said Hendry. "I'm done now, cover story's in. G'night."

He placed his hat on his head, saying to Dewy: "Look at them lads! Do nuthin' all week, then Toosday noight paanic."

"Will you help us, please, Miss Dewy?" said David Cartwright.

"Like hell. Do your own work," said Dewy, trying not to slur her words.

"Catherine always does a bit with us?" said Tim West.

"Your job, *you* do it." said Dewy. She called across to Colin Hendry, who folded a handkerchief: "May I see the main story?"

"Course!" said Hendry. "On my screen, have a look."

Dewy sat to read **Lessons Must Be Learned**, chin resting on clasped hands.

"Awful," she said. "That poor guy. His mother watched him taken away to die?"

"Yup, there's the photo," said Hendry, returning to scroll to the next page. As Catherine had written the picture captions, Dewy didn't expect:

A passer-by photograph of Matthew Willis being put in the back of a police van.

"Hell," gasped Dewy. "Then the guy *died*! And his mom was watching?!"

"Well… he *was* a bit intoxicated, apparently," said Hendry.

"Is that any reason to kill him in front of his mom?"

"They didn't kill him. He died in a police station in Yeovil."

"They *did* kill him! They hoisted him high – this picture shows it – they threw him in a van, slammed the doors and he wasn't seen again. I'd call that killed."

"Inquest said cause of death was heart attack."

"Shifting the blame. Who *wouldn't* have a fricking heart attack, detained unlawfully by guys throwing you in a van in front of your family? Then being driven fast, where to, or why, you don't know? It's Amnesty International stuff. And what's this about 'bystanders'? Look at the picture. Look! Six, seven guys as a team, hoisting a man above shoulder-height to hurl in a van. That is *not* 'standing by'. And who *were* these men?"

Dewy scrolled down:

"Six guys from a *pub* volunteering themselves? The police *allowed* them to violently intervene? Throwing a harmless boy into a van? Where *are* the cops here anyhow? None in this picture, it's all guys from the pub, 'helping' the cops. Helping with *what*? The poor guy wasn't even under arrest, right?"

"I'm not sure he was, no," said Colin Hendry. "The police said they were trying to get him to hospital."

"But took him to a police station? This picture proves no cops were doing anything. And *was* Mr Willis under arrest? Why's that not definite?"

"The inquest hasn't really mentioned it."

"Has it, or not?"

"No, but it seems understood he wasn't arrested. The police're solidly saying they were only trying to get him to hospital. What's clear as day is: they balls'd it up."

"Why hospital? What was the medical emergency?"

"They said: 'behaving erratically'," said Hendry.

Dewy peered at the screen: "Here it is, actual words: 'behaving erratically'. According to *who*? One of the guys from the pub? Erratic's a vague word, hard to contradict. This chair's erratic, the bus station's erratic and so on, til you realise nothing's *non*-erratic. And how was Mr Willis *meant* to behave? Is there a protocol to follow when slung in a van by a male gang?!"

"Them said he needed to go hospital."

"*Who* said? These pub guys? Any of them qualified medics? How come a police van arrived, not an ambulance? How can the cops *possibly* tell the inquest *any medical procedure was being followed* if they *didn't* call an ambulance? Instead, they allowed six drinkers to lift a potential patient completely off the ground and throw him into a van, which was then locked and driven at speed to…" Dewy squinted at the screen: "Yee-ohvil?"

"Yeovil. Pronounced 'Yo-vil'," said Colin Hendry. "Yeah… taking him all the way *there*'s the bit what don't add up, it must be said."

"What, everything else *does* add up?"

"Shouldn'ta took him Yeovil," said Hendry. "An hour away? Crendlesham Royal has a mental health emergency facility. Why didn't they take him there?"

"Or even Exeter?" said David Cartwright. "25, 30 mile whatever, not 70."

"The inquest's continuing," said Colin Hendry. "I'm covering it next week."

"Can I attend?" said Dewy.

"Nah, closed," lied Hendry. Trust he'd built up over years with the town's dignitaries, judiciary, coroner, Councillors and senior police could be ruined if he arrived in the Town Hall chamber with a shoeless woman who looked like a model and who passionately distrusted the inquest.

Amid alcohol fumes, Dewy was glaze-eyed, louder of voice and swaying, but the men didn't hold it against her. Until she'd spoken, none saw the death of Matthew Willis as anything but a sad, everyday tragedy befalling a young man who may have taken mild, legal drugs.

After Dewy left, they clustered round the computer to look at the cameraphone picture of the last moment Matthew Willis was seen alive. They realised Dewy's words: "Six, seven guys as a team, hoisting a man above shoulder-height to hurl in a van" were precise.

ANNETTE'S SWOLLEN FEET were soaked in a basin, then Dewy massaged them an hour. She washed Annette's face again before giving her a long facial cleanse, three basins of clear, hot water to hand. Annette lay quiet as Dewy's fingertips delicately soothed her face.

Annette was cold, from hot, her breathing laboured. Dewy hugged her to warmth, resting her lips around Annette's earlobe light as butterfly wings.

Annette hoped for talk, some focus, or giddiness would become nausea. She whispered: "Do you wish you'd continued ballet, darling?"

"Yes and no," said Dewy. "I *do* want to dance professionally, plan to start over, try contemporary dance, learn Graham Technique properly, join a company. My long-term aim's to be a choreographer."

"You were a beautiful ballerina," said Annette. "Even Mom and Dad came to watch you when you were principal, Clift too."

"They were kind to sit through that. I appreciated it."

"They loved it. They were proud of you. Mom shook your hand…"

"Indeed. The only time she… ah, I shouldn't be like that. Joanna's not my Mom, she doesn't owe me anything."

"She does. You've always looked out for me."

"I will so long as I live."

"Remind me why you stopped ballet?" said Annette dreamily.

"Booze."

Dewy began a long massage of Annette's hands and fingers, saying:

"Plus years rushing from school to the Boston train

Monday to Thursday. Ballet ended 9.15. After stretches, I'd ice-bathe my feet scarcely a minute, skip a shower, bolt for the 9.50 train."

"Mom and I'd go down Newburyport, pick you up," murmured Annette. "You were so tired, hon."

"And so smelly."

"Your footies were in a bad state."

"Yellow, black and green."

"A miracle your long, beautiful toes didn't get bent en pointe," said Annette. She stopped for breath a few seconds. "But your ugly duckling footies have turned into swans! Smooth, perfect and lovely."

"I couldn't expect Joanna to pick me up every night, so two nights I stayed~"

"~ At Georgina Talbot's. They'd moved from Rowley to…"

"Beacon Hill," sighed Dewy. "And there I did stay, Tuesdays, Thursdays. I'd get to their house 10pm, Georgina's brother followed me around: 'Hey, skinny! Do the splits!'. Georgina and her mom watched recipes on YouTube. Their dad, an epic dullard, asked me about your family's Navy activities."

"*Why*?" said Annette, rousing.

"He hadn't much talk in him. Most weeks: 'Hey, the Stephens guys down Norfolk?", or: "Robert was in the Sixth, right? Sons in the Sixth Fleet too?"

"What business of *his*?" frowned Annette.

"I'd say: 'I've no idea, sir, I hardly know the family.'" said Dewy. "He never got the hint."

"I missed you bad," murmured Annette. "Incredible schedule you had, hon."

"16 hours a week en pointe. Saturdays your Mom fixed it Karen or Juan ride me to the morning train, pick me up 7pm. Some of what I say about your Mom I oughtta retract: she always gotten me to ballet Saturdays. She paid me well for cleaning the horse-stalls, enough to cover classes, dancewear, new pointes every week, train fares. I got up 6am every day to clean the stalls, and half a day, Sundays. You'd come by, help service the vehicle engines."

"To be near *you*," said Annette. "But Joe made me watch everything he did, then had me do it. Age 12 I could replace most engine parts."

Annette paused for breath. Dewy rubbed her shoulders and back, saying: "I quit ballet, stopped wearing shoes forever, so no more going to the stalls to muck out. Thereupon remote respect between your Mom and me ended."

"You were so good at ballet. Beautiful as principal."

"Only two times, hon. La Sylphide, Daphnis et Chloe. Rest of the time ~"

"You were *corps* in the main company too. City Ballet proper!"

"Only understudy rota. Danced maybe half dozen times in two years."

Dewy turned on her side to hug Annette. "Georgina Talbot was kinda sweet. One of Nature's annoying-harmlesses, like Vacua. She talked about homework, her expected grades. She'd forget we no longer went to the same school, so asked things like: 'If Scott Pym did fewer sports would he do better at Science? Is Perry *really* cheating on Tori? Should Marilyn Kirsch be hanging with Lindsay so much?'. I hadn't a mule's clue who these people were."

Annette put her arms around Dewy and pulled her close, as Dewy continued:

"I wanted my Annette, I'd think of you, up late at the microscope, making notes, angle-lamp on. Beautiful you in your pyjamas, Bachelor by your pillow."

"Ahhh, Bachelor..." sighed Annette, sleepily. "An angel. Loveliest soul who ever lived. Thank-you for talking to me, hon, I feel better..."

Dewy lay awake. The reality of Matthew Willis and

some of the town's other news stories never left her mind. When 2am chimed far-off in the night, Dewy turned off the light.

IN OPEN COUNTRY, a rainstorm hit. A boom of wind at her window woke Jade. She rose, knelt on the bed to peer at a world pitch black beyond streaming water. An occasional *plap!* meant water leaked in the corner above the wardrobe.

A deeper sound arose and stayed. Helicopters were rare, never 2am, so Jade couldn't place the noise at first. She tried to sleep, wondering why the helicopter wasn't going away. Round and round the sky it gnawed, minute after minute. With vast thudding, a second helicopter passed overhead, shaking the walls, flashlight searing everything hyperbright for a moment. Ocean bolted from Warren's bedroom, barking along the passageway. The hall light went on. Jade heard her father thump down the stairs. Danii's voice spoke, then Brandon's in reply.

Lights slowly circled the sky. One stopped to switch on a powerful beam over the land. Trees gleamed emerald, wheat white-gold. Sirens, flashing blue lights and headlamps converged from all directions. Jade stood by her door in the dark, opening it an inch, letting thin light and house-sounds in.

From downstairs her father yelled: "Tweet from The Plough in Brinton!"

He stumblingly read out: "Helicopters... and boys in blue from all over... For Syrians hiding out near here, game over!"

"Right," said Brandon, "I'd better get out there, offer my services."

"I'll drive you there, son. Good lad."

"Don't be silly," came Danii's weary voice. "You're a security guard, Bran. If they got helicopters they won't be needin'..."

"Listen, love! said Tyler angrily, 'He's doing the right and courageful thing. If it *is* a bunch of fuckin'… Syrian *whatevers*, they fight like animals. Our police aren't protected against beasts like that. Them've got *knives*, they're *crazy*, got no *decentness*. C'mon, Brand, let's get dressed."

"Er… Mum's right," croaked Brandon, sleepier suddenly. "Police probably *are* well covered. Helicopters… ground staff…."

Warren charged along the hall: "Michael Slater, right? Lives in Brinton, he's a dickhead, but his tweets is *well funny*, listen to this: 'Fuck off Syrians come back when you learn to wash and work!'" Warren laughed like a maniac: "Then he says – *Ha-HAgh!* – then he says: 'Nah on second thoughts, don't come back!' Ha-ha-*ha!* Fuckin' *well funny!*"

"Hashtag Howards at Moresby!" said Tyler. "The Howards, eh!" He paused: "Ah, just saying: 'rumours of illegals in area maybe reason for police presence'. Very well put. The Howards – always *pukkah*."

"'Hashtag 'Human Rights Watch'?'" scowled Warren. "What's that bollocks doing on here?" He jabbed a phone button. "Fuck off!"

"Right!" said Danii, more awake. "Sick of this language, don't want effings and blindings. We're *respectable* in Moresby."

"Dale Johnson!" shrieked Warren: "Mr 'I don't use Twitter'. Now he's tweeting: 'Bit serious here. Loads of police. Gone in the woods with dogs.'"

"They should, if it's Syrians," said Tyler. "Hashtag Brinton! Village sealed off. Take alternative route if –' ah, it's just road directions."

Jade sat on her bed reading Twitter too, local entries, drivers who'd had to stop, someone posting thanks he'd found his dog under the bed, "not outdoors missing afterall."

Jade scrolled down, #Jbcv-man again:

this Rain should get the fukin siryans out their holes. 2

caght last week, 10 more near us at least. police r on it now. Go boyz!

Underneath, **#mejesus&nigel** replied:

2 rite. imigrnts buying every other house if we dont protect wahts ours.

Jade looked out the window. *They talk about Syrians like they're foxes,* she thought. Jade almost tweeted this, but knew better. Blocked-out memories came back, made her tense. Those dozens of locals who hid their names behind handles. The *forty-one* replies to her last ever tweet, Christmas Day afternoon's: *Hi! Any1 else bored yet?* included:

#pigsperminator   *if u bored try chok yrself 2 death fat little Moresby cow*

#pikekiller   *Go 4 another shit jade you must go load of times u eat so much*

 # dethbymydick   *commit sjuicide? even if u loose wiegt youll still b pig ugly*

These were milder than some others.

MARLON HEARD THE rain. He put the bedside lamp on. Light made the world normal a moment. Single bed, England FC eiderdown stretching towards the front wall, dark green curtains closed against night, against rain, against outside, against… *them.*

Cars turned up all hours, once, twice a week. Last year, over months, Marlon's bedroom window was smashed, garage door graffiti'd, a firework through the letterbox, youths on the front lawn jeering, knocking on the windows. *I'm glad none of this happened while Eleanor was alive.*

Attacks were fewer, but Marlon's anger had deepened. Last year, he wasn't so badly affected, despite a glazier picking glass off bed and floor, windows converted to Plexiglass, pairs of police (including PC Steven Pollard,

Farrisford Town reserves midfielder and Methodist) calling by to ask if things were OK.

Marlon had flashbacks. He constantly replayed attacks. Cars pulling up, shouts, laughter: "Hey, black boy? Play some reggae! Ha-*ha!* Have a fucking spliff! *T'ya-ha-HA!!* Straight-up, we thinks you're all right. Why ain't you talking to uzz? You fuckin ignoring uz, black boy? *HEY!!* Sleep with that old white man? Do you suck him off? *T-ya-ha-HA!!*"

Marlon was ashamed of what he did in flashbacks. He often acted out dragging youths from the open car window and attacking them. Marlon enacted how his blows would land by hitting his own face hard, over and over. He did so now, stopping an instant before the kitchen door opened. John was there: "Marlon?"

Marlon trembled, his eyes were strange. He scarcely knew where he was, no recall of leaving his bedroom. "I'm all right," he murmured.

"Can't you sleep, Marlon?"

"Going bed. Sorry to wake you."

"If you can't get back to sleep, give me a knock?"

Marlon nodded, averting his face. He didn't want John to see it was swollen. In his room he dabbed a fingertip over his cheekbone. Swelling and numbness tonight, no blood.

NEXT MORNING, CATHERINE and Dewy chased late copy. Print run was tonight. Dozens of minor last stories arrived, including dull ones left until very last:

Leaflet Racks Vandalised

Man Cheated Of £200

Dog–Show Postponed

Walk And Talk Reveals History Of Gas Mains

By contrast, many sports write-ups were so enthusiastic they were deranged, taking time to edit.

A late news filler from Ryan Palmer: "Police Immigration Round-up" stated simply:

A police inspection of woodlands near Brinton last night (Tuesday) led to nine migrant arrests. Seven men and two boys, believed Syrian and Afghani nationals were taken into Home Office custody near Dartmouth.

Dewy didn't like that single paragraph bulletin at all. She wondered what lay disguised in its routine words. The story resonated with the paper's front cover about Matthew Willis.

How far is Dartmouth? Dewy wondered, remembering Matthew Willis's last journey, to Yeovil. *And 'near' Dartmouth – where exactly? How were the nine people taken there? Were they allowed to stay together? Were they frightened? Of* course *they fucking were, and still are, idiot. How old are the two boys? Fourteen? Twelve? Seven?*

The paper was sent to the printers at 4pm, leaving Dewy free until evening. She was to meet Catherine and Carruthers at 9.30pm, to accompany them to printers Ross & Sons at Statterton, 14 miles away. The three would read run-offs at 11pm, final stage of the paper's production. Though Annette was at university, Dewy walked in 88 degree heat to The Lugworm, ran up to the room to tug Mrs Lara Gardner's white Prada shift dress out through a hole Dewy had carved in the padlocked case, and change into it.

Lost in thought, she walked Keeley Lane. A distance past the park, houses ended. The lane narrowed, woods each side, then became a track under high-branched, spreading trees. Beyond a last building by humming transformers, the track was an earth path through grasses and high flowering weeds, to a farmgate into shimmering countryside under clear blue sky.

Dewy walked for hours, wading through streams, edging along fields of breeze-waving crops, walking slowly, curiously through woods, running in a meadow of grass and bluebells, undressing in a waterfall to fully wash for the first time since the US. She flattened her dress and underwear on a large, pale stone to dry, then lay beside them, naked in sun, feet tugged by cooling river-current. All was peace, cicadas light-trilling, a passing bird from time to time, a bee now and again. The river's sounds were gentle, the sun-warmth bliss. Dewy lay as in a spiritual state, moor and river sounds echoing far inside herself.

Burning easily, she wore the dress as sunhat and shawl as she walked a mile of pasture teeming with lavender and butterflies then climbed to a heathery plateau. There, under huge sky, ancient country spread to all horizons. Hills stretched in folds until blue and hazed. A far-off track road meandered in silence. Sheep blocked it sometimes.

Dewy saw meadow pipits, a mistle thrush, black grouse, chaffinches, daws, a wood ouzel and other birds she ached to identify, guesses to be confirmed. **Bird-watching – startled joy!** she'd blogged long ago. **Each new bird a startle then a thrill that lasts til next startle.**

Climbing a hill, Dewy glimpsed a mote of gold – the St Botolph's weathervane. She headed towards there, sometimes climbing higher ground to get her bearings and re-find the vane. At last she joined an overgrown path through fields and over walls to Farrisford.

She'd three hours to fill before meeting Geoff Carruthers and Catherine in the Good Queen Bess. Dewy went to The Fusilier.

She had a routine there, a pint of Rattock's far left of the bar, two empty metres under a bulky, wall-mounted TV that was usually off. The line-up of males accepted Dewy with polite indifference, a nod of greeting from a nearest one, or two. She'd nod back.

Dewy and the young server Jay exchanged words, Jay speaking of things she found baffling or annoying. She chewed gum, never asked questions and smoked in the alley every 15 minutes.

With a second pint, Dewy would go to a small table in a dim corner at the front wall. A black rubber mat under a decayed dartboard ran to just short of the table. Dewy's toes sometimes rolled and unrolled the end of the mat as she sat in thought, blogged, or reread The Tattler. She'd forgotten how, in her months at a Massachusetts paper, she always reread it, feeling real understanding and experience of a place came from absorbing its newspaper. Now, likewise, the Tattler. Alone in peace and Rattock's, Dewy's mind opened to how more ordinary news – car-boot sales, school presentations, farm machinery auctions, darts finals, retirement parties, fund-raisers, dog-shows, an outdoor model railway – were patchwork pieces of the soul of a town and how life felt there. And the Tattler's 11 page farming section was like nothing Dewy had ever seen, not least the Farmer's Bulletin Board:

> Several bulls forward with a best price of 88p/kg for a Simmental from LJ Peake, South Fetton. Beef cows to 130p/kg (102.33p). Dairy cows to 107p/kg (102.33p) Cull bulls to 86p/kg (83.75p). A decent entry of 159 mainly younger store cattle sold to a continued strong trade with plenty of demand. A pen of big-framed ewes from Mr P Hallicock of Treyvyan Farm, Cressy sold to £87.50 (£71) Second quality ewes to £50. An entry of 81 store lambs with plenty of demand for all types.

Dewy's imagination thrived at these timeless scenes, of farms, animals, auctions, noise, life, people, the power, mud, intensity – and stench – of places like Hollenby Market, where:

A good entry of 255 grazing ewes met a strong trade for lean and small ewes on offer. Best meat and better steaking dairy breeds were excellent trade to 144.5ppk for a boat of a Holstein from Mr FW and Mrs LJ Hemmings, Balaton. Tremendous Charolais at 149.5ppk from Messrs J Halborne & Son, Loddleford. Good Blonde at 144.5ppk from Dan and Karen Dalton, Farrisford. Sucklers sold to a superb £1324.57 for one of the Charolais from Mr M. Lodge, Volcombe Basset.

In the Fusilier, Dewy read, dreamed, thought, mumbled to herself or to the Goddess and absently paced the darts mat. If sure no one saw her, she'd pirouette, step into fifth, bend, do three or four brisk fouettés. She'd never demonstrate her ballet prowess anywhere. Only Annette (and by accident, Andrea Millard) ever saw her dance now.

Back home Dewy danced every day without clothes on a 40-foot lawn at the back of her cabin. Waldo and Andrea Millard owned the square-mile forest estate. They lived half a mile away in a mansion by a lake. Andrea had several times chanced upon Dewy dancing nude.

In 2016 no one knew what to do about Dewy, who freeloaded anywhere, after years in New York, where she'd freeloaded everywhere. Wal Millard, lifelong friend of Annette's 39-year-old brother Robert Jnr, uneasily offered a slightly run-down cabin for one year at $300 a month, one-quarter market value.

Wal Millard was nowadays keen to modernise and newly rent the cabin, but couldn't shift its tenant of 37 months, who'd only ever paid eight months' rent, had no apparent plans or employment and, according to his wife, danced naked outside half the day to music from an amplifier. Other days she'd take the second oldest of his seven cars, a 1980 BMW, disappearing to Boston for her weekly pedicure and to teach English to Hispanic children. Or vanish in his car for days with Bobby Stephens's kid sister Annette. The car now had dents, a scrape down one side, a splintered windscreen and a junk-filled, stained interior.

In Farrisford, The Fusilier's always-empty front half became Dewy's equivalent to the lawn behind the cabin at home, a space to dream and be, and be alone to dream and be. Over a new pint Dewy blogged:

> An hour ago the girl behind the bar here, Jay, said: "Right, I'm putting EastEnders on", referring to a British TV show of that name. Men at the bar groaned. Jay replied: "If you don't like it, piss off down the Nor', be saddoes there." I like Jay a lot.
>
> "Right, I *will*," said a man. "And me," said a bigger man, draining his pint, clunking the glass on the bar.
>
> "Diane'll be showing it there anyhow," said Jay. "But *you'll* not admit that. I'll say: 'How was The Nor'gate?', youse'll say: 'nice and quiet, no telly'." As three men trudged out, she yelled: "And youse'll be lying bollockses, coz me and Diane do Twitter in EastEnders coz we both watches it."
>
> Jay put the EastEnders show on. It knocked me to the fricking moon. It's *excellent*. My first experience of British TV. I can't imagine it could have been better.
>
> EastEnders, a British institution, is set in London's east end, a working-class side of town with strong communities, perfect for a soap-opera. Everyone talks like the Small Faces, so I'm up like a meerkat straightaway. I get into the show, figuring it out, Jay whispers a couple explanations to me. Within minutes Jay, men at the bar and I are overwhelmed by pure drama. This is an *outstanding* program. I don't how to talk it up with justice, I'm no critic, but: the acting's amazing and real, there's a lovely sense you're in that community because you always *hear* it. Energy and busy life is always close-by, a market

outside you hear all the time, scenes outdoors in a square called Albert Square. Everyone's hanging out in atmospheric public places: the market, a cafe, a huge 19th century pub with great décor, a park, even a laundromat where a lovely, older woman in a blue housecoat works. OK, I can't hope to make you interested in this program, so I'll stop. But it's real good TV, (my girl and I *can't handle* TV as you long-term readers know.) And Jay, look at Jay, one of society's low-income workers, next-to-no education, yet drinking in this show's complex, often subtle, emotional, intelligent, tense world like soul-nectar – further proof the idea some people are less intelligent is suspect. Anyone's mind can absorb brilliant things.

Three EastEnders episodes a week. What an institution! {Apparently it has a rival, also well-loved, decades old, called Coronation Road. I'd like to see that also.} What a brilliant, lucky first experience of British TV – EastEnders is awesome. I totally recommend it if you go to Britain. Ah-de-o. Xx

Dewy drank sixth and seventh pints over a conversation with a Socialist couple in their 80s, who told her many left-wing and pacifist people began World War II as conscientious objectors, but enlisted to fight when realising the truth about Hitler. By 9.30 Dewy was drunk, "Where *is* the Good Queen Bess?" her last memory.

Chapter 4

NEXT MORNING, DEWY lay asleep on the floor, limbs at odd angles, sun-touched face blotched from crying. Annette knelt over her, upset, trying to warm her: "Darling, my bae? Please wake? I'll get your coat dry-cleaned."

Beverley knocked: "Ready to go, love?"

Annette rushed to the door. "She's out cold."

"Excuse me," said Beverley, entering. She picked Dewy up, flung her on the bed, slapped her half-hard.

"Please don't hurt her!" cried Annette.

"*Uhh*," groaned Dewy, eyes half-opening.

In one movement, Beverley turned Dewy onto her side, recovery position, and ushered Annette out: "Must go, love, it's 8.15. Got everything?"

Hours later Dewy was woken by crashing sounds. As she stood unsteadily, another *BANG!!* She opened the door an inch. Douglas Fent and barman Jon King hurled furniture into the hall from the room opposite.

Fent saw Dewy and shouted how she'd thrown stones at windows at 3am, waking Beverley to let her in, "then you woke *me* singing and yelling!"

Dewy could never say "Fuck off" to anyone. It hurt so deeply when said to her, she'd never inflict it. She slowly closed the door. Fent banged it with the side of his fist. Dewy opened it:

"Sir! £200 a week to be treated like this?"

"Don't *fucking shut the door in my face* and don't ~"

"*Sh,* Mr Fent!" said Dewy.

"Don't *sh! me.*"

"I pay £200 pounds a w–"

"185 *actually*!"

"I'll be less confused when I see a tenancy agreement!"

"Tenancy agr–"

"As promised, sir."

Fent swore and stomped off to throw more furniture.

Dewy sat on the bed hugging herself, lost in patchy, guilty memory. Last night… was it the *printers?* … noise… striplights… big machinery… men in blue overalls… Catherine… a night car journey…

Her phone rang.

"How are *you*?" said Catherine. "Dear God, what's that *banging*?"

"The landlord throwing tables."

Geoff Carruthers had asked Catherine to speak to Dewy. She must never turn up at the Good Queen Bess in that state again. They'd waited for her in the cordoned-off Tattler Room. "We heard bar-staff shouting at someone," said Catherine, "Then your voice. Geoff and I went to look. Staff were really angry – ready to physically throw you out. You were nearly asleep as you stood, saying: 'Who in fuck called this place the gyookeebee?' Geoff said: 'She's with us, can she have her drink? Mineral water?' You said: 'Gimme Rattock's', then fell over. Geoff picked you up, we walked you to the Tattler Room, you slept like a baby. They brought you a pint of scrumpy."

"They did?"

"The Good Queen Bess gives the Tattler editor and his – I hope one day *her* – guests a free drink once a week. Dates back to the 19th century."

"Like, a tradition?"

"Yes, and on Fridays free lunch *and* drinks. That somehow expanded to a free drink on print-run night too. The little room off the main bar?"

"I don't recall."

"That's the Tattler Room. Wednesday night and Friday afternoon it's cordoned off for us. Geoff and the boys go in Friday 1pm. They bash out the next week's page-plan and get hammered. Total boys' club, I can't stand it, you won't either. They draw lots for who stops drinking to ensure the page-plan gets back to the office. I recommend avoiding Fridays altogether and go in Sundays instead, like I do."

Fent's furniture-throwing worsened. Conversation had to stop. Catherine said: "Well… I'm on leave at last! I won't see you now."

"Oh, Catherine."

"I'm officially off. Really glad you came last week, great timing. I wish you all the best, you're excellent, you know what you're doing. Don't let any Tattler blokes get you down. Keep giving it back to them, 'Let no man steal your thyme'. Or my chair, Stuart Dean. And don't let that *landlord* get you down. Why's he so noisy?"

Next day, after short labour, Alicia Wren was born.

ON HER FREE afternoon, Danii Tyler returned to annihilation. Dave Tyler had taken the day off, driven to Exeter to spend hundreds of pounds on a pair of chainsaws and two leaf-blowers, a hand-held and a back-pack.

Tyler and Warren now sat on the patio, happy, wordless, drinking tea, proudly surveying a garden hacked and bare. A dramatic amount of sky was exposed that wasn't there before.

"Where's the trees and bushes!" cried Danii. "What've you done?"

"Relax, mum! They had to go. Them'd aphids."

"Blocking sightlines from the house," said Dave Tyler.

"*Where's the apple tree!?*"

"Had to go," said Warren. "Attracting insects."

A 20 foot hedge had entirely gone.

"There were flowers along there!" said Danii. "And along there! *And* there!"

"Weeds," said Warren.

"They *weren't*! It was geraniums sort of things! You've killed the bloody garden!!"

"Now listen 'ere!" said Tyler. "This is a job of work. Warren here's specialising in this, or will be. So *butt out.*"

Warren put on thick-cased, hearing protectors. He pulled a chainsaw start-cord, the machine roared violently.

"Smooth start-up!" he bawled.

"My afternoon off!" yelled Danii over the extreme noise. "*Thanks!*"

In Homebase, Danii filled a trolley with bedding plants, soil bags and flower seeds. Tired, annoyed, she queued for the till. Shopping suddenly felt like one of the loneliest things in the world.

"Do you need help packing, madam?"

The gentle, rich voice startled Danii. She turned:

"Oh, *my*. Hello."

He is BEAUTIFUL!

"Shall I take the trolley to your car, madam?"

"Oh." said Danii, deep-breathing. She struggled to speak, or take her eyes from the young man's face. "That'd be..." She glanced to his name-badge: "*ever so nice*, Marlon..."

OCEAN HAD MORE energy in cooler evenings, squeezing through lower and middle bars of the stile into the big field. Left to grass this Spring, the land sloped down towards gently rising woodland.

Jade hesitated. She liked to be by the stile – last safety of the settlement, before the vast world. Around her in newly-dense hedges, birds rustled, building nests. Nettles were a metre-high crowd. Some leaned out low, delinquently, waiting for bare legs. Purples and blues of forget-me-nots surrounded Jade. The air was rich with scents and tangs. Jade sensed a force making blackthorn hedges and catkins burst outwards, like a time-frame explosion.

She sat on the stile, hands cupping her face. The meadow was dotted with fresh yellow celandines. Suddenly they glowed against a darkened field. Jade looked up to a vast raincloud. She felt a shock of fear.

The horizon was closed down by grey. Far land was disappearing. Birdsong and bustling stopped. Wind quickened, heralding the huge, grey mass above. Jade saw Ocean down by the wood-edge. She preferred to go to him than call from this distance, in case anyone local and young heard her, then find and torment her.

Jade reached Ocean as rain arrived. They entered the wood and stood, awed by the differentness of its private, quiet world. High trunks of oak and plane trees were spaced apart, ground soft and earthy. Jade recalled hide-and-seek here years ago, everyone running around: when Warren was a friend, the Moresby children a loyal gang, Carol her best friend.

Carol moved away when Jade was eight. No one saw her again. Everything changed that year and wasn't restored. Warren began ridiculing Jade's weight. The Moresby gang formed factions. Miss Jory left school to get married. Her replacement Mrs Stall never wrote kind notes in homework books as Miss Jory had. Why getting married meant Miss Jory must leave Brock Lane Junior perplexed Jade. That, and her parents, put Jade off marriage for life.

Thinking about *them* alarmed and conflicted her. Jade was unmoved by tall, slim, alert Danii's made-up beauty, though in rare moments of little, even no make-up, her mother was ever the good-looking side of plain, under a permanent up-do of gold-highlights. Danii was Head Beautician and Stylist at the salon of Rennicksons department store in Crendlesham. She cut private clients' hair at their homes midweek evenings too. When angry, she made Jade think of a scolding, cigarette-smoking, Rennicksons window-dummy.

But the spectre of her father made Jade feel forgiveness and need for Danii. "I'd rather have *her* a million times!" She wondered what it was like for her mother being married for years ("and *years*, longer than *I've been alive*") to a man nearly a foot shorter, who spoke horrible, racist things, boasted and joked with Warren and Brandon about something called "porn", and at Christmas took the pair on his "works do" to a strip-club at the coast, returning drunk and instructing son and stepson how to blow condoms up like balloons and stretch them onto their heads: "Use blue ones, look like Marge Simpson, ha-*HA*!"

Jade wished her father would finish working on Moresby new-builds and work far away. For weeks she'd returned from school to his grey van blocking the drive, Tyler in the kitchen, showered, smiling, approaching. He usually told her to help him cook. He rubbed her shoulders when they cooked together. She didn't like it. Tonight was Friday though, no cooking. Pizzas from JoJo's in Balaton.

"Ocean?" called Jade. "We're stuck. This rain? It ain't stoppin'."

They sheltered under an oak at the wood's edge, watching rain on the fields. "Where did the old days go, Ocean? Why don't kids play here now? All at computers. I hope no one *is* in the woods though? Just you and me, Oash."

A shudder passed through Jade. Her mind veered into familiar, unhappy thoughts. Breathless and clammy from jogging downhill, she wished she could take her cardigan over her blouse off. But resistance to removing anything over her chest was strong. She again checked the length of her hair. It needed eight inches more to cover her bosoms. As a child Jade asked Danii why women tend to have long hair and men short. "We've prettier hair," was the reply. Jade wondered if women grew their hair in caveman days to protect their bosoms from men, and the habit continued. Now Jade felt this the truth. She desperately wanted her hair to grow. No one must ever see her bosoms. She wouldn't take her bra off, night or day, until her hair grew. Jade sometimes wondered if she was normal being like this, then a numbness in her mind made all thoughts stop.

Hungry and thirsty after a long school day, Jade had brought four slices of bread, sliced chicken and tomorrow's flap-jack ration. Small bottles of water had gone, she'd lugged a two-litre one in her rucksack, plus two packets of crisps from a multipack. If Warren counted the packets, he'd tell Danii – not from concern, but because he liked getting Jade into trouble.

Jade turned to Ocean: "We've got some chicke~"

He'd gone.

Something felt wrong. Jade turned, walked further into the woods, to a part less familiar, tree-covered, darker, lonelier. Thick trees towered amid ferns, fallen boughs, shrubs, mossy roots and last year's fallen leaves. Jade heard sploshy commotion and twig-cracking as Ocean bounded through ferns. She scanned the high, overgrown slope, trying to spot where he was.

Kneeling, half-hidden, returning her gaze, were a man in his 20s and a boy of 12. Both slowly stood. They exchanged brief sentences in Arabic and fell silent.

Chapter 5

SATURDAY MAY 11TH began cold, wet and blowy – Dewy's favourite weather, but an upsurge in: "Where's yer *SHOES*?" from any passers-by who hadn't darted for cover, though many had, thinking 12°C drizzle and breeze a storm. Coatless people winced, hugged themselves, broke into a run, burst into shops, patting their clothes down: "*Bad* out there! *Jesus*!"

Sometimes an elegant fairy, kind and alert, her bearing perfect, would pad in, rain-gleaming and pure. People huddled and stared:

"*No shoes!* / Look at 'er!/ **She must be cold!**/ ***Where's her fuckin shoes!***/ Her feet'll get wet/ *Mummy, why's that lady not got shoes?*/ SOMETHING'S WRONG IN HER HEAD. DON'T STARE.

But after midday, when the sun came out, could arrive an elegant, kind but saddened fairy. Such was the case after meeting Tessa England.

The MP's Saturday morning surgery was upstairs in the small Town Hall. The 1720 building overlooked a square with a weekly farmers' market. Dewy liked the square's ancient, big, smooth flagstones, two sides of Georgian townhouses, on another the beamed, thatched, King's Arms, and the south side's medieval, stone cloisters, housing a gift shop, estate agent, Devon Hospiscare, Ladbrokes and a closed-down bistro. The cloisters joined a bulky, half-ruined, Norman gatehouse and arch at the corner of the square. Beyond the arch, paths diverged across the wide grass common before St Botolph's.

The farmer's market was busy. Food stalls made Dewy hungry, a rare feeling, it meant non-drinking was back. Hunger never troubled her drinking life. Sober since print-run night. Dewy bought a vegan sausage roll and wolfed it down, as she approached the Town Hall's dark green plaster and clean white window-frames. Though accustomed to historic buildings in Massachusetts, Dewy was still moved and awed, like most American visitors, by old British architecture – part innocent visitor, partly a sense here was ancestry, a country older than America (though to Dewy that was a sham. Many times had she blogged:

> **Native American civilizations – worthy of the word, for they *were* civilized, lasted 12,000 years only to be murdered in two generations by Europeans, or killed by diseases they'd brought. Europeans whose "civilization" was guns, slavery, Bibles & land-purchase "rights".**

The Town Hall's doors were set back under a projecting first floor on pillars. Inside, a book-fair bustled before a staircase up to galleries of ornate doorways. After 10 minutes and four "Aren't your *feet* cold!?"s, Dewy left the fair with a 1912 Walt Whitman and a Vernon Lee book then climbed the white marble stairs.

Three people sat along a narrow arched passage. A bulky, florid man in tweeds emerged from a room at the end on the right, booming: "Thaanking you, Mrs England!! I's'll be waiting on the outcome. We'll see wh'haapens."

"Yup! Bye, Richard!" roared a voice. "*NEXT!*"

A woman stood and went into the room. Dewy sat along from two men next in line, nervous.

I'm about to meet a Conservative member of the British Parliament. I will ask: 'Why does the Wall Street Journal

call London 'the money-laundering capital of the world'?
Why are four million of your people below the poverty line?
Why do you claim 100 per cent employment, yet there are
thousands of food-banks? And, three years after narrowly
voting to leave Europe, the UK hasn't done so. Why?

Dewy waited a long time. The first man to go in had been a while, another was before Dewy. Her mind had long wandered from why she was there. She found broadband and blogged:

> Forgive, if you can, my tangled thoughts, I'm off the booze again. Cue the usual withdrawal symptoms: life's a locked door, I'm hopeless, no one likes me and they're right. I'm waiting to see a British legislator right now, but am obsessing on a rude, unhealthy conversation I had last night *at* my darling girl. I hate myself for it. My poor lovely girl.
>
> I told her the men where I work are jerks about me not wearing shoes. They'd seemed over it but aren't. A stare, remark or question every hour. My girl said:
>
> "But your footies hate being covered."
>
> "I *know!*" I cried. "As if it *matters* I don't wear shoes in a fricking office, or anyplace!"
>
> My stupid brain found this one-dimensional subject fascinating. I moaned on like a toothache'd wildebeest: "I don't *understand* these people! And I'm sure one guy has some kind of sexual interest in my ankles or feet. He goes stiff-faced and Draculoid. I saw his reflection in my computer, peering down. But my ankles are crossed, surely he can only see my soles? Unless *they're* what gets him off?"
>
> My girl said: "Morris loves my soles, but knows not to lick the tickle-bits."
>
> {NB: Morris is my girl's Boston Terrier. She and I are in England, Morris in Massachusetts.}
>
> The conversation got worse. "Hey!" I said, think-

ing me hilarious, "Maybe I could write a piece for the paper!? What gets the guys off? Geoff Carruthers: female choirs dressed as ants but with bare legs. Colin Hendry: World War Two munitions girls licking red lollipops. Ace reporter Drac Vampiro: binding, licking or fucking the soles of sub-editor Miss Durant. I'd do my bit too: 'Licking and kissing very clean, medium-thick, eight-inch dicks."

"OH!" cried my girl. Her dear, smooth brow furrowed. "I don't think Morris wants to hear that kind of thing."

"Morris is back home, darling."

"He sometimes comes when I swoon into sleepland, like, when everything goes *wahvravahva*... Maybe he and I connect on the astral plane?"

Instead of saying "Sorry," then shutting up, I tactlessly, soberly *carried on*! {Christ, I *hate* myself. I HATE MYSELF}

"I'll whisper," I continued: "so Morris's visitation won't hear. The times I went with guys, and was drunk enough to cope with the surrealism of penises, it was kinda OK to softly lick and slow-kiss random places of his dick. *Not* sucking – *ugh!* – but licking and kissing. Drives a man wild. Or did. I've not slept with one in years."

My girl went quiet and remote. She looks awful anxious these days. Being pregnant in another country, working two jobs, alone, the man vanished... then your girlfriend comes, she's drunk on your floor, or sober in your small bed saying: "Kiss or lick – not suck – guys' dicks?" That's what my girl is enduring.

Goddess, I can't *bear* what I turn into when sober. I don't know what I say or where it comes from. I don't even *mean* the crap I come out with. People say: 'It's *great* you're not drinking!' but I'm this whining

134

fuckwit. I hate sobriety, I hate who I am, I'm *not me*. Or *am* I? Is this the *real* me? Am I *only, truly me* when sober?! No, Goddess, *please* **no??!!! No! Aaaaarggh!!**

Dears, if you've read this far, thank-you from my selfish heart. I hope you're happy & loved. Delete this whinge, get rid of me. *Argh!*-de-o. Xx

Dewy sat in tears. She blew her nose, using a tissue.

"*NEXT!!*"

A man to Dewy's right: "Miss? You're next."

"Uh? Thagg-you, sir."

Two Georgian arched windows overlooked the market. Mid-room, a powerful woman in a navy Guernsey sat at a large desk, busy.

"Gotta be quick, 'fraid," she said, glancing up, peering over reading-glasses. "You OK?"

"Hay feeber," sobbed Dewy.

"Hm. Get it bad, by the look of it. *Do* sit. How can I help?"

Dewy fought an urge to bolt from the room, sprint to The Lugworm, dive into Annette's bed and tell her she loved her.

"*What* is the subject of yaw enquireh??" barked the upper class, brisk voice of Tessa England.

"Oh... um... I've gone blank. Sorry."

"Okaaay. Who are you?" said the MP, pen poised over notebook: "Mrs? Ms? Miss?"

"Ah. *There's* a question."

"What?"

"I don't feel connected to any of those," mumbled Dewy, "'Miss' is kinda 'nice', but I sometimes don't like 'Miss', especially if people presume it?"

Dewy pulled her hair under her nose, but remembered she had tissues to blow her nose in and did so instead. Failing to see the MP's frowning stare, Dewy continued:

"Of course I oughta be 'Ms', but I never really liked that. The *sound* of it – '*Muz*' – like a depressed insect. Can't I just be Dewy? Or Miss Durant? I'm not keen on *any* term of address, but ~"

"*Fine!* Miss Durant. How can I *help*?"

"Or Dewy Durant? Either is ~"

"I'm *very* busy," said Tessa England. "What can I *do* for you? You're a constituent? Living, working here? From the States I take it?"

No answer. The MP leaned forward: "Do you know what *very busy* means?"

"Yeah, *sure*, I-I…" Dewy sniffed, then: "Like… last month I, uh, bought some raisin bread – cinnamon-raisin bread? So I started making toast, but forgot it? I went into the garden or whatnot, then ~"

"*Christ*," gasped Tessa England. "I *hate* telling people to get out. But *GET OUT!!*"

JADE WAS NERVOUS. Her father took Ocean out at noon every Saturday – "You and me, Oash! Man and dog!"

What if they went to the woods and Ocean led him to the men?

"What's wrong with *you*, pudge?" snapped Danii to Jade. Danii had the day off work for the Moresby May. "Why so miserable?"

"She's looking slightly thinner," said Dave Tyler.

"*Is* she?" said her mother, examining Jade from several angles, squinting.

"All that dog-walking," said her father. "She even took him out first thing. Look at Ocean! Wants his Saturday midday walk, don't you? Can't today, mate. Gotta go back out, help with the fett. Jade'll take you out? Keep her weight-losing."

He wore new slacks and reeked of cologne.

"Them loafers look better with socks," said Danii.

"Why've you got changed anyhow? Don't go back out setting up stalls and stuff dressed like that?"

"You might have a point, actually," said Tyler. His nerves before village social events used to be endearing. Now Jade couldn't bear to look at him.

"Jade, I said take Ocean out!" he snapped. "Always goes Saturdays midday, without fail. He *knows*. He *knows* he's ~"

"One *minute*," moaned Jade, acting. She'd be suspicious if eager. Brandon's near-romance with a Moresby girl years ago saw his sudden keenness to exercise Ocean, an excuse to leave the house.

Jade hoped no one heard her leave with Ocean at 6am, but clearly her father had. She'd gone to the woods to give the man and boy two blankets, Evian, a roll of Andrex and any food she could, though everything in the kitchen was accounted for. The men had thanked her in Arabic, nearly crying with gratitude for four slices of bread, two Dairyleas, a packet of crisps, tomatoes, an orange, a pear.

The sun was out now. Ocean panted alongside Jade. They slowly toured the village. Church Lane bustled with stalls and food vans, a bouncy castle, beer tents, thudding generators, a polished "Green Goddess" fire-engine on display and a sheep-shearing pen. On a makeshift stage, acts would perform through the day: children's dance groups, The Balaton Mummers, a local choir, Brinton Girl Guides Steel Band, a magic show, Volcombe Basset Opera Circle, The Bettle Brass and a folk group Knives To Grind.

The church struck 12, a town-crier bawled, people cheered and the Moresby May began. Morris Men in antlers and bells leapt in formation at the crossroads. Jade and Ocean watched them dance and clack sticks. Jade wondered why people joked about Morris Dancers. She liked them and the strange old music they danced to. Maybe everyone secretly did. It made a change from men parked in vans with their engines running, one in every street everywhere, poisoning the air. Why aren't *they* singled out for mockery instead? *Can't turn an ignition key to the left? Too difficult?*

Jade had to write a story for English homework. She'd write about a village that banned Morris Dancing because everyone said it was stupid. But one moonless night, near the churchyard, sticks were heard bashing, bells jingling, ancient music weaving…

In Church Lane, Danii face-painted children, as every year at the May. Despite her mother's insults and bossiness to her, Jade couldn't stop a slight pride watching Danii here – quick, tall, slender in Jimmy Choos and white Liberty dress, making a boy a tiger. Jade thought her mother only looked good when too busy to care, as now. If anything she looked better than ever. A new light shone in her eyes recently. Maybe she'd won the lottery and not told anyone.

Dave Tyler and Brandon were drinking with men from the village. Jade realised if her family was involved with the May all day (and Warren glued to war-games in his bedroom) she could smuggle more supplies to the woods.

At home, Jade packed a blanket and a sleeping bag into a bin-liner. She'd secretly bought a sponge cake, home-made bread, scones, honey, juice and damson jam at the May. She left for the woods, back turned to the village, no one would see she hugged a bulky bag.

SOUNDS FROM THE May carried over the fields to where strawberry furrows stretched to the horizon. Dozens of people knelt, progressing by inches, three tubs an hour, £2 a tub. The age range was 12 to 80, from Britain and nations all over the world.

Billy Nevin straightened his back, examined his hard, earthy hands. He wasn't working fast after five days' drinking. A heavy cold the cider had held off arrived now, demanding interest and a bed for the night. Yet Nevin still berated himself for wasting £50 on a Balaton B&B that rainy night in the week. He'd had a good bath there, a 12-hour sleep, clothes washed for an extra £5, but it all left him penniless. He'd challenged an Albanian man to fight for money in a lay-by near Fetton. Nevin got hurt and a tenner, enough for a gallon of scrumpy from a farm, where, on the way out, he chanced an open door to a kitchen and took £40, leaving 30, so vanished money wouldn't be obvious. Before long he was broke again, working "in the fecking fields".

He straightened his back, gasped breath after breath. Air felt good.

A small cloud drifted, returning sun's warmth. Nevin stood, shook his limbs, screamed: "*Faster*, ya foreign wankers!!" People around knew his meaning if not his words. A Slovenian woman flipped him the finger. Nevin grinned and held up both in return: "Have *two* ya feckin mongrel! If ye weren't ugly, I'd batter yer man then gi' ye *this* up the erse!"

On "*this*" he pulled down his trousers. Howls of laughter and nauseated moans roared over the furrows. Some people held up their thumb and forefinger an inch apart, laughing. Nevin looked down, saw his penis was like a white brussels sprout. He pulled his trousers up, bawling:

"See how ye's DON'T give me the horn? Tis 10 inches when Nevin's randy!"

He pulled a bulbous plastic bottle from his hold-all, 9% proof cider, £3.29 from CostCo in Brinton. Four swigs later, a rush of power and optimism energised two minutes of frantic strawberry picking. "Billy's in the feckin' lead!" he raved, to no one. "Bionic Man! Da-ner-nah-*nerrrr!*"

The big plan felt possible again. Usually Nevin knew it couldn't begin until he'd raised £350, an amount he'd not seen in years. In better moods like now, however, Billy felt £350 was two days away, the plan imminent: Andy in Swole sold cocaine at £350 per 10 grams, never under 10 grams, and never on credit, unless by precarious short-term arrangement (which, if breached, or believed breached, meant a severe beating from several men).

Nevin planned to buy 10 grams, sell each in Crendlesham for £60, any over in Farrisford for 50.

Sun and cider put schemes in motion. Nevin zipped his bag and stood. "Feck it! I'll go see Andy *now*. He'll give me credit, he's a sound fella. Saturday niiight! I'll sell good tonight!"

DEWY WANDERED THE sunny town, discovering the retail park. In Matalan she bought a deep-red blouse, a floppy green sunhat, two size 14 dresses for Annette, then returned to the town centre. More £3 lurid beach-towels from the covered market were needed. There could never be enough. Annette's nightly foot-wash and Dewy's attempts to wash herself down-below by squatting into a basin, making water flood everywhere…

She walked along High Street, still ashamed of last night's conversation with Annette, wishing she could give Annette a treat – Annette who had such little happiness, yet didn't complain. Annette who ached for Morris, worked every day and often felt ill now.

Oh, Baby Bear – thought Dewy, welling up – *I wish I could give you something you loved. You're so humble, you'll think these dresses and a couple beach towels are precious gifts. I wish I could give you a present that* MATTERED, *a surprise that delighted you.*

She paused at Sheekey Autos while an old, doorless car was hoisted over the pavement onto a truck. Dewy remembered she needed a car for work, and for Annette to use. She glanced into the open, dark cave: cars on high jacks, overall'd men, radio echoing. A sports car the colour of turquoise sea was being pushed out towards the truck.

"Excuse me?" called Dewy. "What will happen to that car?"

"Scrapyard!" called the youngest man.

"But it's beautiful," said Dewy.

"It *is* nice, yeah," said the man, approaching. "1976. Dark green originally. But it's had it. All that rust... see?"

In the truck, Gary Sheekey glanced in his mirror to check the delay – Dale talking to a fine-looking woman with no shoes. Now Dale was coming over.

"Dad?" said Dale. "This Stag. Anything we can do?"

His father sucked in air, muttered "doubt-it", got out, walked to the car, frowning. "Want it gone. Don't like it."

"The colour's so lovely and radiant!" said Dewy. "In today's world of colourless cars."

"A shell. No engine," said Gary Sheekey. "Dale took that."

"Rebuild the engine, put it in another car," said Dale.

"Is it a V8?" said Dewy.

"It *is* a V8," said Gary Sheekey, respectful. His son nodded.

"My girl restores V8s," said Dewy. "She loves them."

10 minutes later, a truck pulled up by the Lugworm, Triumph Stag on the back. Gary Sheekey, a mechanic called Raj and Dewy sat three abreast in the cab. Dale and another man were on their way to to fetch the V8 engine. Dewy got out and beckoned the truck to a far, empty corner of the car-park half-hidden by an oak whose roots upburst the asphalt. As the bright Stag was lowered, Dewy ran happily to the pub to look for Annette.

MARLON HAD MADE a lemon-cream sponge cake with mandarin oranges around the top. It rested like a crown on a rack while Marlon cleaned the kitchen to Radio Four. Despite Bobby's verdict "a cabbage", Marlon followed politics closely. The baffling, febrile, Brexit saga disturbed him, and everyone. Marlon struggled to understand the endless media it generated. So did John Wright. So did Marlon's Homebase colleagues. Even Robert Obogo – a supply teacher with a degree in Politics and Economics – shrugged: "Marlon, I haven't a clue, it's a joke."

On the radio, an MP fussed and lied about "a deal on the table", the Irish Backstop and a third parliamentary vote (aim unclear). He repeatedly used the phrase "moving forward".

"Towards *what*?" muttered Marlon, turning the radio off. He returned to his room to collect laundry, wondering if to go and see Farrisford Town play. He hadn't left the house for two days. Mr Wright was out volunteering at the Hospiscare Shop. John also helped run Our Lady of the Missions food bank on Tuesday nights too, run by a Father Alan, though it was interfaith. No one minded Mr Wright wasn't a Catholic, nor minded a Muslim couple who volunteered. Marlon felt guilt for not taking up John's suggestion to help too, felt ashamed of his two private reasons why: 1. *Doing something else on Tuesday nights would doubly feel I'm not at football training. Another step further away from the club.* 2. *I just KNOW some of these boys who harass me are people who need the food bank. They're all from the Stipley, or Yenton estates.*

Marlon's phone pinged. Probably Robert again, nagging to come to the game. Marlon glanced at the clock, an hour to kick-off. He opened the message and froze.

Hi Marlon, I really enjoyed our chat the other day. Thanks for your number in case I need advice on other things for the garden. I do, as it goe's but easier we talk in person? So look out for me in the week ahead! looking forward very much to meeting again. Danii x

THE LUGWORM'S CAR park was quarter-full most Saturdays. Like the Tattler office, the rest – busy a century – lay empty. In a furthest corner, a spreading oak.

Two young women crossed towards it. One, 5' 10, a dancer's bearing, in white dress and dark-green, floppy-brimmed hat, walked elegantly on nimble, if slightly long, bare feet, hand in hand with the other woman, 5'5, whose long, dark-honey hair was in bunches. Matalan dress tucked into jeans, she wore old Dr Marten shoes, one blue lace, one black. The taller woman hid a bundle under her arm – the other woman's overalls – "part of the surprise."

Annette saw trees ahead, heard birdsong, smiled. The surprise must be the discovery of a nest, or a British bird neither had seen before.

"Oh my!" she cried, stopping near three men busy at a vintage car. "Did you ever see a more beautiful shape of British car, hon? It's a Triumph – the actual name, though a design triumph if ever there was. Maybe a TR6, or a … a Stag? Look: *a V8!* On that pallet? Oh! Do you think these men would mind if… er, we went over and…"

"Perfectly fine, darling!" smiled Dewy, hugging her. Between kisses: "The *car* is the surprise! It's *ours*, hon! I'm buying it! Wanna fix it up?"

"Do I wa- *oh my God!!* Yes!!"

"Fritz, Raj? Dale? This is Annette," said Dewy.

Annette hurtled towards the engine:

"An Offenhauser manifold! Oh, *my*! Look, hon? Look!"

Gary Sheekey had left a while back in the truck. Near the open back doors of Dale Sheekey's van, parts taken from the Stag over weeks lay on pallets. Annette climbed into her overalls fast and helped with parts-cleaning.

Dogs and engines – thought Dewy – *the twin passions of her life.*

"Is this originally a Rover engine?" Annette asked Dale Sheekey, who was only half-sure. To most further questions he helplessly said: "I'll have to ring my dad and ask." When Annette and Raj talked on an equal wavelength about suspension, Fritz and Dale's gazes moved one to the other, as at a tennis match. Dewy felt superfluous and left for the pub unnoticed.

She was woken late afternoon by Annette lightly kissing her face all over. Annette had removed her overalls and sat on the bed near-naked. She gazed down at Dewy wide-eyed and breathless, a look Dewy knew well from other women, but never Annette.

"Hi, hon," murmured Dewy.

Annette cried "*Oh!*" and plunged her face onto the ridge of Dewy's armpit, kissing and inhaling.

"I wouldn't go *there*, hon," said Dewy. "I don't smell too good."

"It's nice," gasped Annette, nearly lying on Dewy, kissing her unstoppably. Her leg climbed onto Dewy's thigh. In hot breaths she said: "You're *cold*, hon, you shoulda… got under the covers…"

Annette tugged and kicked her knickers off, pulled Dewy's dress up and grinded on her naked hip. "I… *Oh! Ah!*" She turned away. "*Oh God! Oh! Oh!! I'm sorry!*" Annette grabbed a towel, bolted to the bathroom, returned a minute later, drying her hands, stricken. "I'm sorry… I… … …" She began to cry.

Dewy, terrified Annette had been miscarrying, hugged her, drew her to the bed, lay by her, sighing: "*So glad* you're OK, hon! Why so upset?" She stroked Annette's cheek. "Hmm?"

"Sometimes," sobbed Annette: "Sometimes I- I… *self-pollute.*"

"Don't be ashamed, poor lamb!" said Dewy, "Everyone does it. I do it *all day* in the cabin." She kissed Annette's face, all her tears, held up a sheet-corner for Annette to blow her nose. Annette reached instead for a Kleenex box Dewy never seemed to see.

"Everyone masturbates," said Dewy. "Back home, after I've filled the bird-feeders, checked the nests, made peanuts and lettuce, danced a couple hours, I go lie down, knead and whizz-off til I shriek like a vixen, rub the gook all over myself ~"

"Ughh! Honeyyy?"

"Well, it's good to keep busy in the days."

Annette confessed sexual feelings for Dewy she'd always had. She cried as she spoke. Dewy cried because Annette cried. Dewy wished she'd realised Annette's feelings, and could have fulfilled Annette over the years:

"It's only *me*, darling," she said, hugging Annette close. "Grind on me, feel no shame. I want you to be *happy*. Don't be bad to yourself about what you *desire*. It's natural. And *you're* natural. You're natural, honest, free and so beautiful, darling."

But both knew Dewy didn't sexually want Annette.

"We've never explored sex," said Annette quietly, "Because we always shared our bed with a person of caninity: Bachelor, then Morris. Every night together, except overseas, someone who is a dog was present. It never occurred to me to be sexual with you, for it would traumatise a coda. I couldn't do that. Neither could you, I know."

(Coda was Annette's private word for a dog with a soul and spiritual/emotional sides. She'd never declared a dog *not* a coda, however.)

Annette kissed Dewy's neck gently, fully: "Ohhh, I've often self-polluted about you, the smell of your armpits and ears, your beautiful hair. *Ohhh*, and when your hair's in a bun and your ears are fully out. That's when I just wanna… … *oh…*"

She kissed, nibbled and licked Dewy's ear. "Ohhaw*ww*!! May I please… give your ears a snoo?"

"Of course, d-darling," said Dewy through quiet tears. "Poor thing! You had sexual frustration."

"It was latent, hon. Like I said, persons of caninity were always with us in bed. Their welfare came first.

"Uh-huh," sniffed Dewy, blowing her nose on a corner of the sheet.

"Can I take your dress off?" breathed Annette.

"I got it!" said Dewy, quick upright, dress off. Annette's mouth glumped onto Dewy's bosoms and kissed them hard. For minutes she kissed Dewy's shoulders and bosoms all over, breath hotter, slower. Dewy knew Annette was beginning to have sex with her. She tried to subdue her mind and pretend all was OK, though no alcohol was here to help.

She softly, firmly returned Annette's lengthening, scooping kisses, hoping these were enough to satisfy. Annette's bosoms, heavier, harder, compressed her own from above. Her ear felt Annette's nostrils, the familiar uprush of air as Annette deeply inhaled there. Usually Annette pulled away to emit a groan of joy, but forgot now, causing loud noise in Dewy's right ear. Annette wrapped tightly around Dewy, kissing her hungrily. "My darling! *Ohhhhh!*"

Dewy felt lightly abrasive hairs and warm wetness press up and down her right hip.

"Is this… *OK*, hon…?" moaned Annette dreamily.

"You bet, darling!" said Dewy, trying. She hugged Annette close, kissed her more, bucked the rhythm, inserted a hand in her underwear as her other hand roamed to embrace Annette's waist and help her ride harder.

Dewy's only hope – it never failed – was to fantasize to orgasm while kissing the woman with her. She excelled at clitoral stimulation of herself and another woman simultaneously, with bouts of swapping, and sometimes going down, though Dewy preferred face-to-face. She kissed exceptionally and caringly, for she liked her partners – some more than others – though Dewy had no idea how gratifying her kissing really was. Three dozen New England married women had never known anything like that. All wanted more. Dewy happily agreed to second, third (or tenth) discreet trysts, for luckily, her keenest fantasies involved married, wealthy women aged 38-45, as many of her admirers were.

Models in catalogues of sensible clothes made Dewy steam with lust. Her pornography collection entirely consisted of booklets from garden centres and furniture stores. Healthy, banal women of 40 smiled from shed doorways, or benignly watered flowerbeds. Others lay on chunky, maroon recliners in mock rooms, smiling at a TV remote. Dewy's favourites were thin-papered home-improvement catalogues that fell out of newspapers. These starred duos of half-pretty, big-boned Stepford Wives in cardigans and slacks, standing in conservatories for no reason. Dewy despaired at herself ("Golden retriever owners with Aga's, ah-*uhh!!*"), but the real-life peak of her fantasies was plain/pretty, blonde, 46-year-old Joni Swan, lawyer wife of Wall Street's Michael.

A bittersweet, hot memory of a 2014 goodbye kiss – dot of wetness on her lip-corner – often triggered Dewy's self-erotic episodes. Once more, the Willetts's, late-Spring dusk, grass-dew soaking her toes: "Bye, Michael. Bye, Joni." *Joni turned, she smiled.* On impulse Dewy went to her. *A firm kiss, two seconds long, half on her mouth. She **did not** recoil... We faced each other, a glow in her eyes, smile widening. Then she sighed, tension-release so lovely... And she took my hand in both of hers!!* In the four seconds until Michael's "Jone! C'mon!", Dewy was wordless. Forever after, she couldn't bear herself for staying silent: five thousand relivings rewrote those silent seconds with: "Would you like a date sometime?" – *She would have said yes, she would have said YES! But I NEVER SPOKE! I stood there like a GOOSE!*

Annette's rhythmic weight, wetness, heat and cries faded as Dewy's mind departed...

HOT today! Empty beach, sand gold, bluest of blue skies, here's the old hut, go in, cool off. Sun-bleached old door's open! Someone there?

"Hello…? JONI! Sorry to wake you. I'll leave you to it!"

"No, come in, Dewy! Michael's gone for ice-creams. Just let me cover myself, I only have this towel? Would you like the mattress?"

"No-o, stay there, you look comfortable!"

"Come rest, I'll budge up. We can both fit? Don't be shy! That's it. Mm, you ARE hot, Dewy! Our arms just touched."

"You're quite cold lying here! Shall I rub your arms?"

"Mmm! Go ahead! I like the warmth."

"Oh, Joni!" **Kiss!** *"Oh-ahh, that was the kiss 'hello' I meant to give you…. ….hmmm…. this is nice…… … You've beautiful shoulders, Joni."*

"They like your warm hands on 'em! Tell me, is the ice-cream place nearby? Mike set off walking."

"It's six miles."

"Oh. He'll be a while. Oops, my towel's slipped!"

"I got it, Joni! Let me… oh, I've dropped it… Oh, Joni…" **Kiss!** *"Ahh … ohh…"* **Kiss!** *"Ah!… ah!… AH!!… Ah!!.. Ah!!… Oh! …Ah!!… Ah!!… Aah!!.. Ah! Ah! Aaah! OH! Ah!* **AH!"**

Dewy's body twisted right, left-hand fingers pressing hard, fast, rotational. Her free arm reached for Annette.

Annette had gone.

Dewy stopped just short of orgasm. Her eyes opened. Annette was sitting on the edge of the bed, looking away. She'd put on a T-shirt.

"Da-hharling?" panted Dewy. "Ya'OK? Huh?"

"I'm sorry," said Annette, in much misery. "I… I…"

Dewy sat up, hot, damp, a pink rash on her neck. "Honey? Wha'… what's up? Did I piss you off?"

"No, *gosh*, no. You never could, hon," said Annette, letting Dewy hug her close. "I'm sorry… I-I just couldn't go through with it?"

"That's OK, hon." said Dewy. "Don't worry."

Annette began to cry. "I think … you and me, I-I think we're… not meant… not meant… for, uh… *that*."

"Sure," said Dewy, rubbing Annette's back. "That's

OK. If you feel it's not right, that's OK. Don't cry, hon? I cry if you cry…"

Annette dried her eyes,: "It's n-nice that you… you felt for me the same as I f-felt for you a little. And of course I still do, you're my life's passion."

She looked at Dewy with a power Dewy wasn't used to.

"No one's more arousing… and beautiful than you, Dewy."

She rested her head on Dewy's shoulder. Dewy caressed her, gazing at space.

After a time, Annette said: "I-I'm sorry to disappoint. But I don't feel the sexualness I thought I had."

"That's OK, hon. Never worry."

"My hormones are crazy. And your smells are kinda…"

"They're bad."

"They're not. But they *are* strong. It makes me wild. Y-you really won't have a bath here?"

"Hell, no, You've seen I try wash my butt and woo in those damn plastic basins, but…"

"Come Exeter, I'll book you in as a sports centre guest? Go in, have a shower, leave?"

"Mmm. Finding time? The newspaper's kinda full-on…"

They fell quiet and held each other. A first ever shared sexual moment, now past, made them silent, each lost in her own, unreachable privacy. In Dewy's case: *"Darn dingblast and horses! That weird, unwanted incident just then… A mistake. A desecration. Sacrifice. All to oblige what she started, then didn't want…"*

Annette raised her face, eyes big and beautiful, making Dewy smile and kiss her, though Dewy's tummy lurched, as it often had when she'd seen Annette's face in the past hour. Now she realised why…

She looks like a grown-up.

She's never not looked like a child before.

Annette is becoming adult.

Chapter 6

NEXT MORNING, A Sunday, Dewy left Annette sleeping and walked to the Tattler. She tried to overrride the second depression that always arrived two days after the first depression that hit two days after her last drink.

Dewy called depression "deadness".

She paused in the woods, placed hand on trowel in inside coat pocket and focused on bodily feelings – nothing, no bowel churn. She walked on, unlikely to dump, having not eaten since yesterday's sausage roll and half a sandwich Annette smuggled to the room in a doggie bag.

As Fent had banned Dewy from all downstairs areas after the Disgusting, and Farrisford Organics was finally off-limits, Dewy relied for food on doggie-bag scraps Annette brought. The arrangement was made more uneasy by Annette's dislike of the term "doggie bag".

A clear, bright morning of birdsong promised a warm Sunday. Dewy padded into Market Street, then an alley between shops to a nondescript precinct towards an old oaken bridge over the Brate into Bridge Street. As Dewy neared the end of the alley she heard a man scream:

"Ya foreign *shite!*"

The depth of rage signified a dangerous man. Dewy froze. "*Feck off back to Romania!!*" bawled the voice against the rushing Brate in the background. Dewy peered from the alley. A down-and-out man, out of his mind, loomed over a terrified woman sitting in a blanket.

The man coughed phlegm, spat it on the blanket and roared: "Your men hide away! Feckin' *cowards*! *Tell those foreign conts* that send ye out beggin' money *Nevin'll kill 'em!!*"

He seemed ready to kick the woman. Dewy ran out and stood beside her.

The man saw Dewy. "*Who the feck are* YOU?" His face was pink with gelid eyes. He stank of pies and cider. Trembling, Dewy removed his spittle near her eye and said: "Leave her alone?"

Nevin grabbed Dewy and flung her aside. She sprang back in front of him, crying: "Leave this girl alone and do *not* handle me!"

Nevin shimmied and danced as his face leaned into Dewy's: "I'm having a *conversation* here, darlin' Get the *feck out of it!!* 'Fore I *slap* ya!"

The young woman slowly stood. Nevin saw her.

"I ain't finished with *youse*," he bawled. "Sit! Sit feckin' DOWN!"

"*Sir!*" cried Dewy, very scared, tearful "Leave her alone! She c-can't defend herself. Isn't that *so* cowardly of you? Isn't it not?"

"*Piss off!*"

"Don't shout at women. We hate it," said Dewy, so frightened she didn't know what she said: "W-we *hate* it. Life might be... *kinder* t-to you if you'd... if you'd not *scare* us ~"

"*Foreigners!*" roared Nevin, staggering zig-zag to the river-bridge. "Foreign *hooers!*"

The young woman touched Dewy's arm, tried to speak, but in panic ran to Market Street. Dewy remained – shaking, gulping, unable to focus.

FATHER ALAN TRIED to make Mass uplifting, but coughs and shufflings echoed in Our Lady Of The Missions' sunlit, blond-wood and blue big chapel.

He uttered final prayer. All fell quiet and stayed so. Time passed. A car with botched exhaust passed far away, then deepening, restful silence. Father Alan looked across. Father Entreton glanced 'Shall I?' and walked over.

"Thank-you, God," he began, "For the privileges and blessings we have,"

A faint sigh of happiness to hear his voice rose from rows of lowered heads.

"Thank-you for this Earth and all life," he continued: "To think it could so easily not have happened! Yet it has. We might be the only speck of life in all infinity. But what funny things we are! Often bored, discontented. 'Life is first boredom then fear' said poet Philip Larkin. Who doesn't feel that at times? But this world existing was a chance in trillions. We live in a *miracle*."

Sensing formal prayer over, the congregation sat up, looked with fondness to Father Entreton, who surveyed all. No one felt missed out.

"And every person is a miracle. Hard to believe at times! But who can deny it? Even atheists can't deny we're miraculous and astonishing creations, as is all that exists. On these points, those who follow Christ, those who believe in a different version of God to ours, and those who believe in no God, can happily agree, and respect one another."

Earlier, in his garden, Father Entreton remembered with sadness and a pang of anger the May 1990 suicide of an exam-pressured Farrisford teenager. Now the priest said:

"Finally – who's got A-levels or GCSE's soon? Well... I believe God wants you to have a day *off* on this beautiful, warm day. No revising. No essays. Go out, enjoy the sun. Enjoy *forgetting*. It'll benefit ye. Take the day off with God's blessing. We in this church condone it just the once, do we not, Father Alan?"

Father Alan tensed. A few in the congregation chuckled.

"Do we not, Father Alan?"

Everyone laughed. Father Entreton often asked Father Alan's consent on unconventional, even rebellious approaches to life problems. The younger priest would roll his eyes, raise his hands helplessly. He did so now.

"There, see?" said Father Entreton. "And he's a tough nut to crack."

Everyone roared. Father Alan folded his arms, mock-annoyed.

THE EMPTY OFFICE glared. Each scattered chair seemed to have the spirit of its owner. Stuart Dean's seat, side-on to his desk, stared at the door, like most of the men's, while those of Tim West, Ian Balloch and David Cartwright faced inwards. "Caveman stuff," thought Dewy. "Aggressive guys ready for invaders, nicer guys domesticated." She saw Michael Fenwick's chair obediently side-on to Stuart Dean's (Catherine's) bigger chair: "That is *so telling!*"

Very few articles had been submitted. This was deliberate. The men wanted her to beg and cajole. Predicting they'd send masses of work hours before deadline, Dewy resolved to make it clear at tomorrow's meeting she'd refuse anything later than Tuesday.

But she was worried. Barely one-fifth of the amount for a usual Sunday was in. Colin Hendry had sent short pieces like: **Quad Bike Pursuit Leads To Arrests** and **CPR Saves Cressy Man's Life**. David Cartwright had sent his listings pages and **New Road Surface Welcomed**. Two Sunday stalwarts – 60% of the Farmers' Bulletin, and the Farrisford Town match report – were in, however.

Dewy edited and laid out the Bulletin for hours until dazed, hungry and ready to leave, but the match report would only take minutes, 400 words by contributor Dennis Fairbairn.

But Dewy had yet to read Fairbairn after a Farrisford Town victory: 12 paragraphs, each 100 words, a fact Dewy noticed accidentally while deleting several. What began as:

Miracle After Penalty Hell

Town	**2**		Wyll Albion	**1**

Cassidy 7, Obogo 90+1   *Preston* (pen) *85*

(H-T 1-0)

(Town's Scott Parkes sent off 85 min
Albion's Gavin Birch sent off 85 min)   attendance 238

became fanatical reams about corners, free-kicks, passes and throw-ins.

The accompanying "Townie Says…" cartoon was in. Signed in tiny letters by its creator, Crange, the small, weekly graphic starred a lumpy man – presumably Townie – in a farmer's hat with FTFC on it. He always held a newspaper with the Town result and spoke the cartoon's caption, this week: *"Where there's a Wyll, there's a way!"*

"Good grief," sighed Dewy, switching off her computer.

Her return to The Lugworm seemed long. Hunger had made her weak, and delirious in her mind. When Dewy arrived through the doors by the Lugworm kitchen at 3pm, the building was hazy with Sunday lunch aromas. She inhaled roast potatoes, gravy, nut and mushroom roast, red wine sauces, garlic bread… Dewy let out a whimper and, to her surprise, actually drooled. As she slurped the wet icicle back into her mouth from the back of her hand, Martin Davidson knocked her over. He'd rushed through with gravy-wet plates from the restaurant. A left-over potato fell and bounced, with a dot of warmth, off Dewy's foot.

"S-sorry, miss!" cried Davidson, panting. "I'm *SO* sorry!"

"My fault!" said Dewy."

"*My* fault," cried the boy. "I-I'm clumsy. Hello by the way! I-I remembers ya, Miss!. Ah-I-I-I now works also the weekends now here, doing washing-up, but also… er, I-I'd better *go*… Nice seeing you. Sorry I er… er…"

He rushed away. Dewy picked up the potato and wolfed it down.

She lay on the bed, closed her eyes, hearing busyness of the pub beneath. The potato had, at least, removed worst hunger pangs, but the smell of food, stronger upstairs, still made her salivate. She dozed and woke thinking, with sisterly love, about Martin Davidson. She briefly cried about him – *he feels the pain* – then drifted to sleep. Suddenly: *Oh SHIT!*

Wide-eyed, Dewy sat upright and struggled to calm herself, *breathe in… breathe!* as she flung herself off the bed into a crouch to examine one, then the other foot.

She saw what she saw, clenched her fists, focused on breathing deeply until calmness returned. But denying the crisis was impossible: *it was 16 days since her last pedi.*

She'd emery-filed her nails daily to keep shortness, but thin lines of clear nail were nearly emerging over cuticles of two toes on one foot, three the other. This was untenable. Dewy's toenails must be always perfectly painted. A pedi tomorrow was urgent. Dewy climbed back into bed, astonished she'd let 16 days pass.

LATE SUNDAY AFTERNOONS were the best time to ask for things.

"Mum, can we get more Evian?"

"There's loads," snapped Danii.

"Three left."

"What?? Supermarket delivery came Monday! Four-packs! 16 big bottles!"

"I've had a bottle a day, I want to lose weight. Apparently, you get more hungry if you're detrayted."

"*Dehydrated.* Where's the empty bottles?"

"Er… I drink them at school…"

"You're lying."

"I… dispose of – *look*, I don't want Brand and Warr knowing?"

"All right. You should be allowed water without guilt, I suppose."

"Um… can I go on packed lunches as well?"

"You *hated* them?"

"They're a lot ~

"~ less fattening than school dinners, too right. Yeah, I'll write a note. Make your own lunches though. Your dad and me ain't got time. This is all good. You'll feel empowered if you lose weight," said Danii, heading upstairs for her Sunday facial. "You might even be in the salon soon. Wouldn't bet on it, mind."

Jade worried how to provide the men food and water every day. She'd bring them her packed lunches, but both couldn't live on those. She called them "the men" in her mind. Though younger than her, the boy had the same spiritual maturity as the older brother, but no warmth in his big, brown eyes.

Jade had to find a way to buy supplies. They needed soap, toothbrushes, a towel, more bog-roll, blankets. The covered market in town would have the lot, but… how to get there?

Mrs Holmes had set a project on any local topic, pupil's choice. Jade had chosen Farrisford's history. Perhaps this could mean an "official" chance to leave school at lunchtimes?

"Mum?"

"*What NOW!*? I get *one day* to myself all week, and ~"

"I need a note. To go into town lunchtimes?"

"Why do you need a note?"

"If a teacher sees me or a police says 'why aren't you in school'?"

"Okaay! Write it, I'll sign it. Hurry up."

"OK," said Jade, only just suppressing: *Yess!!*

To who it mayconcern,

> I give Jade Tyler my daughter permition to go to "town centre" at lunchtime's to research her history project for Farley Wood School until further notice. Signed –

JOHN TALBOT BROUGHT David decaf filter coffee and his favourite chocolate mints in the green foil wrappers. He hid disappointment David was again at the desk near the French windows, working on his laptop.

John placed the coffee down, rubbed David's shoulders. David groaned: "That's nice, dear," breathed out deeply, sat upright, slurped coffee, nodded towards the screen. "Couple of things to do. This bit shouldn't take long, a 'Performance Development Recap Matrix'."

"A what?" said John.

A thick orange hexagon filled the screen. Five sides each had an arrow, pointing clockwise. The sixth had a question mark instead of an arrow.

"A recap on last week," said David. "I'm to select pre mid-year priorities."

"*Pre* mid-year? Why's that part a question mark, not an arrow?"

"I don't know," said David. He clicked a drop-down menu. "These are some of the priorities."

David and John read:

preparation

set objectives for year Ahead

review Conversations and Progress in perfoprmance development record

recap on early-Year review

refamiliarisation with Documentation and& guidance

The list continued, and continued. "I'm to select five,"

said David: "See, if I highlight and copy *this* one…"

He did so with **recap on early-Year review**

"And paste it in one of the hexagon segments… see?"

He did. An arrow changed to a green tick. **recap on early-Year review** replaced it.

"David, this is nonsense. Come on, let's eat out."

An hour on, John Talbot watched sunset from The Bibby's dining room. A thin band of red sky lay low over Flett's Hill, all else was dark-plum cloud of new night. Flat cobbles in the road of Queen Anne houses glistened from recent rain.

"Like Bath or somewhere, Crendlesham," said John. "D'you reckon these are London prices?"

"Hm?"

"Those houses… fancy two next to each other? Get a double basement dug?"

David Bennett narrowed his eyes in mock annoyance. Modern vandalism to classical buildings was his bugbear. John was relieved to see David's humour hadn't deserted him. But it seemed David had deserted David these days. He often seemed not himself, nor anyone John knew.

He reached across and clasped David's hand with both of his.

"I'm sorry for you, love. It's about work, right?"

"Hm?"

"Talk to me, Davie? I won't say: 'Resign', like I've said past year and a half."

Energised, David withdrew his hand, leaned forward on folded arms, said:

"I *could* talk, but…" He sighed deeply. "It's secret. I'm under contract. You're spot-on a year and a half. It *is* 18 months, the 'secret project' – which Alpha spent a fortune on branding. All those 'sex' advertisements and ~"

He sighed again. "But I haven't delivered, the thing's impossible to construct. No one listens when I say this. Instead, the whole company, mostly merchandisers, or young strangers whose jobs I don't even know, glare at me: 'Where's the product? Why isn't it in manufacture?'"

He took a short sip of wine. It went down the wrong way. He coughed and blushed. John reached to pat his back. Spluttering, David continued: "We were to launch the special project next month, another 'sex' advertising spend. Now we're scrapping it."

"'Special project?'" winced John. "Slight delusion of grandeur? Does Alpha realise it makes staplers?"

"And hole-punchers. And desk pencil-sharpeners. And nervous breakdowns."

"If this 'special project's being scrapped," said John, "Is it safe to say what it is, before I pass out with suspense?"

David lowered his voice. "It's called the 'Sexpler'."

"The *what?*"

"A stapler-gun that fires overlapping staplers in an X."

John shook his head, sighing gently: "Don't worry, love. The world will continue belting around the sun without the Sexpler. Let it go..."

BILLY NEVIN WAS brought by police to Crendlesham Royal Infirmary and sectioned under the Mental Health Act. He woke on a bed, slowly deducing where he was: "Ah, shite. The feckin' hotel" – his fourth time in the locked psychiatric unit. Nevin had no memories of the past 36 hours.

He opened his mouth to speak but had no power. After a vitamin injection in his leg and four different pills he felt like heavy sand. When his eyes closed he hallucinated a dark whirlpool. When they opened he saw his scabbed, nicotine'd, work-stained hands. They looked unfamiliar.

Ye've hit bad times when ye don't know your own hands.

He was walked along a corridor and given a bath,

where he fell asleep. He came to as he was being dried, head slumped forward.

"Clean... not in the jail... towels... ah, Jaysus..."

He was put in pyjamas, socks, a dressing gown and led to a big room with a sunset view. Glazed people in dressing-gowns sat around the walls. A TV boomed Antiques Roadshow so loud it lisped.

DELAYED JET-LAG, HUNGER, depression plus trauma at yesterday's sudden, unwanted sex encounter with a childhood friend all combined to make Dewy sleep for five hours from 4pm. When she woke the room was dark.

She lay, very sad, eyes brimming, watching steam from the vent pipe disperse against the night. The far, breathy hum from whatever in the kitchen caused the steam slightly soothed her.

The door opened, light clicked on, Annette clumped in and sat heavily on the edge of the bed, smelling of oil, WD-40, Italian food and a tang of beer. "What a *day*! The guys just left. We got so much done. If certain parts arrive, we'll be on the road next week?"

She hadn't looked at Dewy yet. Her voice picked up: "Today we installed a whole replacement exhaust system, a new alternator, a header tank, and a re-cored, staggered core radiator, which we fitted with an external water-pump!"

"Oh." said Dewy. "Sounds good."

"Fritz overhauled the oil pump then... ta-daah! Dale's dad Mr Sheekey rang to say he has carburettors, and – guess what, hon! They're *Strombergs*!"

"Oh." said Dewy. "Well..."

"We've new drive shafts, new timing chains and ~"

"Oh, hon, give me a hug?"

"Sure," said Annette. "You've been crying?"

"No, just tired. You smell of nice food."

"I do? Are you hungry?"

"Um…"

"Did you eat?"

"Oh, I… plenty ate, hon."

Dewy kissed Annette, who slightly pushed her away, reached for a bath towel, rose and paced out: "Time to get clean."

Dewy sat up, angry. Had an old side of Annette returned, the "I-don't-need-you", which had surfaced in Annette's first year at Smith (Dewy's third year, but circumstances made her leave five weeks in). It recurred when Annette went to Vassar (though Dewy was in New York) and strongly during Annette's first year at MIT.

But Annette's last two MIT years saw a return to old closeness. Annette's father's sister, Aunt Meredith, didn't vocally mind Dewy's unrequested "staying over" in her Roslindale house with Annette, though "staying over" soon meant "permanently residing". Fearing Joanna and Robert Stephens finding out she was freeloading there, Dewy kept a low profile at Meredith's (or so she believed, forgetting drunken disturbances and wine-cellar thefts).

Dewy got up and put Mrs Foster's dress on. It felt cold around her. She decided one bottle of wine would be OK, hoped Annette wouldn't mind sending for one, and counted out money. Annette fell into the room, pale.

"Hon? You OK?" said Dewy.

"No-o…"

Annette couldn't lie down. Dewy sat her on the bed, knelt on the floor, placed Annette's feet on her lap, rubbed them, handed Evian to Annette, who drank half the bottle. Her face was sad, alone and ill. Dewy hated herself for unkind thoughts a moment before.

Annette burst into tears. "What's happening to me, hon? I k-keep *changing*. I'm… undergoing momentous… *strange experiences*. And I-I-I…"

Heaving with sobs on Dewy's shoulder, she struggled

to speak: "I c-can't *bear* to think of the f-*future*. I never felt s-so *insecure*! Poor little Hiram… I know he's a boy? Bachelor, Morris, Hiram… I'm meant to have boys, I feel it. Oh, hon! What will his life be like, with only me? And I'm just… *silly*. A *kid*."

"You'll be OK, darliing," said Dewy, caressing her. "I'll help you, and your child, in every way, forever. We'll be real fine."

Annette reached for a Kleenex and gave one to Dewy, who cried because Annette did.

"Next month," said Dewy, "I'll rent us a li'l house with a garden. Seen 'em in the classifieds. Cheaper than this room! We'll be out of here *soon*, our own place, a garden, li'l rabbits, plenty bird-houses…"

"And Morris can come over?"

"Definitely! We could… figure a way to have Martina escort him over?"

"By ship" sniffed Annette, drying her eyes. "Queen Mary 2, first class, so he can share a cabin. People who are dogs are only allowed in first cabins. Codas from non-first are in kennels on-deck. I hope they're OK."

"We'll get Morris over soon enough! Does that make you feel better?"

Dewy tucked Annette in, then climbed over her to the wall side. They lay in the light of one candle, Annette groaning slightly with each long exhale. She sat up, embraced her knees, placed her face between them. "My head's *swimming*."

Dewy rubbed her shoulders. Annette murmured: "Sorry, hon, I can't handle being touched right now."

"Oh, darling. More water?"

"No-o-uh…"

Dewy wondered if distracting Annette's mind would help. She tried:

"Hon? You know the bathroom? I *found out* who decorated it *and* put all the vile things in there! He visits in the dead of night *to add more!*"

"Really?" said Annette quietly.

"*Yes.* Every rust-rimmed aerosol, stray pubic hair. He comes from afar to scatter them! He has a *huge* personal collection of soiled bathroom products and old pubes."

"Who, hon?"

"*Crange.*"

"Uh…?"

"Crange did it," nodded Dewy, wide-eyed.

"Really?"

"It's him all right."

"Is he like Figbite, hon?"

"*Yes!!*" cried Dewy. "But – unlike Figbite – Crange *exists.*"

"We said that about Figbite though," said Annette. "And Clancy."

"*Clancy!*" Dewy pressed her palms to her cheeks. "I *forgot* Clancy!"

When Dewy was nine, Annette seven, Figbite was a monster in the woods beside the Stephens's house. His accomplice, Clancy, was believed a pale-clothed man who never entered buildings. Though never seen, both lurked not far. Figbite could change his weight to zero to perch in treetops and went everywhere on horseback, no other transport. Travelling by car or bus was therefore safe. But that didn't mean Clancy wasn't following in another vehicle, telling Figbite where you were headed.

AFTER 40 MINUTES fitful sleep, Annette sat up again, breathing deeply. Dewy knelt beside her. Minutes on, half-lying in Dewy's arms, Annette asked for more talk: "Tell me about… anything… like, *oh,* tell me how Bachelor came into my life?"

The favourite story was retold, Annette aged two, father on active service, brothers at boarding schools or naval college, only her mother around, a busy instructor and businesswoman, to whom Annette was hopeless and likely 'on the spectrum' (but less acute than Joanna's older brother's Asperger's.)

Infant Annette never spoke. She scribbled pictures or wheeled toy cars around the floor going *wvvvvv!* If a toy could be dismantled, Annette did so. She was scolded for that, so learned to reassemble toys before anyone saw. Other times, Annette drew vast, terrific abstracts. Many featured a small black and white dog in one corner. Annette had never spoken a word in her life.

On Christmas Day 1995, Clifton Stephens, 13, noting the dog in his sister's pictures, risked parental trouble by presenting Annette with a Boston Terrier puppy he'd secretly bought in Revere. The family froze as Clifton entered the north sitting-room with a bundle in a soft blanket. He set it before Annette, who stumbled forward, enraptured.

Her joy even made her mother's eyes wetten, slightly. No one had ever seen such pure happiness as this tiny girl, not yet three. Rarely had an animal been so instantly loving back. "Almost equine," murmured Joanna.

"Clift, you're a jerk," smiled 18-year-old Robert Jnr.

"Whatcha gonna call your new dog, honey?" said their father, kindly. He did not hope for a reply. His daughter was mute. The family was adjusted to that.

"We could give the dog a name for you, Annette, if you like?" said Clifton.

Annette smiled, breathed in deep, shut her eyes and yelled: "*BACHELOR!!*"

DEWY PAUSED FOR Annette to yell "*Bachelor!*" at the end of the story, as always, but she was asleep. Dewy checked she was warm, held her hands, kissed the top of Annette's head, savouring its aromas, the favourites of her life. "I love you, Baby Bear," she whispered. Her mind was very lost, for another story had played before Dewy's eyes while reciting the Bachelor tale.

In August 2009, Bachelor, slowly, in stages, descended the bed-to-floor staircase Annette built for him, for the last time. He wanted to sleep on a rug in the corner of the room, toy-bear's arm as a pillow. In his last weeks, Annette slept on the floor beside him, holding his paw. He peacefully died in his sleep in September, aged 14, "a good age for someone who is a dog."

16-year-old Annette's heartbreak was incurable. For three weeks Robert Stephens III brusquely dismissed an idea Dewy confided to him, then one day caved in and drove her to Saugus, to buy a nine-week-old Boston Terrier, last of the litter, a morose, slightly lame, small, juddering thing.

They drove back in silence. Dewy and Robert Stephens knew another dog would enrage Joanna, who'd hated Annette's "obsessive, immature" love for Bachelor. Would this begin all over again? Mr Stephens now regretted having let Dewy sway him and Dewy knew it. The journey's silence deepened. Dewy's heart sank. This black and white scowling puppy, who'd peed on her and wouldn't stop shaking, seemed an insult after the majesty of Bachelor. He might even worsen Annette's grief.

Dewy, 18, weighed eight stone, even made Joanna worried (and angry, as ever), and planned a date to take her own life two weeks away, but told herself: *If Annette doesn't like the dog I'll take the poor thing, smuggle him to college. If I'm going to college. Unconfirmed. I won't be alive by then anyhow.*

Annette's love for the puppy was instant. She wept when he leaned up to slurp her nose with a tiny pink tongue. In that instant Dewy was cured. She'd done something right. A reminder why she lived – to look after Annette, as she had since age nine.

The Goddess sent a second sign that day. Notification

at last from the Van der Zee lawyers: her mother's estate would top-up her college part-scholarship "until further notice". Praying the "further notice" was unnoticed, Dewy faxed the document to the tutor who'd interviewed her at Smith. She doubted her place was still available. She was to have confirmed finances months before.

Now, 10 years on, lying by Annette, who quietly slept, Dewy realised she'd never before coincided her illness and suicidal intent with being ignored by her mother's lawyers (and being always ignored by a father she'd met twice). All Dewy had asked her mother's family's lawyers was, if funds were available to pay her through college. So began a 14 month wait for one simple answer.

Dewy snuggled up to Annette now, reminiscing: Robert's 5pm knock: "Fax, Dewy, my office." Bolting along the high corridor, down the first stairs, along the east wing, down the main staircase, the hall, past the family dining room where Connie laid table, *bash!* into Robert's study, fax machine, untorn curl of paper. She lifted it by inches, couldn't bear to tear it off, Smith letterhead, tutor's handwriting: *Dear Ms Durant, Congratulations!*

Dewy returned to the present. She softly kissed Annette's cheek.

"See? Like back then, I hit the worst low then realised why I exist – to look after YOU. I won't let you down, hon. I promise. I won't let you and Hiram down.

Chapter 7

AT NEXT MORNING'S Monday meeting, Dewy's hungry stomach gurgled. Worrying it could be heard, she said anything that came into her head if the room went quiet.

"Why nothing about Tessa England in the paper?" she boomed. Everyone looked at her. "Why always the Labour guy?"

"What do you mean?" frowned Geoff Carruthers.

"That *is* what I mean."

"What, like, we're not giving coverage to the Conservative MP, only Labour's prospective one?"

"*Yes*. What did you think it meant?"

"*I* didn't know, that's why I asked!"

"What else *could* it have meant?"

"Excuse me?" said Stuart Dean angrily, to the group. "Can I clarify something?" He jerked his thumb towards Dewy: "Is Sandie Shaw here the sub-editor, or deputy editor?"

Dewy snapped: "And can this fricking ad-man hurry up submit adverts? We'd 30 this stage last week, today we ~"

"*Oi!*" shouted Stuart Dean, standing up from his chair. "A 'fricking ad-man'! *How fucking dare you*! How *DARE* you!"

His anger was embarrassing. Dewy was overpowered. Everyone stared at her. She wished she hadn't said 'fricking ad-man', a contemptuous thing to say, even if Dean *had* been unpleasant. She sat still, refusing to speak.

Silence worsened. After half a minute, Geoff Carruthers answered quietly:

"Miss Durant here has Catherine's role: sub-editor, occasional reporting, maybe a leaning to women's stuff."

"Women's '*stuff*'?" said Dewy. "Like what?"

"Well… y'know, women's interests, issues…"

"Like what?"

Grunts of discontent, sighing and tuts bristled from the group.

"Er… *usual* issues?" said Carruthers. "I thought *you*'d suggest ideas to *me*, not the other way round…?"

"'Usual issues' include: unequal pay, domestic violence, sexual harassment, exploitation, rape, sex trafficking, denial of education, overwork, mutilation, unsupported single parenthood, a range of under-researched medical problems ~"

"I'm not discussing all this at a ~"

"Men won't," said Dewy

Colin Hendry drew a deep breath and reverted the subject:

"Listen? About Tessa England? She don't talk to us."

"Not since the expenses thing," said Geoff Carruthers.

"And the bypass," said three voices together.

Dewy said: "Once again, our next issue has four picture-news stories about Matt Clissenden, also a mini-interview."

Carruthers sighed: "Yeahh, I suppose you're right. We should have England in, or at least approach her." He turned to Dewy: "You won't have met her yet, have you?"

"Um…"

"Get an appointment and interview her."

Mimicking Dewy's accent, Michael Fenwick said: "Are you the frickin' MP?" Stuart Dean and others bellowed with forced laughter as they shuffled page-plans and notes, end of meeting. But Dewy hadn't finished. "Is this week's cover story definitely decided?" she called.

"Yeah, 'Fresh Bid To Stop Traffic Congestion'" said

Carruthers.

"*That's* a front page story?" said Dewy. "A 'scrutiny committee' saying…" – she read from a press release – "'In our opinion, traffic movements in the town are getting steadily worse.'"

Silence. Stares.

"Who's paying these geniuses to have meetings saying: 'Lots of cars around'?" said Dewy.

"They said a bit more than thaat," said Colin Hendry.

"Indeed!" said Dewy. She read out: "'A County Council officer told the committee a solution was likely to involve major infrastructural works which would not be affordable or deliverable at this time.' Therefore nothing's happening! Where's the 'bid' in the headline? There's none!"

"Perfectly strong front page," sighed Carruthers

"Is it her role to criticise front cover stories?" snapped Stuart Dean. "Got a better story, has she?"

"It's *not* your role, actually," said Carruthers to Dewy. Smiles and spite shone from the men. "Obviously we appreciate input from all corners, *if it's constructive*. Right, let's get on?"

"What about Matthew Willis?" cried Dewy, as everyone dispersed. "That should be front page again and again 'til the truth's out! A boy murdered by a fake cop and guys from a pub? What's happening with *that*, Colin?"

"Update on page nine," barked Colin Hendry.

"How *is* the inquest?"

"Ongoing, I'm down there now. Don't worry, we'll get another front page out of it."

Dewy felt sudden sadness Matthew Willis was commemorated as merely a news opportunity. She balanced this by realising no justice could be done for him without revelation of what had happened.

Carruthers approached Dewy: "Want you to do something, come with me."

"Why?"

"Because the press release I need you to see's in my office."

"Bring it here!" said Dewy. "If I go in your office I'll holler at you about no contract and your vagueness about pay."

"Fine!" snapped Carruthers. Angry now, he marched to his office. Dewy called after him: "And bring me a damn contract?"

She arrived at her desk. A drawing-pin had been placed on the floor pin-up beside her chair. This was the second time. She pinned the tack hard into the edge of the desk with her thumb. Future drawing-pins deliberately placed for her to step on would join it. The office had whiteboards, no pin-boards.

"Right," said Carruthers, returning, calmer. "Alpha Staplers... here's the press bumph. The upshot – this is interesting actually – they're helping out African schools, giving them staplers?"

"African schools need pens, paper and books, not staplers."

"Well the ones what *have* got paper, they'll probably be grateful for a few staplers."

"How will they know which schools have paper?" said Dewy. "Knock on the door? 'Got paper? No? Want a stapler though?"

Dewy and Carruthers unpacked an expensive press pack that unfolded four times then divided into separate modules. Glossy cards bore agency photos of African schools. Pamphlets and postcards showed agency photos, not in Africa, of happy white heterosexual couples in fields, reasons unclear. Alpha's own studio close-ups of staplers and hole-punchers recurred, plus a double page centrefold cardboard pull-out of a green stapler.

"This is horseshit," said Dewy. "Alpha 'Philosro-pry'... a misprint? Apparently not, it's all the way through."

"Someone messed up spellcheck?" said Carruthers.

"No, they spell 'philosophy' correctly when that's used. Look?"

She held up a glossy photo-card of a white couple hand-in-hand on a sunset beach under **Alpha Philosropry and Alpha Philosophy - why we care** *and* **think**.

"Give 'em a ring?" said Carruthers. "Get the story about the African trip…"

"No. Ask someone else. This is patronising, western garbage, instilling 'need' in poorest people for things they've no use for. The cost of this damn brochure would fund 10 schools for a year."

"God, you're cynical ~"

"*This* is cynical. I've been to Africa, seen what the west does there. Alpha Staplers is smug, self-interested and insulting. Anyway, those schools lucky to be given a stapler by kind, white *bwana* – where they gonna buy more staples when they run out? Who sells staples in rural Chad?"

Carruthers, annoyed, gathered up brochure components, scrunched them in his arms: "Fine! I'll get someone else!" His armful was increased by Dewy pushing Matt Clissenden Team Labour leaflets onto it: "Geoff, take this Teeth Labour stuff too?"

In Dewy's inbox: **Village Wins 'In Bloom' Award**, and a piece on the official opening of Sir John Wyce School's new media suite by PTA head and local Councillor, Judith Roper, also Wyce TV's first interviewee. "Well done for keeping Clissenden away from there," muttered Dewy. "Must have been hard."

After working on these pieces, Dewy leafed through the current issue for the Parl Beauty advertisement with the: *We now stock cruelty-free products* flash in the artwork. As Parl was some miles from Farrisford, Dewy left the office for a last search of nearer, potentially suitable nail institutions. Finding one would save time and a round-trip by cab.

"Bye then!" snapped Stuart Dean. Another man muttered: "Is she just *going out* again?" Dewy came and went as she pleased, as at anywhere she'd worked. No reporter is desk-bound. Let Dean and others take issue, she'd ignore them.

Nail-It played loud autotuned pop while 12 women had treatments. Nails + More was again deserted. A woman in a white housecoat stared out, arms folded. Two other nail-bars seemed sinister to Dewy. She was sure people-trafficking of workers was involved but wondered how that might be proved. She inspected High Street's two beauty salons, but their window-lists of services were so elaborate, Dewy didn't believe them specialist enough.

In Market Street, she discovered Greggs, however. She bought three vegetable pasties, ate the first while leaving the shop, was still in Market Street as she began the third, paying no heed to workmen pausing to watch "*Her* again", now gobbling pastries like an animal.

Concluding no failsafe Farrisford pedi existed, Dewy rang Parl Beauty. A woman with a thick local accent answered, a radio played, building work banged, but use of Lauren B products was confirmed. An appointment was made,11am. Dewy booked a cab to Parl.

ANNETTE SLEPT ALL morning, woke at 12.30pm to find Dewy sitting rigid on the edge of the bed, coat on.

"Oh! Back early!" said Annette, throwing herself around her in a mini-frenzy of kisses and snurflings. "Lovely surprise!" She emerged from Dewy's hair. "What's up?"

"Ohhh," sighed Dewy. She raised a leg.

"You've had a *pedi!*" cried Annette. "Oh, your footies look *nice!*"

"A *disaster*. If Mrs Andrinez saw –"

"They look good, sweetheart!" said Annette, leaving the bed to kneel and examine Dewy's feet on her lap. "I like this dark-blue polish."

"A *Draculoidian Satanist* has done this!!" cried Dewy. "This nightmare."

"I see… nothing wrong," said Annette.

"*Nothing wrong*!? Uneven thickness of top-coat on three toes of *this* foot and one on *that*. Almost a half-millimetre gap on the bottom right corner of my left big toe. *Look*, see, naked nail. See? That gap?"

"I can't see… anything, uh…"

"And this *middle* toe's cuticle's outline's visible in bright sunlight!"

"Your footies look *nice*, darling."

"She hadn't the *first clue* about filing!" said Dewy, starting to cry. "She filed *side-to-side*, Chrissakes! You *never* do that! It *has* to be *one side to the centre, other side to the centre*."

Her phone rang. She threw it across the room unanswered: "Go away, Geoff! What do you and your darn paper know about *anything*?!"

"Your footies are so beautiful, darling," said Annette.

"Nothing as bad as this has ever happened!" wept Dewy. "That *horror* of a woman! She *hated* I wore no shoes. 'Need to soak *them feet*', she cawed. Like it's a labour of Hercules? *Of course* soak them! *That's how a pedi begins*! I guess she noticed I don't smell so good, and hated me for that too, though I kept my coat on. Two men drilling into a wall in the salon kept stopping to leer, while that permatanned harpy strafed my nails."

Dewy paused for breath, blew her nose on the sheet, sighed: "I *know* it's the trivialest damn thing. An insult to the suffering in the world, but… oh… I just need *ONE thing about me* I know is *perfect* because everything else is *so, so NOT*. My toenails and never drink-driving are *my only perfections*, the only two I *know* I have. My two medals. But *now*… Ohh!"

"How about a glass of wine and a snack?"

"Booze won't block this out, hon."

They sat side by side. Annette put her arm through Dewy's and snuggled up to her. Dewy woke up to how Annette was affectionate and lonely, and began to cry again because Annette had no treats or excitement beyond work and being pregnant, yet never complained.

Annette handed her a tissue. "Maybe book a new pedi someplace else?"

"Ah, never mind. How are *you*, darling?"

"Had *such* a sleep. Very healing."

"Wanna go up the coast? See some birds?"

"Ye-ah!! Like, *now*??" said Annette.

"Yes! And I can wash in the sea?"

"DON'T TELL MARLON?"

John Wright was trembling.

"I promise," said Millie. "Let me walk you home…"

They walked into Arkwright Crescent, Millie holding John's hand.

She couldn't believe what had happened. A minute before, leaving the JobCentre, she'd seen Mr Wright walking ahead in Danelaw Street. A blue car shot past, handbrake-turned, mounted the pavement blocking his way. He slowly walked backwards. Youths leaned from the car windows. One left the car, rubbing his groin, yelling: "Don't want a white 'un then? Gotta be a black boy's?"

The others screamed with laughter and pressed the car-horn. The youth in an all-grey sweatpants tracksuit swaggered towards John Wright. "Got a cigarette for me, loverr?"

Before John could react, Millie was there, out of breath.

"Leave him alone," she said.

"Tell *me* what to do?" snarled the young man, "You

don't know who you're dealing with, girlie."

"Don't care," said Millie, looking past him. A young boy, far end of the car's back seat looked sharply away. Millie nearly spoke to him, but stopped herself.

"Piss off, girlie," said the youth. "I'm talking to my old mate here!"

"Go harass summing *harmful*, go on!" said Millie. "You've done harmless, let's see you do harmful?" Rage made Millie approach him. To her surprise he backed off, disguising this as a casual choice to return to the car.

"Don't go fuckin' with *us*," he said, getting in. "Why do you keep looking at our car? Wanna buy ut? Two grand and suck our dicks?"

Millie didn't reply.

The youth turned to his friends: "Ha-HA! Look at her! Got herself an old man's dick to play with!!" He called out to John: "Watch she don't rob ya!"

Laughter, thinner now, as the car backed into the road and sped off.

Millie held John's arm and watched them go. In the passenger seat, Tyson Bradley had been first to hide his face from her, affecting to listen to his phone. In the far back seat, 17-year-old Stephen Vanders.

Millie's mother, years ago, babysat Stephen and his sister Ria.

"JADE! HURRY UP!"

Jade passed through the school gates and climbed into her mother's red sports car.

"Why didn't you ask your *dad* to take you?" snapped Danii. "Only gonna be *there* 10 minutes, choosing subjects you'll take."

"And be shown around…"

"NO *WAY!*" said Danii, texting, "Straight in, straight out."

Jade hadn't seen her mother so angry in a long time. Danii used to rage at Dave Tyler, but rarely now. Did their sleeping in separate bedrooms the past two years have a bearing on that? Did it mean Danii's nastiness must find a new victim? *But you're all I've got, Mum.*

Sir John Wyce School's imposing 1659 main house was covered in grey scaffold sheeting. Black and gold gates led straight to Portakabins, skips, a cement mixer lorry and raging noise.

"Visitors and reception, go left, mum?"

"*Yes!* I'm not blind!"

Mrs Kaur's grace and excellent nails mollified Danii, who blurted:

"You from India then, if you don't mind me asking?"

"No, from here. My parents are Punjabi."

They walked through an ancient, grand hall to a very old, low-lit, wood-panelled corridor of oil paintings, war memorials, aromas of the past. Glass cases held shield-shaped trophies, school caps and framed black and white photographs. Jade sensed here was the special part of the school. The only other place she'd seen like this was the small museum in Crendlesham.

Her mother's high heels clacked. She asked the Deputy Head: "Have you been India even so? Like, with your mum'n'dad? Love to go myself!"

"I've been many times, yes. What attracts you to there?"

"Dunno really. I go Dubai sometimes, a lot of people on the plane doing a stopover before India, and I'm like: '*AhH*, I'm really *jealous*'!"

A walkway bridge passed over a walled garden. Muffled school classroom sounds arose as they entered a modern atrium with a vast frieze of the 17th century painting of ruffed Sir John Wyce they'd seen in the old building.

"Big, innit!" said Danii, looking around. "Like a airport!"

"Here's my office," said Mrs Kaur, "come in."

Jade expected more hell on the return drive to Farley Wood, but after a laughy phone call with a friend, Danii turned to Jade:

"Nice, her, at the school? Good-looking. Your dad's right, *you* should stay on at school. Being clever's your only hope, let's face it…"

She dialled another number and stopped the car. "Can't be hands-free, private call with a client." She reached for her cigarettes and got out.

Jade watched her mother on the phone, slowly pacing, immaculate in terracotta twinset, crisp white blouse, strappy high heels. Lipstick daubed the filter of her long cigarette. Playfulness filled Danii's eyes as she spoke and listened.

"Mum's clients must like her," thought Jade. "She's quite glamorous if she doesn't get angry, or pick specks out her eye-corners."

Danii ended the call, dropped her cigarette into a drain, walked back, happy, head bowed, arms folded, unaware Jade watched. She re-entered, saying: "Arkwright Crescent. Remember *Arkwright Crescent*. I'll Sat-Nav it after I've dropped you at Farley."

AN HOUR LATER a gold-plated lift door swished open to the perfumed air of Rennicksons' top floor. Danii and Marlon stepped out.

Marlon saw a bright, long, busy space of windows and mirrors, where white-coated beauticians and hairdressers attended to women in comfortable leather chairs. The air smelt of seductive, rare lotions. Sister Sledge's "The Greatest Dancer" played.

"*Danii*, my God!" said Stephanie, stylist. "Where d'ya get this *man*?"

"Told you'd they'd love you, Marlon?" said Danii, taking his hand. "We're gonna get his ear pierced, then take him to Roni, see if she wants him for the winter catalogue?"

"Course she will!" said Stephanie, winking at Marlon. The woman whose hair she cut gazed full-eyed at Marlon via the mirror.

"Who's this, Dan?" said another beautiful, ruby-manicured woman in a white coat.

"Marlon, this is Liu," said Danii. "She's sex mad, so stay with me."

"Aagh!" screamed Liu. "Is this your toy-boy? He's *amazing*!"

"He's not my toy-boy. Roni needs models, I found this fella in Farrisford."

"*Farrisford!?*" shrieked staff the length of the salon. "No one's good-lookin' in Farrisford!"

"Well *he* is!" said Danii. "Rihanna? This is Marlon, can you pierce his ear? The right one? Still OK with that, Marlon? You'll look *ever so* nice."

AT 4PM, JOHN Wright jumped at the key in the lock, but of course it was Marlon, breathless with Rennicksons of Crendlesham bags and, of all things, a stud in his ear. He seemed… different, but John didn't trust his own perceptions. He knew he was in shock after the incident with the youths two hours before.

To Marlon John looked pale, stooped, worried. After two glasses of wine, his first kiss and a ride in an open-topped Saab to Galar's Peak to kiss more, Marlon *did* trust his own perceptions.

"Dad! How's it going?" he barked cheerily, turning right to his bedroom.

"You missed that girl Millie," said John, "She was here."

"Had my ear pierced," called Marlon. "Stud's tempo-rary. I'm getting one that's better. Wait til I show you something? This is proper good, wait there…"

He changed into a Fendi suit in front of a mirror in his wardrobe door. The door kept slowly closing, annoying Marlon. He propped it open with one of the new, size 11½, Loake shoe-boxes from one of the bags.

Marlon admired himself in the suit, but hated the cheap, shoulder-height, white wardrobe, stickers of footballers from *Shoot!* magazine he'd stuck on years ago, when the wardrobe was slightly taller than him.

I should be in a hotel, sea view, cocktails on the balcony… Marlon smiled. *Danii and her women friends out there?* He imagined Danii: "*Marlon, you look lovely, but try the shirt with that?*"

He emptied the third bag, selected one of four shirts, the one he'd worn in the shoot at Roni's third-floor photo studio, where the public went for portraits or to book a wedding photographer. Danii had led him past a big board outside: **Closed for fashion shoot, open 2pm** to meet Roni. *Very nice lady* thought Marlon. *And that girl modelling womenswear was… woahh!*

"What do you think, Dad?"

"*Very* smart suit," said John Wright.

"Give Obogo a run for his money, eh?" said Marlon a touch coarsely. John caught a tang of alcohol.

"Hope you didn't spend *too* much?" said John.

"Nah-ah!" said Marlon, as if the question was inane: "Did modelling for Rennicksons. Gonna be in their catalogue."

Marlon explained, making Danii's role very slight. He didn't mention her name. John liked listening. Marlon was grateful for a mug of tea. Wine had made him glazed and headachey.

"They let you keep the clothes you modelled?" said John.

"Er… no, a shirt, yeah, I kept this shirt. The other stuff, they gave me, payment in a way." Marlon never lied. John put his vagueness down to wine.

In truth, Danii had taken Marlon to menswear to

choose shirts, a suit, a blazer, two pairs of shoes, four pairs of boxer shorts and various £18 pairs of socks. Unknown to Marlon, nothing was free. Danii had winked to Alan at the till. She'd pay later, 10% staff discount.

The whole store would be talking now. *Great!! Let 'em!* thought Danii. *I've bagged the best boyf since Liu went with that student. AND I'm the oldest!*

AT 9PM, DEWY and Annette returned from the coast. Annette went straight to sleep. Dewy tried not to get worked-up about the Parl pedi again. A positive blog post was overdue. She felt her generous readers were owed one…

> **I haven't bathed or showered the whole British stay. The shared bathroom here is a glimpse of the ultimate horror and I won't use it. So here in the bedroom, I wash what I need to by half-filling a plastic tub with Evian and hot water from my girl's travel-kettle, then dunking myself in it.**
>
> **Water spills and floods the floor. I wash my two *connaissez-vooz* with gentle soap then, front-upwards, walk on all fours to a second, unsoapy basin to rinse. This makes puddles too. I rapidly can't keep up with basin and cloth management, which flannel's soapy, which isn't, then all the water gets soapy, so the only way to rinse is: lie back, kick legs high, slightly part them, prop my back with one hand and, with the other, pour Evian – warm water mixed in – onto my vagina and ass. The floor becomes a damn pond.**
>
> **Understandably, I've almost given up washing.**
>
> **This means committing a shameful crime, forgiven by none, and – I greatly fear – not pardoned by readers either. {When I confess here, I'll lose some of you, so with sadness: adieu, and I'll always love you.} The crime: *I smell.***

When Annette said: "Honey?" I knew. I know all her "Honey?"s by heart. This – one of the oldest – means: *We need to get you washed and your clothes washed. It's kinda urgent.*

Here's how the problem was almost solved: I figured I'd bathe in the sea and be clean in two minutes. Annette agreed. Also we could wash my dresses in the sea, plus my four pairs of knickers – now three, after the pair that had deteriorated to elastic with strips of cloth hanging off was thrown in the trash by Annette. I tried to tell her how that pair, though it *did* resemble a puppet-show jellyfish, was pretty good to wear: several long scraps of various widths tied according to how much base-support and coverage the day needed. Annette's very open-minded, but dismissed my claim adjustable underwear like this is superb.

We headed to the coast, but couldn't figure the buses. We'd gotten one to Crendlesham, but none goes from there to Littleport. So we tried hitch-hiking from a shambolic road system. No one stopped. We walked back into Crendlesham, via a part we'd not set out from: scrapyards, industrial units, office blocks with broken windows and To Let signs. We saw a grass-snake slide into knee-high thistles and weeds. Everything felt so lost. A spire of half-ruined, 12th century Crendlesham Abbey came in view, reminding us where the town center is.

Blah blah, we made it to the coast.

The sea was so cold I was paralyzed & crying out by mid-shin. High, intelligent waves lunged like wolves into huge white explosions that swurked backwards, tugging me out to sea. "Honey, I can't do this!" I shrieked. "It's freezing and *agh!!* - that was only a splash against the back of my kneEAAHH!!"

I sploshed yelling the hell out of there into Annette's warm arms and kisses. How forgiving she is.

We'd been three hours getting to here.

White sky, hard sand, a promenade. Along it, a lavatory block of brown mortar with tiny stone flecks in it, outdoor showers one side.

"Darling, you can't strip off and shower here?" said my girl.

"Dammit, I will."

When no passers-by were very near, I took my clothes off. Pushing a shower button gave no water. I pushed the other: nothing. These showers don't work. It would have made sense to check that before removing my dress, but I hadn't, and was stomping around bare-bosom'd. My boo's looked firmer, more enlarged and goosebumpy, nipples a purer pink and bigger than even when snow-dancing at the Millards'.

Jeering heard. Men watching, leaning over a wall above the promenade, grinning like pumpkins. We fled.

Goddess, thank-you for getting us painlessly by bus to Lifford, then a cab to Crendlesham driven by a cheerful woman who talked about her son in Denver. She boosted our hearts, made us think of home, we got a little misty-eyed.

Missing the last-but-one bus to Farrisford, we stayed two hours in The Wheel Inn, where I drank Coke. (No alcohol five days now.) Annette saw pota-to-skins on the menu. We ordered two lots. They were *Disgusting.* Ah-de-o Xx

Chapter 8

EVERYONE BUT DAVID Cartwright made Dewy's work difficult. On Tuesday, day before deadline, features and photographs weren't in, no ads confirmed. Two-fifths of the issue was missing. The men were bluffing: they couldn't *not* produce material. Dewy e-mailed all, title-only: WHERE IS YOUR LATE WORK?

She still hadn't been given a contract, told what she'd be paid, or when. As yet, no tenancy contract at The Lugworm either, nor had Annette's kitchen-work been reduced. Dewy's sobriety, day six, was unrewarded and difficult, especially with the fraught extra crisis of a flawed pedi.

Dewy e-mailed Carruthers: I can do no more until your staff submit work. *YOU* chase them. And where is my contract? *Am* I on zero pay?!!!

"Got anything sharp, Miss Dewy?" said Cartwright, shunting a cardboard box. "Can't open this."

"Her tongue's sharp!" said Geoff Carruthers, appearing. His habit of being suddenly a foot away was beginning to get to Dewy. In fact, the whole office was annoying her. She also needed a dump. The only article in that morning – **Hospital Ward Bid Rejected** – detailing £22 million withheld from Crendlesham Royal Infirmary for a new ward, angered Dewy too. An accompanying press release from Central Devon Care and Health Trust (saying: "…the Crendlesham bid remains an important part of our overall estates strategy.") enraged her. "How can this

'Trust' say the ward's an 'important part of estates strategy' yet decide *not* to build it?"

Carruthers and Cartwright didn't hear her, staring at the box. "I did *have* a letter-opener," said Carruthers. "Maybe Jane's a box-cutter?"

"I've my trowel," sighed Dewy, leaning over to split the box's tape open with its point. The men exchanged wry looks.

"You, er, carry a trowel everywhere?" said Carruthers.

"You, er, run a paper, 40 per cent missing, day before deadline?" said Dewy. "You, er, have a hospital run by shitheads saying 'no new ward'? Why don't you pair *go away*? I've opened your box, now *go*."

Naturally, the Tattler's tiny, vile wc had never been an option to Dewy, but dumping in East Lane Park was difficult. The park was not large. Anyone trying to hide in its perimeter hedge, bushes or shrubs would be seen doing so. Luckily, today was cold and starting to drizzle, park near-empty, though dog-walkers and parents with toddlers circuited. Dewy headed to a stone wall overlooking the river. Its left quarter was hidden by bushes. Dewy hid herself there, did what she must, but while burying it all with the trowel, a yapping Jack Russell burst upon her. The owner tootled: "Lu-cas!" repeatedly.

Dewy emerged from the bushes, feet earth-smudged, Lucas furious at her ankles. Eight cagoule'd dog-walkers, gathered in concern at Lucas missing, stared at her. Dewy took a breath, walked tall and cheerful: "So *refreshing* today!" she smiled, and kept walking. The people slowly turned to watch her progress to the exit, staring until she was gone.

Dewy returned to the office hearing it silent but for a stark voice from a speaker-phone. Six of the men crowded round it.

"I think it is the right decision, yes." said a man's phone-voice, tone gentle. "Our school has the best standards. We need to ensure these are upheld, by every single one of our clients."

Dewy frowned quizzically. Cartwright handed her a national tabloid, page 22:

Girl, 14, Heartbroken After Being BANNED From The Classroom Because She Is TOO BIG for Uniform Skirt

Dewy quickly read how Kylie Burnett, a Year 8 pupil at Farley Wood High had been excluded for wearing a pleated skirt of a slightly different grey because no brand suggested by the school fitted her.

The 14-year-old was removed from classes and told if she didn't wear the regulation skirt, she would be forced to study in isolation, or stay at home

"It wasn't an easy decision," continued the voice of Farley Wood's young head-teacher, Jamie Felstead. "And wasn't entirely my decision,"

"Hang up on this creep," snapped Dewy. "*SHH!!*" said all the men.

"We *have* to run this story," whispered Cartwright. "If it's in the nationals ~"

"We do *NOT* have to run this and I will *not* work on it!" said Dewy, to louder *SH!!*'s and a "Shuddup, sit down".

"Poor girl *lives* in this town!" snapped Dewy. "We will *not* run this piece!"

SHH!!!!! seethed the men.

"Sorry about this, Jamie," said Carruthers, knowing Felstead heard the disruption. Carruthers continued: "*Now*: it says here, her mum's angry, the girl can't stop crying. Quote: She's a healthy person and quite good at her subjects Unquote. I mean…?"

"I understand that completely," said Jamie Felstead's voice. "Obviously I'm very affected by the reaction it *is* having with Kylie. I want us to work supportively together in order that we find a uniform that *is* compliant."

"Christ!" fumed Dewy.

"*SHHH!!*" said all the office.

"The photograph here," said Carruthers: "In the national paper. It says the skirt's from Asda. Plain grey. It just looks like a skirt. Nothing controversial…?"

"Oh, I agree," said Jamie Felstead. "That's a point that I believe has a definite valid basis, yes. But it's about a solution being found. And it's about the skirt being the appropriate ~"

"*SHUT UP, you stupid cunt!!*" roared Dewy.

The line went dead. Carruthers repeated: "Jamie? Are you there?". Dewy paced to her desk, ignoring uproar, and ignoring Carruther's: "My office, Miss Durant! *Now.*" She began working.

20 minutes on, Carruthers placed an envelope on her desk.

"Is that my contract, Geoff?"

Carruthers sighed. Dewy continued working, knowing the office had stopped to watch. Carruthers cleared his throat:

"I'm… I'm afraid it's a written warning, Miss Durant. We *cannot* allow ~"

Dewy tore the envelope in two and dropped the pieces in the bin. Carruthers walked away, angry.

All Dewy cared about that moment was, she was hungry. *But I ate yesterday?* She'd seen a traditional British chip shop while researching nail-bars. She liked its vintage, blue glass panel with Almighty Cod in gold copperplate.

Dewy left the office, feeling the men staring at her back. Outside was a rainstorm with gusts. Teeth gritted, Dewy headed to the town centre, shoulders hunched, arms folded. Soon she changed course for The Fusilier.

Three hours later the sun came out. Squinting in brightness, Dewy meandered to The Lugworm. She'd drunk two pints of Rattock's in The Fusilier, two in the

Nor' Gate, a half of Wennoxford's so foul and sour in The Bear she'd returned to The Fusilier to erase the taste with a pint of Rattock's.

Dewy had forgotten how delirious daytime drunk was: darkened vision, crushing fatigue, headache, anxiety. People stared at her, "Where's your *shoes*?" medium-often. At Cressy Road Bridge she watched the river. "Why's barefootedness believed an extreme offence?" she murmured to the water-spirits. "What is *up* with people? They presume the right to angrily demand I explain myself. Yet they obey a thousand forms of bullying, rip-offs, legalised extortion, lies, surveillance, coercion and harms – no question or resistance."

She'd recall little between The Swainway and early evening, except the walk got darker and cold, and she'd sat on a mossy wall in the woods, crying about her mother.

Climbing the stairs at 6.30pm, Dewy heard a blastingly loud, wavering screech like a huge, angered hornet. The source was a masked man electric-sanding the floor of the room opposite Annette's. Fent was having it made into a B&B let.

Dewy made a hot water bottle and curled up in bed. But the sander's excruciating noise, at car-horn volume, never ceased. She padded downstairs to sleepily walk Keeley Lane, shivering. Drizzle returned. Dewy stepped into the wood for shelter. Suddenly she remembered ringing Harrods in London from The Nor' Gate. She'd booked a next day pedicure there and bought train tickets online, totalling £198 ($260). A taxi to Exeter at 6.15am must be booked, plus one from the afternoon train to the Tattler, fast, for deadline Wednesday.

In a first pang of sobriety, Dewy totalled the Harrods trip: at least £380. Was this justified for a pedi? Dewy looked down at her toes: *YES IT WAS*. Harrods painted her toenails in 2012, when she and Annette visited for the Olympics. To Dewy, Harrods was the only UK pedicurist of proven competence.

Cold, she returned to The Lugworm, and tried to ask the electric-sander man how long he'd continue. He yelled over the machine: "What's the problem?"

"The noise, sir."

"I don't think it's loud."

"You're wearing hearing protectors, sir. It's *very loud*."

"I've a job to do."

"How long to you intend to continue please?"

"Why do you keep asking that?"

"I'd like to know when quiet will start."

Voices ascended the stairs, Annette and Beverley.

"Oh!" cried Dewy and Annette. They kissed, embraced, kissed again, lost themselves in each other. The man flashed an amused, lewd glance to Beverley, who looked at him like stone and said: "What are you doing?"

"Sanding this floor."

"It's my night off," said Beverley. "Don't want to hear an electric sander. Finishing soon?"

The man stared, lip-curled. Anyone – women, basically – bothered by sander noise was petty. He put his dust mask up, replaced his thick hearing protectors and the machine roared again. The women backed away. Dewy and Annette went to bed. But the sander noise was too much.

"Shall we stroll?" said Dewy. "I'm real tired, though."

"So am I." said Annette. "But I can't take that noise, let's go."

IN THE WOODS, the bivouac had gone. After a second's panic, Jade saw a scrap of paper with a heart next to a drawing of Ocean. On the top right was a cross like a compass, an asterisk next to the right point.

"Is that the direction they've gone in?" thought Jade. "Is it east? How am I to know where east is? Maybe my phone's got an app?"

Yesterday Azdek had spoken at length for the first time. His English was good. Jade loved his accent. He really was from somewhere else in the world. His voice imbued a sun-baked, ancient land of great danger, and beauty, heritage, mystery, scented nights, romance... and ordinariness of people being people too. That last feeling touched Jade's heart and imagination just as strongly.

Azdek said he and Yusef were brothers, 22 and 12. They'd fled Syria last year with an uncle, a brother and men from their city, plus their mother, sisters and aunts. They paid to be smuggled into Turkey in a van, where they were captured and put in a camp. The women were safe there, they hoped, but the camp only allowed men for 48 hours. They bade farewell to the women – (Azdek fell silent at this point, stared at the ground, spoke again when Yusef glanced to him) – then walked across Turkey, staying in refuges – barns with no facilities or bathroom, or maybe one, for hundreds of men and boys. Churches and charities tried to provide food once a day.

Here was as far as the story got. Azdek, usually good-humoured, got annoyed by Yusef, who repeatedly stopped him to show Jade pictures he'd drawn. These were precise: of the internment camp, of himself, Azdek and other men wandering Turkish streets, men around a bonfire, a UN refuge with a nurse and doctor, a night in a refuge, rows of men sleeping on the floor of a high barn, moon and stars through a half-missing, icicled roof.

Maybe Azdek envied his brother's talent. Maybe both were at their wits' end. *Of course they are* thought Jade, strangely reassured by the impatience of the men to each other. They were *people.* Siblings who bickered, not Syrians, not "migrants", "asylum seekers" nor any cold, remote words the TV news and newspapers used. Two brothers bickering, like brothers everywhere.

Today Jade and Ocean wandered deeper into the

wood. Quarter of a mile in was a clearing she remembered from years ago, spaced-apart very tall trees, massive and higher now. They allowed little sky in, only shafts of gold, causing a serene, dusky, comforting light to permeate. Jade heard a low whistle and a handclap. Ocean bounded heavily towards a glade sunk below its surroundings.

Yusef was tense and alone in a new shelter there. They'd brought the bivouac roof from the last hide-out, made it bigger, more dense, now wedged between roots of a beech and a steep earth bank. Carrier bags and bin-liners were carefully used as floor covering. Jade saw her blankets and old cardigan strewn. Soap, toothbrushes, toothpaste lay in a corner on a cut open Tesco bag stretched taut with stones. The soap was depleted, but Yusef looked dirtier. Azdek must only use it.

As Yusef drank water she'd brought, Jade saw paper covered in drawings and doodles. Yusef must be so bored and lonely all day. Jade glimpsed drawings of tanks, explosions, fires, bodies, a skeleton. Yusef covered these and presented her with a piece of paper he'd prepared. Jade smiled, saw Yusef didn't, so stopped. But three pictures of Azdek he'd drawn were deliberately comical. The first, Azdek stripped to the waist, grinning through lather as he soaped his face, the second, pouring water from a bottle to rinse his face, the last, smiling with self-satisfaction amid rays from his clean face.

Then a four-box cartoon: 1. Azdek leaving the wood, face gleaming, following an arrow. 2. Spotting a distant farm – square fields, tractors, tiny people. 3. Azdek with a question mark in a speech bubble talking to a man by a tractor. Finally, Azdek alongside people picking plants in a field. Jade realised he was telling her Azdek had gone looking for work. Yusef pointed at fields on the Google Map Jade had printed out at school.

But Yusef's intensity and fearful eyes made Jade real-ise, to him, it was less a case of where Azdek had gone, as where Azdek was last seen.

Jade unpacked food, and a torch. She flashed it on and off and drew pictures to signify he must do this at night if Azdek did not return. She beckoned Yusef follow her. Jade remembered a short-cut out of the wood, of little use to anyone because it led to no paths, only a very big field. It did, however, provide a new view of Moresby in the distance, including the back of her house, even her bedroom. Bidding Yusef stay at the wood's edge, Jade walked out to the bare soil field. She back-kicked her heel into earth to make a hole and plugged it with scrunched white paper.

Yusef intuited he must find that white mark in the ground in an emergency. It was the spot to flash the torch on and off at night from, so Jade would see.

LATE SUN WON over rain in Keeley Lane. Dewy and Annette headed hand in hand for the park near Londis, stopping to watch the Brate flow past the buttercups and dandelions meadow. "You look nice," said Dewy.

"Dumb blouse, two-piece and tights," said Annette. "Clumpy closed shoes."

"I love you," said Dewy, wrapping herself around Annette and rubbing her upper back: "Your mind will save the world."

In the park they sat on their bench, Dewy drowsy, coatless and cold. Annette wanted to get her back to The Lugworm, to bed. They heard yells of happiness and saw children running.

"They're coming to see *us*," said Annette.

The children arrived all talking: "Can we play with you hair again, miss?"

"Of course, darlings."

Girls searched for bluebells, buttercups and forget-me-nots for Dewy's hair.

A boy said: "Is it true you're American?"

"We are," said Annette.

"Do you have bears and that, and snakes and all that?"

"We *do*," smiled Annette. "Bears, copperhead snakes, mountain lions! Coyotes, raccoons, bobcats. Dewy had a *moose* in her garden one time!" She told of New England's forests and wild Atlantic coasts, of the ancient Pawtucket, Wampanoag, Nipmunk, Mohegan. The children knew what a totem pole was and described one. When a child spoke of a dance they'd done at school, her voice suddenly stopped. The children looked round and up.

Two police had arrived, in peaked caps with pale blue bands, lemon hi-vis anoraks, no markings or police numbers. Behind them a third, on a mountain bike. He wore scorching hi-vis, no hat, and stared at Dewy's eyes.

"All right?" smiled the young woman officer. "What's this then? Bed-time story is ut?"

The children looked at each other, very quiet. The man on the mountain bike's insolent stare never left Dewy. The children carefully stood in ones and twos and began to walk away. Annette and Dewy were exposed.

The policewoman, if she was, continued:

"Flowers in the hair! Kids do that?"

Inevitably: "Where's yer *shoes*? Leave 'em somewhere?"

Dewy didn't answer, but couldn't stop calling to the bike man: "Sir, must you stare like that?"

The man's face intensified to aggression and disgust. The nearer man smiled down: "American then? That's good! What you doing here then?"

"Been drinking, miss?" said the woman, stepping forward. "Been out a while?"

Dewy ignored her and looked at the other man, a foot away from Annette now, smiling inanely down at her. He hadn't stopped talking: "Nice park to chill out in. Is that why you and her's here? You come out for a stroll or something tonight, is that what it is? Nice place to come to. Nice, yeah?"

The woman was furious Dewy had ignored her. The man began to change tone, for Annette, unable to speak, or look vertically up at him, did neither. Dewy restrained not to kick him. She'd have vengeance on anyone pressuring Annette.

The man's smile faded: "Right, mind if I quickly I ask your names?"

Dewy rubbed Annette's tense shoulders, leaned close and whispered: "Fuck 'em."

"Need your *names*," said the man, producing no notebook. The woman stood legs apart, arms folded, staring fixedly. The mountain bike man glared. His small, pink, muscular face had black dots for eyes.

"What's *your* name, love?" said the other man to Annette.

"Sir, why do you want our names?" said Dewy.

"Just procedure," smiled the man.

"That's a non-informative answer," said Dewy. The man looked mortified.

"Do you have your *passport*?" snapped the woman. "Can tell by your voice you're not from our country."

"Ma'am," sighed Dewy "Would you mind – and you sir – taking a step back?"

"Have you a *passport*?" said the woman, louder.

"Step back, please?" said Dewy. "You're in our personal space."

"Fine!" said the man, breezily. "Not a problem." He reached to the woman's arm and tugged her.

"Thank-you," sighed Dewy. "Now: I've visited 10 countries, seen war, civil unrest, dangerous regimes, but never been asked to explain sitting in a park. What is this?"

The woman and the mountain bike man exuded such threat that Dewy's vision, in panic, blotted both out. Ballet training took over, utter stillness, chin high. She heard her own voice: "Where are you three stationed, please?"

No answer. Annette and Dewy watched three lurid anoraks walk away. The mountain bike man glanced back at them, teeth bared.

Annette breathed deeply. Dewy caressed her. She saw the children, far away, watching. Parents stared from windows beyond. The children slowly turned away.

"Oh!" said Annette. "Those cops have made the children afraid of us? Like we're weird and dangerous now?"

"They weren't cops," muttered Dewy.

As the three had left, she'd seen, on each back, a bright blue sign with white letters: Police Community Support Officer.

In this week's update on Matthew Willis's death, the inquest learned how, in the first instance, he was approached then detained in isolation for 11 minutes by a Police Community Support Officer (PCSO).

Online, Dewy had discovered how PCSOs, with near-identical uniforms to police officers, aren't police, but untrained members of the public, not required to have qualifications or employment background.

Even one minute detained by that PCSO with the mountain bike would reduce anyone to an extreme state, Dewy reflected. She hoped he wasn't the man who'd detained Matthew Willis.

Chapter 9

ELECTRIC SANDERS AND other work finished two days later. The room was ready as an online B&B let. To Douglas Fent's dismay, the world's tourism was uninterested. No bookings, not one online viewing. Beverley persuaded Fent to let her and Annie have the room when it wasn't hired, and Annette's old room any night it ever was.

"We're swapping rooms with Annette and her friend," said Beverley.

"Why?" frowned Fent.

"Annette is pregnant."

"Rubbish. How can a…?"

"Lesbian?"

"Look, I don't think she's pregnant, OK? Probably just putting on weight. Americans *do*."

"Douglas, she's having a baby and having our room until they move out when the time's near."

"This is a madhouse. That pair are *demented*."

"Annette's a lecturer, her friend works for the paper. Hardly 'demented'."

The room-swap took an hour. Beverley helped Dewy move everything, for Fent might appear if Dewy was alone, either demanding extra rent for the new room, or forbidding the move.

Dewy was most grateful to Beverley for arranging this, and relieved Annette would be out of that 8 by 12, too-hot, back room.

The front-facing new room had foxgloves, geraniums and sage in an outside windowbox. Annette returned from university and promptly fell asleep in the huge, comfortable bed. Dewy lay beside her, hearing chatter from picnic-tables below, cries of river-birds beyond. Later, when cigarette and vape smoke blew in, she got up to shut the window, not wanting Annette to breathe it.

In last light Annette woke. Dewy was awake four inches away:

"Does Martin Davidson think we're weird?"

"Why would he think that, sweetie?" mumbled Annette, stretching luxuriously.

"Doesn't he though?" said Dewy.

"Well… *Bachelor* always thought we were very compact. Like: 'just so'. Like we *belong* together. I sense BooBoo thinks that also. Please may I give your ears a snoo?"

"Of course, darling," said Dewy, happy Annette was more relaxed here in this room than anywhere yet in England.

TESSA ENGLAND'S CONSTITUENCY office was a barn conversion in a cobbled mews. Dewy had a Thursday 4pm appointment. ("Miss Dee". She was sure Durant would be refused.)

A hearty young woman in old clothes answered the door: "You've no *shoes*!! Ha-ha-HA-ha-ha-*HA!* I'm Helena. Wait *there*, I'll see what Tessa's up to. Can't believe you've no shoes on! That's so funny!"

Dewy's fourth ever blog post years ago was in response to a "so funny!"

Not so funny as your bunions, corns, foot odor, trapped circulation, ingrown toenails, foot deformities, crushed toes, under-nail fungal infections, dead skin, sweating, numbness, spinal problems and the

**thousands of dollars you'll spend in your life achiev-
ing these aims. But accost and terrify anyone who
opts out. Shout questions at them. Scream at them
they're cold.**

Dewy waited, Day Two sober, resenting Helena, then
herself: *Oh, Goddess, I HATE not drinking. All the love in
me dies. Spite and rage spurt up like boiling mud. Everyone's an enemy. It's TEDIOUS.*

She was led up iron spiral stairs to a room more cluttered than the downstairs. Filing cabinets, in-trays and
whole-wall shelves sagged with box files, Parliamentary
reports, books, folders. Tessa England sat as in a trench at
a huge, green-leather-topped, vintage desk heaped with
papers and files. Dewy wondered how it got up those
stairs.

The MP was on the phone. To Dewy's relief, her face
didn't harden on seeing her guest. She pointed Dewy to a
chair, soon ended her call, then: "Right! Have you things
you want to say this time?"

"Why has Farrisford's library closed down?" said
Dewy.

"Oof, good one. Is that all?"

"Why are you not in the Farrisford Tattler? The Labour fellow always is. You've no profile, yet the whole
country's highly politicized about Brexit. That Maurice
Johnston guy ~

"*Boris Johnson*," corrected Tessa England.

"*Him*, yes. He's announced he'll run for Prime Minister. There's talk of another Election, third in, what, four
years? What kind of politics *is* this? It's like South
America, Africa."

"Rubbish," said Tessa England.

"A shambles by a deceitful, myopic, inept, greedy
power-base."

"I hardly think *you* have ~"

"Britain's *very* edgy now," Dewy cut in. "No one can give reassurance, it isn't possible. And *you* have a serious rival in that Labour candidate, He has high media profile, Team Labour were in town Saturday, table at the Farmer's Market, posters hanging off it, sticker-badges given out. Where were *you*?"

"In my surgery getting on with it, you were *there!*"

"I mean in the general sense? Are you complacent you'd hold your seat next election? You only did two years ago by nine per cent.

"Are you a journalist?"

"Temporary at the Tattler, but – listen, please? Please? This is *all* off-record. I *promise* off-record. I asked them: why no Tessa England in this paper? They hardly answered, I thought I'd ask you myself."

"They don't like me," snapped Tessa England.

A pause. The MP looked grimly at Dewy, who braced herself for anger. But:

"I do *like* The Tattler," sighed Tessa England, "Grew up with it. Daily in the 50s, 60s, went weekly… '78 or so. We fell out, few years back. Alleged expenses scandal. I over-claimed four thousand pounds, they went overboard. Then the Bettle to Moresby bypass kicked off. They found out my nephew's wife's a surveyor on it. Even made Private Eye, d'you know Private Eye?"

"No."

"Magazine, satirical. It said because of my relative I, quote: 'turned a blind eye to the public consultation for the bypass' unquote. I did *not*."

"You were accused of nepotism?"

"Yup."

"Not challenging a rotten bypass, so your nephew's wife could work on it?"

"Yup. Expressed like that shows how ridiculous it is, but if said in hints or indirectly, seems whopping corruption. My 'niece-in-law' – if that's a term? – is highly qualified, needs no help from me, or anyone. And the bypass isn't 'rotten' it's needed, but *not* the version decided. Of three options, the Department of Transport picked the worst and most intrusive. They ignored everyone, including me. *Then* the contract was given to a shambles of a company, now bankrupt."

Helena arrived with tea. She placed the tray down and hovered, smirking.

"Thanks," said Tessa England, then continued to Dewy: "But as you lot know: 'don't let truth get in the way of a good story'. As with Private Eye, the Tattler wants to believe I signed away miles of beloved countryside for this bypass. I never signed anything, it was *all* D.o.T. committee."

"*But*," continued Tessa England, "The dark side: I didn't do enough. Sorry, Helena – can you carry on downstairs? Thanks – What I didn't do well, *was*: I didn't ram home the results of the public consultation to the Department. I should have done so again and again."

She looked expressionless, picked up her tea, faintly slurped.

"Excuses are odious," she sighed, "but it was 2015, we were centrifugal about an Election weeks away, I was out campaigning *then* all right, worried daft about UKIP, know of them?"

"Yes. Abominable."

"No comment. Turned out a false alarm, I knew we'd come through, we're good people in these parts, not xenophobic idiots…"

"Historical legacy of Quakers and Methodists, than any Conservative influence?"

"Ha! Spot-on about the history. Unsure I agree with your comment. Anyway, the bypass got lost in the fight to keep my seat, which I did, three thousand majority, down from six.

"And UKIP?

"Thousand. Voters I lost went to Labour, not them."

"But they'll be back. That man?"

"Farage. Nigel Farage."

"Only for voters to see-saw between him and Labour again? Are you going to address that?"

"I'm buried in Brexit and trying to calm farmers."

"You were against Brexit? Do you still feel that?"

"Yes. But over half here who *did* vote, voted we leave Europe. I represent them."

The MP drank tea and said:

"Voter turn-out only 61 per cent. Shame. Brexit's insane for this part of the world. 98 farms in my constituency, nearly all depend on European workers, who work like billy-o. Post-Brexit, many Romanians, Latvians, Slovenians, Poles might leave, or not wish to come. The local population couldn't get half the farming done even if we all did it. Miss Durant, I must get on, but... are we *completely* off-record?"

"Yes."

"Then I'll say *this*: we may as well face, for better or worse, Boris Johnson being Prime Minister. He'll likely call an election straightaway, aiming for a landslide victory in the nick of time before inevitable mess-ups start. But even if an election *does* anchor my party, stability's not guaranteed. We've *still* no practical answers on how to leave Europe, the reality of doing so with no plan is overwhelming. Promises disaster for some regions, including here. OK, I must get on..."

"Thank-you for seeing me," said Dewy, standing. "Would you like to be in the paper? I'd like to interview you properly."

"Uh, n~... I'll think about it. We *can* meet again, Saturday surgery's usually crowded, but try there first. Otherwise ring here to see if I've 10 minutes, I'm here usually one day a week. Ring first, no unsoliciteds. See yourself out, will you? Bit snowed under."

MARLON STARED OUT at evening rain. The doorbell had rung, John had let that... *girl* into the house, then disappeared, leaving them alone on the sofa. *Why*? Marlon couldn't turn his head to even look at Millie, who talked without cease:

"Yeah, he's a black man, my dad," she continued, "But above all a man. That can mean: selfish, untalking, bad-tempered... No feelings he'll show, except annoyance, anger. *You're* not like that."

Marlon's thumb-tip drew circles on the back of his phone.

"I can be," he sighed. "Got a few issues about stuff."

"Aww. It's good you admit that. That's a brave thing to do," said Millie. She touched Marlon's forearm, which he instantly retracted. The obviousness of this caused a terrible pause. Marlon still looked away. Millie tried:

"Looks nice got your ear pierced! What made you think of getting that done then?"

Marlon shrugged a shoulder.

"Where d'you get it done?"

"Why?"

"Well, er... looks *nice*. Oh God, see that lightning?"

Double flash, a thunder-crack. Marlon looked at the sky. Millie watched him. A long silence.

I talk too much. He hates it. I got nothing to say, but say it anyway. I wish I wasn't how I am.

"I don't like to think of you unhappy, Marlon," said Millie, softly.

No response.

"If it's them boys, they're *nothing*, they're cowards, Marlon. These're the tossers too scared to go the dentist. Blubbed when they had a injection at school. Probably get slapped by their mums, hit by useless dads. These kids are desperate to prove they got power. So they attack anything harmless. It's all cowardness. Don't ever let cowards get to you?"

Her voice grew faint as the sky boomed louder. "Any time, if you want to talk, I'm happy to…"

Marlon exerted all mental energies into inventing an excuse to get Millie out of the house. His heart sank when storm rain began. John wouldn't send her out in this. Unless… where was the golf umbrella?

"I feel white with my dad, black with my mum!" said Millie, reverting to cheery. "Her kids are white. They're nice but… the boy don't speak? Stays in his room with the computer. He's called Nathan. His sister's really sweet, she's six, called Gracie. Mum's still called Donna Zena, but her new kids, they're West, not the direction, the name West. Gracie West and… you get it."

Silence.

"Is that you over there?" cried Millie, seeing photos. "Can I have a look?" She sprang up and walked to the sideboard.

I hope he's watching me? My walk's nice in these jeans.

She turned. He was looking at his phone.

Millie saw younger Marlons in photos and began to well up. In the youngest, age seven, he wore a pale-blue school shirt, had two inches of hair growth and smiled with big, new teeth. Millie wondered what he smiled at, someone off-camera making him laugh? It made her happy he'd laughed at least once as a child.

"Er…?" Marlon cleared his throat: "Dad wants to watch something probably in a bit…"

"Oh, of course, yeah! I gotta get back. *My* Dad'll want me to … er… er…"

Marlon saw her to the front door. He opened it to heavy rain.

"Can I say bye-bye to Mr Wright?" said Millie.

Marlon sighed, opened an inch of kitchen door: "She's going."

"Oh! So soon?" said Mr Wright's voice amid radio and cooking noises. He emerged, wiping his hands on a tea-towel, then fussed to find the golf umbrella. Millie thanked him a lot. They turned quietly to see Marlon in the doorway against rain and stormy sky, looking out. Rain was loud. An outdoor halogen lamp glared pale, faintly greenish.

"Anything going on, Marlon?" said Mr Wright.

A lot seemed behind these words. Marlon turned, shook his head, eyes stricken. He looked out again.

Millie suddenly felt afraid of the outdoors as he did, but paced forward cheerfully, to show fear was nothing. "Bye, Marlon, bye Mr Wright."

The door closed.

Chapter 10

FRIDAY WAS SUNNY. Dewy worked hard all morning. Interesting stories sometimes arrived, but so did:

Rotary Welcomes Its New President

Work Takes Place On Bridleway

New Collection Points For Waste-Bins Proposed

Archery Competition Raises £300 For Scouts

Soon a story intrigued her: very aged members of Parachute Regiments 1 and 2, pictured in berets and blazers with medals outside Loddleford Church. Two supported the pole of a tall, colourful flag – their standard. Dewy read the men had formed an association of ex-members in 1969 when two got talking in a Balaton pub. The landlord told them others lived in the area. Soon the Farrisford and District Branch of the Airborne Forces began. Of 34 members, six survived today, all of great age. They'd asked Loddleford Church to take charge of their standard, made by a member's wife years ago. None was able to make public appearances with it now.

The photograph made Dewy well up. Men so old they looked like toads, a sixth skeletal and tall. All stood straight, with dignity, humbly requesting a church let their memory live by relieving them of a flag they couldn't lift.

Luckily, Gregor Finniston was next in her inbox. He always cheered Dewy up. The week's **All Right Then, I'll Say It**, about plastic waste on coastlines, began: I never liked the

hippies, but I admit they were right. Dewy pressed her hands together: "I'll never edit a word of you, sir".

All had gone quiet. Dewy glanced round. The office had emptied.

"Fancy coming along, Miss Dewy?" said David Cartwright, last to depart for Friday at The Good Queen Bess. "You haven't come to this yet…"

"Busy," said Dewy. She wasn't taking her usual Friday off, to atone for her absence on deadline-day two days before, when she'd made an 11-hour round trip to Harrods for her emergency pedi. ("Sounds like you're on a train?" said Carruthers, who'd rung at 11 to ask where she was. "I darn-well am *not*!" said Dewy, under a shrieking tannoy announcement the train was near Waterloo. "I'm real ill. I'll be in later.")

She'd breezed in at 6pm, perfectly healthy, if glazed by drinks on the train, with beautifully ("adequately") applied new red-pink toenail-polish, to find Geoff Carruthers, Michael Fenwick, David Cartwright and Stephen Ellis panicking to sub-edit the paper. Ross and Sons had rung again, warning 8pm latest for next morning publication, staff waiting, distributors ringing for updates.

"Well, Geoff?" slurred Dewy. "Thizsis wh'happens if you don't chase staff to submit work on time! I *told* you, if ardicles miss deadline, *you* sort it. Lemme at my compuder, fellas, skedaddle."

She'd barged through them with crisp Harvey Nichols and Harrods bags. For Annette she'd bought a white Valentino midi dress, sandals, a sunhat and a deep-green Christopher Kane cardigan. For Beverley as a thank-you for giving up her room, she'd bought Harrods Food Hall gifts.

Today, Friday, two days on, David Cartwright tried again: "Come down the Bess, Miss Dewy?"

10 minutes later, at the bar, a male chorus: "Ah-HA!!! *She's* here! Ha-ha-ha! What you having?"

"Rattock's, please."

80 minutes, four pints: "*Stop* askin' if I wanna *eat*, fellas! *I do not!* Let's hear it for ladies *who DON'T lunch*, OK? Screw eating! It's a *PUB*, even if it *IS* decorated *grey* like a frickin' *morgue*. Yeah, another Rattock's, Geoff, thank-you. Of *course* a damn pint!"

Dewy hadn't met Amanda Wilson, one of two people who managed the Tattler's online edition. She arrived now with her fiancé Dean. Dean didn't work for the paper, but the men deferred to this young, frowning, neat-haired man.

Amanda worked the table in a houmous-coloured twinset. Tanned, with long blonde curls, she leaned down to each man in turn: "All right, loverr, *yeahhh*, good as gold, ha-ha-ha-*HA*, been behaving yerself? Ha-ha-ha-*ha*!!"

"Jeezsz Christ," mumbled Dewy, altered and strange on scrumpy, one eye half-closed. Her body faintly wobbled.

Amanda froze in wide-eyed, friendly-trepidation at Dewy: "I'm sorry," she said comically: "I *have* to check something?" She lifted a corner of the tablecloth, peered: "Oh my God, it's *true*! You *really don't wear shoes*!! Ha-ha-ha-ha-HA-ha-ha-ha-ha! Dean! *Dean!* Dean!"

Dean stopped being talked to by Carruthers and Fenwick and stared at her coldly the length of the room. "I'm *talking*," he snarled.

"The American barefoot girl!" yelled Amanda. "It's literally true! It's true!"

Dean silenced her with a look of real violence. Dewy's mind changed. She resolved, no matter what, not to be nasty to Amanda.

JADE FOUND THE bivouacs missing every two days, but always something tied to a low branch, usually long grass tied in a bow, the men's way of signalling: "Don't worry, we're still here."

At school she Googled as much as she could about what might happen if police found the men. They'd be put in an Immigration Centre, any of a dozen in the UK. The nearest were near Dartmouth, or Southampton, but it seemed people were sent wherever had space.

Jade read a Daily Mail article online criticising the cost of the centres, risks to staff and inmates' children, overcrowding and how people could be detained for years. She read a Guardian article on dismal, claustrophobic conditions, bullying by staff, health problems of inmates, particularly women and children, and how people could be detained for years.

Policies were confusing. Some people got "granted" something called "asylum" but weren't allowed to work or earn money. Others *could* work, or was it only those who didn't know if they had "asylum" yet who couldn't work or get food-vouchers? Some people were in Centres, others weren't. No one knew how many "illegals" were in the UK.

"Well, I know two 'illegals'," thought Jade. "I call them 'people'. And how they're living's worse than anything. And where they came from's even worse than that. Where *that* was, people got shot dead in their street."

Jade's rucksack bulged with supplies bought in the covered market: a one-side-waterproof tartan blanket, sliced bread, tinned soup and Irish Stew of brands unheard of, dented boxes of Mr Kipling cakes. She'd bought a contraption that unfolded into a camping stove – it *did* have a nozzle, she saw now, so the butane canister *would* fit – that stall-holder wasn't lying after all. (Full recovery from Danii's mind-conditioning, including contempt for the covered market, would take time. Whenever a cheap product was advertised on TV, Danii sneered: "They'll be fighting over *that* down the covered market!")

Jade had visited there most lunchtimes. Of her £80

savings, she'd spent barely half. All survival essentials in one place at little cost, no risk of being seen by Danii or her clients, ever.

DEWY SAT ON a banquette past the end of the crowded dining table. Amanda Wilson dragged a chair side-on and spoke at length to Ian Balloch and Tim West about her and Dean's Thailand trip.

"No stopover on the way," she continued. "Nor on the way back. So… *no* stopovers, basically. It would've been really good to ~"

"What, like, Dubai?" said Balloch.

"*Exactly.* To look at shoes, get a proper, designer, going-away outfit? I mean *Dean's* sorted, he's got this supercool suit. *He'll* look like James Bond. And *I'll* be like: 'Hello-o-o? Only me-ee!'"

She said those last words in a tiny voice. Balloch and West laughed with her. Dewy left for the wc, then to the bar for a sixth pint. Made to wait, she unleashed another blazing demand the bar-staff tell management: "Whoever renovated this antique pub into a grey *gulag* should be *thrashed* in the **STREET!**"

The staff detested Dewy. She'd yelled things like this on her first visit. Now she again raved: "Renaming this pub 'GQB' on all signage! *Despicable*! Is 'Good Queen Bess' too *long* for your marketing fuckwits to *process*? Do hundred-grand algorithms say millennials can't grasp a name that long, 'so change it to GQB'?" **HeEEk!**

Back at the table, Amanda talked on about Thailand. David Cartwright now listened too. Dewy quietly sat, secure in her decision not to be nasty to Amanda, stuck with a cruel man, soon to marry him.

"Just been saying to Ian and Tim?" said Amanda to Cartwright: "How me and Dean could scarcely get time off work for Thailand *and* the honeymoon in August? So we didn't have stopovers?"

"What, you flew to Thailand, but no stopover?" said Cartwright.

"Exactly. No stopover at Dubai on the way there, nor on the way ~"

"*Christ!*" spluttered Dewy. "Did you ever say anything interesting in your *life*?"

"Excuse *me*?" said Amanda, wide-eyed, mouth open. "Did you really just say that?"

"How long d'you have to talk about damn *stopovers*?!" said Dewy.

Amanda glanced aghast at the men and back at Dewy. "Right then! I'll say something *interesting*, just for *you*." She swooshed her curls back, leaned to Dewy: "We'll build a *beautiful wall*, folks! To keep the Mexicans out! And *they* can pay for it!"

The table burst into laughter and cheers. "Ah, Christ, no. Please?" said Dewy, raising her hands in surrender: "You've won. Touché."

"America first!" yelled Amanda. "America first!"

"Please. I… I've no humour about this."

"*Well* then!" said Amanda, who stopped when seeing Dewy really was troubled. "We can't *all* be *glamourpusses* with… high cheekbones and… sexy feet and gorgeous hair! *You* say something interesting then?"

"Gonna throw-up," slurred Dewy.

She made it outside, stood dizzy between parked cars, didn't vomit, walked, vision spinning, to a bench under pub flower-baskets. Minutes on:

"Feeling better, Miss Dewy?" David Cartwright sat himself along from her.

"Did you puke?" blared Amanda, standing over her. "Were you actually sick? That coat's nice! How much was it?"

Dewy accepted Amanda's hand to help her stand. "C'mon let's get a drink."

"Don't know the coat price? Did you steal it?"

"No."

They arrived at the bar. Staff glared at Dewy. Cartwright bought drinks.

"How comes you got that two grand coat?" persisted Amanda.

"As you'd expect," sighed Dewy, "After I let my girlfriend's brother's friend's wife kiss me and do what she liked, I said: 'Your coat's nice'. A new one arrived for me next day."

Amanda's upper arm was pulled by Dean: "Why you having another drink?"

"Er…" said Amanda nervously. "Go on home, Deanie? I'll get a cab in a bit."

"Waste of *money*! You'll just stay here drinking!"

Dewy moved away in case she poured a drink over Dean. She firmly told herself not to do that. She moved to beside a large barrel by the wide arch into the raucous Tattler Room. Female servers in black and white maid outfits stacked dinner plates. Local businessmen stood drinking with Geoff Carruthers, Stuart Dean, Tim Hall and Ryan Palmer. The businessmen discussed Dewy so loudly she heard parts of:

"Fine piece! What's something like *that* doing here? No shoes, look!"

"Our temporary sub-editor," said Carruthers.

"Yeah? Mm!" said the men. "Checks things spelt right, does she?" said one.

"A bit more than that," said Carruthers.

"I bet she does!" said a man, prompting a wall of laughter.

"A shocker, she is," said 25-year-old Ryan Palmer "Proper nice."

"You like her?" smiled Carruthers.

"Yeah-ah!! If she ever had a bath, a couple of decent meals, wore shoes, shaved her armpits, I'd be *mad* about her."

"*And* shaved her *legs!*" said a businessman, darkly. "Bit hairy, look? Quite rude, that, actually. Lazy to shave, is she? Or just mindless?"

Amanda joined Dewy with a vodka and tonic. "This time yesterday we were in Bangkok…"

Seeing Dewy wasn't listening, Amanda asked: "What you thinking about?"

"1795, when the paper began?" said Dewy, gazing at The Tattler Room. "All the guys in periwigs, velvet coats, clanking tankards together? You and I not allowed: 'Begone, wenches!'"

"It possibly could have been different in some ways, yeah," nodded Amanda.

"I wonder what the headlines were?" said Dewy. "'Tractor Not Invented Yet – can some bastard hurry up on this? say ploughmen.'"

"Would that have been a headline, d'you think?" frowned Amanda. Dewy looked at her half-fondly. Amanda's gaze softened as she studied Dewy's face.

"Cor… you really are *beautiful*," said Amanda.

Dewy kissed her cheek.

"*Don't!*" panicked Amanda, glancing around. Dean hadn't seen, nor anyone. She didn't hear Dewy mutter: "Can't *believe* I kissed someone dressed like you."

Dean was suddenly there: "*Finish drinking*, Amm! We're going!"

He stared at Amanda, then turned to Fenwick. "Mike? Going now? I'll come tomorrah, ain't playing though."

Dean was a cricketer, as were two Tattler staff.

"Just going toilet!" said Amanda.

"Be *QUICK*!" said Dean, slapping her bottom as she ran. Fenwick saw and raised his eyebrows. He and Dean grinned.

"Precious to me, that arse," leered Dean. "For a *much* more important reason than slappin'!"

Fenwick laughed so convulsively he tried to suppress it. Tears appeared in his eyes. He and Dean exchanged warm glances and loudly laughed again. When they realised Dewy watched them, laughter ebbed and stopped. They stared at her.

"Do you brainwashed, anal-sex morons ever think you might be gay?" said Dewy.

Amanda returned to uproar. On the left Dewy, beer-soaked, restrained by Cartwright and Carruthers, yelled: "Girls' online advice pages: 'He wants anal…' 'Will it hurt…?' 'Will I bleed…?' 'Can it injure me…?' Obvious answers *YES!* The agony as our anal diaphragm's stretched, the shit, blood, humiliation, all for your *loveless, guy-power trip!!*"

Amanda looked urgently left to right. Michael Fenwick told her: "American slut poured a drink over Dean! Don't worry, he poured one back." He omitted to say Dean also lashed out at Dewy, punching her arm then collar bone.

"Aren't our vaginas good enough?" shouted Dewy "Gotta inflict anal sadism, cos your man friends say *they* do? Anal sex is cruel to women. Would you tolerate it done to *you*? Would you *hell*. A man inflicting what he can't take back's a *coward!*"

A stocky barman marched Dewy from the pub. Dean followed, screaming:

"Fuck off back to – *shaddup, Amanda!!* – fuck off to the States!! Fuckin' American yank, come near me, I'll *glass* ya!!"

Dewy flung the barman off her, turned and marched at Dean, who backed into a wall, Dewy whispered to his face: "You *ever* hurt Amanda, I'll hear about it. And I'll come – from anyplace on Earth – to *break your arms*."

IGNORING JOHN'S: "ARE you running a bath?" Marlon

wondered instead how to answer:

> *Dear Marlon, Thank God its Friday! Leaving work now. wondered*
> *if you fancy a quick drive to the coast? is lovely evning. I'd like to*
> *see the sea and sunset with you i can come pick you up. xxxxxx*

He had anxiety about texts. He never sent them except to John or Robert. How could he ask Danii to *not* pick him up at the house, but the top of the crescent, corner with Trant Road?

He'd better reply quickly, if she was on her way.

Dear Mrs Tiler, that would be good! do you mind not pick me up at house but at the top of roda. will xplain. Marlon

He leapt up: "No time for a bath, have to be a shower. Ah, *no*. Frying onions, no way!" Marlon paced to the kitchen: "Dad, is it all right I shut this door? The smell, y'know?" His phone pinged, new text.

> Searching for Mr Wright? What you doing tonight? I'm meeting Bobby Z at the Good Queen B at 9. Not drinking because of game tomorrow, so can pick you up and drive you home? Yours, Lord Professor Sir Robert Obogo.

"Making home-made burgers," said John Wright, appearing. "Do you want ~?"
"Dad keep that door closed? Please?"
His phone pinged again:

> *U are the sweetest thing! yes i'll b top of the "roda" 20 mins. Mrs Tyler (not Tiler!!)*

AN ORANGE BIG moon rose over the Brate. It soared high and white, making all the land navy blue. A silver river gleamed from woods near a tavern by a hill of houses.

Outside the tavern were braziers and people's silhouettes. Some to and fro'd through French doors into a restaurant.

In a room overlooking the courtyard, moonlight found a long, white figure asleep on her side, hair and soles black in an otherwise blue-white, moon-sheened room.

Warm light filled the doorway as a woman's outline entered. She closed the door, walked to the window. Anyone outside looking up might see a thoughtful, pregnant girl in a cardigan and orchid-white dress shut a window and vanish.

Annette moved to the left of the double bed, sidestepping a washing-up basin. She softly rubbed the arm of the sleeping form then picked up a coat from the floor to cover her.

"*Uh.*" grunted the figure on the bed.

Annette returned to the door, opened it and leaned on the door-post, waving air with a magazine, face subdued. On the bed, very slowly, Dewy tilted to face the ceiling, eyes scrunched.

"*Uh.*"

"Hi, hon," said Annette quietly. "Opening the door, cigarette smoke's strong from outside."

"Ahh, my *head*…" croaked Dewy.

"Your hair's… different, hon?" said Annette. "Kinda flattened."

"A guy poured lager on it."

"*What?!*" Annette was annoyed Dewy had got into a depressing situation. "Gonna sleep it off?" she sighed.

"Kinda did, few hours," mumbled Dewy. "My head's *dying.* Anvil crushing the backs of my eyes. Two pulses in each temple. Hot forehead."

She rose to sit on the bed-edge hugging herself, facing away.

Annette was glum, though relieved Dewy was no longer drunk, or weeping.

"Well," she sighed, closing the door. "My evening was... interesting."

"Yeah?" said Dewy, rising, placing a hand against the wall to prop herself as she pulled down her knickers, kicked them off and squatted over the basin. "Sorry, bae, gotta piss?"

Annette left abruptly. Realising Dewy's post-drunk blood-sugar would be non-existent, she went downstairs to get chocolate cake. Annette also wanted a minute of uplifting company in the kitchen, a contrast to the scene in her bedroom. When she struggled back upstairs with cake and bottles of sparkling water. Dewy was face-down on the bed.

"Well," said Annette. "I... uh, was offered a job today by Boeing, and also..."

"That's good, hon!" said a muffled, weak voice.

"Kind of, but... it's not what I'm about now. I left flying school, like, seven years ago? British Aerospace were there tonight also. They were interested in the same~"

"Britizh who?"

"Aerospace. They *and* Boeing like the project I did couple years back for Cessna? On how flight-simulator hydraulics can be less delayed? But I don't want to work in aviation. In fact the opposite..."

"*Uhh...*" moaned Dewy. "This is a brain haemorrhage..."

"Let's empty that basin, hon? I'll take it~"

"I'll do it, sweet," said Dewy, struggling to move. Her lifting the basin and attempting to walk didn't succeed. She flumped back onto the bed, basin sploshing. "I'm still listnin' hon. Did you tell these aviation people to, like, fornicate afar?"

"I hinted I was in other areas now. Later I had a good talk with reps from the Graphene Flagship? We spoke about titania nanoparticles then moved onto rising sea-levels. They suggested I help develop improved sea-bed monitoring? Like, the consequence of rising seas is increased volume on sea-beds. Less stable parts risk landslides, earthquakes – meaning tsumanis, but alerting these at source would save many lives. Each hundred miles out to sea is 10 minutes' evacuation time and ~"

Bleh-aachh!! vomited Dewy into the basin.

"Oh, dear. Shall we empty that now?" said Annette.

She took Dewy's arm and ushered her to the hall. Dewy paused, squinting sorely in the light, saw Annette: "Aw, you look lovely, hon."

"Oh, bae," said Annette, voice tired. "You look like Morticia." She kissed Dewy's bare shoulder. "But always beautiful."

Soon they lay on the bed, apart, facing away from each other. Chocolate cake and water lay untouched. Annette fell asleep but was startled awake by fizzy glugging, a fork clacking on plate, then chomping and low muttering:

"…anal sex. Cruel, sad, brainwashed cowards. Millions of guys'd be happy with *real* lovemaking, but are corrupted by bullshit into sexual conformity called: injure your woman's anus and rectum, make her bleed, shit and cry in agony until YOU come. But: 'hey, girls, it's a guy thing, he says he only wants to try it, go along with it!' Hmph! 'Fucked up the ass': an everyday term for 'destroyed' or 'completely exploited'. What does THAT say about the new sexual submission demanded from women? WHY does ~"

"Honeyy?" groaned Annette. "Gotta sleep."

"We're ALL asleep," sighed Dewy.

"DAVID?"

The house was empty, 5.30am. John had showered, dressed, come downstairs assuming David had woken early. The sun was up, third Saturday in May, garden wonderous, flowers big and radiant. John must leave for Asda in 20 minutes. The hour before Saturday opening was manic.

The sliding glass door to the garden was inches open.

John headed there, squeezing between the round dining table and the open drawbridge of David's escritoire. Was the laptop on? Had David been working? John rubbed its contact pad, the screen lit up. He read:

I don't have anything to live for. My 50 years have led to nothing. I've nothing to get up for but the constant rerun of failures and hurt in my head. I am a reject, a failure. Unwanted. Broken. Nothing ahead but more failures. Been treated so badly by those I gave everything to. I am disliked. I just want to escape it all.

"*David?*"

John rushed outside. In a second the greenhouse was before him, morning condensation, David's blurred shape within. John tapped at the door.

"Y'all right?"

"Hello," said David. "Flowers look good?"

"*Yeah*," smiled John, hugging him close as he ever could. "Ahh, pet. Yeah, brilliant, the flowers, yeah." He kissed David. "Want a coffee?"

"Er, no thanks."

"Gi's a hug. I hope you're not too down about going to your mother's later?"

David tensely tried to return John's embrace. "You smell of toothpaste."

"Glad to hear it," replied John. He kissed David again and held him tight. He didn't want David out of his sight.

"David? Will you come Asda with me, please?"

"What?"

"Remember Christmas? I sneaked you in to help with shelf-stacking? It's like that today, a couple of people off."

"I-I… do you really need ~?"

"I do."

"*NEXT!*"

Dewy marched into the surgery room. Tessa England

looked up.

"The Shalton Road care home's being closed by the trust that owns it," said Dewy, "For the building of 'luxury apartments'. Some 'trust', huh? Where are the elderly people meant to go? Why are you allowing this?"

"How can I stop it?"

"And this 'HS2'? A 90 mile replacement railroad, plus 150 new miles, costs 106 *billion* pounds? I read the consultation alone cost two *billion*. How can a consultation for 90 miles of railroad cost *two thousand million* pounds??"

"Sit down? But can this be quick?"

"£106 billion means over £1,600 from every person in the UK! Each family of four pays *five grand*?"

Dewy gracefully sat, livid. "How many working families could do with that sum right now, to spend on essentials – a huge kickstart to the economy? But, no: a replacement 240-mile railroad by 2035."

"HS2 was originally hoisted by Labour," sighed Tessa England. "Though it *was* cross-party debated and passed, but further debates will be had."

"Your Tory government is like living with a drug addict."

"We've created two million jobs in seven years."

"Doing *what*? Hi-vis men with leaf-blowers in empty parking lots, hi-vis men breaking up streets. Roads and buildings renovated for the hell of it. Yet budgets for schools, hospitals, communities, youth clubs, libraries, training initiatives, cut or abolished."

"Where do you get your information?"

"From what I *see* here. And what I read on The Guardian's US site, and ~"

"Oh, *what* a surprise!"

"Washington Post, Boston Globe, New York Times… the world's watching Britain. Your government's oblivious to the suffering you cause. Houses where children are cold, red bills on the mat, missing toys or anything saleable, loud TV no one watches, empty cupboards, undrained sinks, dead refrigerator. Ain't nothing going on but the rent and this lit-up government with monkeys on its back – Trident replacement and railroad rip-offs. But libraries must close, clubs with free lunch for pensioners who fought Hitler cease, no more safe afterschool clubs for children with working parents. *Jesus*, do you bastards know how to hurt people?"

"I *don't* have to listen to ~"

"You *do*, Mrs England. You're not a brick wall, like 95 per cent of your mob. Your party's taken a beautiful, historic, spiritual country, home to some of the world's best writers, composers, inventors, musicians, reformers, scientists, you name it – do you know how *much* your country *means* to the world? You've more geniuses, innovators, dreamers, artists, bands, viragos, firebrands, mystics, educators, poets and holy drop-outs per square mile than anyplace on Earth. Or *did*, until Conservative bullying turned everyone into a worried-sick depressive or thug. In nine years your government's reduced Britain to a laughing-stock. A siphon for billionaires to pump looted cash into its land, so no one can afford to live. Your shallow party should be *ashamed*!"

"Enough! Go please. This surgery's for constituency matters."

"Ashamed of its *stupidity* if nothing else! Two *billion* pounds on a rail *consultation*!? While disabled commit suicide for want of 80 pounds a week."

"More like 180," muttered Tessa England.

"Oh, *180*, huh?! Those poor multi-millionaire rail 'consultants' could've had *more* money if disabled people hadn't claimed half a living wage to employ carers! Mrs England, for the first time in history Britain is BORING! Its spirit is DYING. And YOUR warped *damnation* of a party has caused that!"

Dewy marched out, a tear rolling down her cheek. Faces looked up as she strode past muttering: "Darn, forgot to ask, when do I interview her for the paper?"

"SAY HELLO TO your mother for me?" said John.

They pulled up at lights near Exeter. John reached for David's hand.

"Mm?" said John. "Say: 'Griselda? John says hello'."

David sighed. "Waste of £140, Goring-By-Sea and back."

"Well… you didn't go last year," said John. "She *is* your mother. And we said now's best, next weekend's train prices double at Bank Holiday."

"You didn't go last year?" said John again. He had to repeat everything to David now. "And don't worry about missing work Monday, Tuesday, love?"

David tensed: "They don't like it I'm taking days off. Deadlines ~"

"There's *always* deadlines there," sighed John. "But are they genuine?"

"They need a COMAR by Thursday," said David. "Code One Matrix Appraisal Reach-out'. I'm not actually sure what that is, but ~"

"David, if it's nothing to do with design or manufacture of staplers, forget it."

"But there's pressure to… COMARs are probably quite easy, once I've…"

"Oh, *David*… You're going to your mother's? Three nights. Forget work."

John was trying, but both understood the last thing David, or anyone needed was a three-night visit to 85-year-old, right-wing Flora Bennett.

"Try to relax there?" continued John. "It *is* possible… *perhaps*. Go to the beach? Old haunts, where you used to paint?" John wished he hadn't reminded it was three nights. "I'm booking our holiday when you get back."

"I didn't visit my mother last year," said David. This only now occurred to him.

"She'll be glad to see you," said John.

"She's never glad at anything," said David. "Whenever Mrs Thatcher won an election, Mother said: 'Glad the country's seen sense.' Her only connection with 'glad' I ever knew. She still didn't look it."

"Mrs Malcolm'll be round in the morning," said John.

"Oh, *God*," said David, a flash of the old David. John laughed with joy to hear the return of David's lost self, even for a second.

"She's OK, is June," smiled John. "Then Anthony Not Gay Remotely, he'll be round?"

"Oh, *no*. Poor Anthony NGR. I wonder if he still drives? We're stuck if not."

"Why's that?" said John, nearly crying, so happy to be with the real David again. He hugged David's neck and kissed his cheek softly all over.

"Because Anthony's the only transport," sighed David. "He was very deaf last time. I think he was putting it on to avoid conversation, though. Wouldn't you, if your only social life was Flora and June?"

"Remember, buy flowers at Waterloo," said John. "You've the market-leading Asda fruitcake in your bag too. That and flowers, you're well-armed."

They hugged and kissed before leaving the car in heavy rain to get David's case from the boot. John rushed back to the car: "See you Tuesday, love. Text me, yeah? If I don't hear from you, I get a bit…"

"I'll text late-night in bed," called David. "Can't text in front of *her*." He mimicked his mother's genteel voice – "'The *height* of *rude*ness'."

"The *heiiight!!*" squawked John from the car window. They parted laughing.

Rain had fallen for hours, looked set to last. Jade worried about the men. Were they dry? Had they enough to eat and drink? Ocean refused to go out in rain, so Jade was stuck. Going out alone in weather like this, her father, cleaning the kitchen all day, would ask why.

Danii and Brandon were at work. Warren was… wherever. Jade decided a bath might improve the long Saturday afternoon.

It did. Jade liked the big, warm bathroom, a shrine to her mother's mad mind. "The boys" shared one downstairs, here was for Jade and Danii only. A sunken, peach-hued, shell-shaped bath, three steps down into it, lay in the corner of two bronze-tinted mirror-walls with frosted outlines of huge swans. Across the apricot deep-pile carpet a doorless cupboard of neatly stacked, colour-coded clean towels stood beside a wall of shelves, each a cityscape of Danii's colognes, hairsprays, mousses, Guerlain soaps, sprays in deep red, gold, green or blue glass, 30 creams, bronzers, gels, incense burners, candles, jars, and make-up-stacked in blue and white china bowls.

Jade ran a bath, got in, switched the jacuzzi on and basked exhilarated, and amused as ever by the room around her. Brandon had not taken Jade's favourite red and blue beach-towel for once. Better still, Jade had lost three pounds since last Saturday. She reweighed herself twice. No error: three pounds.

A time later, she left the bathroom wrapped in a towel, humming a tune along the passage. Her bedroom door was open, overhead light on.

Jade walked in to see her father standing on a chair, looking up. His small hands prodded a damp corner of the ceiling.

"I'm just out the bath, dad," said Jade.

Apparently absorbed by the ceiling, Tyler spoke quietly: "Need to get out on the roof soon, check this." Jade caught a tang of alcohol.

Tyler stepped down from the chair, still looking up. He wore a T-shirt, but put his arm around Jade's bare shoulders, shook them affectionately. The arm remained.

"Seen the rain come through there?" he said: "That patch is a stain, see? Like a piss-stain, ha-ha!"

Jade tutted, tried to pull away, but his arm was firm on her shoulders. He finally looked at her: "Unless *you* pissed on it!? *Eh?*"

His eyes were bloodshot. He laughed without warmth, shook Jade's shoulders again. "Could you piss that far up if you lie on your back? Ha-*ha!*" His free hand pointed from bed to ceiling as he made a *pshhhhh!* noise. To Jade's relief his arm dropped. He moved to the door.

"Right," he said. "Better get downstairs – ah, one more thing. I wanted to ask you, er… need to ask something, nothing exactly, just I'm your *dad*, annnnd…"

He shut the door, stood head back, chin forward. He looked mad.

"Quick, just put dad's mind at rest," he commanded. "So's I know you've turned out well and right? That's what I'm asking."

Jade didn't know what he was asking. She looked at him quizzically, but his gaze moved. He stood strangely, an unfamiliar shape. Now he turned, mouth twisted, eyes square and glinting. He approached, mumbling fast:

"I'm a dad, *your* Dad, gotta see you're normal. You'll know what I mean when you have kids. I'm *respectable* about it! Parents now – they wait til the kid's asleep then pull the covers up. *I'm* not like that."

Jade backed away, tightening the towel round herself.

"Listen, Jadey?" his tone lightened, as if beginning a funny story. "A parent needs to know…"

His smile failed. An eyebrow rose freakishly and his nostrils flared. "Yeah? Get me?" he whined. "A parent needs to *know. I* need to know, granny needs to know, part of growing up, letting your dad know all's well."

His face froze, eyes wrong, like in a paused video. He breathed fast. "So! I'd like to see your upper half. Just quick. *C'mon* Jade," he glared, smiled, grinned, blurted: "I'm your *father*. Quick-show the upper half, please, *not* the lower, that bit's *your* business, I presume all's well down there. You *are* peeing, yeah? And the other, y'know, the monthly, I knows you have 'em now. Perfectly natural, hope they're not hard for yer. *I* just need see to the *top* half's OK?"

Jade stood, squinting. Was she meant to take her towel off? Was this what he was asking?

"C'mon Jade!" said her father, seeming to laugh. "I'm your *dad*. Just need to see your upper half? *Thaaat's it…* just drop the towel a bit."

The towel slipped to her waist in three soft falls. Air made her chest cold. Her father moved nearer, glanced to the door, then bent forward, face inches from her bosoms, mouth taut, open. Jade felt his breath on her chest, saw wet, pink, open lower lip and beige, incomplete teeth. His hand shot out, clasped and pressed her right breast for three seconds then vanished.

Tyler straightened up, stepped back, staring intensely at Jade's bare chest. Jade didn't see him. Her vision had shut down. Bad sensation spread like water where he'd touched. Something heavy dredged the base of her stomach.

"Good girl, proud of yer." The voice again, echoing as he vanished in the hall: "Come down when you're dressed? I'll make tea and toast."

Jade couldn't think or perceive anything. She slowly sat on the bed, felt her head crane up to look at the ceiling stain. She didn't like it. Something was trying to get in. Something wet was trying to get in.

A gnawing vibration in her tummy blocked a thought trying to form: *the ceiling leak means he'll come here again.*

MILLIE'S FEET WERE soaked in her trainers. The golf umbrella's blue and white canopy was all she saw. It often collided bendily with lampposts.

I can give him this umbrella back! thought Millie, not caring she'd be left rained-on. *I'll say: 'How about we go in town after you've finished, go Pizza Express?' Oh, I'm mad. I'm sad. But he DOES need this umbrella back on a day like this.*

At Homebase, Millie sheltered in a steamed-up Perspex trolley depot far out in the car-park. She wiped a pane clear to try spotting Marlon. He often helped shoppers take heavy orders to their cars. *There he is!*

As Millie struggled to re-open the umbrella, she noticed a tall, smartly-dressed white woman emerge from a sports car with its roof up. Uncaring of the rain, the woman hurried towards the store, almost at Marlon. In fact she *was* hurrying to him, a short leather coat draped over her arm.

In a moment that would haunt her forever, Millie saw Marlon's joy and surprise to see the woman, who was *nearly 40*, and who laughed, hugged him, kissed his mouth. The coat slipped, she grabbed it, gave it to Marlon – a brand new, hooded, leather, sports anorak. Marlon looked astonished.

The woman put her arms around him, untied his bright Homebase nylon waistcoat-vest, removed it, put the anorak on him. Marlon put the vest back on over it and pulled his hood up. Wet-through now, the woman kissed him, stroked his nose with a fingertip then ran to her car. Marlon smiled radiantly. The woman blew him a kiss, rotated like a dervish, arms out, laughing up at the rain. She climbed into her car and drove off, double-beeping the horn.

Millie walked away.

Chapter 11

ON SUNDAY DEWY worked alone at the office. She hoped Annette was resting, not working all day on the car. Annette had been unwell, dizzy and hot much of yesterday, feet swollen until bathed and softly rubbed by Dewy through the evening. Dewy woke several times in the night to find Annette hot and damp, watching phone-movies of Morris. At 4am Annette became hyperactive. Dewy woke to:

"Remember when BooBoo was confused by the new compost heap?"

"Uhhh?"

The screen was placed six inches before Dewy's face. Annette rested her cheek on Dewy's to watch the film with her: "I open the west kitchen door?"

Annette's on-film voice echoed: *Morris? Go get wet-nose, good boy!*

She kissed Dewy excitedly: "*There's BooBoo!* Out he goes!"

Filmed on a phone from the kitchen, Morris gambolled on a sunny lawn then paused to gaze on a recently-created compost heap in a far corner.

"Look, hon!" beamed Annette "Tilting his head as he stares at it!"

"Yuh. Mm...."

"Like: 'Where did *that* come from?!' Awww! Now he goes way over left, see? He starts doing poop-poops, but *still* looks over at the compost heap!"

Joanna Stephens's film voice blared: *Annette, have you nothing else to do?*

Now, six hours later, Dewy felt bleak and the office was haunted. She felt whatever presence was there might accept her if she constantly worked.

Joyous, elaborate St Botolph's bells rang and splashed late-morning. Dewy liked their sounds and felt revived. She began on Colin Hendry's piece about developments at Sherrier's Waterfall. A minute on, she rang Hendry:

"Why are there plans to wreck that beautiful place, Colin? Who the hell are 'Downfall Developments Ltd'? They really call themselves *that*? Are they aware what downfall means?"

"Miss Dewy, I'm making breakfast for my son, my daughter-in-law, and ~"

"Companies House lists Downfall Developments as a new branch of London company Tanjia-Mathies Investments. They describe themselves as 'Venture Environmentalists'. Their filed accounts of December totalled £94,860. *Today*, from somewhere they're being given £2.4 million for the Sherriers development. Drawn plans show three boxy houses and a 'Visitor & Conference Centre' with a wrap-around balcony, parking-lot and access road. Colin, why is this crap being built?"

"Well… what can we do?" sighed Hendry.

"Object to it!" said Dewy.

"We can't. It's a development, creates jobs ~"

"It's vandalism by bastards."

"Not our place to say, Miss Dewy. We report – plain and thorough, that's it."

"Should be the cover story though?"

"That's for Geoff to decide. Now, if you don't mind… See you at the meeting tomorrow."

Dewy locked up and left at 10pm, had a double gin and tonic in The Bear, where a pub quiz shielded her from notice. She had no other drinks and reached The

Lugworm at 11pm. Fent was locking lantern-lit outer doors.

"Good-night, sir," said Dewy, hurrying past. He didn't answer.

Annette was asleep, room in darkness. Dewy climbed into bed, held Annette's hand, stared at tiny, busy colours in the dark and dwelt on how, first time in years, she worked at a place of scheduled employment. *When do I get paid, and how much?* she thought. *Am I on this 'emergency tax', or paid cash? I oughta pay tax, Britain's half-beat. Didn't Tessa England ask: 'Working here?' Yes I am. So I oughtta pay tax to contribute to a country cut to bits by her Conservatives.*

Dewy guessed it was 4am. She looked at her phone: 01.12. *Why did I have that double grim-and-chronic in The Bear after no food all day? My body's confused, awake and wired with money worries.*

Dewy's last ATM visit showed £172 left of £2,280 three weeks before. Fent's rent and her London trip combined had cost £1,640. Next month's £800 to Fent was due in nine days. No one had discussed financing the Triumph Stag, its new parts and labour yet. How much would Sheekey's garage charge?

Dewy tried to be calm. She had money in the US. Not trusting herself with all the crowd-funding money, she'd put half in a 120-day account then instantly applied to withdraw it, predicting it would arrive when the first money ran low. She'd misjudged by 91 days.

She couldn't ask Annette for money and never had. Annette's money-awareness scarcely existed. Before Annette left for Britain last year, Dewy helped arrange the transfer of Annette's monthly trust fund to the Stephens's housekeepers to look after Morris. His organic poultry and fresh fish deliveries averaged $160 a week. Organic grains, biscuits, rice, pastry, vegetables, artisan treats, chews, supplements, vitamins, glass-bottled mineral water and two new toys all averaged $190 a week, plus his monthly vet check-up and claw-clip, dental check, tooth-clean and specialist shampoo. A dog counsellor visited weekly to spend an hour with him in the gardens. Annette also paid the Hernandez's $300 a week to walk Morris, cook for him and have him live in their cottage. $42 a week remained for herself.

"Dare I ask Mrs Halaton for help again?" murmured Dewy wretchedly. "No. That would be *so wrong*. I didn't thank her last time, never answered her e-mail. Then I blanked her in Boston – though she saw I was drunk with Laura Sturgis. To ask Mrs Halaton for money now would be despicable. I can't and won't do it. A definite no."

Minutes later:

Dear Elspeth,

Predictably turmoil'd. If only you and I could meet right now – honey vodkas at sunset from your big bed, I'd like that so much again. But tell me about you?

"Oh, you sly whore, Durant!" muttered Dewy, deleting all. She tried:

Dearest Elspeth, I'm broke and need help. I think fondly of you regardless if you help or not. 'Miss D'

Finally:

Dear Mrs Halaton,

I'm in Britain and need help. Sorry to approach you, Elspeth, I've no one else to turn to.

Dewy

Chapter 12

CRENDLESHAM ROYAL INFIRMARY'S Hazel Centre had two locked wards and an outpatient programme. Father Entreton climbed stairs to the wards, as every Monday since the centre opened in 1976. Much of his private prayer was dedicated to the mentally ill. The only pastoral care he could offer, that he felt might help patients, was to listen.

He greeted a new security guard in a neon lemon jacket. The guard lazily said nothing. The priest walked to reception. The desk was unstaffed, usual for busy times. Father Entreton could wander into the wards, but always felt he should check-in first, say hello to staff, hear updates on patients.

"Scuse me?" said a hard voice behind him. Father Entreton turned. The security guard's blazing jacket was a foot away. "D'you mind telling me what you're doing here?"

"Visiting, sir."

The guard moved nearer: "You'll need to *check in* then."

"I'm doing that now, sir," said Father Entreton gently. "Waiting for someone to come."

The man stared at Father Entreton's eyes, then swaggered off to lean back against the wall, staring down the opposite stairs, arms folded.

Resentment was alien to Father Entreton, but he couldn't shake off unease at the man's manner. He remembered certain brutal Christian Brothers in his childhood, who specialised in making harmless boys afraid. He'd stood up to one verbally at age nine and received a beating with a strap. The lesson he'd decided to learn from it was: forgiveness can take a long time, true forgiveness far longer, but it will come.

After some minutes, Father Entreton rested his weight on the counter, lost in thought, "my favourite clouds". A ward-door flung open and a dishevelled man in a dressing gown and old shoes, stomped up the corridor: "I'm fit to go! I'm Billy Nevin!" The man's glazed eyes met Father Entreton's. He approached, screaming:

"Who's letting paedo *filth* like youse in here! *Fucked any kids today*!!"

Father Entreton backed away in terror. He glanced round for the security guard. The guard had gone. Breathing hard, Father Entreton retreated along the corridor.

"This ain't the kids' ward!" bawled the man. "That what ye're looking for?"

Father Entreton felt disembodied. He saw a shape in a flapping dressing-gown, heard his own voice say: "You have hurt me, sir."

He tried to keep walking. The man yelled more profanities.

"I am old, sir," said Father Entreton, struggling to walk, a sob escaping him. His arm hurt, his breathing worsened. A low table lay ahead. Father Entreton shuffled there and collapsed onto it, dizzy. Covering his mouth with a shaking fist, he dared look left. The figure had stomped off far, ranting.

"Jesus, break his fall," prayed Father Entreton. "Lord Jesus, break that poor man's fall."

MARLON DID 150 press-ups in lots of 50 then lay on his bed watching a recent Aston Villa v Liverpool match on his laptop. For the first ever time, close-ups of players walking when the ball was out of play absorbed him, epecially if the player was tall, young, black and…

Marlon sprang up to look in the mirror again. *Am I handsome?*

"I just look like *me*," he said, downhearted. He returned to the game. In a long pause before a goal kick, a midfielder walked back to his own half, unaware he was in close-up. Though he winced, sweated and spat, he was good-looking, straight-backed, dignified. Marlon went to the mirror again. *Do I look like him? Could I?*

He reread Saturday night's text:

Hi Marlon, I'm in my little house doing my little things. I look out the window i see the rain I wish I was with you now. Maybe I'm a little broody to-night? Rain has that affect on me. ANYHOW – Dubai on Friday! Sunshine, shopping, us four loose women (not really! except Liu but she scares men off!) Im gonna buy you somehtng in Dubai, u'll look great. You are lovely & special. Dont forget keep Thurs night free xxxx Do you like yr new coat?

Marlon put the coat on again. It looked and felt superb, bestowed power. He sat on the bed, smiling. *Yeah, I look all right. A very beautiful kind lady seems to think so anyway! It's nice to be fancied. It's AMAZING to be wanted like this! First time ever.*

11AM, TWO MILES away, satellite-channel football boomed through the Zena household. Bobby had found an Uzbekestani live match to drink Red Stripe at.

Millie lay on her bed. She'd cried all night.

Her phone pinged a text. At least her mother was replying. But the dialogue wasn't good.

Is there really noweere else u cn go mil? why not tlk to dad + say u need a place of ur own. Ask him2 help with deposit. we havent room. u cn stay a week at most but alan wont b happy and nor me.

Millie began to cry again. She texted:

PLease dont turn me away mum. i need out. its all too much

AFTER QUIETLY WORKING for hours, Dewy was maybe forgiven, and forgiving, about the meeting earlier.

She'd asked for the Sherrier's Waterfall story to be front cover, plus a half-page survey of people in Bridge Street, asking what they thought of the favourite local spot being developed.

"Front cover?" said Carruthers. "No."

"The only way *that's* fair is, if the Matthew Willis inquest update goes front page instead," said Dewy.

"Miss Dewy, you are *not* the editor of this paper," said Carruthers to a bellowing cheer and laughter from nearly all the men.

Emboldened, Michael Fenwick complained last week's decision not to run the piece on the "wrong skirt" schoolgirl, was: "because of *her* there, making a stupid fuss, saying she'd quit if the article went in!"

Carruthers replied *he* had made the final decision not to run that piece. Fenwick countered: "Yeah, because *she* was saying 'It's wrong for the girl's life' or whatever."

"You think it's *right* a girl be humiliated in her hometown paper?" snapped Dewy.

"Oh, we've to be all *PC* and worthy, *yeahh*!" sneered Fenwick, to laughter. He and others demanded Carruthers clarify Dewy had no power to block or approve content.

Now, late morning, as Dewy worked, she became convinced new articles were hoaxes by the men to provoke her. The first was about fracking in Fetton Vale, the second a pointless shopping development.

"Fellas? Can I ask something?" she called. "Has someone made these up to make me explode, so you can all laugh?"

She described the imminent £2.8 million renovation of a shopping street in Crendlesham – Green Walk – soon to be renamed 1 Crendlesham. Holding up a computer image of 1 Crendlesham, she read from a press release: "'To re-clad the outside of shop units, remove low-level canopies, replace with a glazed cover, repave the Walk from Hill Chase Street to Horsefair.'"

"It's real, yes. I didn't invent it!" said Ryan Palmer. "What's the problem?"

"Green Walk's fine as it is!" said Dewy. "Britain's *obsessed* with repaving things that don't need repaving, or 'improving' things perfectly OK. Some tiny company homes in on a place, cooks up a 'need' for improvement, pretends expertise to get government money. They use a fraction of it to pay hi-vis psychotics to build soulless trash, then vanish. Half the country needs tax credits to make wages," Dewy held up the artist's impression: "But plenty money for *re-cladding!*"

"Oh, *look here!*" groaned Stuart Dean. "This… *woman!* She's… she's hardly *not capable this paper* is about, er… nothing that's *herself*, her opinions and that!"

Dewy held up the press release for the Fetton Vale fracking proposal. Some of the men didn't like shale-gas drilling either. They paid attention now.

"Yeah, that's real," said Colin Hendry, who'd written the article.

"Colin, it's Sherriers 2, with names changed!" said Dewy.

"It ain't. This is fracking, totally different."

"I checked Companies House. Marlag Ltd, assets 170 grand, description 'Petroleum Prospectors'. Formed 2017, three staff, London-based. Search engines bring up *nothing*, so they've never done anything. Fetton Vale's their first gig, they've received £12 million 'operating costs' upfront. A local councillor here – Cara Hanson – says Marlag's failed to provide a 3D seismic survey of the site, *or* a Health & Safety management plan. *They haven't surveyed the explosive gas site they're about to drill into!"*

The men tutted, shrugged, continued working. Dewy called to Hendry: "This fracking project it's been *approved*? Eight votes to three by councillors?"

"They want another vote," said Hendry. "But it'll get approved again."

"Without a legally-needed survey or safety plan? We'll see about *that!"*

"No 'we' *won't*, Miss Dewy!" said Geoff Carruthers from his office doorway. Stuart Dean, Fenwick and several others repeated the cheer and mockery of earlier. "Do your job please, as required." said Carruthers. "Leave your politics at the door like the rest of us. And when's your interview with Tessa Eng?"

"Thursday 3pm," snapped Dewy.

She silently worked on, enraged, but not at Carruthers, or the men. UK news that week featured a government ferry contract given to a three-man company with no ferries or experience. Similarly, here, shale gas-drilling, volatile with unknown effects, was being entrusted to novices disregarding safety.

"Things like this are happening all over, through lack of opposition," Dewy muttered. She stared out at Bridge Street recalling lines from "Jane Eyre" learned by heart as a child. "*If people were always kind and obedient to those who are cruel and unjust, the wicked people would have it all their own way: they would never feel afraid, and so they would never alter, but grow worse and worse.*"

"Resist. Resist!" thought Dewy. "But *how*? How to resist this fracking?" She sighed: "There must *always* be resistance to bullying and evil. If it's not apparent, think,

think, think, there's *always* a way. Don't stop thinking til you've found it."

The Sherrier's piece was ready to be sent to Geoff's 'Final' file. Suddenly Dewy stretched space at the end of the last paragraph and wrote in small script: *There will be a public meeting to discuss this issue at Farrisford Town Hall, Tuesday May 31st at 7pm.*

"Christ, I hope Geoff or Colin don't question that," Dewy whispered to herself. "And how will I arrange this meeting? Is the Town Hall even open at that time? I'll cross these bridges… er…"

Bolder still, Dewy planned a public meeting about the fracking scandal too. Next week she'd write a letter to the paper as a Miss Price, who, disgusted to read this week's shale drilling piece, would add: *A public meeting about Fetton Vale fracking is on Tuesday June 7th at 7pm, Farrisford Town Hall.*

All I do then… thought Dewy *…is e-mail the letter to Cara Hanson, asking her and her fighters to come speak at that meeting.*

DANII'S ABSENCES ON weekday evenings were intolerable to Jade now. She texted her mother a third time: **Not heard back frm you. What time u home?**

Jade wouldn't go to her room or upstairs until Danii returned. She hadn't changed out of her uniform. Her schoolbag lay in the cloakroom by the back door. She decided, unusually, to do homework in the sitting room, where Warren and a timid friend Anton came and went, no risk of being alone with her father.

Jade didn't consciously decide these things. She hadn't thought about the incident with her father in her bedroom, only dimly registered she'd not liked it. Dave Tyler had said he was being normal, so he was. One of those things, like cod liver oil – horrible but nothing to think deeply about, just… …*normal.*

Jade had a sudden memory, Dave Tyler summoning her ("Come here. Oi!") from a garden paddling-pool when she was 10. He'd risen slightly from his sun lounger, gazed at her bare chest left and right, pulled a funny face, softly pressed one of her nipples with a curved, stubby thumb and said: "What's going on here then? Still looking like a boy?"

He'd laughed, repeated the question, moved his face around her averted gaze until eye contact. Jade tried to smile back, as her father must have said something funny. Grown-ups laughed at things that made no sense, but Jade wanted to seem grown-up when possible, so she smiled. Haplessly she turned, walked off, hoping she'd not get into trouble for walking away. But no "Hey! I'm talking to you!" was heard. Or maybe it was. The memory ended at walking away.

Warren and Anton played a violent computer game on surround-sound on the TV far-end of the sitting room. Then came words Jade had waited for, her father: "Gotta pick Brandon up. Jadey? I timed that oven to go off in in 40 minutes, check it does, yeah?"

Jade breathed now her father was leaving. She still didn't go upstairs.

Hours on, dinner over, Jade returned to the sitting room far table, trying to do maths homework. Brandon, Warren and her father basked like reptiles around the television. Dave's stumpy feet in baby-blue, stained socklets rested on a tan leather pouffe. Brandon and Warren sprawled on the huge, L-shaped sofa. On the six-foot TV, a police car, filmed from the back seat, accelerated, siren whooping, urgent radio contact: *Suspect heading into Lisson Street, pursuing, over.*

"Proper chase now!" roared Warren. "Get the scumbags!"

"Traffic police'll handle this well properly," said Brandon. "They're on it."

A sonorous man's voice gave pious commentary: **But**

the youths in the stolen car realise there is *NO CHANCE.*

"Aww!" yelled Warren. "Giving themselves up! Fuckin' let-downs."

Jade texted: **Mum?**

No reply came.

Jade checked her phone every minute to see if Danii replied, then couldn't bear checking any more. As the Tyler men roared at another real car-chase, Jade quietly left the room. She locked herself in the downstairs wc, sobbing for no reason she could think of.

LACK OF FOOTBALL was felt most on Tuesdays. Last year Marlon would psyche himself up all day – would *tonight* be the night he'd be promoted to the first team?

But on this Tuesday his yearning to play again was swept away by last night's dream. A smile crossed his face as he walked along Homebase aisle two – *it was no dream.*

They'd walked hand in hand on the beach at sunset, stopped to kiss every minute. They'd shared fish and chips in a cliff-top shelter, watched the moon above the sea, its bright path across the water towards them. They drove through a starry night, stopping by a remote gate. As Marlon pointed out constellations, Danii took him in her arms, kissed him unstoppably, opened the gate, tugged him into the field, flung her coat off, knelt, unzipped Marlon...

"... *three for two?* Hello? I'm *TALKING* to you!" A thin-nosed man in taupe anorak and cap snarled up at him.

"Sorry?" said Marlon.

"I *SAID*: these pot plants, three for two on offer? Only two left of this kind!?"

"*He* don't understand, Jim," said a huge, red-viscosed wife: "C'mon, ask someone else."

"Nahh, let *him* do it," frowned the white-pink man.

"Big and ugly enough."

His wife pulled him away: "You know what *they're* like. 'I'll find you one', then he won't come back."

Marlon stood still a minute. Sometimes it felt any moment of happiness, cherished thinking, *purity* he'd ever had was wrecked by sudden racism and inhumanity. He closed his eyes, opened them, went out to the car-park. How ineffectual the words *Let it go…* sometimes were.

But then Marlon thought of Danii, and that couple in aisle two passed forever.

He remembered today's "Wikipedia rabbit-hole". Reading about Mahatma Gandhi led to reading about Nelson Mandela, then Dr Martin Luther King, the NAACP in the US, then a writer called Dorothy Parker, a white woman, who'd left all her money to the National Association for the Advancement of Colored People. "That's brilliant," thought Marlon. Wikipedia listed her famous quotations. Some of these didn't seem to make much sense – maybe because they were from a different era. But one remained with Marlon: *The best revenge is to live well.*

Yes… the past year's struggles: these youths, the police warning him never to retaliate or the youths would claim he'd attacked *them*. Books on anger management. The self-harming, the anger, the weeping, the violence always in him. The flashbacks, fantasies of punching the youths. *Let it go…*

When I'm with Danii I am living well. The best revenge.

AFTER CRYING ON the shoulder of fellow Yorkshireman Jonty at the Bibby, John Talbot heard his advice. "I'm guessing David's had a breakdown," said Jonty. "That's why he's not come back or contacted. He's coccooned at his mother's. Go and see him. He wants you, but too ashamed of the state he's in to reach out."

On Wednesday morning at dawn, John put gifts for David on the car's back seat and headed for Kent. He pulled up at noon outside a holly-hedged, mock Tudor 1930s house set back from the road.

"Oh. It's *you*," said Flora Bennett 10 seconds after opening the door. A slight, forced smile raised one side of her mouth. "Better come in."

John entered, with flowers: "Looking well, Mrs Bennett."

"I'm not at my best."

"I like your blue velour pants suit."

"*Leisure* suit. Prefer dresses, but I feel the cold now. David's in bed. He's eating. Are these for him? You don't buy him *flowers*, do you?"

"For *you*, ma'am," said John with a slight bow.

"Oh." She sighed. "S'pose I'll have to find something to put them in. You shouldn't have." She took the bouquet and walked to the kitchen to fuss in cupboards. "David wasted money on flowers Saturday," she called, "From a railway station, I could tell. I didn't bother with them."

John hadn't seen Flora for six years. She was nearer to frail, faintly limped, but the big frame and block of head David inherited were unchanged.

The house was always smaller than expected. Like millions identical – John and David's too – the front door faced stairs in a narrow hall that extended on to the kitchen, with front and back rooms on the right. In this house, the front room was forbidden, door closed, the back sitting-room's one always open. John stood by it, remembering tension if anyone entered unbidden. Mrs Bennett reappeared, eyes bulging. "Go in!" she barked, "Sit down."

John sat in a '50s chair the size of a dodgem car. The room had barely changed, wine-red carpet, a bare, too-near dividing wall, which, if demolished, (like at John and David's), would make a large, bright union with the front room, banishing gloom from both.

John surveyed the mantelpiece ornaments, new ones a small, glass clown and an eight-inch owl from the Franklin Mint.

Flora's chair, four feet from a heavy television, was besieged by lilac tissues, local papers and parts of the Mail On Sunday. The room smelt of gas-fire and sandwiches. Snooker played on TV with the sound off.

John noticed no photograph David sent of the two of them had ever made it to the family pictures. These were arrayed each side of a green onyx clock on the mantelpiece. The largest – a 1950 black and white portrait of a thin-moustache'd young man, fear in one eye, friendliness the other – was the draughtsman Eamon Bennett, David's father, who'd died aged 78, in this room. David never discussed him. John gathered over time David's silence about his father came not from unresolved issues or dark secrets, but lack of interest.

Another object of David's indifference – his older sister Lorraine – filled most other pictures. A gold-framed group picture showed her 1989 wedding in Sydney to Andy Hannox, who wasn't Australian either. "I never want to think about that man again," was all David once said about the burly, pastel-suited madman in the photo who – hair vast and broad from the rear of his head – resembled the Sphinx.

Flora Bennett appeared. Her broad face and well-kept, up-swept blonde mane made John think how Jean Harlow might have looked had she lived long.

"You'll take a tea," she stated.

"Oh, yes, that'd be great, thank~"

A wide tray was brought in and clunked onto a coffee table. Three cups on the tray. John tried: "Shall I take a cup up to ~"

"No."

This confirmed his fear he'd be prevented from seeing David.

In silence Mrs Bennett stooped over the teapot, opening it, stirring it, closing it, opening it, peering into it, stirring it, closing it, frowning, opening it, stirring it. She seemed to doubt what teapots do. At last she poured, put a cup on a saucer and left: "He's already got biscuits."

John sat enraged. As calmly as able he called after her: "Can you let David know I'm here?" It came out deeper and louder than intended. Flora Bennett did not reply.

John paced the room, trying to tell himself anger was a physical health problem in its own right, that he should breathe deeply, try to perceive how he might be appearing to others, do nothing sudden. *Breathe in…*

But Jonty's voice cut in from last night: "Don't take crap off his mother. Seems her life's work to screw people up, and she hasn't retired."

John marched from the house, leaving door ajar. He got David's presents from the car: sketch pads, dark mint-chocolate and a rosewood box of 100 paint tubes, slammed the car door, returned to the house, walking in as Flora approached.

"You went out," she said.

"Giving these pressies to David," called John as he ran upstairs. Mrs Bennett emitted a cry like a seal.

John tapped on David's half-open bedroom door. "It's me, love."

He entered the room.

A bulky man with tousled hair sat cross-legged on the floor in pyjamas reading a Noddy book.

A high whirring growl agitated past John's foot, a model train with carriages, fast on a circuit of rails around the edges of the room.

"D-David?" said John.

Slowly the unshaven man looked up, eyes glazed, tomato soup-stained stubble. His mouth fell open. He looked at John in utter confusion.

"Daddy?" said David.

"Geoff, I'm broke."

"Can we talk about this later? I'm~"

Dewy marched into the editor's office: "I've rent and a car to pay. This is my third week, 10 hours a day plus research and print-night. You've ~"

"Calm down, take a seat."

Dewy did neither.

"Everyone works a month in hand," Carruthers began: "What you earn ~"

"Which is *what*?" said Dewy "I work 53, call it a 50 hour week. What rate?"

"Er…"

"What's union rate?"

"I wouldn't know. You'll have to ~"

"I will," said Dewy, leaving. "Gimme two minutes."

Re-entering the main office, she sensed something. Michael Fenwick's face was bulbous with kept-in laughter, Stuart Dean studiedly looked away, biting his lip. Others too-obviously averted their gaze from her. Dewy walked to her desk, looking down to ensure no drawing-pin was placed for her to step on.

Her computer screen had gone dark. She shook the mouse, screamed and jumped back in a spasm, hands by head. The office roared with mirth.

"*Bastards!*" she cried. "Oh!"

Someone had magnified a Matt Clissenden photo so only his teeth filled the screen. Dewy might have let this go if her screen hadn't gone dark. But it *had* gone dark and the sudden, grotesque picture shocked her.

Later she'd realise, shame at having screamed, plus anger at being made to scream, were what provoked her to violence.

Where was Marlon now? Homebase? Home? Or with *her*? Millie got up from the furthest bench on the wide green before St Botolph's and drifted to the arch into

Town Hall Square. She'd never felt so unhappy, or in this particular way. She remembered nothing of her life after the car-park incident. She couldn't even remember if she'd been to the JobCentre today, the vague purpose of a walk into town two hours ago.

She left Town Hall Square by Windmill Lane, up towards the cobbled, gently sloping square, with a clock-tower, between Groats and High Street. Millie was too preoccupied to see a colony of youths in grey hoodies around the bench before Willow's bakery.

A wolf-whistle jolted her. She looked round, confused.

"Where's lover-boy then?" jeered Carl Hughes.

"He's smokin a spleef, mahhn," said Tyson Bradley. Two youths and a girlfriend clacked with laughter. Millie walked on, scarcely taking this in.

"Oi, girlie! I asked a question! Where's your boyf?" shouted Hughes.

"Talkin' to me?" said Millie, stopping.

"Who's your boyfriend get his weed from?"

"Boyfriend?" said Millie.

A youth next to Tyson Bradley now turned. The one who'd threatened John Wright. Millie froze.

"Ex-boyfriend, innut?" grinned the youth. "Prefers white pussy I hear?"

Millie approached The Bone (as Darren Tibley pre-ferred to be known) with such strange and determined rage, his face dropped. He backed off, pretending to laugh. Millie noticed Stephen Vanders.

"*You*," she said. "What you *doing*, Stephen? What you doing with them *cowards*? Are *you* one as well? Scaring old men on their own? Is that how you want to be, Stephen? *Is* it?"

Millie's voice rose. Pigeons by the tower burst into flight.

"Is that what you want to be?" she bellowed. "Like *these fucking COWARDS*!"

"Yahh," crowed Darren Tibley – The Bone – drifting

away. Bradley followed, body language *let's go, we've stuff to do.* All got up and left.

"*Cowards!*" roared Millie.

"Least we're white," said a girl quietly.

Millie picked up a half-eaten egg sandwich on a bench. She charged at the girl and rammed it in her face: "You're *BRIGHT YELLOW now!* Inside *and* out!"

"Get her off!" shrieked the girl. "HELP!"

"*They* won't help you, they're *scared.*" said Millie, shoving the girl.

The whole concourse watched. Faces crammed windows of Willow's, Bennett's dry cleaners, the toy-shop, a Good Queen Bess back window.

The gang kept walking, straining to seem casual. As Millie followed, they walked faster. "I know you *all,*" she screamed: "I'll have you *fuckin' dealt with!*"

None turned or spoke. They walked quickly and didn't stop.

ALONG FARR'S LANE, Dewy recovered herself. *Do not drink, do not drink… do not go to the Fusilier…*

Last-ditch alcohol-prevention kicked in: seek immediate food, Coca-Cola and a bottle of fizzy water. If all are gulped within minutes, alcohol craving diverts. *French fries. Known here as chips. UK chips from a fish'n'chip shop. With those weird peas they have, like green lava.* "Oh, hi, Millie!"

Millie looked up. "Oh… y'all right?"

"What's up, hon? Wanna come get some chips? I need them, like, *now*?"

They sat on a bench eating chips from Almighty Cod. Neither spoke much. Millie felt uneasy if a passer-by noticed Dewy's bare feet and stared furiously. Dewy, years accustomed, was oblivious.

Also, Millie felt ashamed to think it, and told herself

she wasn't *really* thinking it… But… this was *weird* because…

…*because… she's "the other way". A "lezzer". And older. And American. I like her though. I don't think she's after me. But I'll have to be politely clear… I'm not gay, I'm not that kind of ~ actually, no, I'll not say anything. Not a thing.*

"Want some alleged peas?" said Dewy, offering a Styrofoam tub.

"Listen, I don't like women, in a sexual way? Do you understand?"

"Uh?… Sure. So what?"

"Sorry," said Millie. "That was rude of me. I'm shit. I can't communicate."

"You're not shit. Never think that. I don't care if you're not gay, be as you are, that's the point."

"I've no problem with gays. I've just not met many. You and Annette are lovely. She's *ever* so nice.

"Aw, I'm glad. It makes me happy when people like Annette."

"Then Beverley and the Scottish girl? It's like 'Wow! All these lezzers!' Sorry, is that the wrong word? Why you laughing?"

"Atrocious word."

"Wha's it I'm meant to say then? It fucks me off how like, the world's like: 'you can't say this, can't say that'. Most people aren't intelligent like you, we didn't get chances. Tell us which words you *want*, we'll try say 'em, but don't treat us like we're shit. We don't *mean* harm, I don't think people *mean* bad." She reflected a moment. "*Most* people anyway."

"Oh, Millie."

"I'm in a fucked-up place. My… ah, it doesn't matter. Sorry I said 'lezzer.'"

"I don't mind what *you* say, Millie. Your heart is good and you're brave. But evil words in cowards' mouths spur them on to worse things."

Millie laughed bitterly: "Ha! I know all about *that*."

Dewy *tsch!*'d open her Coke can and glugged enormously, head back. Millie turned to look, aghast at a flawless, lily neck guzzling like a pump. Dewy flung her head upright, wiped her mouth, then: ***Burrrp!***

"Fuck!" said Millie. "My old man don't belch like that. And that's really saying something."

Dewy looked at her phone. 1 New Message G. Carruthers She fell into reflection.

The flimsy folding-chair she'd thrown had crashed onto Michael Fenwick's desk and broken in two. Coffee, papers, pens and a lap-top went all over him. Dewy shoved his desk over, Fenwick falling under. She'd picked up one of the chair halves and began beating him – width of the chair, not side-on, not dangerously. He'd crawled out from the mess, leapt straight into Stuart Dean, who fell across a desk. Dewy pursued Fenwick taking swipes with the chair. His mouth bled, he cried: "Enough! Please! *Please*?!". Geoff Carruthers grabbed the chair-half from Dewy. Stuart Dean attempted to march her to the door. Dewy seized his wrist and twisted hard. He screamed in pain. The door was near. Dewy left.

She took a deep breath and opened the text:

After u interview T. England as arranged, regret to say your services no longer reqrd. Trowel fell from yr pocket during incident. If want us forward it send address. G. Carruthers

Dewy and Millie sat in separate silences. Breeze fluttered their chip-shop wrappings at the top of the nearest bin. Millie sometimes stamped a foot to shoo two pigeons away.

Dewy absently looked to Millie, glad she was there. To be alone now would be unbearable. She must interview Tessa England at 3pm. Thanks to Millie, she now would. Alone, she'd have gone to The Fusilier.

Millie, meanwhile, looked ahead, unblinking. *Marlon doesn't want me. He never will. I am a poison to him.* Wearily she clunked a foot near the pair of pigeons again. One spruffled into a four-inch flight of retreat, the other walked.

"Is that an i-Phone?" said Dewy.

"Hm? Yeah. Wanna buy it?"

"I'm broke, hon."

"Gotta sell it," sighed Millie, running her hands through her curls to spread them. "Need money to go my mum's."

"What you doing this afternoon? Got school?"

"School? I'm old.

"I meant, like, college?"

Millie giggled. "That was *so* American! '*Like, cahllege*?'"

"I don't speak like *that*, biddy hoodsie!"

"*Cahhlege!*"

"Listen, come take pictures of your MP, on your phone, for the newspaper?"

"Eh??"

"SORRY WE'RE LATE, Mrs England ~"

"Tessa!" said the MP. "We've 12 minutes." She peered past Dewy and blared "Hello?" to Millie.

"A'right?" said Millie, nervous. She'd bumped against stacked wallet files, scrabbled to stop their avalanche.

"Millie Zena, photographer," said Dewy.

Sun made a four-pane skylight's shadow stark on a whitewashed wall. Tessa England stood as she usually did, hand on hip, faint frown. She faced Dewy: "Well? Get on with it."

10 minutes later:

"... Brexit probably *will* be a shambles. Impoverish the country, increase unemployment, weaken the pound, see falling investment, thousands of tiny changes, many large ones. We currently have free, easy European trade.

Spanish leather, Swedish furniture, Greek olives, you name it – in it comes, transport costs only, everyone happy. Only a destructive fool or a lunatic would change that. I tried and tried to say this pre-referendum… you know the rest."

"I do," said Dewy. "Rich, white men from your party lied to the country, then ran away, leaving Selena May ~"

"*Theresa* May!" barked Tessa England.

Dewy continued: "Who's now resigning, leaving the Prime Minister role open for any of those smug, male, right-wing, time-travellers from 1950."

"No comment. Rashid's picking me up in one minute, you need a photo. Ready, Millie? How do you want it?"

"Um…" Millie turned in panic to Dewy, who smiled, held up crossed-fingers like a parent urging *go on!*

"Maybe n-near the white wall here?" gulped Millie.

"Yup!" said Tessa England.

"Taxi!" Helena called up the stairs.

Millie took photos. Dewy bought time, asking:

"But your Remain voters? Don't they feel let-down by you?"

"They know me," said Tessa England. "They know what I do. Constituency MP first and foremost."

"Mr Clissenden says his Labour party will try to stop Britain leaving Europe?"

"Some of his party. There's nothing *they* can do. It's done. We're stuck."

Tessa England turned round at Millie's request for a side shot and fell into thought: "I *do* wish our exit from Europe wasn't happening," she sighed: "It's like dragging a fishing-net over rocks. Snag after snag. I hope I'm wrong about… about what I think Brexit will realistically be."

THE MILL HOTEL near Crendlesham overlooked a sky-reflecting lake then woods. Sunset drinks were served on a terrace. A velvet-gowned woman played a harp.

"That shirt's *so* you, Marlon!" said Danii. "I'm bringing you more stuff from Dubai what'll make you look a million dollars."

Danii wondered about the cocktail. It was strong. She felt floatiness and acceleration.

"Isn't this place beautiful here, Marlon?"

"Yeah. Built 1680, says out front."

A maitre d' led them to the upper terrace. The table had far views. They ate lobster thermidor, beef wellington with asparagus and creamed potatoes, chocolate ice cream with cherry compote, then coffee, no brandy, for the half carafe of red wine after cocktails was all they could take.

Unease about over-drinking was one subject they discussed with meaning. Danii told of passing out at weddings and Ascot. She slipped her shoes off to hug her feet around Marlon's new, suede Guccis as she listed drinks she'd never have again, each with a story attached.

Danii was going to Dubai next day with Liu, Stephanie and two others from work. She smiled at Marlon adoringly, a look both thrilled and serene. Marlon gazed back. He found her very, very attractive. Her attention and fondness made him glow inside. Yet sometimes his mind flashed a horrible, intrusive trick: *she doesn't say much.* Not compared to Eleanor Wright, nor Jocelyn – the vast, benign, chain-smoking key-worker in Bristol years ago – nor Farley Wood art teacher Mrs Storer. No other women had ever had time for him except these three, he reflected. Danii was the fourth.

But he knew little about her. *She's married, got kids* was the fact Marlon and Danii mustn't say. Their bond relied on ignoring that truth.

"Old enough to leave home, nearly," was all she'd said about her children. *What if that's not true?* thought Marlon. *What if they're young and want their mum?*

Suspecting Danii a liar troubled Marlon's conscience. She was so kind to him, boosted his confidence and… that night when she'd stopped the car... *that felt incredible...* her smooth hands rubbing him everywhere, kisses to the side of his face, the *sound* of her kisses, her perfume *ah....*

Sunset colours deepened. Danii's red cardigan glowed. Her eyes shone. She and Marlon leaned to kiss.

"Come on then," she whispered, gathering purse and cigarettes.

"Oh. OK." murmured Marlon, trying not to sound sad. He'd have loved to stay in the moment longer. "Got to get back, yeah?"

"No," smiled Danii, taking his hand. She gestured at the glowing, quietly bustling hotel. "We've got a room."

DEWY LAY AWAKE, reliving Tattler incident, Tessa England interview then Millie sobbing on her shoulder at Cressy Road Bridge. She'd said her heart was broken by a boy, how she'd no hope of a real job, and couldn't bear empty days at her father's any more, no day different.

Dewy had written up the interview within an hour, emailed it with Millie's best photos to Carruthers. After agonising what to write personally to Carruthers, she decided: Geoff, here's the interview, photos by MILLIE ZENA. Can she be credited please?

Dewy worried how she'd look after Annette and the baby. She must find a job immediately.

Annette kissed her awake next day: "8am, bae. You look *beautiful*, so sleepy!"

"I'll go to work late," drowsed Dewy. She hadn't told Annette about yesterday. Annette left to work on the Triumph Stag, Dewy lay worrying about money.

She totted up her hours at the Tattler. A website confirmed union rate £15.10 an hour. She was owed £3,020.

Dewy emailed an invoice, hoping Carruthers would forward it to the parent company. She wondered if the parent company was reliable, and felt the "uh-oh" every freelancer knows.

She Googled 'employment agency Crendlesham'. Three came up, one on Pottergate.

In Crendlesham's central streets, estate agent windows showed cottages with gardens, £700 a month. One with a swimming pool was £780. Rather than angry at being very overcharged by Fent, Dewy felt optimistic she and Annette would have their own house soon.

tHE gIG eMPLoYMENT aGEnCY was up narrow stairs to an office over a dry-cleaners. To Dewy's relief, the two staff – Karen and a nervous girl, Caz in thick glasses and long floral dress with buttoned collar – were insane. Caz stood before Dewy, talking unstoppably in high notes. She had bad teeth and unsaveable hair. Dewy felt a surge of love for her. She registered with the agency, but the only jobs were night-carer, or door-to-door sales as a charity fundraiser, commission only: "No, we don't know what the product sold is. They tell us on the day. It was cat food last month."

Near Crendlesham bus station Dewy passed a newsagent. She'd forgotten the Tattler was today. She rushed in to buy it. The bypass was front-page again, no "see inside" of a Tessa England interview. Had they run it?

They hadn't. A final indignity. Page 18, 24, nothing…

Dewy sat on the edge of a stone trough of summer flowers, opening pages so fast they tore.

"*Yess!!*"

The interview took up page 40, Millie's black and white photo filling two-fifths and stunning: the MP's profile bright amid sloping shadows of the four-pane skylight on the white wall. The picture captured her reality. Under one corner: Photo: Millie Zena. "Geoff, you're not all bad," sighed Dewy. She winced at headline **This Is England** and skimmed:

She says an election's "inevitable", some Labour MPs are "good sorts" and she'll do as Brexit insists, but loathes it. And the bypass, Tessa?

"Oh *no*," she groans. "Must we?"

"Of course!" I reply.

She looks annoyed. Tessa England annoyed is not an easy experience. I worry she'll clam up, give stock answers, even cancel the interview.

"Are you going to be grumpy and cold?" I say. She smiles, slightly. "Well, I can be, but, no, let's have a decent interview. If I'm stitched up, so be it. A free press is more important."

Dr Tessa England MP is 68. She spent 12 years of her childhood in Farrisford, attending Sir John Wyce ("Happiest school memories probably") then boarding school in Somerset. For 22 years she's lived in Pegasus Lane.

Dewy never liked reading her own articles and skipped to the end. A last paragraph she'd been proud of was cut altogether. Instead:

I tell her she's at least respected for accepting Brexit. Tessa sighs: "I'm past caring what anyone thinks of me personally. I care about their views on what's going on, and what they want. At present a lot's happening, with much worry and discontent."

"Dumb ending," muttered Dewy. "Dumb article." But again she saw Millie's name under the photo and sighed with happiness. She also saw on page 10's piece about Sherrier's Waterfall her *A public meeting to discuss this...* included. Dewy reminded herself she must find a way to make this meeting real.

At the bus station she waited with 30 people for the 13.30 to Farrisford. Local service between the towns took 40 minutes. Dewy realised how much transport Annette had endured three days a week for eight months, plus the hour-long Exeter bus from Crendlesham. She was glad

Annette would soon drive the Triumph Stag.

When Dewy appeared in the Lugworm car-park Annette nearly cried with happiness. Gary Sheekey and all the men were there. "You couldn't have timed this better!" Annette called to Dewy, turning the ignition key. The car roared.

"Get in, hon!" yelled Annette.

Dewy opened the stiff passenger door and got in. Annette released the brake, they left the car-park and headed for open country.

"It's amazing, hon!" called Annette. "Certainly *throaty*!"

"Feels exciting!"

"True old British sports car!"

Both were overcome by the experience of this low-slung, blasting, beautiful car to say much. They smiled, hair blowing wildly, Annette occasionally yelling about technicalities. Dewy nodded, preoccupied now at how to ask Gary Sheekey how much was owed.

They returned to the car-park 10 minutes later, Annette slightly crestfallen, as the engine was overheating slightly. They hadn't exceeded 50 miles an hour. Annette, Dale and Raj opened the bonnet and began a discussion. Gary Sheekey answered Dewy's question directly: "£1200 all-in, within 28 days please".

"Oh, I'll pay before then, Mr Sheekey, thank-you," smiled Dewy, terrified.

"Lunch, everybody!" said Annette. "Come on in! My treat."

All walked to the pub, Dewy last. Still banned from eating downstairs, no hope of food smuggled to her under Fent's watch, she'd go to bed.

"Buffet-style, help yourselves, loads there," said Beverley as they filed in.

Fent was there. "Is this being paid for?" Beverley said yes and cast her eyes upwards. As Dewy passed Fent on her way out he snapped: "Rent in three days!"

"*Six* days. And I'll need your bank account numbe~"

"*Cash.*"

"Sir, I ~"

"I want the money!"

"Do *not* talk to me like that, please."

Everyone was watching. Defeated by the day already, Dewy ran upstairs and threw herself on the bed. At 3pm Annette found her face down, cheeks blotched, hair plastered from crying herself to sleep.

"Oh, *darling*. You must have needed all this sleep," said Annette. "Will you come down? It's sunny."

"Staying here, hon."

"Oh, darrling," Annette hugged her. "You're terribly sad. Is it because of your job?"

Dewy told her she was no longer working at the newspaper.

"Aww, hon," said Annette. "You tried so hard. I'm proud of you."

"Th-that's nice," said Dewy welling up, throwing her arms around Annette.

"Oh!" cried Annette suddenly, holding her abdomen. "*Oh*... oooh. Did you feel that? Did you feel that through me?"

"Did the baby kick?!"

"Ye-ahh!" gasped Annette. "Real much!"

"Oh!"

"Someone's alive! *Three* of us are here! Oh! Morris would be thrilled!"

"Has the baby kicked before?"

"Not on this scale, hon. Oh, my, did you hear that?"

"There was a *noise*?"

"No, out back, the Stag, revving? It may only need more transmission fluid."

ASDA DEPUTY MANAGER Susan Thompson had been fantastic all week. She loved John and wanted to give him much leeway, especially as John cheerfully covered shifts for her and other staff and never asked favours back. She gave her blessing to John's request she cover Friday while he drove once more to Goring-on-Sea.

Flora Bennett greeted John as though he hadn't left. "I've made tea, about to take some up to him."

John tried asking how David was. She ignored the question, handed him tea in a rattling cup and saucer, then took tea and biscuits upstairs, returned, crossed the room slowly to her chair, levered into it and stared at a quiz show on the mute television.

Five minutes passed. John's "How's things been, Flora? was ignored.

A low hard voice began. John froze.

"*You* made him like this. He didn't want to be... *homosexual.* Look what it's done to him! Lorraine doesn't want him in the family. Would have broke Eamon's heart if he'd thought his boy wasn't going to... *settle down.*"

Effortfully she rose, struggled like a clunking old robot to the door and disappeared. John remained still. Flora Bennett returned to the doorway.

"I've no more to say," she rasped.

"Flora? Can you sit down a minute?"

"I'm not a sitter. I've a meal to plan."

"Please – come in a minute?"

"Why?"

"Please?"

She moved to the fireplace and stood, hand on the mantelpiece for balance. "Is it money?" she said. "Don't *you* come here thinking you've rights. His inheritances are in an account."

"I don't care about that," said John, pleasantly. "I wondered if the three of us might stay at a hotel up the coast? I know a nice one. All of us, have a break a couple nights? Sea-views, lovely food…"

The idea bewildered Mrs Bennett. John re-explained. When he repeated "sea views", Flora snapped: "What, and look at migrants drowning as they come in boats? No thank-you. *Silly*, these people."

John took a deep breath: "Then I'll take David to a hotel myself before we go home tomorrow."

"You will *not*."

"Flora? He's *your* son."

"Yes he *is*."

"And he's *my partner* of 16 years. And I'm *his*. I love him very much."

"Why's he like this?" said Flora, trembling. "What do you people *do*?"

Emotion escaped her as she spoke that sentence. She was trying not to cry. Despite everything, John couldn't not feel compassion for her.

"He's had stress at work," he said.

"Rubbish!" snapped Flora Bennett. "Absolute bolly-cock." Her emotion had passed. She was angry again. "He's got a *very good* job, senior position."

John stood: "Sadly… senior positions can be stressful, Flora. 'Tough at the top' and all that."

"*Get out.* Get out of this house."

"I will," said John. "Shortly."

He summoned up what Jonty had said: *Stand up to bastards calmly, they don't know what to do. They thrive on drama and yelling… if you grab the cake off them they'll scream. So don't grab it, you've won. It's a leap of faith. Get ready for the fact you've won, it's a shock.*"

He proved right. John calmly climbed the stairs. After: "Where do you think you're going?" and "Come back!" nothing further was heard from Mrs Bennett.

In the hour he spent cuddling David, it crossed John's mind Flora might call the police to have him removed. She was someone who could do that. "Stay calm," he remembered. "Calm begets calm."

"Oh, John," said David, speaking for the first time. "Oh, *John*." He began to cry. "I'm g-glad you've come."

ON FRIDAY EVENING Millie replied to an e-mail from Dewy.

> **hi**
>
> **no didnt get paper   i'll buy it. thanks.**
>
> **is there anyone who might buy my iphone.**
>
> **brand new 3 months old. 200 cash.**
>
> **sad 2 sellit but need money 2 get to my mums + have £100 so's i can get back here if she doesnt want me.**
>
> **2morrows my last day at the pub unless dougliss wants me over weekend bank hol;iday and whaever. [plse dont tell any1 im leaving?]**
>
> **do u knw its a bank holiday? do u know what they are? its a day off. love Millie**

Dewy wrote back:

Hey, Millie!

Don't sell your your i-Phone. Please? If you need to come back from your mom's, write me, I'll help pay. Don't feel embarrassed, people helped me when I was young, now I'm passing it on. Pay me back by helping someone younger when *you're* a creaker.

Did you see the paper yet? Isn't your photo not AMAZING??!!

This may sound like a patronizing grown-up (please don't think I'm a grown-up) but … *you have a huge future as a photographer for magazines and newspapers.*

Now you have your first professional portfolio

piece! Buy a good scrapbook – a photo-album with black pages is best. Cut out the Tattler photo with your name credit, paste it in. Also paste a clear print of the photo on the page opposite.

Start buying Elle, Vogue, Harper's. See the photos they have, read articles that interest you. Also check out a British magazine Huck.

When you get to Manchester look around for cheap (some are free) media courses that include photography, better still photo-journalism. You'll be taught the basics, expand your portfolio and apply for internships. That's when your grounding in reading the best magazines comes in. Aim by Christmas or Easter to be interning at Elle, Harper's… they all have UK editions and offices around the world.

Go for it, honey. You've a talent.

Dewy

PS: Boring intern applications work best. Do this: *Dear Vogue, I love your magazine and wondered if I might please apply for an internship? I'm 18 and studying photography at xyz college. I enclose my resumé and two reference contacts. Yours sincerely…*

PPS: I indeed know what Bank Holidays are. We have them in the States, but ours honor Martin Luther King, war veterans, laborers, George Washington and the fight for Independence (there also should be Native Americans' Day, Rosa Parks Day, Rachel Carson Day, Stonewall Day and John Brown Day).

The UK has Bank Holidays instead, honoring destructive, criminal gluttons called "banks". Can your generation please change that? Honoring your great people instead of banks which fund planet-killers, oil-drillers, arms-dealers, and steal trillions of dollars from poorest countries through a con-trick called You Owe Us Interest.

Also, demand *52* one-day holidays, not three!. One a week. Why not? 50-50 the planet's dying, why the five-day week? Clinging to that work ethic's what's *got* us into this mess. Let it go! Every Wednesday a public holiday! *C'mon*, Britain! 52 "Bank" holidays a year honoring 52 Great Britons instead:

Mary Seacole day, Mary Wollstonecraft day, Wat Tyler day, Charlotte Brontë day, John Lennon day, Nancy Astor, Percy Shelley, Kenneth Grahame, Mrs Pankhurst, Olive Morris, Emily Brontë, Tom Paine, William Shakespeare, Annie Maunder, Mary Astor, George Harrison, Nell Gwynne, Ian Curtis, Mrs Gaskell, Caroline Norton, DH Lawrence, Edith Cavell, Poly Styrene, Jessie Donaldson, Mary Shelley, George Orwell, Elizabeth Browning, Anne Brontë, Josephine Butler, LP Hartley, Emily Davison, Jane Austen, AA Milne, Wilfred Owen, why am I choosing? I'm not British – you do it, everyone choose. A new British holiday each Wednesday! *Demand* it! You invented the industrialized working week. Now dismantle it. Lead the way again.

PPPS: The attachment's an invoice to the paper for the photo you took. I put it at £40. Add your address and bank details, send it to G. Carruthers at the email included.

DEWY WORRIED HER e-mail was wrong. Hours passed, no reply. She kissed and massaged Annette to sleep, then checked her emails again. Nothing from Millie. But a new inbox arrival stared, no message, title only:

Elspeth Halaton   *Stay the hell out of my life!!*

Stunned, desperate, sober, Dewy lay listening to night birds and Annette's laboured breathing. Tomorrow

Sunday, then Bank Holiday, then rent due. Did Annette have bus-fares even? *Was* there £30 for a pedi at that Crendlesham beautician/ holistic place Earth & Sky? There would *have* to be. But that would mean under £50 remaining.

Dewy logged into her Bank of America account. Was there *any way* the 120-day account might be accessed early? There wasn't a hope, she'd tried twice last week. But… might there be even just a chance?

When her details came up, Dewy cried out and dropped the phone. She looked again. The balance really was $5,104 and six cents. She clicked her online statement. Under Payments Received:

Mrs E. Halaton #3 a/c   **$5,000**

"Oh, Elspeth," sighed Dewy. "Oh, Elspeth…"

BANK HOLIDAY POURED with rain. Annette felt unwell. Dewy lay next to her, reading bell hooks, Angela Davis and Bella Thorne's "Life Of A Wannabe Mogul". Men hammered, clunked and drilled in the cupboard across the hall. Dewy forgave the noise – Annette was sleeping through it, and the men were making an exclusive shower-room/wc for the B&B guest-room. Dewy was determined to use it.

She still had no washing options. Need was increasing. Weather had been too rainy or glum to go to the moors to wash in the waterfall.

Noise stopped. Dewy peered through a key-hole to see Fent and the men switching the shower on, agreeing it worked. After checking the wc flushed, they left. Dewy pounced. Her first shower in weeks veered hot to cold – Fent had bought the cheapest – but it was a shower.

At 9pm Dewy and Annette heard a faint knock. Dewy put the bedside light on and opened the door to flowers.

"For you and Annette," said Millie.

"*Oh!*"

"Thanks a lot for everything – hi, Annette!"

"Hey, Millie!" said Annette squinting in light, trying to rise.

"Don't get up. Listen, Beverley's bringing you food, she worried you ain't had none. I gotta go now. I'm leaving tomorrow."

"*Oh!*" said Dewy and Annette.

"I'll do them things you said," said Millie to Dewy. "I read your e-mail."

"Oh, Millie," said Dewy, tears welling. "Take care of yourself. Please don't sell your i-Phone?"

"I promise!" said Millie. She hugged Dewy, blew a kiss to Annette.

"I'll miss you, Millie," said Annette. "Good luck."

"You too!" said Millie. She tried to smile, but was tearful and walked away.

She doesn't want to go… thought Dewy sadly *…or know how to go, or where to go. Oh, Goddess, that's painfully familiar. Please can she not end up like me?*

TUESDAY'S WEATHER FELT strange. Jade had a maths test, her strongest subject, though not her best-liked. That was English, or used to be, for the harder she tried in English the worse her marks got. She'd never recovered from Mr Lyon saying in front of the class: "Jade, the question was: 'Explain how Atticus Finch defends Tom Robinson'." He'd held up her answer-sheet and to rising laughter read out: 'To Kill A Mockingbird is a book that makes you cry and realise you should always be justiced and racism is evil but people who do it think they're normal. This book must be the best thing ever in the books world. No surprise the cover says millions of it have been sold.'"

The school bus climbed Brinton Hill in a hailstorm.

New sunshine burst through streaming windows at the summit. The view had different weathers and types of light. Far north-east was lost to a rainstorm, middle distance baked and gleamed in sun. Moresby was invisible in fog, the abandoned bypass too, a half rainbow rising from it. Jade stared at the grey wall where the raised brown scar usually was. She enjoyed it being invisible, though, like everyone, rarely noticed the earthwork these days. An outrage at first, the two-mile mess was usual now

"Dad said he'll be late," said Brandon by way of greeting. Unemployed a week since the closure of the Tilhampton branch of Rennicksons, where he'd been the security guard, he spent his days around the house in underwear and socks, vaping, eating Dairylea triangles and watching Police File dvd's.

His behaviour to Jade had changed in the four days since Danii left for Dubai. On the first night, fearing her father might come to her room, Jade had rung Brandon at midnight: "I hear a strange noise". Her plan was to make him get up, so her father would know Brandon was around – a witness to anything. But Brandon had yelled: "Fat little cow, you've woke me up!" and ended the call. Jade had rushed to knock on his door instead, but stopped on hearing her father snoring – safely asleep, for now.

On the second night, Jade crept out into the passageway. Again her father snoring. His new contract saw him leave the house before anyone was up, back 13 hours later, "two beers, a burger then bed".

Another blessing – of a kind – was Warren's schoolfriends Michael Brown and Michael Ansell staying overnight on the third night, then all weekend. Some Matthew boy and others arrived. Computer games boomed, a football match using leaf-blowers lasted hours in the garden, the microwave was beeped all night until food ran out. The only time the house slept was 5am, when Jade dared leave with Ocean for the woods.

At weekend dawn, Azdek was always sleeping, Yusef awake. Yusef looked excited and fond of Jade when she arrived now. He tried to rest his head on her shoulder sometimes when they sat beside each other. Jade pushed him off. She did not want to be touched. He was a little boy anyway, 11 years old, *three years* younger, like the Farley-first-year munchkins. But Jade couldn't help something... something *deeper*. An anger. *Don't want to be touched. Not by ANYBODY. I don't even like Ocean coming up to me.*

Yusef always wanted her to show him photos from her phone, the more ordinary the better, preferably from several angles. School buildings, the covered market, the Town Hall. He loved the old, red telephone box in Town Hall Square and made three sketches of it. He had dozens of pencil drawings Jade thought dull: trees, leaves, fallen logs, one of his battered old shoes. But she noticed each drawing was precise and had taken hours.

Azdek still worked on farms. On Sunday at dawn, he slept heavily while Yusef showed a bundle of bank-notes, maybe £300. He produced a strip cartoon he'd prepared, depicting the woods and an arrow pointing to a house. Next box, Azdek, drawn satirically, hands money to a figure beside the house. In the last box, Azdek and Yusef wave from windows of the house.

"You're saving to get a house?" whispered Jade.

"House." nodded Yusef. He smiled broadly, eyes shut, and took her hands.

Now, two days on, Jade gazed from the kitchen window, remembering. *I wish I'd hugged him. What is WRONG with me? Why am I so weird about boys?*

Brandon's voice awoke her to the moment. He was *always there* now, intrusive, dominating.

"What you about to eat, Jadey?"

"I'm not eating anything!"

"You're about to! You *look* like you're about to!"

As with her father, there was no telling how far he might go. Jade was sure Brandon went into her room during the day. In fact she *knew*. What did he do in there? Jade believed her father went in there alone too.

"Leave me, Brandon," said Jade, climbing the stairs. "I'm tired!"

"You're tired because you overeat!"

"I'm tired because I want to be dead," murmured Jade, unheard.

Chapter 13

NEXT DAY, JUNE 5th, Dewy and Annette made a late greeting to their favourite month with a midnight walk.

"I know where we'll go!" said Dewy, excited. "Did I tell you the secret shortcut to the town? A while ago I found it, end of Keeley Lane, old green sign, 'Footpath to Farrisford', into a wall of weeds, brambles, overgrowth. I ploughed through, not thinking, then: 'ah my legs are cut, I'm nettle-stung' but *amazing* countryside, hon, like I'd gone through the looking glass! Little hills, stone outcrops, the wildest of wild trees, vales of flowers. Wind blew my dress. I climbed stiles over ancient walls of stacked rocks."

"I *love* those British stone walls in fields!" said Annette. "Remember 2012, after the Olympics, hon? The train to Scotland, these walls going high up in the hills?"

"I remember," said Dewy. "They have them here too!" They kissed and planned what to wear for the special night to greet June.

"The shortcut passes a hidden old bridge by a waterfall," said Dewy. "I stayed, watching water burst on boulders. People for centuries must have stood there, seeing what I saw, feeling the same peace and loss of time. A place where two waterways join must have been important to early peoples? It's *gorgeous*, hon! Spiritual, mystical, blessed. Shall we find it for the Goddess months May to June changeover?"

"*Yes!!*"

Dewy kissed Annette's hands. "Tonight we shall! If it's

moonlit we'll get to see *all* the landscape. the little, endearing hills – *hillocks* are they? What is a 'hillock'? Is it a hill that hiccupped and became smaller ones?"

"Isn't it when a fairy changes a bullock into a hill?" said Annette. "So he becomes a hill-bullock, hillock for short?"

"You're *right!*" said Dewy. "A lot of bullocks don't get on with their bull dads and don't want to be like them."

"So they ask fairies to change them into little hills," said Annette, "for beautiful moo-moos to rest on: *hillocks.*"

"Exactly so, darling."

At midnight they slipped out the fire-exit and into Keeley Lane, wearing dresses and flowers in their hair, Annette an open duffle-coat over her dress. Though one side of the lane had streetlamps, the women saw this night was clearer than any they'd seen in Britain. To their left the river shimmered by tree-silhouettes under stars. Its sound soothed. Night-birds' odd cries and songs resounded.

The playpark was foggy beyond railings one dim lamp overlooked, all else darkness. Annette tensed and stopped. "I don't like it there. Didn't like that day."

Dewy's eyes gleamed. "Never fear, dance badness away!"

She struck an arabesque, darted to the gate, pushed it open and entered the park in a ballet walk, head high. "A little light, hon?" Annette switched her torch on full. Dewy began to dance.

Annette saw immediately Dewy danced her *Danse Macabre* solo from a group show at Jacob's Pillow in 2010. White-blue tip-to toe, hair a tight bun, dark blusher each cheekbone – this was the last time Dewy ever danced before a formal audience. Annette had watched all four nights. In six minutes of Saint Saëns' music, Dewy, blending ballet and contemporary, solo'd the first two and was principal in the fifth. Annette knew every movement, especially when Dewy followed the lead violin. Now Annette saw these movements, knew Dewy could hear Saint Saëns in her head. If Dewy knew any music well, she'd dance to it in silence easily: "I hear it inside."

Eeriness and drama of *Danse Macabre* was interpreted by Dewy so powerfully Annette, having seen it, had thrilled to watch the audience agape in the last-but-one minute where Dewy was whisked and slung like a rag-doll by an imaginary partner – possibly Death itself. Her reactions to a tough, unpredictable dance-partner at volatile speed were so real, the eye constantly turned to the bare space her arms embraced, or which tugged her. The fact only thin air danced with her seemed impossible. The piece earned a standing ovation every night. Already slim, Dewy lost 30lbs that week.

Now, in torchlight, a night-mist backdrop, Dewy ended the two-minute opening with a weaving run around the space. Onstage she'd lightly touched nine hidden ghost-dancers, bringing them to life. Here, instead, Dewy bounded to her coat, took out a new trowel and acorns or tree-seeds she'd collected. She danced a circle around where the PCSOs had been. Nine times, in a move of mere seconds, she scooped earth, dropped a seed, earth-covered and stamped it flat as her ever-changing body glided on. She danced a last time round the site, low-curtsying in motion to each planted tree, grabbed her coat while pirouetting, then ran to Annette, who hugged her.

Annette was glad Dewy hadn't attempted her bravura fifth minute of the dance from years ago. "D'you know, I don't remember that?" panted Dewy. "I know I did *something*, but *what* I don't know. Never rehearsed it, like I did the opening. Whatever it was stayed there and then. Much dance can only be in one space and time."

At the hidden footpath Dewy backed into the wall of hedge and high weeds to clear a way so Annette was untouched. They burst through into pure space. Night was so clear, the best-known stars had tiny, very far ones dusted around them. After awed silence, Annette clicked low-beam on: "We're on a grassy path. Snails, darling! Like spilt beads."

Holding hands, Annette and Dewy carefully landed each step in a radius of torchlight, avoiding snails and slugs. Dewy's cherry nails gleamed in emerald grass and buttercups. The path became a meadow. Annette switched off the torch. They stood in each others arms, astounded by stars. "Saturn and Mars so clear," breathed Annette. "Venus brighter than ever I've seen."

They kissed.

"I hope we see a shooting star?" said Dewy.

"So do I."

"I wonder if we make the same wish?"

After a long, dreamy hug, Dewy whispered: "Let's find the bridge? Surprised I can't hear the waterfall."

"What if someone's there?"

"There won't be," said Dewy, but her voice was one per cent uneasy.

She sensed Annette wanted to turn back. They'd been out enough now to remember nights are cold.

"Take you back to bed, tuck you up?" said Dewy. "Would you like that?"

Back on the path they kissed and watched the sky a last time. Annette said:

"Why no shooting stars, I wonder?"

"I don't know, my love."

AFTER YESTERDAY'S SADNESS Jade felt alive tonight, joyous, fast-thinking, laughy, *strange*. Yusef, earlier, had hugged her. She lay on her bed now, remembering, gazing out at a night of serene infinity.

She relived a shape had loomed to her right, a tang of something odd, not unpleasant – musky. Suddenly she was being gently, firmly held by two arms, Yusef's cheek touching her own. She'd pulled away. He'd not persisted, but had reached his forefinger under her chin to lift her head slightly. He then drew a smile over his own mouth, a direction to Jade to smile too.

Jade had slightly smiled, for it was funny to be urged to by someone who didn't. Then Yusef *did* smile, faintly. He seemed manly, not boyish.

Jade knew Danii's phone was switched off in Dubai ("100% MY time, leave well alone."), but Jade took comfort from texting anyway.

Mum my periods starting agian. sorry. u dont want to know that. but theres no one to tell. A boy hugged me today. he probaby wont agin but he saw i was depressed i think and put his arms rounbd me. i swaer im not making this up!!!

Jade pressed send. She couldn't bear to not have some connection with Danii, even if it was one way. She wondered how Danii – if she ever read the text – would take the news of her first ever boy-hug. Would she ask a lot of questions? *'Just a boy' is all I'll say, I won't go beyond that...*

"I hope Yusef's OK," thought Jade, kneeling to look up at the night. "He's got blankets, an anorak, plenty food. But he sounded a bit ill. Maybe tomorrow... I'll get some cough mixture! There might even be some in the storage box from last year?"

She switched her bedside light on, leaned off the bed, looked under it upside down, reached for a plastic storage box.

Dave Tyler entered the room.

"What's a man to do, eh?" he sighed boozily: "What's a man to do, my little girl?"

Jade scrambled up and off the bed. Her father sat heavily on it: "The wife's in Dubai, the blokes want a pay-rise, I got a unemployed stepson. Jadey, *siddown*, yeah? I'm talking, need a sympathetic ear. You're the woman of the house now *she's* away!"

He was drunk. "Been at a works do." he blared. "Cab back – 30 quid! But I... I mean, what that is, is..." His words tangled up and he hiccupped.

Jade backed against a wall. Her energy drained sickeningly downwards into the floor. She'd read websites about abuse, how to not appear a victim. None of this surfaced now. She needed to say: *Get out please!* but couldn't speak.

Tyler stood: "Jadeee?! Why you no' talkin'"

He began to leave, but turned. "What'smatter, Jadey? Shy?" Jade pushed back into the wall so hard, she moved sideways. Tyler got nearer. Alcohol fumes filled the air.

"What's up with my little girl?" he smirked, "Somebody want a hug?

He blocked her view. Jade ran to the door, her father's arm stopped her. She cried out.

"What's up?" snapped Tyler. "Daddy's having a talk! *C'mere.*"

Jade couldn't process what was happening. Her father's weight now pressed against all her front. She couldn't breathe or see, his hand clamped her head to his shoulder, bending her nose. His other hand rubbed her back. "Losing a bit of weight!" he growled.

Jade fought, thrashed, her head banged the wall, dizzy as her father's face got nearer, filling all vision. He suddenly kissed near her mouth, his nose wet, cold on her cheek, his stubble smelt – *tasted* – of beer and kebab meat. Jade pushed, gasped for air. Her hand banged the bedlamp, it smashed, room pitch dark.

"What you *doing*?" snapped Tyler, "Wanna *see* my li'l girl!"

Jade shoved him hard. He retaliated. A fist struck Jade's shoulder then her father grabbed her. As he did, Jade saw far torchlight, flashing on and off. *Yusef.*

A scream escaped Jade: "GET *OUT*!" She pushed, pushed, kicked the man, pushed again, kicked again, again.

"All right!" yelped Tyler. "Temper temper! *OK, OK!!* Ha-ha!" Light from the hall as he escaped. Warren's faint voice, her father replying to him: "*Very* touchy little madam. Only said 'good night' she has this *fit*. Ha-ha-ha!"

Jade stuffed clothes, cash, phone in a rucksack and bolted downstairs. If her father stopped her, she'd scream. But she heard him talking to Brandon over TV in the sitting-room. Jade grabbed any food she could and fled.

She ran to the stile as the church chimed 12. As the bells ended, a vast, familiar sound filled the sky.

"No!" cried Jade. "*No!*"

The helicopter joined another poised above the woods. Light-beams flooded on hi-vis police near the trees. Jade fell to her knees.

"I LOVE NIGHTS when it's you and me snuggled up, kissing forever then sleep," murmured Annette.

"My darling," whispered Dewy.

"I wonder how Beverley's getting on?" said Annette. "At her sister's in a place called Southampton? She goes one night a year. Her brother-in-law's awful. Beverley uses the pub as an excuse to leave at 5am to drive back."

Soon the starry window overlooked two sleeping figures. One lay her head on the shoulder of the taller who held her in her arms. They'd seen no shooting stars. One – very brief, very small – passed now as they slept.

At 2am Dewy woke, knowing Annette was awake.

"Darling?"

"Something's not right" Annette's voice was shaky and quiet. "I can't, uh…"

She tried to raise herself: "*Shit.* Aagh. *Aagh!!*" Her back arched. Dewy sprang up: "We'll get you to hospital, sweet."

Annie had woken. She opened her door to see Dewy struggling into a dress:

"Annie? Please come?"

They helped Annette downstairs. She was in pain. Soon they crammed into the Triumph, Annie back ledge, kneeling sideways.

"Where are we g-going?" gasped Annette. "I'm *wet*. Why'm I *wet* down here? *Oh!! Oh! Ah!*"

Dewy lowered herself into the driving seat, turned the key. Nothing.

"Work, Staggy, please, darling?" said Dewy.

She tried again. *GAVRRRMMMM!!!* went the engine, deep and deafening. Annie rubbed Annette's shoulders: "Don't worry, darlin'."

Dewy drove fast, praying they'd enough fuel. She slowed to 70mph for a roundabout, took second left, Charford Lane, to Crendlesham. The headlights seemed weak for the unlit road. Dewy tried to recall the route from her one journey to Crendlesham by bus.

Annette gasped, strained, clutched Annie's hand. "Annette?" said Annie. "Tell me things aboot America? I've never been. Tell me nice things?"

"M-Morris is there," struggled Annette, panting. "We have... l-lovely walks. Dewy lives in a wood. It's nice there! Sometimes we... Ah!! *AHH!!*"

"A'right, pet. You'll be OK."

"Dewy?" said Annette.

"I'm here, hon. We'll be there real soon. Ah, *hell*. What's this fricking red light?"

A traffic light in pitch dark:

WHEN RED LIGHT SHOWS WAIT HERE

"Horseshit," said Dewy, accelerating.

An arc-lit scene of road-cones, digger-trucks, vans and workmen appeared.

"*Great!*" said Dewy "The hi-vis army on night manoeuvres." She kept her speed up. Even Annette said: "Honey?"

"Drive through 'em, don't care," said Dewy. Annie held Annette and gripped the seat. Dewy braked two metres short of a busy scene, right side of the road resurfaced by a truck pouring asphalt, men tamping tar, left side all road-cones, parked vans, men standing around.

Two approached: "What you *doing*, love? Red light back there!"

"Need to get to hospital, sir!"

"Ahh!" cried Annette "Oh God. *Ah!*"

"Clear that left lane, please, sirs?" said Dewy, "We're coming through."

"Listen love, it's not our ~"

"This woman's in labour. *Don't fuck around.* Prove for once men don't."

Annette cried louder. Dewy revved the car. Men panicked and cleared the lane. *BVRMMMM!!!* – the car shot forward. "Thank-you, Goddess!" cried Dewy, staring up. She kept up high speed around the Tassen hills. Crendlesham's lights began, ones and twos, then all the town lit-up before them. Dewy drove faster.

JADE WALKED AND walked, further than ever in her life, glad she'd a torch and spare batteries, the roads were utterly dark. Cars were rare. Headlights gave miles-away warning, so Jade could hide. Sometimes she stopped crying.

The villages were miles back. Jade no longer saw lights when she looked round. A signpost said Farrisford eight miles, so she'd maybe walked 12.

Her mind processed last minutes in Moresby. She'd stumbled to the woods, crying words she couldn't control. A police van drove fast over the field, then another.

Helicopters hovered, booming, searchlights on, bright coloured foliage and grass, like a hallucination, Jade yelling at an officer: "I know these men! Where are you taking them?"

"What you doing out this time of night?" said the WPC. "How old are you?"

"*Where are you taking them?*" screamed Jade. "You've got to tell me!"

"Doesn't concern you, love," said the woman. "Get yourself home."

"*You've taken them away!*" howled Jade, beating her fists against the woman's body-padding. "*Where are you taking them?*"

"*Hoy!*" roared a man, swinging Jade round. He leaned his face at hers: "Do *NOT assault police officers. Get home!!*" He shoved her hard.

Jade remembered nothing afterwards, except a feeling that nothing could stop her walking. Hour after hour, her legs would not stop walking, they had endless, free energy. She was heading south, a motorway's line of amber lights far ahead. Jade wondered why she was going there, but didn't stop.

Two miles on, night was brighted-out by floodlit warehouses by the motorway. A night-lorry roared past.

Jade looked back a last time, saw blackness beyond the industrial estate's strong lights. Somewhere back in that darkness was the past – her past – and it had ended. She faced forwards again and walked from the dark into a lit-up, busy, strange world. There she must find a man and a boy, two people who, Jade realised now, she loved.

"WHERE *IS* THE hospital?" said Annie.

"Look for signs?"

"I cannae read."

They'd never recall the next minutes. A minicab-driver saw a Stag emit smoke and hoarse noise, and followed. When it stalled, the cab driver took them to Accident and Emergency free of charge, maybe assisted them in.

Annette was rushed to intensive care on a trolley, Dewy and Annie running, holding her hands. The trolley crashed through doors. Annie was nudged out the way by someone wiping Annette's face. Annette gasped short cries, looked crazily at Dewy, who held her.

"Oh darling!" wept Dewy.

"I can see the head!" cried a voice.

Annette gasped, shrieked, gasped, turned to Dewy, tried to smile, thrashed side to side then arched upwards, eyes shut, clenched teeth.

A terrible scream…

A terrible silence…

Annie and Dewy turned frantically to the medical team.

A senior ward sister approached.

"We're so sorry," she said.

"Wh-what's happening?" panicked Annie.

"He wasn't alive," said the nurse. She bowed her head. "He was 23 weeks. He was lovely."

Annette screamed unknown words and buried her face in Dewy's waist. Dewy was too in shock to blink or close her mouth. She juddered as she held Annette: "My darling… oh… …oh, hon…"

At 7am Beverley was shown into the hospital room. Annie, by the door on a plastic chair, woke as Beverley hugged her. They surveyed the bed. Dewy dozed beside Annette, who lay facing away, holding a bundle in a light-blue crocheted blanket. Beverley looked hopefully to Annie, who shook her head. Beverley's body sagged. Annie stood to hold her.

"Hi, Beverley," murmured Annette, unable to look round. "Thank-you for coming. I'm sorry to tell you

Hiram Stephens was born passed away."

The world died.

It slowly restarted. Annette's lower lip quivered:

"He's so b-beautiful. He would have been loving and good. And he *is*. His soul is good."

Dewy stirred, held Annette's heaving shoulders. Silently the four women cried, none looking at the other.

IN CRENDLESHAM PARK Hotel, Dewy and Annette shared a deep bath, emerging in hotel bathrobes and turbans of towel to sit on the bed. Annette's eyes were unseeing. Her movements were steered by Dewy's constant hug.

They climbed into the large bed and slept. Dewy was woken by whooping snarls of a petrol-chainsaw as men dismembered a tree. A loud, growling roar filled the street for an hour – branches being mashed in a shredder. Then 40 minutes of leaf-blower began, a machine that enraged Dewy always.

She padded to the window. Across the road, corner of a park, a healthy tree had been felled then decapitated. Men in hi-vis and orange hard-hats milled around a fresh tree-stump. One picked up lopped, full-leaf branches.

The blower was worn on a man's back. He fired it at empty path, inch-by-inch, blowing dust which thickened the air. The noise was shockingly loud and strange, like a hair-dryer played through a stadium public address system.

Women with pushchairs and small children passed. If the man noticed, he'd stop blowing for four seconds and stare at the women. One appeared to thank his consideration in stopping the machine. He nodded and re-revved the 100 decibel machine, to blow more empty space. Dewy blogged:

> **Today's mad men. "Leaf"-blowers? The guys blow dust! Dust all year-round, and a few days' leaf-fall**

through Autumn.

Their blowers pollute and distress. The dust & fumes harm children. The 200mph air-jets kill insects, small wildlife and pollinators. The extreme noise disturbs birds, animals and us.

Are leaf-blowers and other macho, new gardening tools the swansong of machismo? Alpha Male is unneeded. Evolution's finished with him. In desperation he reaches for his blower, chainsaw, power-washer, anything with *noise*. Alpha Male's done, but he ain't going quietly.

Cheerio, then, sirs, thanks a bunch for the greed, aggression, oil lust, missiles, drones, male gods, and wars, wars, wars.

Thanks for the bullying, rapes, mockery, huge cars, fighter planes, warships, banks, pornography, machine guns, Republican presidents and sadistic leaf-blowers. Hey, guy, strap that blower on all year round and blow dust to... er... to *slightly further away!* Scare away birds and hibernators! Drench flowers, bees, trees and bushes in engine fumes!

But it's not these guys I'm angered by. Many would ditch these machines if told how harmful they are. What gets me, are *environmentalists* who ignore the animal cruelty and pollution of new, mass-market, gardening tools. How can they *not* be aware of these mass-market noise machines, all year, every park, school, hospital, library, college, church, sports facility, playgroup... in every neighborhood in the world?

'Ha-ha, she gets *worked up* by blowers!?'. Why don't *you*? Why aren't you standing up to *every fucking form of male tyranny*? How cruel and insane must today's mad men get before you speak out?

My girl is sick right now. Asleep in a beautiful room in an English hotel. Chainsaws and blowers across the road drove me out my mind, but she slept, thank-you Goddess. She's suffered the worst anyone can in the past 24 hours. I'm gonna calm down and be serene for her. I love her so much. If you pray, please pray for her? Ah-de-o. Xx

Chapter 14

DANII, LIU, STEPH and Tanya talked, shrieked and drank on the London to Exeter train. Other First Class passengers complained to the guard.

Danii checked her phone after days off: 15 missed calls from Dave, 12 from Brandon, 22 new texts. *I'll deal with this tomorrow. Can't be anything bad, or Warren would text too. It'll all be: 'Which freezer drawer's the steak in?'*

Liu, Steph and Tanya lived in Crendlesham. They threatened a change of plan: "Cocktails in the Mill Hotel with you, Dan!"

But tiredness set in 10 minutes out of Exeter. Britain was rainy and cold. The four had so many shopping bags they couldn't see out the cab windows. Steph had left a Moschino suit on a seat in Departures.

Back to work tomorrow…

The last gleam of spirit was Danii dropped off at the hotel. All hugged her and yelled lewd remarks.

Danii waved the car off, looked up at the warm hotel, took out a small, teal velvet box, opened it, saw the square, diamond ear-stud.

Predicting two and a half hours of accumulated delays Dubai to here, Danii had asked Marlon to arrive at 9.30pm. She was accurate to within the minute. A cab approached in rainy dusk, circling the big stone fountain. Within seconds Marlon was in her arms.

They showered together, kissing. They dried each other, kissing, then ran to bed to make love for an hour, often fast.

Danii lay, glowing. Marlon kissed her where she liked for a very long time. Afterwards, they lay entwined, drifting in and out of sleep.

"What you thinking?" whispered Danii.

"Never felt like this," whispered Marlon. "It's like drugs or something. Everything that's been hurting me is cured. This is *living*. Living well."

"Hmm," purred Danii, kissing him.

"Have you heard of Dorothy Parker?" said Marlon.

"You're thinking Dorothy *Perkins*."

"Er…"

"Aww, it's nice you think about shops," said Danii, stroking his chest.

When Danii fell asleep, Marlon carefully reached for the TV remote.

"*Wha' you doing?*" murmured Danii.

"Mind if I watch a bit of Newsnight, with the sound down?"

"Don't want TV," said Danii, waking, sitting up to drink water.

"You're right. It's all depressing anyway," said Marlon. "Conservative leadership race. They reckon Johnson'll win. We've no say in it. Did you vote last time, Danii?"

"No," said Danii, nestling into him. "My daughter said I should. She done a project how women weren't allowed to vote once, and chained themselves to fences. Saw a picture of this woman carried *upright* by a policeman while a man shouted at her. Big hat she wore. They wore a lot of clothes then. If you had a good body, no one saw."

"You've a daughter?"

"I tell you what else I got," said Danii, handing him the velvet box: "Can you open this? I'm useless at boxes."

Marlon took the box and gazed at it.

"Got to be opened gently," said Danii, eyes smiling. "You've got the touch."

The diamond was bright as the sun. Its rays changed colours.

"My God," said Marlon.

"Try it on."

"Need to get a bit dressed first? Diamond on a naked man?"

"Why not?"

FOR TWO DAYS and nights Annette never spoke. Dewy held her, kissed her, massaged her, bathed her, read to her, asked if she'd like to rent *Frozen* on TV. Annette lay inert. Dewy held and kissed her hour after hour. Room-service meals lay cold. On day two, Beverley and Annie visited, with tea, juice, cakes, cornbread, Oreos, flowers, night-clothes from Rennicksons for Annette, and all her Bachelor and Morris prints. Annette tried to say thank-you, but started to cry, hugging the photos.

On the third day, Beverley and Annie returned to take Annette and Dewy to Hiram's burial in a special garden east of the hospital. Dewy left beforehand to find anything Annette might wear. In Devon Hospiscare, Dewy saw a perfect black dress for Annette, size 12.

Shame she's almost a 16, now she's pregn~ Oh! Dewy cried and hugged the dress as she bought it.

In a womenswear shop, she found two black pillbox hats with veils.

Beverely drove Annette, Dewy and Annie to the hospital. The four entered a small chapel. A pleasant, older woman in a purple gown waited. Before her was a small white casket. The woman recited a prayer and asked if Annette would like to say goodbye to her son. Crying, Annette stepped forward, clutching Dewy. Someone lifted the white lid.

His face was perfectly-formed. All else was covered by white silk. Annette placed Bachelor's blue, half-chewed ball where his hand must be. "Give this to Bachelor please, and t-tell him Mommy loves him? And I love you, Hiram."

She leaned low to kiss his brow. Dewy held her so she wouldn't fall.

Outside, Annie, Beverley, Annette and Dewy linked arms to watch the short burial. They thanked the pastor and left. Dewy paid £140 at a bursar's office and joined the others in the car park. None had felt worse at any point in her life, or not for a very long time.

At the hotel, Annette sat on the edge of the bed. Annie sat with her. Dewy and Beverley went out of earshot to discuss what to do. Dewy wanted to take Annette home for two weeks. Beverley helped her find last-minute tickets online and two more nights in the hotel. She suggested they move out of The Lugworm now, on her free afternoon.

Dewy felt awkward and didn't know how to thank Beverley.

"It's the least I can do," said Beverley, pulling up at The Lugworm. "Shall I bring everything down? I presume you don't want to bump into Douglas?"

"I'll help you," said Dewy. "I don't care if Mr Fent's around."

"I'm sorry you had the worst of him. He can be a bastard."

"He is one," said Dewy. "But not evil. Evil smiles and asks questions."

They passed the shut door of Annette's old, first room. Dewy shuddered.

"I shouldn't have brought her here," said Beverley.

"Of course you should," said Dewy, taking Beverley's hand. "She was wandering with a rucksack and suitcases. You did her a kindness. The deal seemed OK, free board and food, an apparent few hours' kitchen work?"

They packed and took Annette's two big cases, rucksack, Dewy's case, and nine carrier bags down to the car. Dewy looked at the bare room a final time and walked downstairs a last time. Never again the descent to a waft of pub food and old beer. She glanced in the main bar to say good-bye to Bernie, but she was serving, and hadn't much liked Dewy. Fent was nowhere to be seen.

Dewy padded through the empty Angler's Bar. Relief at leaving yet another traumatic place where she'd been unwanted, was – as always – edged with slight sadness felt when departing a place forever.

She helped load the car then: "One second!", and raced back to The Lugworm. In the kitchen, no one was there. Dewy turned, dejected, then heard a clatter behind the plate-wash machine.

Martin Davidson looked up in time to see Dewy throw her arms round him: "I'll never forget you, Martin!" She kissed his cheek and vanished.

DANII AND MARLON made love at sunrise, had breakfast brought to the room then slept. At 10am, Danii surveyed crumpled clothes, shopping bags, opened suitcases, breakfast plates, damp towels and scrunched sheets. A corridor vacuum-cleaner whined. The holiday was over.

She heard Marlon splash in the en-suite, and smiled at his cleanliness addiction. Danii wished more men had one.

She switched on her phone. 22 missed calls. 24 new messages. She lay back, sighed, began on the texts. After three she sat bolt upright. On the fourth she paced the room. Another text arrived:

Three days now. we hope shes at her friends or gone a school trip? theres a inocent explantion surely. But get in touch soon as u land. need to discuss if to tell the police. Brandon say's we should.

'…soon as u land' reminded Danii her family thought she was back from Dubai today, not yesterday. She'd lied about being away seven days, not five, so to spend nights with Marlon before and after.

She affected calm as they packed, but couldn't speak. She was too preoccupied to notice Marlon was good to be around in hard circumstances. She hadn't told him about Jade.

They checked out and rang Marlon a taxi. As it drove away, Danii gave a frightened sigh and rang Jade's number. Several attempts went straight to answering machine.

She stood in the rain, bags and cases surrounding her. She told herself over and over this was "only" a cry for help from Jade. Danii recalled how she and Lorna Green ran away to France at 13, getting no further than Canterbury.

It's nothing. Jade'll be back by tea-time.

But Danii was so worried she felt ill.

She shakily rang Liu to say she'd be late for work. Liu laughed as she answered: "*What was last night like?*"

"Oh, er, ha! *Later*," said Danii. Rain fell harder. She ended the call.

An hour on, in the hotel lobby, Danii knew her rain-flattened hair, unmade-up, tense face, two cases and wilting bags from expensive shops were being noticed. When she ordered more tea, the server frowned: "Still here?"

For the 12th time she rang Jade.

For the 15th time she rang Jade.

On the 16th try, a ringing tone. Danii let out a cry. A receptionist looked up. The phone rang three times, four. Danii's left fist banged the chair-arm fast. It could not happen that Jade wouldn't answer. Jade *must pick up*. If Jade didn't answer... Jade *had* to answer. *No way* was Jade not going to answer. That *couldn't happen*.

11 rings, 12...

"No, Jade, *no*," cried Danii, standing. "*Jesus Christ*, answer the damn ph~"

"Mum?"

"*Aaahh!*" screamed Danii. "*Christ*, Jade! Have you *any idea*, for *fuck's sake*…"

"I don't want to be rung," said Jade's voice, far-away, tired. She had a cold. "I'm OK. Good-bye."

"Jade?"

"I've left home."

"I know, Jade, I know. Whereabouts to? Can I come?"

"No."

"Just me. No one else?"

"*You* don't want to see me. I'm your fat, ugly disappointment."

"*Jade, I love you*, I don't give a *fuck* what you look like!"

The line went dead.

TESSA ENGLAND SPOKE with her nephew Anthony on the phone an hour, a rare call. "Aunt, look after Beezer another year, can you?" He worked for the British Diplomatic Service in Lima.

Tessa England tried to sound agreeable to his request while watching the dog dig a hole in the back lawn, go mad chasing birds then do a large, unfirm dump.

Her nephew asked about Britain.

"I don't what to say," said Tessa England, relieved to, for once, not have to conjure a half-positive spin about the imminent future.

"It *will* be Boris Johnson next Prime Minister, yeah?" said Anthony.

"Yes," sighed Tessa England. "So help us, God."

"Don't you like him? He's all right. Few of us met him once, quite a laugh."

His aunt banged on the window: "Beeze! Get *off* that! Anthony, I must go, he's chewing the hose."

"Thanks for looking after him, Aunt?" said Anthony. "No trouble I hope?"

"None at all," said Tessa icily. "Quite a laugh."

She threw a lurid chew out the window for Beezer, gave Rudyard a Bonio, poured an ale, skimmed The Economist, Spectator and Times' worked-up assurances of Brexit uncertainty then decided to forget it all and try bettering her 1998 record of finishing The Times Crossword in 22 minutes. Rudyard rested his chin on her lap.

Five minutes on, she'd managed only: THINGS | FALL |APART 11 across, SEVERE 14 down, TOAD|RATTY|AND 20 across, MOLE 28 down, HUBRIS 24 across, PARAPSYCHOL-OGY 30 across.

She told Rudyard: "Recess soon, I'll be home more. Will you like that? And when I go back in Sep~... what's the matter, Rud? Hmm? Yes, I *am* sad, how clever of you to sense that. Thank-you for your paw. That's *very sweet* of you."

She held Rudyard's paw. A sigh: "Ahh, Rud! Ken Clarke said today he's resigning. 49 years in the House. Wish he'd make it 50. Other resignations too – or *are* they? If those *rats* hanging round Johnson try freezing *me* out, good luck to 'em. So long as this part of the world wants me, I'll keep on til I drop, or grow old."

Part Three

Chapter 1

IN SUMMER SOLSTICE heat, the 605 pulled into Farrisford. Last to alight were two women. One wore a straw hat, summer dress and sandals, the other a short, white dress and wide black sunhat. She'd no luggage, but pulled her friend's case and slung her friend's rucksack over a shoulder. They stopped to gaze at each other and kiss. One stood on tiptoe to sniff the other's left ear.

Market Street's roadworks had increased, the right-hand pavement smashed up to Farrisford Vapes. The road lay silent. Workmen hadn't been seen for days. Dewy and Annette walked along planks, around barriers and tall sand-heaps and stacked plastic pipes. The Grand Hotel stared down. Dewy dragged Annette's case up its 18 steps one at a time.

"Hope they've forgotten me, and let us stay?" she panted.

"Of course they will, hon," said Annette. "Couple nights til we find me a room or apartment."

"Surprised the University didn't arrange anything," gasped Dewy, pausing, very hot. "And this thing you must live in Farrisford, not Exeter?"

"So I'm near Farrisford campus?" said Annette. "Though why I must, or where that is…"

They entered the cool, dark foyer. Dewy removed her two-and-a-half foot-wide sunhat.

Damian looked up. "Welcome to the Grand Hotel, Fa – Oh, er… no rooms." He vanished into the office and slammed the door.

Sun glared on Market Street. Annette slept against Dewy's shoulder. The steps got hotter. The women stood, steadying the other. Dewy fanned Annette with her hat. "Bus back to Exeter?"

They slowly descended the steps. "Can't face that construction site again," said Dewy, "Let's take a right, the old lane?"

After a rest in the lane's shade, they emerged at the top of Beech Hill. A dual carriageway hurtled down, leaving town. Dewy and Annette leaned against an oak, holding hands, viewing countryside bake in sun.

"England, hon," said Dewy. "We're back."

"Mm-hm," said Annette.

Dewy hugged her joyously. Annette was responding consistently for the first time since losing Hiram 14 days before. By good chance Annette's parents were away in Virginia when Dewy and Annette had arrived home. For a week Annette lay in bed, hugging Morris. Dewy told Consuela she'd been overworked. Connie was no fool, but didn't press for the truth.

A Beech Hill timetable showed a next Exeter bus in two hours. Dewy and Annette wandered, rested, got distracted. On the verge of a tree-lined A-road, Dewy struggled with the case through long grass while fast cars and lorries passed. A blue and white road-sign ahead had a new strip beneath: *University of Exeter, Farrisford Campus 1 mile*

10 minutes on, a similar sign pointed right, to a lane into open country. Soon the A-road's sounds receded. Dewy was hot, pink and soaked. Annette made her sit under a tree, poured Evian on her feet and fanned her with the sunhat. They slept an hour in the tree's shade. Dewy woke first, delighted to see Annette's sleeping face wasn't tense at last.

The lane ahead shimmered in heat-haze. Tarry bits looked wet. Dewy and Annette walked in silence but for case-wheels trundling. Dewy saw houses on a ridge far to the right. *Back of the Yenton estate. The Lugworm's a mile over that hill. Annette might prefer not to know.*

A long, two-storey 1960s building lay ahead. Behind it, two low-rise halls-of-residence nestled in hills. All seemed empty.

They arrived at shut gates. Annette pushed a buzzer. Nothing. Then: "Yes?" from a grille.

"G-good afternoon, sir," said Annette, "I-I'm with the... um... university? I was kinda sent here, but that was a time ago, sir."

"Ah, OK," said the man, tone softening. Replies as vague as this often signified an academic. "I'll buzz you in. Follow the left path."

A uniformed man beckoned from a site-office. Annette presented her staff lanyard and some papers. The man rang a number as he looked at a clock: 5.20pm. Speakerphone rang on. At last: "Admin. Yvonne speaking, how can –"

"Ah, glad you're still there! John. Farrisford." He switched loudspeaker off, took the call out of earshot. Soon he returned.

"OK, all set?" he smiled, "It's been confirmed."

Dewy and Annette leant against each other, near-asleep.

"Better late than never!" continued the man. "Everything's ready, has been since October."

"'What is ready, sir?" said Annette nervously.

"The cottage?" said the man, taking keys from a drawer. "Part of your contract? Free accommodation. Stated on the contract's last page?"

"Oh," said Annette. "Does that mean I have a place to live?"

"Since 4th October last year. This way, Dr Stephens."

They followed him up a path through honeysuckle shaded by cherry trees. A high, old wall appeared left, a

cottage roof a distance behind. Trees on the right gave out
to sunny meadows of bluebells and buttercups sloping far
down to a rocky, slow stream with woods on the opposite
bank.

Behind the left wall, a third house's highest window
shone gold sun under blue gables.

The man, John Fielding, unlocked an old green door
with a rounded top. It scraped open to a half-acre garden:
apple and plum trees left, vegetable bed and an old
greenhouse right and a lawn up to a white cottage with a
red rose bush over a blue back door. House and garden
basked in late sun. The wall shadow's invisible advance
reached halfway up the lawn.

Dewy surveyed the garden then kissed and nuzzled
Annette. They hugged close. John Fielding pretended to
search for the door-key.

"So beautiful and peaceful, sir," said Annette. "Am I
allowed in the garden?"

"All yours. I've kept an eye on it, gave the lawn a mow.
Carrots and potatoes in that patch, dunno when they'll
come, planted 'em April."

"Oh!" said Dewy, happily, stepping out to the lawn.

"Fruit'll fall soon," said Fielding, nodding at trees. "A
lot of it."

"How lovely," said Annette.

"And this, sir?" said Dewy, crossing left.

"Oh, *that*," said Fielding. "Nothing very exciting, just a
bit of kale."

"*Woaargghh!!*" roared Dewy, rearing back, knee up.
She shot forward and sloshed through the kale:
"*Ohhaarrgghhh!!*"

"*Whoooo!!*" yelled Annette, emotion escaping after
weeks of exhaustion.

John Fielding thought he'd seen the run of academic
types in 30 university years: bores, scruffs, madmen,
snobs, beauties, frauds, madrigal singers, out-of-date

dandies, smilers with gold wire round a dark side-tooth. But these two American women were sweeping the board.

"*Phwoaaa!!*" yelled the barefooted one, a ballet dancer maybe, or a model, picking her way through kale like a flamingo, leaves earth-powdering her legs. She threw her head back, hand on sunhat: "*Goddess*! These blessings! It is *primal love*!!" She looked to Dr Stephens: "We'll *drool it* tonight!"

"*Kale*! Oh, crinkliness and toughness!!" moaned berry-brown Dr Stephens, arms swaying. "Kale's raw-growth state brings feeling of things needing felt! A tipping point! A *disgorgement*!"

"I love you," wept Dewy into Annette's hair. "My Proserpine! Back from the underworld. We'll be DISGUSTING tonight. I *so* promisely mean that! Ohh!!" She blew her nose on the hem of her dress. John Fielding looked away.

An hour on, Dewy and Annette lay upstairs in the only bedroom. The window was all blue sky. Annette slept. Dewy left a note saying she'd gone to find a store, and put 50 x's for kisses.

The front door opened to a steep patch of grass by a car-length driveway. The pavement was eye-level. When Dewy reached there, she was nearly tall as the house. The upper storey had no front windows. Dewy blew a kiss to the slope of roof Annette slept behind, walked past the other cottages along a lane with far views of farmland, up to a wider road intersecting. There she turned right, towards an edge of the Yenton estate in the distance.

Beep-boop!

"Lucky still open," said Barbara, by way of greeting. "Five minutes."

Dewy gathered what she could, and the Farrisford Tattler. Halfway back to the cottage she stopped, for it was red-time, the name Dewy and Annette gave to a 10 minute phase during sunset or dawn when reds richly glowed. Dewy sat on an ancient milestone to watch this extraordinary phase. A parked red car, her toenails, bricks of a wrecked byre in a field, stones with a sandstone tint, all deeply radiated.

The paper fell out of her bag with a *fhmph!* shaking Dewy from reverie. Time in New England had made the Tattler a memory. Now it was back.

She nearly laughed at headlines: **Houses Still Being Built** and **Hot-Air Balloon Lands No Problem** and: **Parish Council Discusses Issues**.

She sighed at spelling and grammar errors. In the letters page, Father Entreton's poem seemed lines short (unless meant to be. Dewy was sure not). And Colin Hendry's front page on town-centre parking problems began:

As controversial tariffs being seen to be ongoing and affecting where to park, strength of feeling at a Council meeting were high-running what to do about it.

"Colin, you wrote this after the Bess, didn't you?" sighed Dewy.

Back at the cottage, she cooked a meal then woke Annette. They ate Findus vegetarian pancakes with a panful of kale, Smash potato, tinned mushy peas and Bisto onion gravy from granules. Dewy never trusted cooking instructions, if she even read them. The pancakes box said grill 16 minutes. After 10 minutes squinting and tutting, Dewy decided the instructions were wrong, took the pancakes from the grill and dropped them into the boiling kale.

After messy eating, Annette and Dewy hand-washed their dresses in the sink. As Dewy had no other garment but knickers and sunhat, Annette wrapped a towel around her. They padded outside to hang their dresses on a washing line.

"The stars are out, hon."

"And fireflies, look, do you see?"

They lay entwined in bed, watching stars through the opened window. When Annette slept, Dewy looked up at a solstice night which never fully darkened. Breeze rustled trees by the stream. Dewy felt Annette was at peace.

An hour on, Dewy lay awake. *I can't give my girl what she wants, or needs and deserves. I'm cruel to be unsexual to her. I'm her frustration.*

A second wave of guilt: *I can't look after her. Why didn't I realise she was entitled to this free house? Why didn't I check her contract last October? Why was I so useless not to escort her here then? I haven't looked after her. What Annette endured for eight months in The Lugworm was my fault, all of it.*

Dewy placed her face in Annette's hair and inhaled – the favourite scents of her life.

And like the tolling of a deep bell, Dewy's soul knew she must leave Annette forever.

She lay very still, beyond tears.

Everything must change.

"Oh, Goddess, please can Annette not be lost, alone and helpless again?" whispered Dewy to the sky. "Goddess, please bring someone from the universe to take her hand? Someone who Annette feels sexy and hot for, and it's mutual? Goddess, please hear this prayer. I've not had a drink for 19 days, so it must be a real prayer? It's clumsy enough to be real…"

DANII WOKE AT 2am on Liu's sitting-room sofa. The small, new apartment and duvet in moonlight made Danii think she was back in Dubai for a moment.

Liu did well to buy this place, especially in Crendlesham, where the prices ~ ah, God, what is this CRAP I'm thinking?"

Danii grabbed her phone, texted:

Jade I'm not at home either. Looking at the moon. Are you awake somewhere? Can u see it?

In the open-plan kitchen, Danii poured water, leaned on a worktop and cried. She'd had enough of sending texts to nothing but Am fine mum every two days. *Nothing I think, say, feel or do is any use to this situation.* thought Danii. *What can I DO?"*

Danii had fled the house after Social Services visited in hi-vis vests to stare, fire questions, even open cupboards. One counted beer bottles in the fridge. Danii and Dave Tyler were led to separate rooms for questioning, Tyler 10 minutes, Danii half an hour. The house-search continued to Tyler's van. "Anywhere she might have left a clue where she was going, a scrap of paper with an address…"

Social Services left after two hours. Shocked, scared and enraged by them, Danii drove to Liu's. Liu suggested she tell her husband she'd heard from Jade. He'd tell police Jade was alive, so ending the pressure Brandon had caused. Brandon, itching to go public (held back by Tyler's: "Wait, see what your mum says") had emailed photos of Jade to 40 regional police forces: Caucasian white girl IC1,14 year's old, of overwieght build and quiet of nature. This is official amissing Person. Within an hour every newspaper in the west of England had rung. Then Social Services arrived.

Two weeks on, Danii was still at Liu's. She went home some afternoons to drop off groceries, wash the boys' clothes and chastise Brandon to tidy the house. After Warren returned from school, she'd leave. She didn't want to see her husband, but couldn't place why. "It's like I feel Jade's exclusive to *me*," she'd told Liu. "I don't want to share the problem with him. I'm being unfair – he must be cracking up too. But I don't want to *know*."

"Danii?"

3am now. Danii in a trance. She didn't hear Liu.

"Danii? Can't you sleep?"

Liu made tea. They sat under the duvet on the sofa,

kitchen-light spreading into half the unlit room. Neither spoke awhile. They often didn't. Liu felt proud to be so comfortable with her boss they could be silent together, and that she'd provided a safe space for two weeks.

Danii spoke of being taken to a fairground as a child and dreaming about it afterwards. In her dream she returned to the fairground at night with a grown-up, maybe her mother. She saw rides, roundabouts, stalls, a high big wheel, all very bright, all in motion, but the fairground was deserted. The adult urged her to go in alone: "Only *you* can go."

Danii wondered why she'd remembered the dream. Did it relate to now in some way? Had Jade become the girl in the dream, and she, Danii, the adult pushing her away, alone, towards something more frightening than enticing? Or were she and Jade both wandering, separated, amid night fairground's noise, speed and coloured lights? Would they find each other?

"More tea?" Liu whispered, getting up. She called through from the kitchen:

"Red dawn from the window here."

Danii sighed. Dawn. Another day. To do what? To do what *where*? She hadn't been working, for either Brandon, Tyler, or a Social Services person often contacted or appeared at the salon to look for her. HR had signed her off another week, but this couldn't go on indefinitely. Danii absently picked up her phone: 1 new message Jade.

saw the moon b4 i went sleep in a bushes in the mid of a roundabout. am in somerset. id like to see you but thres <u>no chance if anyone else knows where i am or you tell anyone</u>.

Danii replied:

I won't tell a soul. please where are you? im not at home so no 1 will ask or follow me.

Chapter 2

"THAT'S SO GOOD of you, Jonty! Thank-you."

"Everything on the house for you, David!" said Jonty, pouring champagne. "Not for *you*," he added to John. "Oh, OK, you too, you're a dear little cattersmoot."

"You don't have to," said John, "We pay our way. Will you join us?"

"No," said Jonty. "I run a pub-restaurant, have you not noticed?"

David and John ate vegetarian moussaka with salad and garlic bread. Before rhubarb crumble arrived, David produced a battered postcard. He handed it to John: "This arrived today". The card had Technicolor photos and *BRIGHTON* in a red central band. John turned it over:

June Malcolm in hospice. Funeral probable. Would you attend? "Mum"

"Oh." said John. "Shall I drive you up there when it happens?"

David looked solemn. "I... don't really know," he said.

"Is Flora all right?" said John. "Writing's scrawly and slopes down."

"She's indestructible," said David.

"She's not," said John.

On John's last visit to Goring-on Sea, after David had been taken to the doctor, given pills and was in bed asleep, prior to going home next day, John had come downstairs at 10pm, intending to find a B&B on the sea-front. Flora

Bennett peered from the back room. "Might as well stay here. Have Lorraine's old room. Drink a brandy first. Eamon and I had one every night."

John followed her into the back sitting room, which was half-lit by a table-lamp and the silent TV. Flora produced a bottle of Waitrose cognac and pushed a corkscrew into the screw-top lid. It plunged instantly, a rattlesnake sound.

"I've opened this in a mistaken way," she muttered, tugging the corkscrew out, noise a death-rattle. Brandy was poured through the torn tin lid.

John and Flora sat late-night drinking, looking out at the garden. His attempts to talk met silence or "Hmph". She didn't want communication. John wondered if silence was how she and Eamon spent late, last nights. *What were 'normal' parents LIKE?* John often wondered. He'd been brought up by his mother and two older sisters.

John never told David about drinking brandy with Flora. He couldn't decide if it had been wrong, especially as he'd found the experience relaxing, with a feeling of safety. He wondered if it was her way of saying: "I accept you both." At all other times, Flora was intolerant, with a ready supply of crypto-racist or homophobic quips. But John couldn't find it in his heart to hate her. His heart couldn't hate anyone. And she'd given the world David, a love like he'd never known. She'd *made David*.

But her son didn't love or like her. He visited every year, or other year, until that night this year he'd turned up, saying: "Mother, I'm going to bed," and doing so for three weeks. Now the crisis had passed, John sensed David would want distance from her, through shame.

"Know what?" said John, ignoring a tiny inner voice: *you've had too much champagne.* "Why don't we invite your mum to visit?"

"Are you joking?" said David.

"No," said John. "I think she'd be reassured to see us

happy, that *you're* happy. Lovely house… little lane, English country town."

David looked vexed. "No. I don't want her here. She'd ruin things."

"Don't worry, love, just me being daft," said John blithely. "C'mon, forget it."

John did not want to see David's vexed expression – the face of vanished David, the David whose spirit and self had slowly, steadily deserted David for two years until the day he recognised John in his childhood bedroom in Goring-on-Sea. That's when David had returned. The David who *didn't* say: "But my work's too important" when the doctor in Goring signed him medically unfit and advised psychiatric help when back in Devon.

"Wasn't she *great?*" said John when they'd left. The visit had instantly boosted David's recovery. David's reply: "We've got good doctors in this country, haven't we John?" was the first positive, vital thing he'd said in months. John had hugged David euphorically, agreeing: "We have indeed! And it's all free! There's so much *good* in Britain, so much to *protect.*"

Now, in the Bibby, John strived to stop David sliding back into darkness.

"Hey, love!" he smiled, grabbing David's hand. "Let's go in the Bali Hai!"

"No. *No*, I don't want to be sociable."

"We don't have to be. Come on."

John half dragged David across the main bar to the Bali Hai, a dark but colourfully-lit, South Seas-themed chamber. A pleasing, lurid scene took up one side under a huge backdrop of tropical beach and sky. Within white-picket fence, lay a world of flowering, equatorial plants, realistic palm trees, exotic rockery and a waterfall by stages into a 12 foot pond, where, on a sandy shore, and in little caves, lived Jonty's iguanas Lagney and Casey. The backdrop sky behind and above changed in real time, day to sunset, to moon and stars. Martin Denny's "Forbidden Island" played on a turntable somewhere.

Jonty was holding court. Though he'd created one of the merriest, best-run pub-restaurants in the country, he was often grumpy at 60. He greeted John and David: "Come in, you know everyone? Just saying I'm having no more weddings in this room."

"But we *want* to get married in here!" cried a regular, Mike. His partner Tim nodded. "We've wanted a Bali-Hai wedding at the Bibby *so much!*"

"Well you can fuck off," said Jonty.

"But we've told people we're having it here!" said Mike and Tim together.

"Tell 'em something else, then!" said Jonty. "Sick of kitsch weddings. They should be real, and special. We've fought for equal marriage, we shouldn't be clowns."

Everyone tutted and rolled their eyes.

"Straight people like Lynne Featherstone fought for us too," said Jonty, "So don't be berks with Bali-Hai weddings. Lagney don't like the flashbulbs anyway."

His partner Jason arrived to take drinks orders. "Put these on the house, love?" said Jonty. Everyone cherished Jason's usual deadpan look of reply. A working-class, taciturn wisp of 28, Jason had served five years for armed robbery. That wasn't a problem, the problem was, he was an intelligent workaholic who ran all areas of the Bibby, leaving Jonty little to do but sit around being a curmudgeon.

"I'm OK thanks," said David when asked what he'd like.

"Have an ale, love?" said John. "You like ale, you've not had one for yonks."

"18 real ales here now," said Jason. "Tried the Mumbles Gold?"

David and John spent a blissful hour gazing at the faux South Seas, vaguely hearing Jonty entertain or grumble.

Suddenly they heard him say:

"I tell you what we've *not* had awhile – a proper, stylish *laugh* of a wedding. Not since Lisa and Bea in France. Now… I'm thinking: *you two*."

John looked up: "Uh?"

"Yes, *you pair*. Get married!"

"Eh?" said John, exchanging glances with David.

"Yes, *married*," said Jonty "Is the word new to you? It's in the dictionary – between man-up and moron."

"We've never thought of getting married?" said John, snuggling into David.

"Suppose not," said David, shyly.

"Aw, go on!" said a man called Anthony. "You're lovely. You should do it."

"Hear-hear," said Jonty and others. "But no wedding *here*," added Jonty.

John would never know why the moment seized him. In a gold-white haze, all he saw was David's serene, loveable face, as he heard his own voice save: "David? Will you marry me?"

A cheer from the nine present made David chuckle nervously and blush.

"Well, John… I…" he couldn't stop smiling. Tears filled his eyes. "John… I…"

"Speak up, love!" said Jonty.

David cleared his throat and said: "Why, *yes*, I'll marry you, John!"

They hugged to cheers, cameraphones, tears, "Jason, bring five Bollies?", hugs, raised glasses and Jonty's: "How about a wedding on t'steam railway? 23 mile. They do weddings. Two private carriages, all afternoon, vows at a tiny old church en route."

"Yes!" cried everyone, except John and David, who couldn't stop hugging and murmuring "I love you". No one had seen them so happy. Some had never seen David happy. Everyone felt joy.

Chapter 3

DEWY SAT NAKED on the patio in her sunhat, frowning through The Tattler again. Annette was indoors, catching up with work, ringing her students. She came out, hugged Dewy: "Going down Exeter, hon. A subsidised bus leaves at 9am, 11 and 5pm! Only 40 minutes, 60 pence each way. No more £30 a week-pass or changing buses at Crendlesham."

"That's wonderful!" said Dewy.

They kissed. Annette left. Dewy picked up the paper, tutted at: **Man Loses Holi Day Refund** and impulsively rang a number.

Geoff Carruthers answered: "Is that who I think it is?"

"Why's your paper moronic and where's my money?" said Dewy.

"I admit we could do with a hand," sighed Carruthers

"I could do with money owed. I called the parent company. They never received the invoice."

"Well… we could talk about that?"

"We are."

"Er…"

"Mr Carruthers, what's *happened* to this paper? It's full of mistakes."

"I'm just back off holiday, half the staff are on theirs. Could do with a hand."

"If you want help, one issue only, I'll work Sunday for 200 cash plus confirmation the company has my invoice."

"Um, today's Friday? This afternoon we ~"

"I know where you all go. And I'm not."

"Meet me there an hour early. Back room of the Bess, entrance in the clock-tower square."

He ended the call. Dewy stood, annoyed. "I'm just gonna, like, *obey*!?"

But she realised her other reason for strangely return- ing to the paper on Sunday: to make sure Annette could cope alone in the cottage. Dewy absent 12 hours the day before flying back to the US would help ease Annette into her new life.

Dewy took her dress from the line, pulled it on and rang Rashid's taxi.

GEOFF CARRUTHERS SAID Dewy couldn't be owed £3,020.

"Union rate. 200 hours, four issues," said Dewy.

"A lot of days off. You weren't in Fridays."

"Sundays instead."

"Not an official day," said Carruthers.

"You are truly the weasel!" said Dewy. "I worked hard, did a good job."

She drained her fizzy water and called to a barman: "Excuse me? A pint of Rattock's, please?"

"Oof, you shouldn't drink that in the day," said Car- ruthers.

"I need it to smother anger so I don't assault *you*. OK, maybe I shouldn't drink it. Sir? Hold the Rattock's? Merlot instead, please?"

The barman apologetically said he'd begun pouring Rattock's. He held up the glass, under an inch full.

Dewy realised the combination of Carruthers and being told one spurt of Rattock's was a problem, was changing her into someone she didn't like and couldn't stop being. Gunship-grey walls and chalk-boards surrounded her in a 1590 tavern of dark beams, low ceilings and labyrinthine layout.

"Okaay," she sighed, "A *half* of Rattock's, *and* the Merlot. Actually, I don't want anything."

"Have to charge you for a half, I'm afraid," said the man. "The system will ~"

"The system! Look at *you*! Tattoos, beard and piercings, cringing to 'the system'? Some rebel, huh! Think you're *radical* looking like that?"

"£2.65 please!" snapped the barman.

"Pay the hipster, Geoff," said Dewy swinging her coat over her shoulder as she walked out. "And, yes I'll work Sunday, 200 cash, and a three-thousand-twenty invoice signed by yourself."

ANNETTE RETURNED FROM Exeter with gifts for Dewy: a cherry-red cardigan, vegetarian sausage rolls, a book called Betjeman's England and a flagon of organic lemonade. She found Dewy on the bed.

"Oh, honey! Did something happen?"

Dewy began to cry again. Annette lay next to her, rubbed her cold arms.

"Have a bad day, hon?"

"Mmm."

"You've not drunk? Oh, you *are* good!" said Annette, caressing Dewy. "Was someone bad to you, darling?"

"No."

"Were… *you* a little bad –

"*Yes*."

"Oh, hon, I'm sure you weren't."

"I was obnoxious and said ignorant things. Meant them though. I'm horrible. I shouldn't be alive."

"Oh, honey, no, not this again?" Annette hugged Dewy close. "*No*. Hear me? We're not going there again? We *said*, remember? Look at me, my love? Look at me?"

They touched faces. Annette kissed Dewy: "I have things for you, hon? Come see?"

"Sure," said Dewy. "And *you* have a car, hon. Sorry it's the same one."

"Car?"

"The Stag? I wondered what happened to it. I rang Sheekey's. Police had contacted them and they towed the car back, fixed it up, I've paid the balance. They're all asking after you, hon. The car's yours now, documents in your name."

They kissed. Dewy said: "It's parked down the street, the driveway here's steep, it'd never get out."

Later, Dewy cooked. Gravy was poured on fried vegetarian sausage rolls, kale, tinned mushy peas and Smash potato thickened by peanut butter.

Chapter 4

Mum im 3 or 4 miles near a place called Bruton look 4 a roundabout

Danii drove fast to Somerset, parked in a lay-by near Bruton and smoked. A new text from Jade arrived: In this vilage called Hodington

Danii was there in five minutes.

Hoddington had an In Bloom award, pink cottages and a war memorial. In the lych-gate of an ancient church, sheltering from drizzle, sat an apathetic, grubby girl with bulging rucksack and Rennicksons carrier bags. She stirred to see a woman in twinset and heels clack awkwardly along a path to the church. The woman tried to protect her hair from rain by holding a hand flat above it, like a school-play halo. Danii often did that, Jade remembered. It was really embarrassing.

"Mum? In here."

"Oh my God! *Oh my God!*"

"All right! I don't want fuss."

"Cuddle me. *Cuddle me.* Ooh, you stink."

"*Great*!" yelled Jade, "Have a go at me after two seconds!"

"You stink in a *nice* way," wept Danii. "Oh, Jade."

"You're crushing me! Stop kissing my head!"

"*Of course* I'm kissing your head."

"Well *don't*. And stop crying."

"No one's here to see, are they?" said Danii, looking round, holding Jade tight. Jade looked too. Bright grass at eye-level, old graves rising. A robin hopped.

In Bruton they found an unmodernised cafe, quietly busy, serving drinks and fresh-cooked food quickly. Danii and Jade relaxed to a depth not possible in global coffee-shop chains. They looked out the window at a rainy street.

Danii told Jade to eat as much as she liked. Jade said "I don't get so hungry now". She drank much tea, juice and Ballygowan.

"Where you been sleeping?" said Danii.

"I told you I've slept... in a garage at one point. I always found some kind of shelter. I'm not answering any more questions."

"Weren't you *cold*?" implored Danii, taking Jade's hand. "Did it rain? Were you dry?" She pressed Jade's hand to her chest. "Did anyone... ...? W-were you... approached?"

"No. Being fat and ugly has its advantages."

"You're not fat, you're not ugly."

"I pretended I always looked like I knew where I was going? If you look like a drifter, just... drifting around, trouble will find you."

"Exactly. Clever girl."

Tension rose. Avoiding talk of what must happen couldn't last.

"I'm not coming back, mum. Don't try to make me. I know where I'm going. No one's stopping me."

Danii believed her. "You 'know where you're going'? Where, Jade?"

"North. I finally found out where two friends are. In a 'detention centre'."

MARLON LAY ON his England FC duvet cover, staring at the ceiling.

I lost my virginity. Then... she wasn't there.

He checked his phone for messages every 15 minutes. Nothing.

Wish I was with someone I could talk things out with. Wish I was in bed with that someone.

He understood Danii was unavailable now. More bluntly: he'd been dumped.

I can't be in touch at the moment but pleae don't think I've forgotten you was her last text, two weeks ago.

Like everyone, Marlon had longed through his youth to meet a partner. Who would she be? What would her company be like? Would they love each other, hug in bed, talk, and listen?

"*That's* what I always wanted," Marlon realised aloud. "I thought I wanted sex, now I've done that, it's nice, but what I *really* want is… someone *with* me. With me *always*."

He felt a strange sensation, a new yearning, a door opening inside him, ready to receive something wonderful. There *was* someone he knew, and who liked being with him. "Really pretty as well. Bit daft, but…"

Marlon turned on his side and hugged a pillow. "I wish she was here. I'd love to be talking with her now. I'd cuddle her too. She'd be nice to cuddle. I never thought that before…"

Fondness for Millie overwhelmed him. He hungered for her company, even desired her. *She IS nice.* Marlon reached for his phone. *Agh! Never took her number. She gave me it one time… I threw it away! I never gave her mine.*

Happiness welled up in him. The side of him that always knew being with Danii was wrong, won through now.

Lovely lady, but… married, twice my age?! I'll see Millie instead. I'm gonna ask her out. Might have to call round at Bobby Zee's to find her. Lovely girl. Why didn't I realise before?"

DANII LEFT THE north Somerset B&B room to smoke outside and ring Liu.

"I'll be back tomorrow or day after. She says she's got plans. I'm hoping after a couple nights of warm bed and meals she'll feel different and want to come home…"

Danii returned to the room, lay in the smaller bed, watching cloudy night sky. She got up at 4am and walked over to Jade. She slept beautifully, so young and smooth. Danii gently swept hair off Jade's brow. Why had Jade broken down so pitifully when they'd got back to the car? Why did she keep saying: "Please, *please* never try to take me home?"

"Little drama queen," murmured Danii, placing a hand on Jade's sleeping form. But a frown stole over Danii's features at remembering the depth of Jade's desperation and hardness of determination *I'm not coming back. There's nothing you can do about it.*

At 6am Danii returned from a cigarette to find Jade awake, packing fast.

"I don't trust you!" Jade fumed. "You've spoken to… *him.*"

"I haven't spoken to anyone," said Danii. "My phone's over there, look."

Jade seized the phone to examine it. No contact except Liu. Danii felt suddenly annoyed.

"What do you mean *'him'*?" she snapped. "He's your *Dad*! He's worried sick about you. You've put him through hell these two weeks, *you really have!*"

Jade froze. Danii glanced away, but turned to look again. Jade's glare and stillness conveyed something.

Danii went still too. She saw her daughter as never before – ageless, defiant… a woman. And infinitely, terribly hurt.

"Jade?" said Danii, softly. "Gimme a cuddle."

Jade let her mother hug her. She stared at a wall.

"Jadey, did something happen?" said Danii, suppressing tears.

Jade fully tensed.

"Oh dear God," whispered Danii. "*Oh*, I'm sorry. Oh dear God."

ON SUNDAY NIGHT, Dewy left the Tattler, having done all she could, including the Farmer's Bulletin and listings pages. She'd be remembered on a good note by certain staff. Returning for 12 hours had been strange, as was leaving for good, setting the alarm, posting her keys through the Tattler letterbox at 8pm.

Dewy walked in last midsummer sun, revelling in birdsong, through Paddock's Wood, onto Keeley Lane, up to Londis. There she gathered three drums of Smash, tins of mushy peas, a bottle of Merlot, dry-roasted peanuts, Bisto gravy granules and Paxo. Findus Crispy Pancakes had been reasonably Disgusting, but nothing like they looked on the box after Dewy boiled them. Now her gaze fell on Bird's Eye Potato Waffles under a new heap of Magnums in the jingling tub-freezer. She tugged a red box out, causing a Magnumlanche, and examined it: "Now *these* look like they know what they're about!"

She approached the till. The usual people turned to look. Dewy tensely smiled as she entered their staring, close midst. In silence Barbara beeped the purchases. Needing an activity to avert nervous collapse, Dewy reached for six Caramacs to add.

"I'm going back to the States tomorrow, Barbara."

"Hmph," said Barbara. She paused, looked at Dewy clearly, gathered Caramacs and the last basket item – Ribena – and dropped them straight in the bag unbeeped. "Take them then. Mind how you go."

Later, the kitchen took a while to clean after Dewy and Annette had eaten.

Both were happy. Annette had befriended Florence and Ada next door.

"Ada's a Holocaust survivor, she lost most of her family."

"Oh my. *Oh.*"

"And Florence is amazing. Very opinionated. A botanist, been to every country in, like, the world? So serene and gentle, all vegans, they don't like cars. They don't like petrol-engines. I told them you started going barefoot because of that. We talked about how technology for hydrogen-powered, electric, even solar-batteried cars is on a plate, but oil companies ~"

"Are gangsters," said Dewy. "The underworld – apt word, in their case."

"And in the cottage beyond is Matthias!" said Annette, "A 76-year-old microbiologist from Zambia, still teaching, wears big colourful patterned robes."

They sat entwined on a garden seat, watching the rise of the moon. An owl called, stars were bright, they saw Cassiopeia and kissed.

Annette asked if Dewy would like a bath. She loved to bathe Dewy, soapily scrubbing the soles of her feet, soaping her long back, bosoms and thighs, pouring warm water on her head, Dewy's hair tapering sleekly, eyes shut, lips pursed.

"Kinda tired, hon." said Dewy. "I'll shower in the morning."

They went to bed. Annette fell asleep in Dewy's arms.

The room was blue-white and ghostly. Dewy's red toenails looked black, the white bed sepulchral. Dewy and the moon gazed at each other. A fox barked hoarse. Annette stirred.

"Oh, darling," murmured Dewy's mouth on Annette's restful head. "I love you. But… we cannot go on. I'm sorry. Someone better will come. The Goddess won't leave you alone and unprotected."

Dewy tried to speak more, but nothing came. She saw the room from above, her own long, white body caressing Annette.

The moon rose higher than the house. Dewy fell into twitching sleep of muttered words, English, Spanish, or madness.

She dreamt she watched Annette and herself on a long, high bridge in white mist. They happily shuffled towards each other, half-dancing, hands as paws, as they often did as girls. Dewy felt immense happiness in the dream at that moment. She watched herself and Annette hold both each other's hands, Annette on the left. They gazed at each other kindly then parted, backing away, watching each other, then turned, ran and dived over the bridge-rail into mist. The empty bridge remained.

Chapter 5

ANNETTE'S LIFE SEEMED stable, but she missed Morris sorely, and wished Dewy hadn't left so soon. Annette booked a flight home for early August to attend her father's 70th birthday. She began counting down the 812 hours until she'd next see Morris. She wanted to send him postcards, but if Joanna Stephens found out that was still going on, she'd be sour and intercept them.

Annette tried to settle. Campus canteen served free breakfasts and evening meals. Transport to Exeter by old, blue, double-decker bus meant lovely rural views from the top deck. Annette liked Exeter and the work she did, spending hours in faculty, roaming the old city, taking trains to nearby towns to bird-watch and explore.

But she was always alone. When term ended, Annette wasn't prepared for complete isolation, nor weeks-long overcast that can happen in British summers: unmoving, low, grey cloud blocking all sky. Annette had never consciously experienced depression, but a fourth day of weather like this made her not go out.

Dewy had broken contact again. Annette anxiously hoped Dewy wouldn't fade from her daily life for months, as she often had over the years. She texted Dewy: *No point researching Seasonal Affective Disorder, all of Britain has it. Successive days of prison-gray overcast.*

THAT SAME MOMENT, 3,000 miles away, five in the

morning, Dewy sat in the cabin, read Annette's text and replied: Rainy here. The Millards hate me. Roo's here. I miss you. I love you. Wish I'd stayed with you. Men chainsawing trees in the days here because Wal's a pea-brained, property-renovation victim.

Dewy didn't send the text. She rarely liked what she wrote, and wanted distance from Annette, praying each day someone Annette deserved would appear to fill the vacuum. If this hadn't happened by Annette's visit home in August, Dewy would reconsider. But she'd blogged:

I'm no good for her. She needs someone who gives her love, sex and daily help. Her life needs new direction and, hell, doesn't mine not? I want to throw myself into dance, ask around this year's Jacob's Pillow, give out a resumé, talk to people. Could a contemporary dance company adopt me as stage-manager/driver in exchange for studying new dance and choreography?

But how do I earn money to pay for tuition and support myself? thought Dewy: *That ol' Moebius.*

ANNETTE FELT SHE was distancing from Dewy too, for she took up running. She'd wanted to awhile, but hadn't, as Dewy's ire and contempt for aggressive, modern runners was often voiced. Annette bought a pair of running trainers, but no commercial running-wear besides shorts and T-shirts.

Dewy herself had been a runner in last years of High School (described as "the barefoot running girl" in the 2006 yearbook). She ran some days nearly all two years at college, and even in bouts of reform in Medford.

Then, in 2011, the entire middle-class took up running overnight. Streets were unrelaxed, as every 20 seconds a Lycra'd apparition sprinted not past, but *at* people. In drink, Dewy ranted on the matter, or posted variants of:

> **Runners today are fascists. Fascism = bullying. And bullying is what modern runners do, right there, in your street. They deliberately run straight *at* people. Or go right up behind them and make them jump. Notice they don't run at lamp-posts? They manage a wide berth of *those*. But families with children, elderly, or partly-sighted people, you, me – all trash for this cowardly super-race to shove out the way.**
>
> **The agony is: *it's so easy to run with consideration*. It's *zero effort* to see an obstacle, human or otherwise, 20 yards ahead and gently change course, twisting your waist one inch in the direction of the empty space beside the object. But today's runners refuse to (unless you're a lamp-post). Their attitude: "*NO!* Everyone must move *out the way* of the great *ME!*"**
>
> **Historians – look no further than the above to understand these times. Conformist, dull, brattish and proud.**
>
> **And look at today's sports fetishwear! The middle-class has *en masse* adopted an obviously psychosexual, weird, tight-black-clothes fetish to run or cycle in. Every last contour of genitalia and ass blatantly defined. Most of the wearers are too vacant to notice even that. They dress up in these hornet-costumes because advertising said so.**
>
> **The Third Reich worshipped body-perfection and sex-power-clothes too. Instead of jack-boots and kinky uniforms, today's Nazi clone wears shrink-wrap, elastane sportswear. No swastika armband, instead a little computer on upper arm. Now get out their way. *Out the way!!***

But Annette enjoyed running, and found herself good at it. She decided not to tell Dewy, though Dewy never contacted now.

By early July campus was deserted. Ada, Florence and Matthias left for a French holiday in an electric van. Annette was to prepare for a one-week summer school at the end of July. Her solitude deepened.

Transport from campus to Exeter stopped in holidays. Annette tried to drive the Stag there, but turned back at Galars Peak. She didn't like the engine noise, it brought back the night of the hospital. The Stag would stay parked along from the house for a long time.

But lanes in high country to Galars Peak were beautiful, Galars a stop on the 605 to Exeter. Four weekdays of five, Annette walked three miles to the bus stop, and ran back on returning from Exeter late afternoon. One time a man who seemed blind and 90, gave her a lift on his uncovered 1950s tractor. Annette's joy in that moment almost alleviated not hearing from Dewy, or anyone in the world, except e-mails about Morris from Consuela or Martina. If it rained Annette couldn't walk to Galars Peak. She lay in bed, drifting in and out of thoughts and feelings

Why do I feel different towards Dewy? When I got sexy that time, she'd been nice, but I know she didn't like it. I wish it hadn't happened. Did it break our window? Was it that *that broke us apart? I don't think it's healthy we –* I - *did that. Did it cancel out our childhoods together?*

Childhood. Annette relived certain happinesses. From their earliest days, Dewy's calm, medium-low, slightly lilting voice reading to her in bed. Winter nights, summer evenings, rainy afternoons like now. Jane Eyre, The Chalet School, David Copperfield, Little Women, Puck of Pook's Hill, Ballet Shoes, Roots, The Hitch-hikers Guide To The Galaxy, Sweet Valley High, Heidi, Watership Down, Frankenstein, Huckleberry Finn, Shakespeare's sonnets, Sylvia Plath, Christina Rossetti, Walt Whitman, Emily Brontë, Robert Frost. *Thank-you for reading to me, Dewy. No one else did.*

But these memories made her loneliness and recent loss of a child feel more intense and deeply sad. *What is wrong with me? Is this madness?*

One early evening, house under raincloud, Annette got up. Every room was a mess, in each square foot either a book, shoe, saucepan-lid, phone charger, plate, four peanuts, pencil, "Scientific American", tea-bag, coat-hanger, torn packaging, fork or sock.

Annette walked into the rain, pulled kale, picked up plums, apples and pears. She boiled the lot in a pan, adding scrapings-out of honey and peanut butter jars, plus a last handful of home-made muesli Florence had given her. She almost enjoyed the meal then sat very still, watching the garden. The day went black.

ON A RAINY Wednesday Annette stayed later and later in the university library. By 9pm the last bus had left, she must get a cab to Farrisford, but wanted to run awhile. Dark wet streets glistened. No one was about.

She ran along the river, out of the city, to a suburb. Light rain felt refreshing, but she'd run miles, mostly downhill. She must now get back, and remember how to. All around her were house-shapes and streetlights, no far perspectives. An alley between back gardens joined a dark path, amber streetlit every 200 metres. Annette walked briskly but became afraid. Noises burst from bushes – crows, foxes. She saw no city lights, and no suburban ones now either.

A figure was 50 metres ahead. When he or she passed under a lamp Annette a bulky upper back. The person was slow and stopped frequently. For 10 minutes Annette carefully followed. Some suburban lights returned. The person stopped to cough, bent double. Annette felt if that happened again, she could run safely past towards a road, four streetlights away. But pitch dark lay between each light. The figure had vanished into one of those darknesses now, and did not reappear.

Annette waited then moved slowly. She called out: "Is anyone there please? Are you OK?"

Oh! Stupidest thing I've ever done!! If it's a man and he has a knife…!?

Rain pattered on trees. A pained, loud cough began, and continued, like an old car trying to start. Annette called:

"Are you OK? Do you need help?"

An exhausted voice replied. Annette couldn't hear what it said. She edged forward, saying: "I'm coming along the path! Can you head for the next light? In case I bump into you!"

The cough again, then, through big breaths, a voice mustered strength:

"Is that you, Annette?"

"*Annie!!*"

They stumbled blindly, hands foraging empty air. They touched, they hugged. Annie sagged in Annette's arms. She was thin and didn't smell too good.

They walked, wet and tired, trying to talk. City lights appeared. Annie said she lived in Exeter and worked in fields fruit-picking. She'd missed the last bus and walked from a farm, her cough a 'wee cold' she'd picked up.

Annette told how she and Dewy returned to America, Morris was well, but 11 ounces heavier, she hadn't told her parents about her pregnancy and had hardly seen them, for when they returned from Virginia, Annette and Morris decamped to Dewy's cabin for two nights. "Morris takes a *long* time to settle out there. So many animal sounds and scents, he gets real excited, especially at night."

Annie tried to explain The Lugworm crisis of weeks before, but had spoken more in the last 10 minutes than in a month. She didn't want to relive how Beverley had broken down and run outside, crying to Annie: "Please don't leave me," while Fent clutched his broken nose, screaming: "I'll get the *law* on you, you little Scottish cow!

This is *assault.*"

She did not tell Annette she'd arrived in Exeter half an hour before with nowhere to go after walking for days. Her fingernails were black. Annette saw her mud-caked shoes, remembered when she'd got them new in Crendlesham, real Dr Martens, Annie was so happy that day.

They reached the bank of the Exe and walked up to the city. At a crossroads they hugged.

"Nice tae see you," croaked Annie, eyes half-closed. "Ah'll be getting hame."

"Oh, Annie. Bath and warm bed, I hope?"

"Aye, nae bother." She began to cough.

Rain strengthened. Annette led Annie to the shelter of a shop doorway.

"Where do you live, Annie?"

"Er, near the station. Y'all right getting hame yurself?"

"I'll get a cab," said Annette.

"OK. Take care, eh?"

"Oh, Annie? I liked seeing you."

They hugged, Annie uncomfortable. She hadn't expected a firm, endless hug, but Annette wouldn't let go.

A coughing explosion made Annie slide downwall to a sitting position, rucksack shunting her head forward. Annette took her hands and rubbed them. They'd got cold since she held them a minute before. When at last her coughing stopped, Annie tried to free her hands. "You've grabbed me," she said, trying to seem amused. "Ye no' letting go?"

"Where are you going, Annie?"

"Home, darlin'. I'm tired. Nice seeing you. But I need to go."

Annette helped her stand. They looked at each other, half-lit by window displays. A minicab swished past. Annie needed to end this moment. She'd have hardened by now, but couldn't. Annette was so beautiful, her touch smooth, warm, gently strong. Annie didn't want to let go.

Annette's hands felt like someone reaching to her from a lifeboat. A lifeboat in a sea of cold pavements, cold every day, every day.

"Annie?"

"Uh?"

"Are you homeless?"

FOR TWO NIGHTS Annie lay in Annette's bed, overwhelmed by more gifts, nourishment and affection than she'd ever known. She'd never been given flowers before, let alone a cashmere blanket.

When better, Annie slept with Annette properly for the first time, each in a realm beyond words. Never had Annie experienced such perfect alignment of her body with someone else's, nor felt so ecstatic, so *loved*, full-filled and safe.

Next day Annette woke thrilled with affection for the woman in her arms. The experience felt different to waking with Dewy. Annette knew now she'd felt smaller, younger, less worldly than Dewy (though Dewy never intended this). But with Annie she felt like an adult, not an awkward, less beautiful, younger sister. Something very new was happening. Excitement, peace and joy glowed deeply in her abdomen. These feelings increased by the hour.

Annie woke, stretched, opened her eyes, looked startled. When she saw Annette, her face changed to pure adoration.

"Oh, Annie," said Annette. "You're beautiful."

"Ah wouldnae go that far, pet. But see you? You're *gorgeous*."

They hugged. Annette whispered:

"Annie? Will you come to America?

Part Four

Chapter 1

ANNIE CAMERON HAD never flown. She sat at a window-seat mesmerised by the world from above. A screen map traced the plane's progress north over England, then west, within miles of Annie's home-town Ardrossan.

As a child she'd looked up at high vapour trails, knowing those planes were going to America. She'd never dreamed she might ever be in one. Now she really *was*, and in love, and… and… so many positives, Annie was in life-shock – a pleasant form of it, but shock.

When Annette snuggled up to her and fell asleep, Annie gazed down at Scottish sea islands, then examined another novelty that amazed her: something she'd thought she'd never own: a passport. It was in her birth name, Ann Jodie McClure, of no criminal past. She was free to enter the US.

Annette stirred. She and Annie gazed down at the ocean.

"We're coming back by sea," said Annette.

"Really? On a ship?" said Annie.

"So Morris can come."

Near sunset they were met by silver-haired estate manager Juan. He drove them north in a lacquer-black Landcruiser seven feet high. Annette thrilled to watch Annie entranced by sunset forests left, pretty pastel towns against plum-dark Atlantic right.

The Stephens estate gates opened to a gently rising lane through woods and meadows. In very last dusk, three women led horses. "Karen, Stephanie and Lois," said Annette: "The red roan's called Chastain, I can't see the others."

They pulled up at a colonial, white-blue, weatherboard mansion overlooking a mile-away sea estuary. Far in the water, green lights and red lights blinked on and off across distances of night. Annie believed they'd arrived at a hotel. Lanterns and windows glowed, cicadas chirruped, flower scents richly filled the air. A man's silhouette at one of many windows raised a hand in greeting. His other arm cradled a dog.

Juan typed a code in a door-lock. They entered a very large hall of crimson walls, chandeliers and gilt-framed sea paintings.

Morris tore round a corner, crazed. Annette cried out and sank to her knees on the immaculate old lacquered wood floor. Morris zig-zagged, sneezed, rose on hind-legs, cried, rolled on the floor, burst into a run, slid, turned back on himself, charged back, jumped about.

"Oh, Booboo! Mommy's missed you!" sobbed Annette. She glanced up to Annie: "He runs around before Mommy gets a kiss. Welcome, by the way, Annie, I'll show you the house in a minute…"

"H-*house*, er, aye," said Annie.

Head-bowed, gnashing with joy, Morris fell on Annette's lap, nestled into her arms and stretched high to press her mouth with his own.

"Oh, BooBoo!" wept Annette, kissing him back. "Awww! Will you say hi to Annie? This is Annie! You're gonna know her *real well*."

Retired two-star admiral Robert Stephens III appeared, lean, calm, mountainous in navy shirt, chino shorts, very black socks, dark deck shoes.

"Daddy, you're tanned!" smiled Annette. "Been sailing a lot? This is Annie, my friend from England, who's from Scotland."

"Hello, Annie, welcome," rumbled a deep, precise voice. "Thank-you for coming to stay and escorting Annette. Visited New England before?"

"Er, n-no," stammered Annie, blushing as she shook Robert Stephens's huge hand. She'd never known anyone like this man. Very tall and broad, black hair scarcely grey, dark blue eyes, unlike Annette's.

"Mom's at the stables," he said, curtly embracing his daughter, "She's happy, Courtney got the all-clear, dropped off by John's assistant, she got her through this."

He turned to Annie: "One of my wife's fillies had EPM, uh Equine Protozoal Myelo… um ~"

"Myeloencephalitis," said father and daughter together, Robert continuing: "But she's OK now. C'mon through, have a drink, girls?"

They followed him along a passage to a large, traditional kitchen of blue china-tiled walls, rosewood dressers and copper pans hung over a hearth. Robert Stephens said: "Afraid you're both in the old rooms a couple nights Friday, when everyone comes."

"Daddy's birthday Saturday," said Annette to Annie.

"90 staying," added Robert Stephens, "Hundred more in hotels, friends' houses. Annette, will you help Consuela and Juan a little on the day?"

Annette was unreachable. Holding Morris in her arms, her face caressed his face, and his caressed hers. She kissed his head, sniffing near his ears.

"Fix you a Martini, um, Annie?" said Robert Stephens. "Whiskey?"

"No thanks, Mr, er –."

"Bob. Want a beer?"

"No thanks."

"Annette? We have…" He opened a huge refrigerator. "…this stuff, brewed in Andover?"

"Mm? Sure, Daddy, I'll have one. We're gonna take Morris out first."

"Con made you guacamole and vegetarian mince. Like it I make tortillas?"

"We'll make 'em, Daddy."

"Righty." He left for a lamp-lit corridor: "Watching 'Strong Island' right now." He raised a hand, said: "Welcome, Annie, hope you enjoy your stay with us."

In the grounds Annette and Annie watched shimmering coastal lights, dense as diamonds out on Plum Island.

Footsteps along a path, a dark moving shape, white trousers waist to knee.

"Hi, Mom!" called Annette.

"Ah, Annette," cut a clear, sharp voice. "Good journey?"

"Fine thank-you. This is Annie!"

"Yeah, you said you'd bring someone – dog on the leash?"

"Yes, Mom," sighed Annette. "The long leash."

"Good. Hello, Annie? Joanna Stephens."

Annie nervously greeted a handsome woman with high cheekbones and eyes like Annette's only less kind. Tall, straight in riding boots and jet-black blazer, her profile was lit by a wall-light with insects whizzing around.

"The Meakins wanna see you Thursday, Annette."

"Oh, that's nice. Um… long way for Morris."

Joanna tutted. "He'll sleep won't he not? Couple hours' drive."

"Plus the boat?" said Annette.

"Wanna call them, say you're not coming?"

"No, I…"

"Annie's welcome too. What you doing tomorrow, girls? You ride, Annie?"

"Annie doesn't ride. We're going down Newburyport, see if we can't buy something to wear for these… 'engagements'."

"You needn't sound like that. It's only the Meakins, Bob's 70th then the Woolasons. Callaghans on the third, Macphersons fourth, then nothing til The Dennisons."

"And Booboo's birthday, August 7th!"

"Not on *our* calendar," said Joanna Stephens. "You're not having that here."

"I *know*."

"Annie, you post-doc too? Same school?"

"We're learning many things, Annie and I," said Annette happily.

"Good," said Joanna Stephens, uninterested, walking away: "Welcome, Annie, good to have you here. Come see the horses sometime."

Annette was surprised by her mother's slight warmth to Annie. She didn't know how glad Joanna was, to at last see someone with her who wasn't Dewy.

ANNIE PRIVATELY CAME to terms with the truth this vast, astonishing building was no hotel, but *Annette's family home*. Rooms were known by points of the compass, to not be confused with duplicates elsewhere in the house: the *east* sitting room, not the south-facing one, the north kitchen, not the east, the west bedrooms. While passageways and stairs (except for white marble staircases) had deep red, or gold carpets, most floors were of smooth, dark antique wood, like treacle toffee.

The largest hall was the north-west (not the everyday-use south one where they'd arrived). Its atrium rose four storeys above a marble staircase to walkways with maple banisters. Paintings of landscapes, horses or ships, never abstracts, hung on teal and gold-leaf walls. Three 100 foot rooms led off in different directions, respective colour schemes gold, red and dark green. Tiffany lamps stood on burl and walnut sideboards. Four velvet sofas in each room's centre, faced outwards, four more (three if a hearth was there) each end of the room, facing inwards. Silk banquettes lined walls, taffeta drapes half-shaded two dozen windows and four French doors. Somewhere in each room was a 15 foot hearth. The rooms were for entertaining, Annie guessed. Two opened out to terraces and lawns. A fourth was dark-blue with a foot-high stage and a hundred silver service settings on long tables. "Daddy's lodge meets here sometimes," said Annette.

That night, Annette left Morris snoring and crossed the passage to Annie's room to make love. They returned to Annette's room as Morris was stirring. He led them downstairs, to be let out to pee. All three ate breakfast as dawn rose. They held each other, glad they cuddled easily with Morris held between them. They returned to bed, to warmth, to whispers. Annette spoke of her childhood and growing up.

"You inspire me to talk," said Annette. "I've never really talked before."

"It's lovely, pet," said Annie, holding Annette close. "Nobody's ever spoke to me. Talk as much as you want, darlin'."

ANNIE LEARNED HOW to safely hold Morris in the baby-sling, so he could ride in a convertible. Annette led them along a path between gardens to a huge red barn. "Where are we, Booboo? *Yes!* We're going for a drive!"

The barn was dark, but sunrays from high flooded old, unusual cars, the nearest a cheerful red, mostly covered by tarpaulin.

"These are my projects, most of them roadworthy now," said Annette. "The Mustang always has been, I only upgraded its engine. And this red one, let me show you it…" She pulled the tarpaulin. "A 1967 Shelby Cobra. Friends had it lying in a barn for, like, 40 years? I'll show you pictures of what it looked like. You and I can go out in it sometime, but it's too loud for Booboo. Isn't it, Booboo? *Yes! We* always go in the Mustang!"

They drove to Newburyport in Annette's 2003 sea-blue convertible, roof down. In a boutique the owner greeted Annette by name and enquired after people she knew. Annette bought Annie a white and navy sheath dress and navy court shoes. Annie trembled and fought tears. No one had been so kind to her before. Annette half-calmed her afterwards: "Only dollars, not pounds, darling. Six hundred eighty-nine dollars is about nineteen pounds or something? The shoes were scarcely half that."

They kissed amid radiant buildings under bluest sky and morning sun. Annette said: "I wanted to buy you these things because Booboo and I love you, and want to say thank-you for coming here to be with us."

Near sunset, Annette's Mustang roared along the Plum Island turnpike. They watched the sky from the furthest tip of the shore.

Late that night Annette and Morris crept into the large guest room to join Annie's four-poster bed. All slept deeply after the day's coastal air.

"Jack Paton's on leave," barked Joanna next morning, striding through the east kitchen to leave the house. "He'll fly us to the Meakins."

Late afternoon, Joanna and Robert III drove them to a small airfield of neat grass where, to Annie's astonishment, Annette climbed up into the front of a four-seater aeroplane, put mike-headphones on, fiddled with dials and called to her:

"Please can you take BooBoo in the back-seat with you? Hold this towel loosely around the back of his head to cover his beautiful ears, so it's not too noisy?" Annie did so. Joanna loaded cases into the back of the plane then climbed in beside her. Mr Stephens sat beside Annette.

To Annie's increasing disbelief, while all around were indifferent, the plane – taxiing now – was being operated by Annette. Suddenly the thing shot forwards, roaring and bumping at increasingly alarming speed, then lifting up, and up, rocking, dipping but gaining power, going higher, the land smaller, there was the sea underneath them now… and *Annette was flying the plane.* 15 minutes on they landed well on a private airstrip at a country-club by a lake where a sea-plane waited.

Jack Paton's bulky small plane held 11 passengers, drinking Pimms and mesmerised by sunset from the air. The plane landed on sea with an immense *Boomfffshhhh!!!* Everyone laughed or cheered. "We've arrived" whispered Annette to Annie, yearning to kiss her. "This place is called Martha's Vineyard."

A cable-car took them up rocky cliffs to sunset gardens and a house of ochre rooms where a hundred guests talked, drank, or gathered outside by either of two pools. A concert pianist played indoors, a Spanish guitarist on a terrace.

Annie was often separated from Annette and Morris. Handsome, tall people with ice-blue eyes tried to converse with her. "Have we met?" or "How'd you do?" Annie's uneasy answers lasted a few seconds. She was concluded to be from Europe. An "Annette" had been spoken of, so she must be an assistant to the Stephens girl, or Annette Fallon, Annette Machin… no, on reflection, the Stephens girl, she's always been slightly… *um…*

Annie settled in a downstairs cinema where children and nannies watched "Snow White". Annie had seen few films in her life and knew nothing of Disney heritage. Snow White was bizarre and frightening at times, but it absorbed Annie. Upstairs she at last saw Annette, cradling Morris asleep in his baby-sling. She looked alone and tired. As Annie approached, her face turned to joy.

"Wanna kiss you bad," Annette whispered. "Let's go to bed, we won't be missed." Their four-room suite looked over a moonlit harbour, sea-planes bobbing near yachts.

ON RETURNING TO the Stephens's, work must start for

Saturday. Annie and Annette helped Consuela and teams of caterers in three kitchens. Annie grated cabbages and carrots for coleslaw, made potato salad for 200, prepared fruit. Annette washed up continuously. On the day they scarcely had an hour to bathe together, nap, then dress for the evening.

Sunset was beautiful, Venus low on the sea, the evening warm. Blue-white fairy-lights sparkled in trees. Braziers and lanterns lit paths and terraces.

On arriving downstairs, Annette and Morris were led away by a delighted, older woman in dark-green elbow-length gloves. Annie was alone now and relieved to be anonymous. She helped to set tables in a room where a jazz band warmed up. She to'd and fro'd through increasing numbers of tall, strong, elegant people, beautifully-dressed, with American voices (everyone American was still most exotic to Annie). Never had she seen such intense women's clothes, often navy and white, with nautical details, anchors sewn onto shoes, commodore stripes on sleeves. Annie's new Tory Burch dress fitted in.

Many people arrived. Annie wandered in a talking, perfumed forest of fascinating outfits, striking beauty, glowing complexions, beautiful smiles, conversations, musical laughter, Swiss watches, diamonds, clutch bags, sapphires. Perfect forms relaxed in Chanel suits, deep-coloured gowns, sparkling dresses, hair high on intelligent brows, lustrous down bare-backs.

Annie stood until so awkward she'd move to another burstingly busy room. At last she saw Annette in a quadrangle of crowded sofas, Morris in her arms. A woman knelt at her feet, dark head and lily-white arms resting on Annette's lap.

Angry at the woman's intimacy, Annie moved forward, but stopped herself. She paced outer reaches of the room, gaze never leaving the black-haired woman, whose face, mainly hidden, flashed purest white. "Get rid o' her," thought Annie.

But family friends surrounded Annette. If Annie appeared, she'd be awkwardly introduced while angry with the woman, who'd doubtless be powerful and clever, like everyone here. Nonetheless, anyone sprawled all over Annette's lap must be ousted.

Rounding a circle of talking people, Annie emerged to a new view of the intruder. She saw the woman's soles – bare, dark, hard. "Ah, it's *her*," sighed Annie, "I'd forgot about *her*."

She walked further until Dewy was in profile. In a glistening black short Dior dress, Dewy's skin shone as the moon. Lipstick and fingernails were red-pink, toenails not yet seen.

Dejected, Annie headed for a kitchen to offer her services. As she helped uncork vintage bottles of wine. Annette entered, pursued by her mother:

"*WHY is she here!?*" said Joanna, striking in heels and blood-orange shift dress with pink, diagonal band. "You *told* her!"

"I didn't!" cried Annette, caressing Morris. "I've had no contact with Dewy in *weeks!*" Morris trembled and slurped, tried to stand in his baby-sling.

"I can't believe her *nerve*," boomed Joanna.

"She knows we always celebrate Dad's birthday Saturday nearest."

"She drinks, I'll throw her out! I caught her picking at the midnight buffet. Does *that* again I'll knock her block off."

"Mom, please calm? This is unsettling for Booboo. Dewy's here because she has a gift for Dad."

"She can leave it in the east hall and *go*." said Joanna, bashing through the doors.

Annette comforted Morris, saw Annie and smiled. Annie glanced around then kissed her. Morris reached to touch Annie's nose with his own.

"A'right, weeman?" said Annie to Morris.

"*So glad* Morris and you were instant friends," smiled Annette. "I can't tell you what that means to me."

A door slowly half-opened. Dewy peered in. She didn't look alert. Her gaze glumly scanned the kitchen, saw rows of bottles and many caterers. She retreated.

"Honey?" called Annette.

Dewy started, saw Annette, relaxed a fraction. "Gotta eat," she said weakly. She kissed two fingertips, placed them lightly on Morris's paw, looked vaguely at Annie.

Annie nodded curtly: "How you doin'?"

Dewy didn't perceive her. It seemed a snub.

"Honey?" said Annette: "Annie's saying 'hello'."

"Uh? *Oh.* Annie? Hi. Why the misshapen face?"

"Honey, that's not nice," said Annette.

An amplified voice resounded through the ground floor: "WHOA!!, kinda loud!" Feedback shrieked. "Is that better?" continued the voice of Annette's eldest brother, Robert Stephens IV…. "Welcome everyone!"

"The speeches," flustered Annette, "I've to stand onstage!"

In seconds she delicately freed herself from the baby sling, put its loop over Dewy's lowered head and neck, while Dewy held Morris still in it. A move perfected over years.

Annette rushed: "I'm onstage with Mom, Dad, Bobby, Celia, the children," She took Annie's hands. "So sorry – no place set for you at dinner."

"Nae bother, pet, I prefer doing this. I'd feel out of place sitting in there."

"Dewy's not dining either. So you won't be alone."

Annie and Dewy eyed each other blankly.

SOON DEWY SAT in a large, empty room by the end of a long, covered, buffet table. Furtively taking food from beneath its cover, she ate non-stop. Morris agitated until Dewy occasionally fed him, but her own eating entranced her. Annie approached. Dewy munched a vol-au-vent.

"Ah'll take him oot for a pish," muttered Annie. She'd fetched a leash from the kitchen.

Alone now, Dewy gazed into space, eating potato salad, rye bread, quiche, small sandwiches, cheese and oatcakes, grapes, baked apple tarts, a pear, a wedge of Camembert, half a fresh baguette, spinach-and-ricotta pastries, brie with melba toast, cherry tomatoes, vegetable samosas, guacamole and crackers. At 10.15 she groaned: "Annie?"

Sitting elsewhere in the empty room, Annie ignored her. Dewy gasped "Annie?" twice more.

"*What*?" said Annie, startling Morris, who climbed on her, gazing quizzically.

"Can you get me some water?"

"Get it yurself!"

Surging voices indicated dinner was over. Doors opened, trolleys with coffee clattered in, the band began "Sweet Georgia Brown". Annie turned. Dewy was beside her.

"I'm sorry," said Dewy. "I'm glad you came with Annette. I really am."

Annie turned away. Dewy looked on helplessly. Morris looked up.

"I'm not gonna leave you," said Dewy, "I've a role. You're about to see it. The dining room will now invade. Women converge in the centre, while men, roaringly bored, spread out like rings from an atomic blast. A shockwave of jerks and interrogators. I'll protect you."

Annie got up, said "C'mon, son," to Morris who jumped from the sofa. They walked away.

Double doors opened. Crowds in peak conversation poured in. Many men moved to outer territory. Annie and Morris were straightaway talked at by a salamanderish man in a cobalt suit and gold watch. "Oh, fuck" sighed

Dewy. She weaved towards them, heard the snappy, trading-floor voice say:

"*C'mon*, girl! You went to a fancy dress party as Orphan Annie *one time,* right? Don't say no!"

Dewy arrived. "John, how are you? You look nice."

The man turned: "Hell's sake! On drugs, Durant? 'Look *nice*'? Don't creep me out!" He turned back to Annie: "Cute dog. But why the baby-sling? Child substitute? Get over it, girlie! It's a *doggee,* not a kid!

"How's your uh… *friend*?" tried Dewy, louder.

"Which?" he snapped. "Some of us have more than one a lifetime, Dewy."

"The woman at Christmas?"

"The blonde?" said John Tillotson.

"Is that how you define her?" said Dewy.

"Whuh?"

"By her hair colour? Has she a name, an identity?"

"You *correcting* me? I can't say 'The blonde'? Are *you fucking correcting me*?"

"What do you call men?" said Dewy, "The 'grey receding', 'pate churlish' 'bald direct'?"

"Fuck you," growled the man. Taking brandy from a waiter's tray, he saw a male friend: "Hey, *Bullfrog!* Whoa!" and marched towards him.

"Don't look at me like that, Annie," said Dewy, not realising Annie stared at the man. "I came to protect you. Don't worry, I'm *going*, but I'm nearby. If anyone who I know is a wanker – *oh* that *brilliant* British word! – if anyone like that hits on you, I'll come over strai~"

She stopped. A passing, tall, handsome man sighed: "Hey, Dewy."

"Graham," she said. "How are you?"

"Good." said the man, bored, not seeing her. "You?"

"Thank-you for asking, I –"

"It's standard to ask back." He stopped, frowned. "Still writing?"

"I-I try. It's… kinda difficult to ~."

"Yeah, publications closing down, we know. Toughen up! Make a living or give up."

"No one should give up," said Dewy. "*Never.*"

They stood in silence. The man looked pleasantly at Annie.

"Hello, you with the dog?"

"This is Annie," said Dewy. "Annie, Graham."

"How y'doing?" said the man.

"Fine, thanks. Yurself?" said Annie.

"Stressed," sighed the man. "A lot going on at work – all good I add, plus *two* renovations, one in my office, one in my home." He said "home" in a delicate, high note. "So, I don't really know *where* I am, or ~"

"Graham, you're boring the crap out of us," said Dewy.

"Dewy, you're *back*. That 'thank-you for asking' bit spooked me."

"Hey, Connaught!" roared a giant, whacking an arm on Graham's broad shoulders. "Get away from that shoeless whore, wanna ask you a buncha stuff" They walked away. Dewy and Annie were shunted aside by two fresh-faced burly men, one saying:

"9.4 seconds gain a day. Same distance exact. My sprinting's faster."

"How many days?" barked the other.

"81. But 9.4's *median*. I started lower, now I'm faster each time. My average in the past 20 days alone has been ~"

"*I am Retainio!*" boomed Dewy, in the man's voice.

The men turned to her. Morris was alarmed. Dewy and Annie escaped, but soon blocked by people. An older woman in slacks, gold-trimmed blazer and oxblood lace-ups said: "Cough better, Dewy?"

"Uh, *yes,* Lucille, thank-you, I forgot about that."

"*Forgot*? You coughed like a ram." To Annie she said: "Went on *weeks*. Andrea Millud said 'no surprise, doesn't look after herself'."

She peered up to face Dewy: "Whatcha doing now? Anythin' on the 'rizon?"

Dewy shrugged a bare shoulder.

"Ah, *come on*," said Lucille, "You must have a *bit* of fight? What's the story?"

"I teach children English in Roxbury a couple hours," said Dewy. "Most days I stay home, look after the woods and the birds, then I dance to Ella Fitzgerald and Jimi Hendrix."

"Saw 'em both, Ella twice."

"*Really?*"

"Carnegie, and Philly, '72,'73? She was the power."

"And *Jimi Hendrix*…? Y-you *saw*…"

"Woodstock."

"You were at…?"

"Couple hours from here. Wild. Lotta people."

"I love dancing naked to 'Stone Free' and 'Manic Depression'. I wish everyone did."

Lucille pulled a face: "Dewy, get a *job*!" and walked away.

"There aren't any," murmured Dewy. She softly, tone-deaf, sang: "Fourth estate is falling down, falling down, falling down…"

Surrounding voices closed in. Dewy called to Annie: "Let's go outside, the terrace?" Annie cradled Morris and followed. Dewy said "Excuse us, please?" to most people, but sometimes yelled: "*Move!*" One man squared up to her, swearing. Dewy diverted round a group listening to a man saying: "…then rebuild the room. That way, we'll have a supporting wall for ~"

"A *building renovation*!" cried Dewy. "How *exciting*! Mind if I rub my cli ~"

"*Shut up, Dewy!*/ Get outta here!/ *Fuck off*/ Go away!" roared the group. Dewy changed course. Annie planned to abandon her soon.

Two men blocked a terrace doorway, deep in talk:

"I refill the bottle every 5k."

"Right."

"It's made of iodised aluminium."

"Interesting. How much does that weigh?"

"*Retainio's bottle is 2.84 ounces!*" bellowed Dewy, tugging Annie between the pair. On the terrace, Annette rushed to them: "We need to talk, all four of us? Now?" She kissed Morris's head. "Booboo, this will be quite a moment in our lives, and it will be *lovely*".

She took Morris from Annie. Kissing and sniffing the backs of his ears, she bade Annie and Dewy follow her. They walked to a further terrace door, Dewy last. Sleepy from overeating, she walked on her heels, slightly waddling.

They crossed the recent battlefield of a dining room, to a shortcut into the south side of the house. Wood-panelled passages led to a sitting room with rounded bay window. Annette pressed a wall-button. Flames rose in a hearth beneath an aerial-view painting of a gunship in white-crests sea.

Dewy poured brandy from a crystal decanter and stood by the fire. Annette sat on a dark leather sofa. Morris climbed onto her. "Wanna give Mommy's ears a snoo?" said Annette. She offered an ear to Morris and smiled, eyes closed, anticipating wet nose, jolting with a happy cry when it touched.

"Now, Booboo?" began Annette. "We're in this room because Mommy, Aunt Dewy, and Annie-Mommy, yes, that's right, she's *Annie-Mommy*... and there's a *reason* for that. We're gonna *tell* you that reason. It's *real important*, but *real good*."

She glanced to Dewy. "Honey? You didn't tell Booboo, did you?"

"Uh?" said Dewy, glazed by food and brandy, "Tell him what, hon?"

"What I e-mailed you about?"

"No wi-fi, so I've seen no e-mails," said Dewy. "Avoiding the Millards, I don't even go stand by their house at night for wi-fi, like usual."

Dewy saw Annette and Annie were holding hands. Annette looked at Annie devotedly. Annie replied with a tight-lipped, happy smile. Dewy had never seen Annie smile. She looked kind when she did, Dewy thought.

Dewy poured more brandy: "Can't go to any wi-fi place, not had money… So… …totally out of contact…"

She turned. Annette and Annie weren't listening. They embraced, Morris between them. "Booboo?" said Annette, "You know how *you*, *me* and Annie-Mommy shared the bed past three nights? That's because Mommy and Annie-Mommy *always* share a bed now, just like Mommy and Aunt Dewy did. But that was different. It's different because Mommy and Annie-Mommy are very, *very* close – in a thing called a *relationship*."

Dewy looked on, stunned.

"And Morris makes three," smiled Annette tearfully happy, kissing his furry cheek. As the three hugged again, Annette glanced to Dewy ecstatically: "I think this has *gone well*," she stage-whispered. "He's happy. You can see that." She buried her face in Morris, who snuffled and licked Annie's neck.

Dewy stood very still. "I'm so happy for you," she said, voice trembling. "It's a blessing. A *blessing*. I-I didn't know you were together. I love you both. I love you *both*."

They didn't hear.

"Best get back," said Annette. "Only me and Robert Junior here, Clift and Jack away on active service. I sense Mom and Dad want us around tonight."

The empty south hall echoed with voices and music from the rest of the house. Annette and Annie waited for Dewy to catch up. She emerged from the corridor behind them wide-eyed, hands clasped to her chest.

"You OK, hon?" said Annette.

"My darling," gasped Dewy, "I'm so happy. What you've told me, and told Morris."

"You're tired, hon. Planning to stay? We three are in the old rooms."

"Could I sleep in my old bed a couple hours?"

"Go right up. Booboo needs to sleep. Would you –"

"Of course," said Dewy, receiving the baby-sling. "Bye, honeys," she gasped, "See you in a l'il while." She climbed the staircase, reached the turn, looked down to bravely smile at the pair. They'd gone.

Dewy hadn't seen her old room for eight years. High in a new part of the house, along a passage past Annette's old playroom, she'd lived there aged 10-18, though always slept with Annette in the playroom, or Annette's bedroom downstairs.

The playroom was now a bedroom for Annette and Annie while the house was full. Dewy felt a pang of sadness to see its double bed out of bounds to her now. She carried on towards her old room, grateful Morris had stayed in her arms and hadn't pressed to be placed on Annette's bed.

Dewy's old attic room was bare. A single bed remained, new eiderdown with a busy pattern. The room was painted white again, carpet mid-grey. A bare eco-bulb drooped overhead.

Morris returned to the other room. Dewy heard him jump onto the bed and his sigh of settling. Dewy sank down the wall. Her forehead rested on an arm across her knees. She remembered she'd often sat like this in here, her teenage room, where she'd never belonged and rarely slept. Happiest memory, two beds at different places, Dewy reading on one, Annette the other, arm around Bachelor. As they grew older they lay together, crossing to the other bed several times in an evening, it always felt a novelty. In heatwaves, too hot for each other's arms, a bed each, talking for hours under breezes through open front windows.

Dewy's essays and homework, hours every night after the ballet years, were done at a long-gone desk by these windows. Annette would busy herself in her bedroom home-laboratory downstairs, microscopes, test-tubes, bottles of chemicals, thick books of physics.

Dewy now put out the light, lay on the bed. The cover smelt of dye chemicals. She hoped Morris might come, but his snores were loud along the passageway.

She imagined the '50s and '60s, when this part of the house, not built yet, was trees and mid-air. A young girl, Joanna McCoy, passed this way on her foal each day. Her brother Aaron didn't like riding. He read science-fiction and believed humans would get to the moon by 1970. No one believed him, nor: "and Mars by 1980." They'd stopped listening to him by the time he'd got onto: "By 2000 everyone will have several computers and carry one in their pocket."

Aaron learned and spoke Esperanto, refused to get his hair cut after 1964, age 12, and was hospitalized in 1971. He now lived in North Dakota, married to a woman with milder Asperger's who taught in an elementary school. Aaron inherited enough from Joe and Dorothy McCoy to never work or pay a mortgage. He helped at a Lutheran church sometimes. Annette asked Joanna if he was a father: "Not that I've heard," shrugged her mother, mind elsewhere. Her brother may as well have been a vague neighbour who'd moved away. Annette had never met him.

Dewy's mind moved from Joanna and Aaron to one of her life's fascinations: Catriona, the beautiful, wrong, middle sibling McCoy. She imagined the 1972 Catriona in jeans, plaid shirt tied in a knot above her waist, hand in hand with some shirtless, wild-haired, guitar man.

Dewy's mind went further back. Joanna's parents

Dorothy James and Joseph McCoy – Grampa Joe – had married in Newburyport in 1946. The James estate centred on the beautifully preserved 1820 house, connected to the 1900s main house by a covered courtyard and walkway Dewy loved – trellis one side with roses and views of the estuary.

The 1820 house was the James Riding School's headquarters. The old coach-house was a tack room. In some bedrooms lived Karen and another groom, currently Lois. Joanna sometimes stayed in a bedroom where she, her siblings, and their mother, were born.

Presently, in that very room, Annette kissed Annie. They'd escaped the main house to warm night, making love in a clearing of moonbeams near lilies and honeysuckle.

Afterwards, Annette took Annie to the old house. Dionne Warwick played while Karen, Lois and Stephanie cheerily readied to go to the main house as after-dinner guests. Annette led Annie on a tour of the antique house's paintings and photographs up the staircase: "Mom's family lived here from 1860. There's the first ever photograph of the house, the Civil War."

Annette pointed to another sepia photo, a handsome, physically strong woman with a resemblance to Joanna and Annette. "Mom's grandma, Corey James. She founded the Riding School in 1919."

Annette led Annie to the first floor hall. "The James's were from Dorset, England. They sailed for America in 1659. These 12 paintings are James men from the 17th to 19th centuries, all sea captains: merchant ships, or Navy."

Annette and Annie walked slowly from painting to painting.

"Mom was the second James woman to marry someone of no sea heritage but who was in the Navy – my Daddy. His background was department stores. Robert the First founded them in nine cities, New York 1897, Newark

1901, Boston 1904… The empire declined in the 1930s. Dad joined the Navy at 18, earned a scholarship through Naval College and captained supply ships to Vietnam at 23. That's where he met Todd Durant, Dewy's father.

"Mom married Dad in 1974. Joe and Dorothy's wedding gift was the annexe we're staying in, built onto the big house. Maybe it was intended as a hotel Mom and Dad could run in retirement, who knows? Only Dewy and I lived in it. Guests were there during bigger social occasions, like now. Clifton said how until the 1990s, New Year lasted late as mid-January."

AN HOUR ON, Dewy was woken by warm scrabbling of Morris waking as Annette entered the room.

"Sorry, darlings," said Annette, backlit by passageway light. "Oh, Booboo, we *saw* you'd been under the covers, then you came to sleep with Aunt Dewy!" She leaned over Morris, rubbing his chest. "*Yes!*"

Dewy sat up, eyes adjusting to dark. She leaned up to kiss Annette, but froze. *She couldn't kiss Annette now.*

Something Dewy hadn't placed all evening hit now: *Annette is out of my life…*

Annette was at the door, long hair and flowing, Morris in her arms. She'd never looked so pretty, and sexual, to Dewy before.

"Staying tonight, hon?" said Annette.

"Um…" said Dewy. Annette hadn't asked that question ever. Dewy's lifelong unconditional acceptance here was over now, she knew.

"Stay, have a quick night-cap with us?" said Annette. Dewy sprang up and followed her. *Annette knows I never drink-drive?* she thought. *A night-cap must mean I can stay tonight?*

Annie didn't look up from her Dr Seuss book, except to thank Annette for a cup of wine. Annette poured Dewy a coffee cup of red wine too.

The wine was deep and good. Dewy wanted more.

"Stay the night, hon?" said Annette. "I'll go put a night-light in there."

"Thank-you, sweetheart," said Dewy, reaching for her hand. It connected with air. Annette had left for the passageway.

Dewy turned to Annie and nearly yelped. Annie's feet were unfortunately ugly. Each big toe protruded an inch longer than the others, which were scrunched.

"These are *crustaceans*," muttered Dewy, hurtling to the passageway.

Annette was returning,: "I'll make a glug-glug for you, hon."

"Don't worry. Is it OK I take this wine?"

"All yours hon. I'll bring you a glug-glug, we got Uncle Kettle through there."

No kiss.

Dewy re-entered her room wondering if Annette still called hot-water-bottles "glug-glugs" from childhood nostalgia, or because she still believed a water-spirit called Glug-Glug lived in them. As a child Annette declared the faint 'glug-glug' sound of a filled hot-water-bottle was Glug-Glug "telling us he loves us". Hot-water-bottles were always called glug-glugs (and kettles Uncle Kettle, reasons unclear). Annette hadn't liked it when Dewy once questioned why Glug-Glug and Uncle Kettle were definitely male ("Does Glug-Glug have testicles?"). Apparently they "just *are*" male.

Annette extended her arm into the room. "Glug-glug here, hon!" Dewy rushed to the door: "I love you, darling, I love Annie. I love you both."

"That's nice, hon, thanks. See you tomorrow."

Annette flicked off the light. Dewy lay on the bed, hugging the hot water bottle, realising she'd been cold.

Here was the first place with broadband she'd stayed

in since England. Dewy switched her smartphone on, to three-week-old e-mails. Four personal ones, all Annette, the first, two weeks ago:

Dearest, I've much to say, it's crazy in my head.

I've fallen in love with someone. We've had sex!

It was amazing. I had an orgasm, a real one. An ecstatic tingle rose from the base of my spine. It rose on up, and up til sparkling in bubbles from my crown out to the darkness of space. I felt all of time, plus purest energy of the universe pass through me. My chest, tummington and lips were suffused with a gorgeous tingling. I saw myself from a height, all in colors made from dotted lights, like far firework displays. It was kinda wonderful, and I guess sounds crazy too, so I won't go into other perceptions I've had while in that state.

We've had sex about five times now. I cannot hope to convey what each meant and felt like. But there is such a thing as transcendence, and there is a powerful energy of love in the universe. We are crazy to pretend there isn't.

You're right, hon, we are insane to believe we should all be atheists and worker-ants, driving cars, staring at TVs and computers, working, commuting, paying, obeying. You were always right, my dear: humans get warped contentment by shutting down all chances of happiness. Hell-bent on making life hard, in pursuit of doing everything wrong. All could be effortless. New ways of living could easily arise, if we'd open our hearts and minds.

I'm worried you'll be sad to read this, especially as I'm on a cresting wave of life and love and hope, and so soon after losing poor Hiram. I even wondered if all this is a gift from him, his way of saying: "Mom, don't worry, you did your best, me and Bachelor want you to have love and healing, here it is…"

But you are always my girl and my love. If you don't want me to go ahead with what's happening, I'll stop. That also, of course, applies to Morris. If either of you is unhappy, I'll stop. Or might you be happy for me?

I've never felt like this. I'm different from how I've ever been. (Is this not the longest e-mail I've ever sent?!) I feel like an adult. Do you remember when I finally learned to swim – how it took me years? Then one day I could do it! Now one day I could do <u>this</u>! I can do <u>adult life</u>!

Dewy glossed over Annette's remaining three e-mails, relieved Annette didn't think Dewy's no reply was a snub: *I guess your phone's off again and maybe you can't get wi-fi. I know you'll make contact when you read these.*

Dewy looked out of the window, drank, and wrote in SAB:

Tonight – first time out for weeks {my ex-girl's father's 70th birthday} – I was asked about 80 times: "What's happening at the Millards? I heard they're fed up with you?"

When I replied Wal nearly shot me one night in his vegetable patch they ignored me. Rent arrears was what they wanted to hear, so they could say: "Hmm, I've heard they're fed up with you" again.

One thing *is* happening at the Millards': men "clearing" a path through the forest from the road. Chainsaws a quarter-mile in now. {NB "clearing". Paths through forests are "cleared", never chopped down, annihilated, butchered, killed. Nature's *something in our way*. "Clear" it!}

"We hope to make the cabin an exclusive B'n'B let," said Vacua pleasantly. The unspoken end to her sentence – *when you move out* – was the elephant in the room. {We were out by the cars. Godzilla trashed the garage.} And the first phase of "upgrading the cabin" is to kill trees to make a road to it.

As you know I've vast anger at a new, mass-market epidemic of loud, violent, inhumane gardening tools. At any or no excuse, Chainsaw and Blower Man is revving near you. Plumes of toxic fumes spew, while extreme noise strafes the nervous systems of every human, bird and animal around.

Now, today's mad men are murdering ancient woods to my cabin yard by yard. Last year, some of you may recall, saw the murder of hundreds of trees in woods of the estate adjoining the Millards' {the Burrages', who don't live there.} I wept and raged when half a wood, way left, across the last part of the lake, was razed by men with chainsaws and digger machines. In morning cold, the machines' emissions were visible – dense, gray clouds drifting up. Birds' shrieks echoed all over the lake.

A scorched-earth heartbreak of stumps was left, limbless trunks uphill to bare sky. No grass, flowers, even weeds grew there this year. These men killed the very earth.

How well I'd known these woods. Then I watched their death. No need to ask why it happened, it's everywhere now, because men have new, macho machines they're bursting to use. Unsilent Spring. Any excuse, or none. No one's asking them for an excuse anyway. No one seems even to notice them.

Now, a year on, the same urgent shrieks of birds terrified by the monsters. Monsters are what new-style chainsaws sound like if you don't know what they are. And what they sound like if you do.

Yes, "ex-girl", you read that right. And like all freaked-out, new-heartbreak casualties I'm wittering on about other subjects to avoid facing up. I can't discuss the end of me and my darling because I cannot think about it.

Late-night here, I'm running out of wine. If you're reading this I'm so grateful, thank-you for making me feel not-alone. I wish we could meet. I'd try to look nice, have a bath first, make peanuts and lettuce for you, have wine ready…

Tonight is so still. I hear nothing.

My girl has met someone else and is happy. I'm happy too. I *wanted* her to meet someone who isn't a selfish mess like me.

Such stillness here now. Did you ever know Coleridge's poem "Frost At Midnight"?

Tis calm indeed! So calm, that it disturbs
And vexes meditation with its strange
And extreme silentness.

I'm standing at the window of the attic room where I lived long ago. It overlooks roofs of this vast sleeping house, then night. A couple little lanterns on the driveway, enough to show the darkness is two types, lawns, then woods. I know the estuary's beyond these, purest black.

Coleridge was English and lived 1770 to 1835 or so. Maybe he saw a similar view that still, frosty night:

Sea and hill and wood,
With all the numberless goings on of life,
Inaudible as dreams!

I found out this evening I'm no longer and will never again be my girl's lover/partner/ sleep-girl/childhood sweetheart/ define as you will.

I keep skirting around this. Bless you if you're still here with me.

I feel strange. Something huge hasn't hit yet.

Five minutes have passed. Someone got up, went downstairs, my darling's partner gone to sleep on a sofa because of Morris's snoring. Annette said she did that last night.

Morris sure snores. I guess 80 decibels. My girl – no, she's not my girl. My dear darling friend always sleeps peacefully through it. So do I, after years sleeping with her and Bachelor, then Morris, but for someone unused t

oh shit I'm crying like hell

Dewy rose, blew her nose into her cupped hand, opened the window, shook her hand clean, wiped the rest on her leg.

Annette is out of my life. She is with someone else.

Dewy sat hunched against the wall, absently stroking her toes, sipping wine, staring ahead, not blinking.

She posted:

A sign from heaven that true love is true. Do you remember I wrote my girl needs a deep, mutual relationship? Someone with her always, to take care of her and give her fulfilment (ie, sex), love, help and understanding?

It's happened.

'My girl'... After 18 years she is *not* mine. I'm upset, but want to light a candle, not cuss the darkness.

My darling friend's happier, stronger, secure, excited, and has better life prospects than ever. She's slimmer, taller. Her eyes shine, her emotions are loving, she's eloquent, her movements graceful. She's always been brave, so will easily find courage to come out to her Republican, traditionalist family.

My darling is happier than I've known anyone be. So is her partner. I've never seen such profound affection and peace between two people. When they kiss I feel bliss in my chest. I've not seen purer love. I know it exists now.

Just when you thought real love was up there

with the Tooth Fairy or Trump's tax returns, here's proof from heaven true love is true. Love is love is love is love is love is love is love is love is love. True is true is true. I now raise a drink with all love in my heart to Annette and Annie. Please do the same, dear readers? Their love is the hope for us all. Ah-de-o Xx

MORNING WAS SQUINTINGLY bright. Dewy, Annette and Annie stepped onto the south terrace, each raising a hand to visor her eyes, except Annette, shielding the eyes of Morris in his baby-sling.

"Booboo wants the shade by the bushes, Annie?" said Annette. They moved away, leaving Dewy alone.

Henry (Henrietta) Worth cawed: "Good *morning*, Durant! How are you?"

"OK, thank-you, ma'am. How are you?"

A faint 'Ha' from Henry Worth, six foot two, 71 years old.

"Dewy Durant, woah-woh" came a Kermitish voice from the sun. Dewy couldn't see which tall shape spoke, possibly Dale Wallace.

"Look like shit, Dewy" said a louder voice next to him. *That* was Dale Wallace.

"Language, Dale!" joked his cousin Malc.

"I apologise," said Dale Wallace. "She looks *fucking shit*. Ah! G'morning, sir!"

People along the terrace stood, calling out and clapping. Robert Stephens III and Joanna approached across the lawn, hats underarm, fawn moleskins tucked in riding boots, he a light-blue shirt, hers navy-white stripes.

"Good morning!" said Robert, trying to not be awkward. "Uh... thank-you! Well... um... who's had breakfast yet? Is that underway?"

"Just outta bed, Bob!" said Richard Seagram.

"Good, no one's been up hours? We thought 10am

would be the uh… *humane* time."

"Everything's inside," announced Joanna, "Grab a plate, stock it up, sit indoors or out here."

People stood, moved, gathered things. Robert Stephens said: "Hey, Dewy."

"G-good morning, sir," said Dewy.

Why me, Robert? 40 people out here, you choose me?

"How are you?" said Robert Stephens.

"Fine thank-you, sir." *Stop fucking glaring, Joanna.* "H-how are you?"

"Real good, enjoyed last night immensely, did everyone el~"

"Yeah!/ *YOU BET!*/ Sure did! /**Yeah, whoa!**/*Yes thank-you*/ Indeedie! Yessir!/Yusthanks/ ***Sure did, Bob.***/Certainly did/YES THANK-YOU, ROBERT."

"Thank-you for the book, Dewy," Robert Stephens continued, 18 feet away. Their interplay seemed public. He'd hardly spoken to her in six years.

"Book?" said Katherine Jensen. "*She* gave you a gift?"

"Yes," said Robert Stephens to whoever listened. "Walt Whitman. Very tasteful, uh, edition. I shall look at it." Voice hastening, he announced the day's plans.

Dewy darted inside. Guests arrived from bedrooms, seating themselves at white-cloth'd round tables. Annette, Annie and Morris arrived and sat.

"Dewy, sit with us? We're gonna get food," said Annette, standing. "Please hold Morris?"

Joanna's voice carried: "Dewy? Girls? *No*. You know the rule."

A smattering of nearby laughter.

"Up, Dewy, please?" said Joanna Stephens. "Go sit on the other side of uh… *Annie*, is it? Sorry to involve you, Annie, but this pair have a history…er, they're banned from eating beside each other. Disgusting carry-on."

"*So* 10 years ago," said Dewy, changing seats.

"Even so, a life ban's a life ban, Dewy."

Dewy suddenly felt lost and sad.

We'll never have Disgustings again.

Morris climbed onto the now-empty chair beside her. He pawed her forearm, looking imploringly at her. She saw him, began to cry, quickly stopped.

Annette returned with breakfast "Hon, I bet no parking's left up the island. We oughtta head to Crane Beach, or further?"

Dewy didn't know she was included in her and Annie's arrangements, and was glad, though shaky, and wanting to be alone. Annette found her later in shade at the side of the house. They walked towards the garages. Dewy looked back and saw Annie arrive. To her horror Annie was barefoot in an old pair of Aztec print sandals.

"She can't come in the car like that!" said Dewy to Annette.

"What?" said Annette.

"She must cover those or I'll be sick."

"Are you *serious*?" said Annette quietly. "You'd better not be."

"I can't go in a small car in proximity to…"

"Go home."

"Wh-what?"

"*Go home!*"

"I ~"

"How *dare* you talk about Annie like that! I'm sick of you running her down. I *love her.*"

Annette angrily walked away. Annie, unaware, carrying a coolbox, beach bag and parasols, drew level with Dewy: "Can ye take they umbrellas please?" A parasol fell to the ground. Dewy didn't move or look. Annie let another parasol drop and followed Annette.

Dewy's mind reverberated. Her vision darkened. Footsteps returned, Annette, her voice. "Are you coming?"

Dewy tried to say "I'm sorry." Nothing came.

"Don't say anything nasty again." said Annette sharply. "Annie's tried so hard in her life. She's never had anything, or anyone."

Dewy felt destroyed.

The road was busy, traffic slow. No conversation, the sun strong. Dewy felt destroyed still. Morris was perplexed and hot in her arms. He never relaxed in cars, looking frantically around: why did the world rush past? Why did it stop sometimes? Where were these new places? When Annette drove, someone must hold Morris or he'd panic around the car, striving to understand.

The Mustang stopped in a tailback. Fumes became tasteable. Annette said:

"Can you put his mask on, hon, and his sunhat?"

"Sure," said Dewy, glad to be called 'hon' again. Her spare hand rummaged through a tote bag for a child's smog mask Annette had reshaped for Morris, and his floppy, baby's sunhat. She and Annette gently fitted them on.

They'd briefly held up the traffic, 10 yards of open road had opened before the stuck traffic before them. A car from the other lane darted in, enraging a man behind the Mustang. Deprived of 10 yards' progress before the next halt, he pressed his horn loudly.

"Go wash your balls!" yelled Dewy.

"Darling, don't argue with anyone?" said Annette.

A land-cruiser pulled alongside, window whining down. A heavy, sweating, white man stared from high over Annette and Morris. "Nice dawg!"

Annette tried to look up but it was too vertical. The man continued:

"Daddy bought you da car, didn't he tell ya: 'don't stop middle of the freeway?'"

No answer.

"I *said* – ah forget it."

"No, *please* share your views!" said Dewy in a deranged voice, smiling with her lower teeth. "We like to meet new people in Jesus!"

"*Huh?*"

"We are the Christian Women's Softball Federation, sir! We believe Jesus Christ would have played baseball, Mary Magdalene softball!"

"You're fuckin' bananas. Where d'ya get the car? Rich daddy, huh?"

The traffic moved five yards then stopped.

"Got an Orphan Annie stowaway!" barked the man. "She's *poor* trash, you're rich-girl trash. Some mix."

Dewy stood on her seat, waving her arms, bawling, to the tune of "Everything Is Beautiful":

Hallelujah SOFTball!!!

Play it every dayyyyy!!

then released an enormous fart, five seconds.

"Oh!" said Annette. "That ruffled my hair, hon."

Dewy directed Annette off road, up a lane through farmland. "I know a way," she called. "I often drive these roads, escape from the cabin."

On the beach they were approached by college men with a frisbee.

"Hey, girls! Lookin' *nice*, wanna play? Is that a *dog*? Look at that! His own two little parasols! Ha-ha-ha! L'il guy sleeping away there, *ha-ha-ha*!"

Dewy let out a four-second fart. The men's faces dropped. They walked away.

Half an hour on, a middle-aged man tried to tell Annette and Annie he was a "published poet" and asked if he might sit. Dewy farted, three seconds, straining now. The man left.

"Honey?" said Annette to Dewy. "Was that a fuffy or poop-poops?"

"Mmm. Had a bubbliness. Better go sit in the sea."

She stood carefully, began walking to the sea:

A dim sound of laughter, even cheers. Annette said urgently:

"Hon? Your boo's!"

Dewy looked down. She was naked from the waist up: "Ah, so what? Why *can't* I be like this? Like in Europe…"

"Is that the po-liss?" said Annie. A black SUV crept along a heat-shimmering path between beach and low dunes.

"It is!" said Annette. "*Honey*? Lie on your front, the police are there."

Dewy dived onto Ella Harris's new cocktail dress, now a sandmat, muttering: "Repressed, invasive, dystopia we've become."

She tugged and kicked off her knickers, clenched them in her fist, sprang up and ran nude to the sea, yelling: "Fuck the police! Fuck Trump! *Fuck the modern world!!*"

Terrible minutes passed. Annie said: "Don't look at the police car. There's a wee chance they didn't notice. But if they see ye looking at them, they *know* something's up."

"Oh!" trembled Annette. "I hope Dewy's not so stupid to walk back from the sea full frontal."

"She's no' daft, pet," said Annie. "She can see the police car's right there. She'll put her knickers back on at least."

But nearby laughs and wolf-whistles heralded Dewy's fully naked return. She shook out a towel and dried herself.

"*The police are THERE!*" cried Annette.

"So what?" panted Dewy. She dried around her loins: "Got real washed. Sea-water, though, kinda stinging. Swam underwater, *boy* is it cold?"

"*Lie down*!!" wailed Annette. "Morris is *stressed*."

Dewy lay on her back, resting her weight on her shoulders to pull the dress on upwards, then rose to jump wildly around to de-sand it. Annette and Annie lay in silence. The shadow of a man in a peaked cap lengthened over them.

"Afternoon, Ma'am? My duty to inform you, dogs are not ~"

The policeman looked over at Dewy dancing and swaying five yards away.

"OK there, Ma'am?"

"Sure, pig."

Annette and Annie heard her. Maybe the man heard "Sure thing".

"Okaaay," he said. "I suggest you all head home. In future please don't bring dogs onto the beaches. It's a felony. And um…"

He was trying to convey something, looking at Dewy, who danced elegantly, ignoring him. He continued:

"…uh, beware sunstroke, girls, keep properly covered? 94 degrees today…"

Hallelujah sunstroke!! sang Dewy, loud and bad. *Pig-sty every dayyy!!*

"Thank-you, sir," said Annette, panicking. "We're going now."

"Good," said the policeman, walking away. "Have a nice day, girls! Definitely keep *covered up*."

Dewy growled. Annie and Annette hurriedly gathered things, avoiding gazes of people who'd watched everything and still did.

"'Calling us 'girls'." said Dewy with derision. "Does he like to be called 'kid'?'"

"*Shut it!*" snarled Annie, thrusting her face into Dewy's.

Annette drove. Dewy remained afraid of Annie. Morris slept. Dewy rested her hand lightly on his sunhat to keep it on him, and hid her face in his neck.

"We'll drop you off." said Annette, voice like stone.

"Oh, hon? My car's at yours."

Annette sighed and accelerated through a changing light, forgetting the power of her car.

They arrived at the Stephens's to splashes and shrieks of a pool party and a live band. Annette turned to Dewy. "Parked down there?"

A moment that haunted Dewy arose. A tableau of unlove faced her, Annette, Annie and Morris, blank-faced. Dewy had no control over how she reacted. She muttered she needed a shower, to not wait hours for water to heat at home.

Annette tutted, stamped a foot: "OK, *have* a shower! Then *please* ~"

"Go?" said Dewy sulkily. "Yes, I'll *go*. You needn't say it!"

"You nearly got us arrested!" said Annette.

"If I get nicked in this country, I'm straight hame!" cried Annie, approaching. "And if they nicked Annette, I'd go so mental they'd shoot me. That's what they do this part o' the world. That cop was the one in three that's a lenient human being, pure luck."

"Are you not gonna like, apologise?" said Annette to Dewy.

"Well… death before bullshit," shrugged Dewy. "I don't *feel* sorry, so can't say I am."

"I thought you *respected* the police," said Annette.

"I do, if they're real ones, upholding the law."

"He was, and he was," said Annette. "Even if that law *is* discriminatory against people who are dogs, and I'm sorry Booboo. I let *you* down. But I couldn't discuss it with the policeman, because *she* was behaving like a…"

"Like a *what*?" cried Dewy.

"'Fuck the police?'" said Annie, "Hey, pig'? How old are ye? *14*?"

"Don't *you* talk to *me* like that!" said Dewy, with such vile superiority she'd later cry recalling how awful she was.

"Don't *you* talk to *her* like that!" cried Annette. "Annie can say what she likes!"

They walked away, Annette saying: "It's OK, Booboo, Mommy's a li'l upset."

Dewy smirked at them, lying to herself she wasn't hurt, or in the wrong. But a far voice inside said: *They really are walking away from me.*

She climbed through a ground floor window of the guest block, listened outside a bedroom door, tried the door. Locked. The next door wasn't. Dewy entered to strewn clothes and open cases. She had a shower in the en-suite.

As she dried herself, the bedroom door opened. Footsteps clacked in.

"Going back out soon, just a quick nap," said Lexina Hartley's voice.

"Kinda my thinking too," said Michael Hartley.

Lexina's voice approached, louder: "Gotta get out this wet swimsuit and ~"

"Don't come in here!" called Dewy.

"*Waah!! What the –?*"

Dewy peered from the bathroom.

"What are *YOU* doing here, Dewy?!" yelled Mrs Hartley.

"Having a shower."

"A fucking *liberty!*" boomed the man. "You *walk* into *people's rooms* and ~?"

"*Sh,* Mr Hartley!" said Dewy. "Lexina, do you have more waxing strips?"

IN LONG SUMMER days the adults sailed or rode, while Annette and Annie looked after Celia and Robert Jnr's children Robert, Patty and Olivia, nine, six and three. They adored Annie, Morris and Aunt Annette. They ran through the garden sprinkler for hours, splashed in the pool and made glacé ice cream with Consuela. Annie had never felt so wanted or happy.

On days of no sailing, Annette, Annie and Morris drove in the open-top Mustang: through lanes to wide, bright green valleys, a red barn every mile. The weather was perfect, the country teeming with wildflowers nuzzled by bees and big butterflies.

Music boomed from the Mustang's back speakers, less so from front ones for Morris's sake. Annette played

Annie her favourite music. Annie loved all she heard. Roberta Flack, The Carpenters, Dusty Springfield, Dolly Parton, Simon and Garfunkel (especially "America"), Nina Simone, Halsey, A Tribe Called Quest, Al Green, Stevie Wonder, John Denver, "Ruby Baby", Oliver Nelson, Grace Jones, Billie Eilish and the West Side Story soundtrack (especially "America").

Nowhere was beautifuler than summer Massachusetts, "except," Annette promised, "in fall". They toured the Berkshires, stayed a night in Lenox and visited Smith College next day. Annie was overcome by its beauty and scale. Being there made her closer to Annette, for here was Annette's past.

DEWY WASN'T SLEEPING. Nights felt tropical. Storms boomed 20 miles out at sea, Dewy prayed no hurricane would come. Most 3ams, she paced the cabin's back lawn, night dew soaking her feet, her straight, slender shape passing back and forth from darkness to darkness via dim light from the sitting-room. Bats looped crazily, amphibians raved, owls screeched. A maniacal coyote pack often fought or attacked something in the woods in the small hours. One overcast night was so dark Dewy couldn't see her hand if she raised it, as she did, twice, to beat her face hard with her fist.

Goddess, help me! Help me be unselfish. PLEASE, please help me?

At 4am she sat on the sitting-room floor writing:

Annette is with someone else. I'm redundant, gone.

> **But without her I'm nothing. Without her I can't bear to live.**

> **No more will she put her arms round me, no more will we share a bed. No more will we kiss, no more will we *kiss and kiss.***

> **Without kisses I cannot live.**

Never again will my bare breasts be her pillow. No more will I rub her shoulders and kiss them to sleep No more will her kissing give me slow-burn, deep healing in my chest.

She stepped outside. Clouds parted to a crescent moon and Gemini. "I'm cracking up," said Dewy to the sky.

She woke at 4pm. The chainsaws which disturbed her dreams had gone. Cold, squinting, Dewy wrapped Wal Millard's discarded old waxed Barbour around her and stepped out to a hot day's wall of warm air.

Another time of no food or drink except water and fruit-fall lay ahead. Waldo was back from Manhattan, so Dewy couldn't invade the allotments for food. The Amory's' summer party was two days away, but Dewy lacked the nerve to show up there uninvited again.

Waldo hating her was painfully awkward. Wal, who'd fixed a bicycle-puncture for her when she was 11, and obliged for hours when Annette said: "Can you teach us how to do that?" Wal, once so pleasant, tall and gentle, a practising Christian. Dewy feared their next chance meeting would begin: "Dewy, can I talk to you, please?" The blow would fall, a month's notice to go, "we'll help all we can", but out, shift, *go*.

Dewy stood on the front veranda looking blankly at flowering weeds and grasses stretching far to sugar maple trees. Bees and butterflies weaved among harebells and orange lilies. A tear fell down Dewy's face.

I've never been so low.

Yes I have.

A horrible gravity pulled her back to bed. Turning to open the front door, she jumped. A note pinned there stared like a face before her own.

Hi Dewy, Annette Stephens called, she and Andy –? (maybe Anny) & doggie visiting you 2morrow at 11! Andrea x

NEXT MORNING DEWY danced on the back lawn, braless, in her most intact knickers. She rarely danced fully naked now, for at least one man from the chainsaw crew saw her months before. Dewy had spotted movements behind nearby spicebushes.

After dancing she sat on the lawn, panting. By sun-reckoning it was 10am, Annette in one hour. Dewy felt joyous.

Two hours on, she sat on the uncollapsed part of her sofa and hung her head. Annette wasn't coming.

Chainsaws ripped and wailed from 400 metres.

No one had visited Dewy here. She and Annette always arrived together. No one called round, except Andrea to relay a message, give food sometimes, or in very cold weather check Dewy was OK. (These visits led to Dewy staying at the Millards' at least once a year – nine days in 2017. Fearing pleurisy or pneumonia, Andrea had arranged a doctor visit twice to examine Dewy's chest infection.)

At 1pm, for the 10th time, Dewy stepped onto the front veranda. At last she heard footsteps on stones near the bridge over the stream. Dewy ran uncontrollably up and down the veranda, whooping, the Barbour clutched around her, light-plum corduroy trousers rolled to the knee, so not to colour-clash with her pink-red toenails.

Footsteps louder, flashes of clothes behind bushes…

"*Ahhhhhh!!*" yelled Dewy.

Annie saw a dark, wooden, sun-blocking building, like an old barn with a veranda, which Dewy ran from – if that joyous, approaching scarecrow *was* Dewy. Annie had only seen her wear dresses, not trousers, and Dewy looked unfamiliar smiling broadly. She'd never seen Dewy really smile, or her teeth, white, American-perfect, even pretty.

"*Thank-you for coming to see me!*" cried Dewy.

She hugged Annette close, face in her hair. Annie wished the embrace would stop. She turned to watch

Morris, who sniffed dense weeds under the veranda's first step.

The looming cabin's lack of light was compounded by trees and shrubs each side. Dewy led the way to a cold, dark passage that smelled like nutmeg. A room left was padlocked shut. The light-source was a doorless room on the right, whitewashed walls, bare floorboards, one window with a broken blind. Dresses lay on a bed-base. On the dusty floor Dewy's travel case and a pair of stilettos, one on its side.

The kitchen mid-cabin was windowless, beige, lit by a weak strip-light. Surfaces and sink were stained. Empty cupboards had missing doors. A table in a murky alcove was heaped with newspapers, sketchbooks, books, bags of crushed plastic bottles and a bowl of used coloured pencils. A rust-speckled fridge trilled. Dewy reached for a small velvet case – her lipstick – from the bowl of pencils.

"Sorry we're late," said Annette. "Andrea was outside, she said 'come in, I've made lemonade.' She said to bring *you* some." She handed Dewy a plastic bottle.

"For me?" gasped Dewy, forgetting the lipstick, wrenching the bottle and gulping like an athlete.

"It's nice!" she panted, stunned by calories. "Andrea's good at lemonade. Come through, darlings, let's go out?"

Annette continued: "Andrea said: 'take her this tea and these soups.' She unloaded Earl Grey and tins of Amy's Soup. Dewy leapt back into the kitchen to handle these like archaeological finds. Annette opened a coolbox she'd brought: "And we've left-overs from Tuesday's family gathering, Daddy's actual birthday. Aunt Meredith came. She asked after you. Here's potato salad, coleslaw, Pasta with olives and something …"

"Oh!" cried Dewy. She grabbed a container, flung the top into the sink and crammed potato salad into her mouth. She rose to full height and relaxed as she chewed, eyes shut, breathing through her nose.

Annette entered the main room to open its brown curtains to sunlight and lawn. Annie followed, surveying the cabin's first area of no icy chill or darkness. To the left a collapsed green sofa lay between kitchen and a double mattress on the floor in the corner, Dewy's bed. The sofa was covered in sketchbooks, magazines, bags of crushed plastic bottles, papers, clothes, take-away food containers, a laptop, its flexes, and a watercolour set.

The right half of the room, curtained, was unenterable. A maze of antique chairs, cardboard boxes, school desks, empty wine bottles, a gaping bookcase with a few books and magazines, more boxes. An electric lawn-mower with encrusted grass lay bulkily by a collection of rakes, ladders and home-gym parts. On a floral-painted old chest of drawers (two drawers missing) a dented CD player stood, wired to a knee-high amplifier on the floor.

Annie tripped over another bag of plastic bottles. She stooped to a wine-stained old carpet to pick them up, unhearing Dewy say she collected plastic bottles to take to a recycling place for ten dollars.

The lawn was well-kept, size of a tennis court. A high hedge ran the far width, a windbreak blocking view. Annette led Morris and Annie around it, where the garden dropped to a half-mile marshy meadow of weeds and flowers, then fens and reeds. The sky seemed higher and a deeper blue than Britain's, Annie thought. The far view spanned forests and lakes half-full of water-grasses. Sounds of humming insects, cicadas, peeper frogs, yelping birds, tuneful birds and tree-drilling from woodpeckers seemed loud and constant. Depending on the mood of the hearer, it was manic and monotonous, or a lulling symphony of tones and melodies.

"Wetland." said Annette. "Far left's the end of the lake we saw from the Millards'? It ends at those trees, though half have gone – that bare grey hillside? It broke Dewy's heart when they chopped them down."

From the opposite direction a chainsaw ripped. Annette pulled a face. She'd already told Annie about the path being cleared.

Morris was pulling the leash, keen to explore the field.

"No, you'll get lost and Mommy will cry. Let's go back to Aunt Dewy."

Dewy sat, legs straight, eating from an old saucepan. She'd heated an Amy's Soup then added potato salad. Annie noticed Dewy looked pale, a pink spot on her chin, even three. Among first things Annie ever noticed about Dewy, besides shocking foot-soles was how, like herself and Annette, she rarely used make-up. Annie wondered if Dewy had spots like these often, but used concealer.

"I'll make us tea," said Annette, taking Annie's hand. In the kitchen, they unearthed nearly clean takeaway cups. Annie looked around, preparing to tidy a little, but no space existed to tidy things to. Clutter had reached a logical end of being no longer amendable, things must be thrown away now.

Annette prepared tea, foraged in the big room, returned with a lacquered black tray with gold floral motifs.

"My brother Clifton painted on this," said Annette, turning the tray round. On the sleek black underside were two oil paintings of a ballerina, in arabesque from a distance, then in fourth position, arms outstretched. Tiny writing in a corner: *"Dewy"C. Stephens 2004*

Out on the lawn, Dewy lay on her side, saucepan and salad tubs empty.

"Tea, hon?" said Annette.

"Oh!" said Dewy, rising. "That'd be so welcome right now."

The three sat close. Morris looked happy, panting in shade of the hedge, a towel from the coolbox covering his back.

"You went to the Millards?" said Dewy.

"Mm-hm, sat in their new kitchen," said Annette.

Dewy sighed. "They're crazy on renovations and cruddy furniture, like all middle-aged doofs now. Yet the locked room here's full of antique furniture, paintings, heirlooms. *These* would make their house better. Those antiques are getting damp."

She lay back: "I don't understand the Millards. I don't understand modern thinking." She sighed: "Modern thinking – how's *that* for an oxymoron?"

"Why's the front room padlocked?" said Annette.

"They thought I'd sell things from it," said Dewy.

"No," said Annette.

"Wal suspects me of *anything*, after he and his square-jawed Princeton bud surprised me one night borrowing from the vegetable garden. They'd mistaken me for a prowler. Wal's friend didn't lower his gun when asked. I was frightened. He knew it, and wanted me frightened. Next thing, an automatic night-light was fixed by the vegetable beds. Day after that, a man banged on the door here: 'padlawk on a bwacket for Mistuh Millud'." He bashed it up in two minutes.

For a time the three and Morris sat, watching birds come to one of the feeders. Annette pointed out a grackle ("Dewy's favourite word") to Annie and a stunning scarlet tanager.

Raspberry-red, busy birds arrived at a feeder and bird-bath. "Purple finches!" whispered Annette to Annie. "Even though they're red. The men that is, the poor women are a bit plain and brown, there's a woman, two now. They're *all* wonderful." She turned to Dewy: "Purples, hon!". Dewy was asleep.

Annie said Dewy should be covered if she burned easily. Annette fetched the large black sunhat to cover her face and a towel for her feet and legs.

After pausing in the kitchen to rinse containers they'd brought, Annie and Annette left. Annie hoped never to return.

An hour later, Dewy woke to black fabric. Her hands

pulled her hat away, feet kicking at a towel. Disoriented, headached, she saw the sun had moved. A chainsaw roared up-curves like whooping cough. Dewy peered in the cabin, called Annette's name.

She went to the trees, listening, hoping Annette and Annie were exploring there. When she turned, empty lawn and side-cabin seemed to rush at her. Sometimes this happened to Dewy. She'd blink then see a stage-set, envisage a dancer, two, more, a dance unfolding. Like a bubble-burst the vision would end. Dewy would rush to a sketchbook to draw what she'd seen. She'd hundreds of sketchbooks, crammed with coloured-pencil drawings of stage sets, human figures, arrows for direction of movement, scribbled notes, close-ups of limb and hand movements with arrows, drawings of costumes. Some double pages were watercolour set-designs.

But Dewy rarely liked or looked back at what she'd created. Many of her sketchbooks were lost or had pages torn out. Now, as Dewy searched for one, she saw a note from Annette:

> *Honey, you were in a deep sleep. We're going down Meredith's Sun, Mon, but please come to Morris's birthday in the park, 3.42pm Tuesday? Are you free earlier to help with sandwiches, cooking, wrapping gifts etc? If so, I'll clear it with Mom you come.*
>
> *Thank-you for having us visit. I found $5 in my pocket, I thought you might like it. It's in the refrigerator. See you Tuesday (today's Thursday 3rd). Morris, Annette, Annie. xx*

Dewy blogged:

> **The loves of my life were here but I fell asleep binge-ing on carbs they brought.**
>
> **I woke to a loving note:** "*Hostess with the leastest – do you suck or what?? Snoring and drooling like a pig. Even Trump doesn't treat guests this way, or not often. We won't visit again.*"

Sorry I've uploaded no Dull Films a couple weeks. I hope to soon. A lot new is going on: two horned owls, a colony of Great Blue Herons in treetops along the lake west of here, more than last year. Not so many snowy herons, but they're breeding, their incredible yellow feet have gone flame orange. No green herons yet, I miss them, they're so observant and thoughtful, they didn't come by til August last year, I hope they're here soon.

Rapture Of The Week: no, the rapture of *last* week first: two yellowthroats in courtship dance!! Sunny long grass, edge of the woods. Leaping, vanishing, popping up someplace else, singing beautiful, strange, many-mooded songs and duets.

Now This Week's Rapture: *Baltimore Orioles are back*, beautiful, songful and crazy on the feeder. They love sweet stuff, so I put grape jelly out there last week and, oh my word... Four females, five males (hmph!), all energized, big, golden-orange, robust. When they fly off they go fast and high south-east. My aim is to try find where they're nesting this year. When I next buy jelly I'll lay it at the feeder then head south-east, hoping they pass overhead so I can figure out where they go. They're nesting distant to previous years, *and I'll bet those fricking chainsaws are the reason.*

So... the chainsaw men, ah heck, I'm *always* going on about those bastards, you're fed up, I'll change the subject: I want to give birth.

I want children. The ache is big. Annette pregnant brought deep feelings of want in me. I want to be pregnant, I want to give birth. I want to have done it – to cross that line, pass from the BCE to the AD of life, the Old Testament for the New, join the line of women stretching back to the dawn of time.

These feelings in words here look dumb and

flippant. I therefore lack adequate words. But I *need* to do this. I want it soon, I need to do it soon.

But the whole thing's tripped up, as ever, by: "Pregnant by whom?". Seeing as I can't attract a man to save my life and don't want one.

Then comes: "Am I WASP-bait in denial?' Pretending fake-egalitarian horseshit to herself? Will my radical, 'true bohemian' self-flattery end the instant a hedge-fund manager waltzes up? Will I be a Hamptons mother of three with secret girl-lovers?

At this moment I need Jimi Hendrix. I'm gonna take all my clothes off and listen to "Manic Depression". I hope you can do that too, wherever you are. Dance your life and story out, sing with Mr Hendrix like he sings, especially that *WoAGH!!* he throws in a couple times. It is life, it is *living*, it is LIFE.

Jimi Hendrix's defiance is for these times as it was his. You'll know if you play loud and dance the heck. And sing. Much is made of Mr Hendrix's guitar, a few talk of his songwriting gifts, fewer still praise the powers, sensuality, honesty of his voice. A messenger, healer, releaser, mystic and natural enemy of authority. We need his like more than ever. You'll know what I mean when *WoAGH!*-de-oh Xx

FEW EVENTS RIVALLED the Dennisons' summer party. A loyal guest was the weather. Never wet, dull or bad, it led the party by example. Stephen and Cara Dennison were graceful, spoke rarely, enjoyed people's talk and gently laughed often. Now in their 70s, they inspired even the worst people to step out of their selves and become good company.

Ever more informal, the Dennisons never stinted on hospitality. No one was invited or uninvited but knew if they should go. Dewy had been absent for years, drunk by

6pm in her last visits. In 2013 Cara walked in on Dewy naked in the Dennisons' bed with Mrs Greenway halfway down her. Next morning Dewy apologised to Cara, who fondly waved her away: "Well, the children have grown-up. Drink and make love."

"The children" alluded to Dewy's unofficial role for years as keeper of guests' children, who flocked to her for a five hour riot. On today's drive to the Dennisons, Annette (at summer school that fateful 2013 day) told Annie: "A stampede of children followed Dewy everyplace, through gardens and woods. Dewy was indifferent, let them do anything. They'd swarm through the house, bounce on beds, throw mattresses from windows to jump out onto. A music machine player was upstairs, they'd dance like crazy. Grown-ups stopped talking, looked at the bouncing ceiling. They acted disapproving but were secretly glad their children were laughing and muddy-kneed, with big appetites."

Annie tried to feel accustomed to arriving at parties to see dozens of SUV, sports or classic cars parked, an immaculate grass strip for light aircraft, an enormous, colonial house.

This overwhelm came second to remembering to never reach for Annette's hand or signal anything but chaste friendship. She tried to convince Annette she didn't mind this charade, nor mind Annette having to circulate among family friends, while Annie found her own places to go, usually a kitchen.

But in these nine days their love had very much deepened.

Mostly their days were spent alone together. They drove, found places to sit outside and dine with Morris. Annette showed Annie her old schools, the church she'd been baptized in, places she'd played as a girl. They drove to Plymouth to watch a street parade of residents dressed as Founding Pilgrims. Tomorrow would be the Berkshires again, a Tanglewood concert by an orchestra whose cellists included Aunt Meredith, then a soirée at her house in Roslindale. Annette and Annie would stay in the beautiful bedroom where Annette, Morris, and frequently Dewy stayed during Annette's two years at Massachusetts Institute of Technology.

Annette was overcome with love, desire and security with Annie. To lie to the world they weren't in love was unbearable. Annette repeatedly begged Annie they announce it.

Annie advised not yet, but couldn't explain or understand her feelings why. One was her embarrassed awareness of her educational inferiority in this new, opulent social world. Being sudden focus of attention and questions might be unsurvivable. Annie also believed that Annette telling Mr and Mrs Stephens and their friends she was gay, then introducing to them, as her new love, a manual worker (who couldn't read, barely spoke, and had spent six of 23 years in correctional facilities) would be a terrible crisis.

More deeply, Annie worried she might only be Annette's infatuation. Annie did not voice this, and chastised herself for thinking it. Of *course* Annette's love was real and lasting. But life had taught Annie: trust nothing, people change, things go wrong, nothing good lasts or repeats. A bravery in her began to see these hardwired notions were in fact a dim form of comfort, and can be defied.

Now, at the Dennisons, Annie discreetly separated from the Stephens's to wander a large, historic room of Shaker furniture and faded paintings. A live band played old happy blues-rock. Placid talk and comfortable laughter surrounded Annie. What did the people talk about? Who were they? What were their lives, feelings, loves, concerns? Annie wandered out to lawns, trying to seem relaxed.

With a crystal tumbler of water she sat in a marquee

corner, pretending to read her phone, so no one would approach. She even half-wished Dewy was around, at a distance. Dewy's occasional protection at parties had been a help. But Dewy wouldn't be here tonight. She'd stayed away years.

A man pushing a trolley of covered dishes "excused-me" a group of women who reassembled, still talking. The youngest was dark-haired, nearly tall, a level gaze, kind eyes, perfect features. Perhaps mid late or late 30s, she wore a white-trim, navy Chanel two-piece and slide sandals. Her older companions thronged like seagulls across her. One said something funny. All stepped slightly apart to laugh, then stopped to stare at something.

Dewy unsurely approached them, eyes glazed, hair messed, mouth purple from wine. She stopped walking, swigged from a bottle and stood, swaying and scowling. After a blink that lasted four-seconds she heaved out a greeting: "Gwad*eev*nin!"

The group glared. The handsome woman sighed with a look nearly fond and said: "Well, well."

Dewy pouted, frowned: "*Gadda...* theahma *fug*, y'knaw?" She staggered backwards, flailing an arm: "Uh... fugkin'... ah... *fugg aff!*"

"And good evening to you, Dewy," said the woman, without malice: "Maybe *you* fuck off?"

Annie escaped to a white, L-shaped kitchen. A table spanned the length of a bright orange alcove. She sat there and looked through USA Today, The Boston Globe and local papers, wondering if she'd ever be able to read. Annette had been teaching her from her old Dr Seuss books. These made Annie laugh sometimes. She couldn't believe such crazy thoughts could become books.

Suddenly Annie realised she knew, for the first time, what a newspaper was saying. A photo of people, dressed in a certain way, was a hint, but Annie instantly gathered a theatre show of this picture was in Boston for three nights soon, and the dates.

She'd never forget the photo: a girl with pig-tails holding a dog, a grey-painted man in some kind of cylinder, another in a hat with straw, a woman in a gold animal costume. Annie didn't know words on the page said The Wizard of Oz, but knew 'of', and figured the next word must sound like 'of' but with a z, so 'Oz'. Another 'z' with its 'zuh' sound was in the long word, which must be 'wizard'. The Wizard of Oz playing at a Boston theatre on these dates, immediately figured its own self out. Annie was amazed it solved itself before she'd tried to.

Women arrived, pulling chairs, pouring drinks, talking. Annie stood to leave as three shuffled under the alcove to sit at the table. The first frowned: "Wanna get out?" and stepped back. Annie moved quickly, muttering thanks. Stepping back to let her through was the stylish, beautiful woman from earlier: "Don't leave on our account?"

"Er, it's-it's nae bother, darlin'," said Annie.

"We've ousted you" said the woman, "I'm sorry."

Annie wondered what person she would have to be, what other life to have led, for this woman ever to be her friend. Yet here they were, an inch from each other. Closer, but further, than anyone.

Annie glanced past her: "Oh *no*."

The woman turned, saw Dewy too, glanced back at Annie, amused.

Dewy crashed into them: "Roberta, you were *horrible to me* back there!"

She slumped into a chair and sulked at the woman, who said: "But you were drunk and abusive."

Beautiful, tall, Alice Worth loomed in tan suede and gold bangles. She pulled Dewy's hair: "Off the chair."

"You're pulling my *hair*!" cried Dewy.

"You deserve it."

"I do *naat*!" screeched Dewy, thrashing to stop Alice

Worth, who said: "Mess with *me*, Durant!? *Do* carry on. You're quality! Worth your weight in gold plate."

"*You*'d fuckin' know."

Dewy stood, banging her head on the alcove arch and fell into Annie. Roberta sat on a banquette, took Dewy's hand and tugged her to sit.

"Durant, you were improving," said Roberta Georgiana Paley neé Westcott.

"Least I don't pull people's hair like a three-yaar old!" slurred Dewy, glaring at Alice Worth: "Your brittle extensions'd fuckin' *snap off* anyh~" She stopped, dizzy. Roberta passed her a Perrier bottle. Dewy gulped from it noisily.

"I'm told you're messing up again," said Roberta, "I don't like to hear it."

"Whadya *mean I~*" **Burrrp!!**

"Andrea was at Celeste's," said Roberta. "It's a story how you're living. Wal wants you out. You sit outside on your bare ass all day listening to rock music."

"I listen t'*all kindsa* music and I *dance*, I dance, OK? Not 'sit on my ass'!!"

Jennifer Hughes was also drunk: "You *don't* sit on your *ass*!? So, you *are* part of the *human race*, Durant!? *We* all *work*, we raise *kids*, we ~"

"Shuddup," said Dewy.

"*WE* raise kids," bawled Jennifer Hughes: "Walk our frickin' dogs, run 9ks, go for blow-outs. And *you*. Dance. In your bare ass. To rock music."

Pointing long arms with swirling forefingers at Dewy, she yelled: "Between a rock and a Millard place, ba-boom!".

"You *do* look good for it," said Roberta Paley to Dewy. "Perfect skin, as always."

"Piss."

"You're a beauty indisputably."

She turned to talk to Alice Worth, then saw Dewy

weeping and shaking.

"Oh, dear," said Roberta. "Anyone got a tissue? Shannon? Shannon! Can you tear a piece of kitchen towe – ah I'll get it." She climbed over Alice Worth's legs, smooth hands on Dewy's heaving shoulders for support.

"*Why* was Andrea t-talking about me?" sobbed Dewy. "And wh-who was *there* at Celeste's?"

"Durant, quit drinking!" said Alice Worth.

Dewy charged out to the hall, to interrupt people and rant. Annie left her to fend for herself and, as she often did, found Annette sitting halfway up a staircase, cradling Morris, who slept.

"Oh, Annie," trembled Annette. "I've missed you bad tonight. I love you."

"I feel these things too darlin'," said Annie. "Sat here long?"

Annette's hair was one half behind an ear, the rest sleekly down, half covering an eye. Tense with desire, Annie couldn't let go of Annette's hand.

"Let's find Mom," murmured Annette. "Ask when we're leaving."

They departed at midnight, passing Dewy, who, half-lit by garden lanterns, danced a fine, hopping, bashing Sabotière on an SUV roof. Joanna was glad she'd made it widely known they'd not brought her here.

"Green! Circles!" Dewy roar-sang. "G- *HeeEEek!!* Circles!"

"Dewy, can you get off our car?" repeated Jack Summers.

Dewy bounced hard and flew backwards into a bush. Leaves sloshed and writhed. Onlookers helped free her, someone saying: "I shouldn't say: 'you look like you've been dragged through a hedge, but –"

Dewy zig-zagged back to the house, turned down for a ride home by all.

TWO DAYS ON, Annette cried on Boston Common and

Morris was hot. Some people smiled to see a dog in a baby-sling and sunhat, the owner's free hand aiming a small, whirring fan at him.

In Commonwealth Avenue's shade, Annette cried.

"I hate it we can't be *us*, Annie! This pretence we're dull, quiet friends, for if seen in love, it risks Mom and Dad being embarrassed, even 'disgraced'. The consensus is: I – like everyone 'respectable' – am *of course* not gay but simply had a teenage 'thing' with Todd Durant's wayward daughter who, it turned out *was* gay after all – 'Hardly surprising – *that* one!' they say."

"Your parents might no' think that?" said Annie. "They don't seem bad people, like."

"I guess they wouldn't feel *disgraced*, that's too strong," said Annette. "But it would be uneasy. You and I instantly public, all those voices telling us they '*don't mind*', while avoiding eye contact."

Morris stirred, rose out of his sling to face Annette. Annie hugged them both.

"I feel so bad for *you*," said Annette, crying anew. "What it must be like to be with someone's family, but suppress their *self* and behaviour? It's *so unfair*."

"Darlin', I'm happier than ever I've been," said Annie. "I never dreamt nothing like this. And it's *real*. It's reality! It's… it's *real*."

The three closed their eyes nearly half a minute enjoying a coastal breeze. Annie opened her eyes, saw Morris, ears back, eyes shut, a dot of sun reflection on his black, wet nosetip. She saw Annette's smooth hair and lovely, still face, eyes closed.

Annie fought tears. *I'll remember this moment forever.*

Peace. Annette breathed deeply, breathed out. Her eyes opened, she leaned to kiss.

Breeze rustled the Avenue's trees. Annette and Annie kissed on, opened their eyes, smiled, looked at each other, smiled again. Morris snuggled into deep comfort in his sling.

"Annie?" said Annette. "Will you marry me?"

NEXT DAY THEY'D leave Boston for the Stephens's, but Morris's birthday breakfast was first. He had chicken-breast, truffle, boiled quail egg and basmati risotto. They walked him in Roslindale, played tug-of-war with him, let him doze in Aunt Meredith's sunny garden and sang 'Happy Birthday' again. On the train north he looked out the upper deck window all the way.

Dewy was waving by Wal's BMW (which she'd bashed again) in Ipswich Station parking-lot.

"Thank-you for meeting us!" called Annette, cradling Morris. "Look who's nine today!"

"Happy birthday, darling" said Dewy, shaking his paw. kissing his head, "You don't look a day over seven."

They drove to the house, the east kitchen. Joanna Stephens marched through the back door, grabbed Gatorade, drank, wiped her mouth, sat, held a plum from a bowl in her teeth and swung a leg over her thigh to tug a riding boot. Annette pulled the other for her. Joanna removed red socks to reveal no-polish, slightly male feet. Morris watched. She nodded to him: "hi".

"Say 'happy birthday' to him, Mom?"

"He's a dog, he doesn't know it's his birthd–"

"He *does*!" said Annette and Dewy.

"How long you want the kitchen?" said Joanna.

"Two hours?" said Annette. "We're making lasagne and a cake and ~"

"Hurry up. And clean the place thoroughly."

"Yes, Mrs Stephens," said Dewy.

"Don't *you* primly reply. When did you clean any-thing?"

"Your stables for four years?" said Dewy. She'd won, but for Annette's sake avoided a fight by looking away.

"This party *is* going on someplace else?" said Joanna to Annette.

"Yes, Mom, in the park." She glanced to the clock: "Oh my, 13.12!" She picked up Morris. "Two and a half hours to go!" *kiss!* "We must make cake!" *kiss!* "And other eatables for the persons of caninity coming to see Booboopaws!!" She kissed his nose: "*The codas are coming!*"

THE AFTERNOON WAS warm with slight breeze. First guests were Lady, a greyhound cross, and 11-year-old Doberman Rosalie, who, with a daisy-chain on her head, lurched aimlessly around in a heavy dance, front rearing up and down. "Woo*woo-oo-oo! Woo-oo!*" sang Rosalie deeply. A stout man in camouflage clothes and a red Make America Great Again cap arrived with a mastiff called Victory, who tried to mount Rosalie. The man stared through mirror-sunglasses at Dewy: "Careful barefoot! There might be dog… uh…"

"Dog-shit?" said Dewy. "I can see where I step, sir."

The man's body tightened.

"Sir?" said Rosalie's owner Jacqueline: "Could you please get your dog off mine?"

"*VICTORY C'MERE!!*" screamed the man. The park echoed. Victory cringed to the ground and crept to his owner.

"Here's Sherilee!" said Annette. Morris bounded happily to a tall, springy poodle with a pink bow on her head. They ran tumbling over each other. Rosalie lolloped up and down behind them at one mile an hour.

Gustav the bulldog, labradoodle Ollie, retrievers Archie and Sally, Orion the pointer, Rum the Chihuahua, Dakota the Bracco and Homer the Shetland Terrier arrived. A big running around game lasted a long time. All halted a minute while Sherilee squatted, arched back, panting grin. Dewy picked up after her, then Rum squatted.

Most guests were with a cheerful female owner and children who learned riding at the James Academy. As Annie replenished six dog bowls with water, black labrador Mowgli, red setter Jess and Louie the Old English Sheepdog arrived.

In the shade of sugar-maples, rugs were spread, a hamper unpacked. 14 panting dogs ate roast chicken, lasagne, salmon, rigatoni, caviar, white rice, biscuits and a range of treats. The meal was in very gradual stages so dogs wouldn't be sick after running around, though four were. At 15.42, believed the exact moment of Morris's birth, all humans except the camouflage man sang Happy Birthday. Rosalie howled along.

The party concluded each year with Morris taken around each dog to say thank-you and talk with the owner. Nearly all had long connection with the Stephens's. Victory's owner delivered hay-bales to the Academy.

Dewy noticed how Annie stayed in the background. She thought how hard and enraging it must be to have to pretend not to be Annette's lover amid the Stephens's and their friends.

Dewy disliked her own attempts at friendliness to Annie, and knew Annie hated them too. They were worse than rudeness. *She'll never feel that I love her*, thought Dewy, and *will never know I want her to be with Annette always*.

She hoped Annie knew she wasn't a rival, and hoped Annie saw she'd given her blessing instantly to their partnership, no intrusion or comment.

The last dog had gone. Morris was happy and hot. Annette peeled the wet face-cloth from his back, squeezed out a fresh one from the icebox, placed it on his head and shoulders. She lay with him amid the whirr of a fan.

Dewy and Annie cleared trash, gathered rugs, toys,

gifts, then lay under the tree sipping lemonade. Dewy felt delighted to be accepted. She closed her eyes, heard a prairie warbler's songs and far calls of mallards. A distant car passed sometimes. The sun was lower. Dewy opened her eyes. Annie was looking at her, unintentionally, lost in thought. Dewy smiled without trying and gazed fondly. Annie didn't respond, but Dewy's heart had spoken.

The end had come. Annette, Annie and Morris would sail for England next day. Dewy didn't know when she'd see them again, maybe Christmas, maybe years. Whenever it would be, Dewy knew her closeness to Annette would be gone forever.

She bit her lip, trying not to let emotion spoil this last hour. But the day was over. She was being goodbye'd. It was happening now.

Dewy placed her face against Morris's, unthinkingly saying: "When'll I see my little friend with his ears and paws?"

She faintly heard Annie and Annette agreeing something. Annette turned to Dewy: "Tomorrow Mom and Dad drive us to the ship. Wanna come?"

THE FIVE HOUR drive to Brooklyn saw Joanna Stephens at the wheel, husband beside her. Behind them were Robert IV's wife Celia and their three children (Robert IVth returned to Virginia days before). Dewy was stretched along the last row of seats, her back against a door, for suitcases filled the footwell. Annie, Annette and Morris lay on bean-bags and cushions in the deep well intended for luggage at the very back of the SUV.

Two hours in, Annette and Annie lay asleep with Morris between them. The sight made Dewy glad and achingly sad. She looked away, gaze straight ahead, Connecticut blurrily rushing by side-on. To look any further right risked meeting Celia's eye if she turned to her children. Dewy tried to have something to do. She tried blogging:

> **This should be one of Annette's and Annie's happiest moments – departure to a new life together. If I cry, it'll tarnish the occasion.**

Morris woke, softly left Annette's embrace and stood, front paws up the back of Dewy's seat, licking her arm over and over.

Three-year-old Olivia asked to "lie on Mommy". Celia Stephens née McConnell rearranged to lean back against the door, diagonal to Dewy. If either even slightly moved their eyes would meet. Ignoring each other was tense too. Dewy hoped not to seem crying, but was. She needed to blow her nose. She'd been ready to, into a cupped hand, to be wiped in the seat-well, but now Celia would see.

Celia had ignored Dewy for 11 years, since a spring Sunday incident not long after her engagement to Robert.

Dewy, 16, Annette 15 sat entwined and lost in thought that day in the big middle chamber of a lighthouse at the McConnell's Nantucket estate. Robert Jnr and Celia had been engaged a month. Today was a party for 50 guests after a private engagement weeks before.

Celia's extrovert brother Topher paused opening bottles to point at Dewy and Annette: "Look at those little owls!" The circular room gazed fondly on them. They sat up nervously. Bachelor woke on their laps and climbed Annette for a mutual hug.

"Guys?" said Topher. "I mean…?" Everyone laughed. Topher's timing made plain things funny. "You pair are always in this *trance*," he continued, "What do you *think* about? What're you guys thinking *this precise minute*?"

Brave and blushing, Annette began: "W-well, sir, I ~"

"Speak up, Annette!" said Joanna Stephens.

"I was th-thinking about lizards, sir!"

Everyone but Dewy erupted with laughter.

"*Lizards?*" roared Tophe McConnell. "Okaayyyy, *lizards*, everyone!"

The room laughed louder. "M-mainly geckos," trembled Annette. "How they-they… have adhesive paws?"

"*Whoooooo!!*" roared the room. Clutching Dewy, Annette added: "I w-wondered what adhesive *is* that? Can it be synthetically replicated, for use in industry?"

When happy noise subsided, Topher boomed: "And *you*, kid? 'Dewy' is it? What were *you* thinking about?"

"My vagina," said Dewy truthfully. "I may have cystitis?"

Already excluded as a bridesmaid, she was now barred from the wedding.

JOANNA WAS IMPATIENT at the ferry terminal. Annette and Annie had left for Departures, but Robert Stephens V wanted to see the Queen Mary 2, having never seen a civilian ship of its size.

Dewy, Robert III, his grandson namesake, Celia and Patty stood on Pier 12 among hundreds watching the liner. Breeze blew strong. Annette, Annie and Morris were on a high bridge deck. Dewy smiled and cried at the same time, waving one hand, the other holding Robert V's. The stately navy-white ship drifted out, blasting a horn.

Dewy watched and waved long after the QM2 passed the Statue of Liberty. Most of the crowd, and all Stephens's had gone. Dewy's emotions rose.

My time as your sister is over.

Your lover is with you now. It is right.

The ship rounded Red Hook and inexorably vanished. Dewy couldn't move from the quayside, wind in her dress.

"Crying because you've lost her?" said Robert Stephens III.

Dewy jumped. She'd not seen he'd returned.

"You lost her a long time ago," he continued.

"N-no, sir," gulped Dewy. "I don't think so."

"You did. But we're grateful to you, those early years you protected Annette. Wanna be dropped in New York?"

"No, sir. I-I'm gonna stay."

"Ship's gone, Dewy."

Dewy turned, surveyed all New York Harbour and the sweep of Manhattan. "I'll b-be fine, sir. Please let me go."

At 6pm she flew to Boston. Only on the train up to Ipswich did she remember Annette saying: "Here's a letter I wrote you." Dewy now opened it.

My darling friend,

I'm sorry you've been overlooked, especially as you showed no selfishness, only love and encourage-ment for Annie and me. You were once or twice a little smart to Annie, but I know you feel love for her. She knows this too. I hereby thank-you from both of us for being so wonderful about Annie and I being together.

I am filled with gratitude and pride that Annie now sees the good-natured, loving friend I'd always told her you are.

It's not been a successful visit for us, and I'm frus-trated. I want to tell my parents Annie is my girlfriend. I hated putting her through this fake role of 'British friend, almost a maidservant", and keeping up a pre-tence. Many would be righteously bitter in that situation, but Annie's never pressurizing, self-important or demanding. She loves me, sees everything clearly and is always on my side. Her only discomfort is me being fraught.

I will follow your advice and send Mom and Dad a letter. I'll tell them I'm very happy in a loving partner-ship with Annie and want to be with her a long, long time.

I want to write them we intend to get married. But shall I write that? They may object, offer no support, and that will break my heart. They'll insist Annie's someone of no account or background, even accuse her of trying to marry into a rich family (which we aren't. The James School just got out of debt first time in six years).

But Annie wants nothing from anyone. She doesn't care for material things, or even like them much. She hungers to be able to read, learn to drive, and properly train as a chef.

But Mom and Dad will believe what they want about her. They're Republicans. They stick to limited views and can't be moved. It worries me people of a right-wing persuasion are losing what they had of a willingness to at least hear differing outlooks and accept some as at least credible, even if they don't agree. But now that's gone. Debate is unknown. Self-searching likewise.

Darling, I'm sorry. I've been selfish and preoccupied. Please, I hope you aren't lonely? I've paid you no attention or asked how you've been, how you got through July. Were you sober? Did you see much of Jacob's Pillow? Did you talk to people about employment?

I'm sorry I spent no time with you. We didn't even go see any birds. It's been a tangled two weeks, happy but strange.

Will you visit us before the end of the year? Please? I could never bear to be without you long. My sister. My darling big sister.

Love Morris, Annie and me.

Dewy sat amid empty rows of burgundy seats on the train's upper deck. Her face glowed in last sun. Shadows of buildings and trees flickered fast across her.

Part Five

Chapter 1

AUGUST BROUGHT HOT days of gold fields and dreaminess, another dimension, like no other month. People who could afford a holiday left Farrisford. Others basked in sunny back gardens, dug allotments, took picnics to Sherrier's waterfall, East Lane Park or meadows along the Brate.

In fields, workers sweltered, gathering hay, picking apples, night-harvesting vegetables in warehouses with transparent roofs, too hot to work in by day. Silage on fields gave a bodily tang to the air, reminding the town it was country at heart and glad to be.

Tessa England never holidayed. Each Parliamentary recess was her chance to visit each farm and business in her constituency, a favourite activity.

But tension was high this year. Nobody smiled. Anxious, wordy Opposition supporters wanted Britain to stay in Europe. Others demanded immediate action Britain leave. Everyone wanted facts. There weren't any.

The MP was nonetheless welcomed wherever she went, given farm produce, apple juice or eggs as gifts (thankfully no live hens this year). Those who loathed Conservatives, or politicians generally, valued her honesty at least. To: "Why haven't we left Europe?" she'd say: "No one knows how to. That's the fault of pro-Brexit politicians. If you want to move house but have no idea what a removal company is, don't move." To: "Brexit? It's a disaster." the MP replied: "I don't disagree, but we're more resilient than we think. Children fearing the dentist, but when the day comes, the hour, the minute… it's not so bad as you thought, and the relief after is *huge*. Optimism will sweep the country after Brexit because the worry's over. That could see us through…"

Nancy Brown of Cleme Farm stopped her at this point: "Mrs England, are you whistling in the dark?"

Tessa England paused.

"Yes," she replied.

EVERY AUGUST THE Tattler was thin and struggled for stories. But this year saw violent youth crimes, including three stabbings, one near-fatal. The annual problem of no direct ("nor coherent") bus service to the coast was partially blamed and took up a front page.

David Cartwright and Ryan Palmer were laid off but offered telesales for the parent company in Bristol. David Cartwright accepted.

The crisis of no reliable sub-editor after Dewy's departure was solved by Catherine Wren's return, working from home three days a week. For office days she requested a rudimentary crèche and playpen in the office. The men were fond of Alicia. Some brought teddy-bears and toys. Alicia rarely cried. In a rare personal visit to the office, Gregor Finniston, hip-flask in hand, paused in his speeches (about the town, the bypass, Farrisford Town FC, the county, Westminster, Britain, America, Russia, Brussels, Balaton's Sainsburys) to say loudly: "Tis a softening, civilising improvement to any workplace, a crèche. Maybe not to abattoirs, but many places."

News had dropped in tone, Catherine noticed. Violence and affrays, usually two a month, were several a week. "A murder 'fore long," chimed Colin Hendry, adding the town's last was in '04. (Either he'd forgotten Matthew Willis, or agreed with the inquest's "open verdict".)

Catherine ran a wordcount on the word Brexit in one

issue. 146 in 44 pages. Farmers spoke of European workers starting to leave. Farm equipment auctions were cancelled. Recent ones had sold nothing. Six shops in Farrisford closed. Two more nail-bars and an eighth computer/mobile-phone repairs shop opened. 14 local businesses, including Roy's Plumbing, Farrisford Mouldings and Devon Kennel Supplies ceased trading. No new businesses started. St Botolph's' second weekly food-bank began.

Angry confusion filled local and national media. The country waited for the exit from Europe like innocents awaiting punishment for something the culprits would emerge from unscathed and sneering.

Farrisford's third oldest pub The Bear was up for sale. All knew that was the end. Rapid descents of The Bull, the Weathervane and other pubs now boarded-up, had begun with For Sale signs. The Bear dated back to 1670, though no one was sure. Parish records and archives in Farrisford Library vanished when the library was shut down by Conservative government cuts.

Catherine Wren and Gregor Finniston continued to ask the Council to find out where these records and archives had gone. 21 different people had answered their e-mails in 34 months. Some said they'd address the question to a committee. Others wrote to say the archives were "in Council storage". Letters asking *where* weren't answered.

This summer Catherine and Finniston waited weeks to hear back from their last letter on the matter. A reply came, not from the Council, but a company called Communica (*"Helping you to be YOU"*) It was unsigned and said:

> *A search of documents and-or a piece of equipmetn you allege to be looked for cannot be actioned without proven evidence this item(s) were placed. You mustprovide written reference to what docunents and other item you claim are to be searched for within 14 (fourteen) day's.*

Market Street was at last completed but couldn't re-open because Helvia plc had gone into administration. From Catherine to Colin, Carruthers to Finniston, the Tattler's best minds couldn't deduce who Helvia had been, why it had had a controlling share of Farrisford Market, why the market had an owner anyway, and who'd made money by selling it to that mystery owner (trick question: *the Council.*)

"Market stalls open by Christmas" was promised while a new backer was sought. "Why do they need a backer? Why can't the 41 stallholders simply set up again and sell things?" was never answered.

Finniston spared no dislike for the new, expensive Market Street design:

> Gone are the colourful, shaky-framed stalls with hand-painted signs and traditions. Each now a thick, stainless steel wall at the back, nothing each side, no hooks, or any way of attaching things, and a forward-curving half-roof that barely covers the stall-holder. Rain will cascade onto all produce.

His prediction the market's "temporary" relocation to a miles-away hangar near Swole would last over a year had proved correct. Unlike his prediction the £1.8 million cost to renovate the market would double. It tripled.

In August came his 11th **All Right Then, I'll Say It** in three years on the subject:

> The new market is dysfunctional, arrogantly-designed, not-needed and characterless in a way that blocks all hope of character. Our 700-year-old market's heritage and atmosphere have been erased by one stroke of greed and ineptitude. Meanwhile eight of 43 traders went bankrupt at Swole.

But August's atmosphere was a balm. Few failed to

look out at sunset over miles of haystacks and feel peace inside – a rare, warming reminder why it's worth bothering to keep on being alive. In the heat of endless afternoons, Farrisford's surrounding woods, hills and meadows were explored by strollers and lovers. Search for a peaceful clearing would lead to a good spot soon enough, timeless and safe. Far St Botolph's hourly bell made drifting-off sunbathers smile slightly.

"SO… HAVE A think about joining me here in Huddersfield?" said Danii.

"It's a Yes!" said Liu. "I'll come. I won't tell the girls, though everyone wants to know what's happened. Your husband… …he's… er… he's been in the salon again, asking questions."

"Forget *him*," said Danii.

A pause. Liu wondered: had Danii *really had* walked out on her marriage?

"How's Jade?" she said.

"Er… she's OK. Wears a hijab."

"*What?!* WOW!! Ha-ha-ha! That's *amazing*! Er…?"

"She's started school here," said Danii.

"Really? You *are* settled."

"Done my best. Finally got a bank loan, two grand, that's how I set up the business. Doubled the money I got from the diamond – d'you remember that boy?"

"Which one?"

"*Which one?* Only been with one."

"Two."

"Two? Oh… *the surfer*? No, that doesn't count. I'm talking about the *other* one."

"The black lad? Aw, he was *lovelyy*."

"I know. Bought him this diamond in Dubai, right?"

"I remember."

"He gave it me back."

"Whaa? Ah, that's so sweet!"

"I sold it – that and the bank-loan I've opened the little salon in a terraced street. It's not like Rennicksons, I tell ya! Hope you'll like it. It's really different up here though, quite full-on. The people… …they're a bit *common*, but I don't mean that in a bad way."

"Daniii!"

"It's true though. The whites are scruffy and talk funny, but they're nice. Very nice. Jade gets no hassle. Her Muslim friends at school – their mums came to help us set up the flat. There's such kindness in this world, Liu, things that'd break your heart."

"What's Jade being all Muslim for then?"

"I'll tell you when I ~"

"She's in love…"

"How did you guess!?"

"What's he like? Is it a he?"

"He's in a detention centre."

"*What?!* Oh, *no.* Is he a bad 'un? I've fell for a few of them."

"Not a bad 'un, no. He's her age, bit younger."

"Aww. What's he doing in one of them places?"

"Nothing," said Danii wistfully. "Came from Syria with his older brother, they got caught."

"Where's the brother?"

"Sleeping on our couch, sometimes. Gotta go, Liu. so much to do, salon's 8 til 8, it's *mad*, I'm desperate for a nail technician and…"

"I said I'll do it!"

"Are you sure?"

"*Ye-ahh!*"

"Business partner too? Equal with me. But you *mustn't* tell no one we're here? Think up a story…?"

ONE SUNDAY AT noon, Rashid drove Father Entreton

home from Mass. They passed a rough, dirty, ranting man with a hold-all, staring ahead as he marched like a maniac.

"Would you pull up, please?" said the priest. "I know that man."

"So do I," said Rashid. "Are you sure about this?"

Father Entreton got out the car.

Nevin's hair-plastered, sweating big head nodded upwards: "*Ohaah!*"

"Are you OK, sir?" said the priest. "Do you remem~"

"*Aye*, I rembr ye," gasped Nevin. "How's it gaun yerself?"

"I'm well, thank-you. Are you OK?"

"Tooth."

Nevin tried not to gasp and whimper. His lower cheek bulged with a dental abscess. "*Agh!*... Any tablets, Father? Agh! Painkillers?"

"Come to the house, I've clove oil…"

Nevin got into the car. Rashid didn't reply to his slurred: "You're the Indian drives the cabs, I knows ya."

They pulled up outside one of five bungalows circling the summit of Calls Hill. Normally priest and cab-driver parted now, or, if Rashid wasn't busy they'd go to the house to drink tea.

Father Entreton and Nevin left the car. The priest said: "Thank-you, Rashid, see you soon?" The driver meaningfully replied: "I'll come in if I may?"

Nevin lurched through the door and staggered after Father Entreton along a narrow, '50s-decor hall to a racing-green kitchen. Rashid followed. Father Entreton explained clove oil to Nevin.

Nevin rubbed some on his gums and drooled into the sink. Rashid winced. Father Entreton said: "Clove oil makes you salivate."

"Agh," belched Nevin over the sink.

"Spit it all out," said the priest. "Is it working yet?"

"It is, ackshlee. Pain's gone down."

Nevin's stench permeated the kitchen. He'd peed, maybe soiled himself worse, when drunk hours before. He spat and drooled in the sink again.

"How's the pain now?" said Father Entreton.

"When's Billy Nevin felt pain? Don't know the word." Coughing, Nevin stood to full height. He nodded to a photo on the windowsill: "Who's the fella?"

"Father Hall," said the priest. "Led me through the priesthood. Passed into spirit 1961. I sometimes feel it a shame he missed out on The Beatles. He'd have liked them, I think. 'All you need is love" is something he actually said himself. A true man of God. And, no, he didn't abuse children, if that's what you're thinking, and if you are, I'll still never stop trying to respect you, Mr Nevin, and with hope. Now, will you eat? I've scones, other things. Come to the garden, I'll bring food. Are you hungry?"

"Aye, rav, like. But I'm what you'd call a fussy eater. Allergies, y'know?"

Later, Rashid stayed on the patio as the priest and Nevin toured the garden. Despite "allergies", Nevin had devoured quiche, crackers, spreads, chicken slices, a bowl of hot ravioli and half a loaf of fruit-bread.

They returned, Nevin quiet, his toothache returned. He took more oil of cloves, but alcohol withdrawal seemed a worse problem. His body shook, head lolling.

Father Entreton asked if Rashid might drive them both to the Hazel Centre. "I've told Billy I'll go in with him to admit himself as a voluntary patient. He'll be fine to stay a week. Longer if he wants. And there's a dentist."

ON SUNDAY EVENING, "after weeks asking" Robert Obogo at last got agreement from Marlon *and* Bobby to go for a drink.

"Good Queen Bess?"

"Nah," said Zena, climbing into Robert's car.

"You've said 'Nah' to every pub."

"You never said Kennedy's."

"Ah, you're *joking*?" said Robert.

"Where's the kid anyway?" said Zena.

"We're picking him up."

"What's wrong with his damn legs?"

"I picked *you* up, I'm picking him up."

They drove down Hare's Hill. The town and a vast sunset filled the windscreen. Both men fell silent.

"What's this music?" grunted Zena.

"Vaughan-Williams. Like it?"

"Pfff. Where's the boy live now?"

"Same place."

"Not left home yet?"

Silence. The words "left home" struck a note in Bobby's heart. He began thinking of his daughter again. He missed her painfully.

They pulled up at 23 Arkwright Crescent. Bobby stayed in the car. Robert got out. Bobby watched him wave to John Wright at the window then make mock boxing moves as he approached Marlon at the door.

"Prat," muttered Bobby, turning away. His gaze caught a man watching from a window over the road.

"Yeah, three black men in your street!" barked Zena, "What ya gonna do, ring Special Branch?"

Marlon climbed into the back. Bobby turned, eyed Marlon, nodded "Mmph!", turned away. Robert smiled in the mirror at Marlon: "You're in favour! That's his *soppy* greeting!" He started the car: "OK, where to?"

"I don't want ~" Zena began.

"I'm asking Marlon."

"Er…I'm easy, y'know?" said Marlon nervously.

Robert and Bobby bickered. Zena insisted they forget pubs and go to his house to watch football and drink cans.

"Up for that, Marlon?" said Obogo. "A visit to Zena

Castle?"

"Um… y-yeah," said Marlon. He wanted out of the car. The presence of Bobby overwhelmed him. *The father of the girl I love… Oh God…* He looked at Bobby's hands, spread on the knees of his tracksuit bottoms. Was any trace of Millie's hands in his? There *was*.

Millie's *dad*. His voice, Caribbean with a layer of Nottingham. *Millie's DAD.*

"Guys? I-I gotta go home," said Marlon.

"Er… really?" said Robert, concerned. He pulled over, turned to Marlon: "Wanna talk about anything?"

"Nah. See you later," said Marlon, getting out.

Robert jogged after him.

"Marlon?" He put an arm around him: "I'm sorry. You know what *he's* like. How about we all play football next week, yeah? Get you out playing? Is that a yes? Good man. I'll arrange it."

NEXT MORNING, JOHN Talbot pulled up near Alpha Staplers. In the driving seat David took a breath.

"If it's like before," said John, "Walk away. OK? Please? I can support us both."

"I'll be fine."

They kissed.

"You look good with a tan," said John. "The sun's always good to you."

"And you," said David. "Glad we had the holiday."

"That girl on the train!" chuckled John "'*You two been to Myknonos?*' I thought: 'Are we that obvious?' I nearly said: 'Have you been to Ayia Napa?' Turned out she had."

Noise of drilling cut in. Two last, high walls of the old factory formed a V round a hill of smashed masonry. A crane swung girders. Earth-movers roared at low-frequency. The shrill, hard drills never ceased.

"Better go," said David, "Two minutes to eight."

An agitated mob of grey hoodies, tattoos and ruck-sacks crammed Alpha's main entrance. One door was open. The hi-vis concierge peered through glass of the other, eyeing the queue, admitting one person at a time, inspecting their ID card.

Everyone shuffled backwards as three people were let out – a managerial man in denim, grey T-shirt and Birkenstocks, and two very young women in white plimsolls, grey jeans and white shirts with an orange name-badge. The manager held a piece of card with writing.

"Bye, love," said John: "Good luck. You're brave coming back here."

"A job's a job," said David. "And the pension."

David joined the bottleneck at the narrow open door.

"Shit!" said a man in front. "*C'mon,* guy, let us in? We'll be *late.*"

"We *are* late," said a woman. She turned round to bawl: "Stop *pushing* please? I'm spilling my fucking latte!"

A man sighed furiously: "Jesus, *come on*, it's *TWO MINUTES PAST*!!"

David's attention wandered left, to the loud demolition site. Its vibrational noise seemed to bypass hearing to go straight into the chest, where it sank to the stomach and stayed. David's gaze fell on the piece of card the young manager held up.

Welcome David Benett, Dan Hanson, Laura Tallie

Chapter 2

FOR THE FIRST time back in England, Annette rang Dewy. Dewy was relieved. She wasn't deleted from Annette's life, as feared.

Annette had written to her parents two weeks before, saying she and Annie wanted to marry. They hadn't answered. Annette was hurt and distressed.

"Annie's never been loved," she told Dewy. "I want to love her with all the world. I want the world to *show* her she's loved. I want my family to love her. I want us to have a wedding."

Dewy was enraged at Joanna Stephens, and disappointed with Robert III. *Surely he realises not replying is destroying Annette?* she told herself. *He could surely e-mail her? 'Thanks for your letter, glad you're both happy, let's discuss this in future?' Can't Robert not even do that? Why not?*

Annette stopped ringing. If Dewy rang, she got answering machine. But one late-August day Annette answered. She spoke of Morris, who thrived in Britain, had a garden to himself, "a meadow and woods, new scents and sounds. He's real happy." Annette's voice stopped.

"Honey?" said Dewy.

"I c-can't bear it," said Annette. "Mom's never much liked me, but *this*…" She broke down. "… this feels like *hate*. They've ignored *every* communication from me."

She cried for half a minute, then apologised. Dewy

cried too, in anger.

"Why should it *matter* if I love a woman and she loves me?" said Annette. "What harm is it to anyone? Is it arms manufacture? Diesel pollution? Fracking? Anything wrong *at all*? No! It's *love*. Why does love *bother people?*"

"I know," said Dewy, surprised to hear Annette infer arms manufacture as wrong. *Is she defying what her family stands for now? Can anyone blame her?* She and Annette had disagreed for years, Dewy urging pacifism to someone from a Navy family, Annette arguing defence, attack if needed, to ensure peace in an ever violent world.

Dewy drove to the Stephens's in a record 18 minutes. Robert III stepped out to meet the abused car. He'd heard its noise from a mile.

"Dewy, what have you done to ~?"

"*I've done NOTHING to Wal's car!!*"

"Hey! Less of that. This car urgently ~"

"*Fuck* the car, Robert!"

Stephens's iron stare froze Dewy.

"Sorry, sir," she said quietly. "Why haven't you contacted Annette?"

Robert Stephens sighed, nodded, made a phone-call: "Juan? Could you come look at a car, please?"

He turned, "Gimme the key," snatched it from Dewy, paced to the car, scowled at the state of it and placed the key on the dashboard for Juan.

In the house, in silence, a bay window each, Robert and Dewy watched birds in alders and oaks across the east lawn. Robert had rung Joanna, conveying in hints Dewy was in a state of war.

Ever aiming for calm, he demonstrated activating the imitation fire with a phone app. Then he walked to a far wall's brass plate of light-switches. "See, Dewy? The fire's also controlled from here?" He twisted a dial. Flames in the grate rose. "Pretty good, right?"

"Yes, sir," said Dewy.

Mention that fire again, I'll piss on it.

Joanna Stephens arrived, leaned on a doorpost, folded her arms, eyed Dewy. "Get me a brandy, Bob."

10 minutes on, the meeting reached angry stalemate. Dewy had persuaded the Stephens's a two line e-mail would mean a lot to Annette. They seemed prepared to send one, but Joanna objected when Dewy said it might say: "to discuss your plans."

"We don't *want* to discuss her 'plans', her marrying this... *Annie*."

"Why not?" said Dewy.

"We're not giving our blessing to *this*!"

"At least *tell her that*! Instead of leaving her hanging."

Silence.

Joanna Stephens crunched a corn chip. She watched Dewy. So did her husband. They surveyed the decayed, green Barbour Waldo Millard stopped wearing 20 years ago. Beneath it were Wal's ancient, dark-pink corduroy jeans, grooves worn away. Too long for Dewy, she'd rolled turn-ups which unravelled over the ever bare, if meticulously nail-polished feet. Try as he might, Robert Stephens's lifelong attempt to believe in anyone he met wasn't working here.

All three sighed, Joanna hardest.

"Where's this going, Dewy?" she snapped. "We're to give our blessing Annette marry this... 'friend'? No. The answer's No."

"That's for *you* to tell her, not ~."

"Don't tell *me* how to treat my daughter!"

"I *will*, because you've *always ignored* her!" shouted Dewy, standing. "When you gonna *stop* ignoring her? *It's all you've ever done!*"

She turned to face a window, afraid to face Joanna's response.

"Dewy?" sighed Robert Stephens, patting air to calm his rage-pale wife. "Isn't marriage... a little *far*? I mean, why not… a *relationship*? A little experimentation?"

"*What*?!" said Dewy, turning to the room. "Why do straight people call other lovestyles 'experimentation'? Like gay's a form of vivisection?"

"Fine!" yelled Robert Stephens. "*Be* a smart-alec! Pick things apart! But answer my question: why not just, er… er…"

"'Experimentation'?" said Dewy sarcastically.

"A *relationship*?" said Robert Stephens, while Joanna cut-in: "Don't be so *fucking rude*, Dewy!"

Robert Stephens tried to sound more settled: "Dewy… this Annie – we don't… even know her surname –"

"McClure."

"–unknown woman, no family, no money."

"Annie wants nothing!" cried Dewy. "She loves Annette. *Loves.* She'd love Annette no less, and in the same ways – protectively, romantically, companionably – if your daughter hadn't a dime."

"Dewy, do you believe your judgment on Annette's life is sound?" said Robert.

"Yes. And a little no, to make sure. Are you certain of yours and Joanna's, sir?"

"*Yes he damn is,*" growled Joanna Stephens, approaching. "Have you *any* idea what it's like, to have some… *person*… claim to know your child better than you?"

"I *do* know her," said Dewy, tears welling. "Spent more time with Annette in all her life than anyone! I *completely* know her."

"*So do we!*" yelled Joanna. "And from a *real* perspective, not that of someone who *sucks Annette's fingers*, spits food into her mouth and gets blind drunk!"

"This isn't working," said Dewy, "I've fucked it up. I'll leave."

"Please do," said Robert Stephens III.

LOVEWORT AND WEEDS grew fast and wild in the two-mile scar of earth from Bettle to Moresby. In a hi-vis coat and orange plastic hat, Brandon Tyler paced its borders. His job was to stop children climbing the fence, or adults stealing (non-existent) equipment. No one came near the place.

Every 100 metres a sign: **UNSAFE GROUND – KEEP OUT**. Brandon sometimes checked if the signs were securely fixed to the fence. They were.

He missed Danii. And Jade. He wanted his mother. But she was angry with him for telling the police about Jade. Worse, when Danii finally took a call from him one night, and told him Jade had befriended two Syrians, he'd laughed: "Silly cow," expecting his mother to chuckle. But she went silent then tersely ended the call.

Long, quiet days were often hot. Fields shimmered gold. Sheep gathered on hard mud around thin streams. Sometimes Brandon stopped to look east. The 30-mile view made him feel things he didn't understand. *People a thousand years ago looked out at this, just like me* he thought, then disliked himself being "soft".

After each 90-minute circuit, he noticed the country-side's greens and golds tones had changed from the sun moving. Faraway, small, flat-based clouds hung at the exact same height. Brandon watched their slow shadows across the land. Sunrays slanted under furthest, huge, cumulus clouds.

Them Syrians must've mattered to Jade, And we laughed at her for being fat. So she ran off. Mum went after her. Maybe if we don't laugh at Jade, and are nicer about the migrants, Jade and Mum'll come back?

August's only incident was two boys on BMX bikes riding up to peer through the fence. Site manager Les emerged from his small Portakabin to speed towards them in a silver-grey pick-up truck with *Warrior* across the foot of each door in a martial-arts font. The boys calmly rode off before Les got there.

Three other staff, a mile apart, walked the double tyre-tracks outside the perimeter fence too. For variety they might step between the tracks, trampling weeds, dandelions, wild flowers, insects.

A man with a strimmer was coming, it was said.

Certainly this was said. Twice a day *Warrior* bumped and growled round the site perimeter. To the Polish man, Les nodded, to the woman, likewise. But he'd pause the truck to speak to Brandon, or the man on the opposite side. He'd nod at the weed-filled centre of the track ahead: "Fuckin' ridiculous, innut? Bloke comin' with a strimmer soon, they reckon."

No other communication occurred day after grey or sunny day. The perimeter track was four and a half miles. Brandon earned £8.10 an hour.

MANAGER STEFAN PIERCE hadn't processed David telling him twice: "I work here. I'm back after two months off". Instead, David was introduced to: "Your Kickstarter Engagement Officer, Rachel Meadows!!"

David thought Rachel Meadows looked 15. "Welcome to Alphaaa!" said a high, droopy voice: "We work on five pillars. These will be talked through by HR…"

David simultaneously heard other Kickstarter Engagement Officers tell newcomers: "… we work on five pillars. These will be talked through by…"

"We're going to Upper HR," smiled Rachel Meadows, over many echoing footsteps in reception, where the walls were bare grey, no billboard photographs now. Rachel Meadows stopped at the top of the green marble stairs. "I think the others go to Upper Plus HR…"

"*Two* HR departments?" said David.

Upstairs, someone called Lanson emerged from a door plastered with designer graffiti around the A-in-a-circle

Anarchy symbol.

"Welcome to Alpha, David," she said. "Am I right you've been here before?"

David explained he'd been 12 years at Alpha until two months' medical leave. Lanson frowned: "I'll check this" and marched away. David sat with Rachel Meadows for 10 minutes. She told him about employee parking, canteen sandwiches and the location of departments in the building. Rachel Meadows would never grasp that David wasn't new.

Lanson reappeared: "Probably a mix-up, but go with it? You're re-kickstarting, basically? What's your job-title again?"

When David was led to his new desk-pod in a room called Blitzkrieg Bop, five people stood applauding: "*Whoooo!* Welcome aboard!" David recognised Sarita Sumal but no others. A young man presented David with a plastic flag on a 10-inch pole, a white flag with the black A anarchy symbol, circle around it formed by the words Alpha Staplers.

"You put this on the desk, see?" said Rachel Meadows.

David tried to smile to everyone. All had the flag on their desks. Unable to speak, he was grateful now for Rachel Meadows, who talked all the time.

"Open your presents, David!" she said. "From the company and your team?"

David unwrapped vegan chocolates, a zebra-print i-Pad cover, fair-trade cycling gloves, two £3 Farrisford Organics vouchers, a DVD "The Five Pillars Of Alpha Staplers by CEO Luke Hill", and a grey T-shirt with Alpha's A-for-anarchy logo in white.

Chapter 3

DEWY SLEPT DAYTIMES, to block out chainsaws. They invaded her dreams. On waking she'd drive to the coast, walk an hour, buy pizza and Merlot, stay up all night in the cabin drinking, thinking, listening to country music. At first light she'd go out to greet birdsong.

Once a week she drove to Boston, taught English and literacy to 11-year-old Benitez and his neighbour Angel. Then, two streets away, she taught Juanita and Pedro, 12 and 10. She'd taught the children for three years. Dewy worried they'd outgrown her. They seemed unhappy, tense, sometimes angry. President Trump's policy was to repatriate Mexican children by rounding them up in schools. The children knew this was happening. It had happening to friends, it had happened to Angel's cousin, to people up the street.

A browse of websites about 1930s Germany brought sharp comparisons.

Dewy was enraged and afraid. The childrens' English quickly improved, near-fluent. But Angel, the oldest, was silent, unknowable now. He was giving up. The atmosphere in houses where Dewy taught had changed, smiles rarer, voices strained, people dropped things, forgot the TV was loud, snapped at each other, didn't listen, shut doors loudly. Fear had erased all well-being and shut down awareness.

Angel nestled against Dewy on the sofa, quiet, except if Dewy sang. Her donkeyish terrible singing, and apparent outrage if mocked for it, still made Angel laugh. Dewy charged $15 per lesson, not per child, nor per hour. Lessons could continue indefinitely, especially if dancing began. From the two weekly lessons, after $10 gas in Wal's car, Dewy often lived two weeks on the $20 left, half of it spent on a home-pedicure from Benitez's aunt, Mrs Andrinez, who wouldn't take more than $10 from Dewy.

One afternoon Dewy's nail-polish dried in Mrs Andrinez's cluttered parlour. Amid loud Spanish TV, Mrs Andrinez talked on her phone, forced a second quesadilla and more black coffee on Dewy and filed the fingernails of another client. Dewy's phone rang.

"Clifton Stephens, is that Dewy?"

"*Clift!* How are you?"

"Good, thank-you. In New York right now, with my son."

"Oh! I'm happy to hear that."

"Rang Annette from Italy couple days back. She OK, Dewy?"

"She's depressed."

"Can't hear too good. Someplace busy?"

"Shall we speak in a while?"

"I'd like that. Bye now."

Dewy wondered how to discuss Annette. Did Clifton know she wanted to marry? Had she told him? Had he found out from their parents? "She OK, Dewy?" was direct. Clifton always was.

"I ought to tell Annette I saw her parents," thought Dewy. Worrying her disastrous visit might filter back to Annette second-hand, Dewy felt best to tell her. She pulled over near Beacon Hill. Annette answered on the first ring: "Hi, hon!"

"Darling!" said Dewy. "You sound happier!"

"On the bus to college, beautiful morning teaching at a summer school! Booboo's good, he *loved* his breakfast! Chicken in herb gravy with fresh fusilli, then a green chew that strengthens his tooths. We have a good vet here, a Mrs Lowe. Booboo's gums are fine, breathing's good, weight's near-ideal, he's in perfect shape!"

"Great!" said Dewy. "And *you*, hon?"

"Uh… yeah… I… …."

A pause. Dewy said: "Clifton called me. He said you'd spoken."

"He did?"

"He asked if you were OK. I said you'd been depressed."

"Oh. I… I think I talked to him pretty well? I didn't say I was depressed."

"Were you tired?"

"Maybe." Annette's voice had dropped to monotone.

"Did you tell him about you and Annie," said Dewy, "How you plan to marry?"

"No."

"Mind if I tell him? If only because your parents might?"

"I guess," sighed Annette. "I'm trying to not think about all this for *one hour*?"

"Sorry, darling. I'm sorry."

After calling Clifton, Dewy blogged:

Ah, Clifton Stephens, loveliest man on the Eastern seaboard. One of the few people who always treated Annette and me like humans, not weeds in the Essex County social garden.

Clifton is of the souls who know we're not here long, each day another reprieve from the inevitable, so let us love, share this passing moment, find laughter and interesting things, freedom, and freedom from strain and fears.

36, and the ultimate All American, New England boy, Clifton's physical perfection is enhanced by humility and unfailing courtesy. Such men do exist. I should stop so much WASP-swatting, they've some

sweethearts too.

Clifton married Lulu and Bob Willenhall's daughter Carla in 2010. They divorced four years later, no surprise, Clifton on active service, rarely home. Today Carla has custody of two-year-old Robert Willenhall II. He is loving and excited about a half-sibling soon from Carla and her new husband Bruno, who manages one of the NYC opera houses.

Clifton's the best driver in the world. I've always admired that {and his beautiful, too rare paintings.} He's driven Annette and me around since we were children and he 17. How can this relaxed-driver, Syd Barrett-loving painter and young father be in the US war machine?

Like his brothers Clifton inherited Joanna's intolerance of hesitation or indirectness. Therefore: "What's up, Dewy?"

"Your sister wants to marry a British woman. Your parents don't wanna know."

"Hmm. You OK about her marrying?"

"Definitely. I went to your parents and pleaded they bless it, but I'm not the best ambassador."

"How do you feel about Annette wanting someone else?"

"Um…"

"Are you hurt, Dewy?"

"No, uh… *no*, I-I'm through it. I couldn't make Annette secure, or… or fulfilled. Her new partner does."

"Most unselfish of you."

"Her name's Annie."

"Dewy, do you believe my sister and Annie are happy?"

"Yes I do."

"Are they right for each other?"

"I'm in no doubt, Clift."

> "Then I'm in no doubt. Mom and Dad can jump
> in the horse-bath."

Clifton sounded nearly as always, but Dewy sensed he'd had experiences off the Syrian coast. His father had been similar after both Gulf Wars. His brother Jack was after the second one. She recalled their absent-mindedness, silence and desire to be alone. Dewy decided to make an open arrangement to meet Clifton, saying she'd wait for his call. She prayed he'd not forget. But two weeks passed. He was on leave four more days.

BRANDON CHECKED HIS Sent Items. Eight texts to his mother this week, no reply. He checked his phone every 15 minutes. Nothing. Sighing, he texted:

> **dear mum it wld be 'nice' 2 hear back from u**
>
> **Brandon (hope u are ok)**

Evenings at home were strange. The three men affected cheeriness. Mention of Danii or Jade an eyes-upward: "Ha! *Women!*"

"They'll come back," said Dave Tyler. "Let them have their strop. It's Jade basically, got attitude problems. Makes up stories in her head, needs a bit of Mum time."

But permanent lack of contact from Danii worried Tyler. Jade had "probably turned her mum against me, shit like that happens."

Brandon couldn't keep up with father-son team, Dave and Warren, and wanted to move out. Tyler never emphasised or mentioned Brandon wasn't his natural son, often addressed Brandon "son", but Brandon always felt apart. Aware his foppish looks added to this, he went to Balaton for a number two buzz-cut.

"You look like a ostrich!" roared Warren.

"Looks all right, son," said Tyler. "Proper man's cut.

That's what we want!"

"My head's cold," muttered Brandon.

"Get a hat then!" shouted Warren. "'My head's cold' – *get a fucking hat!* Ha-ha-*HA!*" He and Tyler laughed heartily. Warren's wit always hit the spot.

Brandon was glad when the pair left for the kebab shop in Brinton, glad dinner was kebabs again. By unspoken rule the three didn't sit together eating these. No desperate cheeriness around a table. Tonight was the fourth night of kebabs in a row.

"It's because of me," thought Brandon, lying on his bed under posters of racing cars and undressed women. "I'm the odd one out." He sprang up, opened his lap-top, ran his fingers over his head, expecting to touch hair, but only air was there.

After browsing pornography, Brandon looked at Job-CentrePlus online. A job advert showed uniformed men and women staring back at him severely: **HAVE YOU GOT WHAT IT TAKE'S??**

AT 10AM DEWY danced nude, lay on her back, raised her legs, did scissor kicks, parted her legs to let warm, dry air circulate, caressed her labia…

*"Fancy bupping idto you **here** od Fiff Abbenoo, Joni! AH-CHOO!"*

*"Dewy, you should be in **bed** with that cold! Come to ours. Michael's in Japan. I wanna feed you, get in bed with you, warm you up…"*

Dewy stopped herself. *Third time today! I HAVE to snap out of this, lead a productive life.* She opened a bottle of wine.

The Farrisford Tattler finally paid $3,007 to Dewy's account. What remained of June's $5,000 from Mrs Halaton (after paying off the Stag, and flying with Annette to Boston and back) had supported drinking until late

July. Thereupon Dewy lay ill and penniless until her 120-day account cleared the day Annette, Annie and Morris left on the ship. That too went on drinking, donations to homeless people and pizzas. Today, 8th September, she had $3,372.

Besides a Boston trip for a pedi and to teach, Dewy hadn't seen or spoken to anyone for 12 days. Long nights were spent with Hank Williams, Joni Mitchell, Debussy, Tim Buckley, Miles Davis, Patsy Cline and two or three bottles of wine. For a third hot month (and fourth summer) Dewy spent her days naked in a sunhat, lost in thought, sipping wine, pacing garden and woods. Her mind veered from joyous and inspired, to insane, vengeful.

Clifton not contacting made her worried. Impulsively Dewy rang Roberta Paley, telling voicemail:

"Roberta, something's going round in my mind. It's like, totally private, involves others, but I'm a catalyst. And useless."

Next day, Roberta Paley rang: "What's up? Where are you?"

"Plum Island!" cried Dewy, delighted to be rung. She backtracked about her voicemail. "It's… ah… a small tangle… um…"

"Millards?"

"No."

"Stephens's?"

"Um…"

"Obviously the Stephens's.

"It might not be?"

"Don't evade. Come visit, I guess, if you're sane?"

"*I'd love to.* Are you sure?"

"Looking in my diary, ahh, Thursday? Rhode Island, we've a house here. Are you flyi – oh, you'll be driving won't you?"

RACHEL MEADOWS WAS to chaperone David for six weeks.

His only time without her were visits to the wc. Returning from one, he walked along a corridor sunlit by windows on one side. Echoing footsteps on hard, waxed floor increased as two men and a woman neared. As they grew imminent, David knew he was being studied. A man blocked his way.

"Hi! We've met?" said new board member, Mal Harris.

David didn't know. He only saw silhouettes in sun-brightness.

"One of the existing seniors," explained Harris to the others.

"Well, *obviously* he's existin'!" snapped the hard Liverpool voice of the female silhouette.

Mal Harris touched David's arm: "The name?"

David said his name. His eyesight had adjusted to see the second man, who – tall, handsome, if short-foreheaded – watched him unpleasantly. David rightly guessed the woman was Trish Hammond, an executive from Crellan plc, new owners of Alpha Staplers. She looked 40 or 30 in an elegant twinset, hair like a Sindy doll's. Her intelligent, loveless face frowned.

"How's it going, Dave?" she klaxoned. "What's your role, might I ask?"

"Sorry?" said David, sun-blind, perspiring.

"Who you? What do?" sing-sung Trish Hammond. Pursing a thin, wide mouth she absently inspected David while the tall man glared at his eyes.

"H-Head of Technical Design," said David.

"What's that in English?" said Trish Hammond. "Head of *Design*?" she pulled a face.

"Um…?" said David, blushing.

"In what *way* 'Head of… *Technical Desiiign*?"

"I'm… the-the Head of the Technical Design department?"

"Not getting anythin' from that, Dave. Doesn't tell me

nothin'."

"Er... I... I um...."

"You haven't told us *anything*!" wailed the tall man very loudly.

"Head of-of Technical D-Design," gulped David. "Responsible for the team that-that designs our products."

"*Thank*-you!" said the man, annoyed.

"Nice to meet, Dave," said Trish Hammond, walking away. David felt the man stare at the side of his head as he passed. Mal Harris had dematerialised.

Receding footsteps echoed. David heard the tall man: "Seen everything wrong with this fucking company in 10 minutes."

"There's potential," said Trish Hammond. "But 'drain the swamp', like that Trump fella said."

"Shoot the cripples, more like," said the man.

"*Steve!*" said Trish Hammond's hacking laugh, "Stop it!"

David was relieved to see Rachel Meadows, bland and faithful, by his chair. "Remember you need to log any time away from your desk," she smiled, bringing up an online form. "And give the reason?"

"Oh, yes," said David, sitting. "I'm getting the hang of this now."

"We send it to HR 1 every day last thing."

"Yes, I've been doing that. Uh... How long was I..."

"11 minutes," cooed Rachel Meadows. "10.41 to 10.52."

"Oh BONDING up *yours!!*" pealed through the offices. Everyone stood. David said: "I'd forgotten *those!*"

"Company bonding meetings?" said Rachel Meadows. "Quick, let's go!"

She led David fast into a corridor, explaining: "A company bonding meeting means everyone heads straight for Something Better Change and ~"

"I remember," said David, unheard.

Urgency was permanent at Alpha now. No more arriving at a Bonding within 30 seconds. 12 was imperative. Someone crushed David's foot, another nudged his back persistently. Rachel Meadows's hand on his arm was barged off by someone pushing between them. Rachel tugged him through people into Something Better Change's wide, white, echoing expanse, towards a young man holding a placard **Newhire**. "New Hire *Here!*" he screamed. David saw groups form around similar people with **Social Media** and **Influencers** placards.

Rachel sat David in a block of chairs where eager people each had a Kickstarter Engagement Officer talking at them.

Applause and cheers erupted. Someone whispered "Stand!". All stood clapping as three men entered the centre of the space. New CEO Luke Hill, 30, unsmiling, in fake-old jeans and grey hoodie, plus Mal Harris and Toby Fanshawe, who, once in David's team, was deputy CEO. What had happened to Pip Runcolm, no one David had asked knew, or knew his name. Where too was Sahid Verhouzian?

Luke Hill advanced, to huge applause and cheers. He shook a fist and yelled: "INDUSTRY DISRUPTORS, GOOD *MORNING!*"

"*YEAHHH!!!*" roared 104 people.

At 7pm John Talbot returned home to find David staring disconsolately at a computer. John did not like to see this.

"All right, love?" he said, cheerily. "Not working, I hope?"

"No… er, not really, just an appraisal. There was a two-hour bonding meeting… I'm to 'write a letter to myself of a month ago' describing the meeting, and also er… what is 'Outreach Axiom' do you think? Do you have you things like this at Asda?"

John rubbed David's stiff shoulders and read on the screen:

TEAM SCRUTINY/ OUTREACH AXIOM

Dear TEAM MANAGER AND-OR DIREC-TORATE MODERATOR
name: David Benet
Tthankyou for agreeing to participate in out-reach axoim.

Outreach Axiom aim's –
* To symbiose working frameworks re a multi-connectional hub.
* To provide fresh-water assessments of modula-tion and progress-tracking agendas.
* To reveal meta-targets.
* To encourage transparency at both framework and cog-and-wheel strata.

*Please print questionaire attachment to this e-mail and fill in **twice** aweek for 4 weeks.*

David clicked on the attachment. It requested he record his five staff-members' time-keeping, appearance, and "conversation themes &content (CT&C)". He was asked to award weekly marks from one to nine on: attitude, collaboration, individual contribution, shared ideas, linear approach ("I don't know what that is" said David) and Alpha Five Pillars Awareness. David must also put the previous week's score in brackets and explain any change, or why no change. A final blank page said simply: *What are your coments on the Ground Atmospherrics of your hub this week?*

"It's for something called HR 2" said David, as John left the room.

Alone in the kitchen, John placed a fist on his forehead and silently cried.

IN EAST LANE Park, eight young men and three women colonised a bench and low wall. They wore cheap, new sports clothes and gold-plate jewellery. The evening air was thick with ganja smoke.

"Got my own business now," said Tyson Bradley. "Don't need to work, help my dad. He's a millionaire, does all sorts. I get cash like water outta taps."

No one ever questioned anything he said.

"You fell out with The Bone then?" said someone.

"Hssssk!" said Bradley. "He's a fuckin' idiot."

Two or three grunted agreement, others listened keen-ly. Surely The Bone – Darren Tibley – wasn't out of favour?

"What's he done?" said a girl.

Bradley inhaled a thick, oily spliff, exhaled grey-brown smoke, and in a cracked voice said: "He's a fuckin' idiot."

Several *yeahs* were sleepily moo'd. Any drama within the group – power struggles, fallings out, betrayal, fights, bullying, loves, hates – led to discussions of at most 10 words.

"Aye-aye," said a girl, looking right. "Nice legs."

All stared as Robert Obogo entered from the corner in full Farrisford Town home kit. Marlon followed, in a vintage navy Adidas Firebird tracksuit. Robert booted a football towards empty bandstand.

"Big dark for my liking," said Tyson Bradley.

"And mine" said Richard Simm. "Ask 'em for some bananas, I'm hungry!"

Wondering why no one laughed, he threw his head back to shout abuse, but someone prodded him, another placed a hand over his mouth. Simm saw why. Bobby Zena had arrived.

All looked away, a few whispers: *Dangerous fucker.*

Bad man. Psycho. The group began small-talk to try and impress each other they were relaxed around Zena.

He kicked a ball so hard it disappeared, clanged off the bandstand's copper green roof and soared to far in the park. Marlon turned, to sudden shock. Not only was the group who'd terrified him for years staring at him, but three yards away Bobby Zena was too. Father of the woman he loved (ached for and never saw).

Receiving a long pass from Obogo, Zena did ball-tricks with no effort then ran with the ball to within 10 yards of Bradley's group, who he didn't care were there or not, and whacked a shot at the bandstand. As intended, it crashed vertically down from the roof-underlip, bounced fast up and down then lay on the bandstand platform. A woman in the group spontaneously cried *Whooo!*

Bobby gestured Marlon pass him another ball. Zena kicked it clean through the bandstand, no sound. "*Damn*," he said, advancing on Marlon, hands on hips. Marlon tensed, remembering Robert's dreadful instruction on the phone last night: "If Bobby ever says to you: 'Get that ball', say to him: 'Get it yourself'. Don't be afraid to say that. It's scary, but he'll respect you. He won't if you trot off to get his ball."

Marlon braced himself but Bobby turned to observe Obogo, who sprinted superbly, back and forth, one side of the park. "Pfah!" said Bobby.

He faced Marlon. "Right, bends with *me*. Legs apart. Right hand onto left knee, then ~"

Robert jogged towards them.

"Big athlete!" jeered Zena. "Running a hundred-yard park? Now do *this*."

They watched Bobby's brisk, one-handed press-ups. After 10 he switched hands mid-air.

"What *is* this?" said Robert, "An 80s hip-hop video?"

"You can't *do* this!" said Bobby switching arms again.

"It's a case of wanting to. I can't play tiddliwinks either, but if I *wanted* to ~"

"Bullshit!" Bobby switched arms a third time. Obogo sighed: "Effort, Bob. *My* exercises are relaxed elegance, not a performing seal."

Zena sprang up: "I'll relaxed elegance *YOU*!"

Years a kickboxer, he high-kicked to a half-inch from Obogo's chin.

"T-ha! Ya face a picture!" laughed Bobby. "OK, *relaxed elegance*, go over there. Take free kicks to Marlon, he heads to me, I score."

The youths watched them, fazed by Zena's kickboxing move – a reminder he could kill if he chose, and nearly had in the past, it was known. They watched Obogo's precise free kicks to Marlon heading to Zena, who volleyed hard. One or other wrought-iron post in the bandstand went *punnnng!* and bounced back every time, as intended.

Marlon hated being watched by the gang. But it crossed his mind: *there's been no hassle from them since... ...since...* He tried to cast his mind back. The only story in his life was Millie. It seemed forever since she'd gone. Oddly, no racist hassle in that time. No cars in Trant Road, no night visits in the Crescent. A coincidence.

"Oi! Wake up!" yelled Bobby.

The group watched Zena, annoyed, walking at Marlon: "Standing there like a pylon! Go get that ball!"

Every gaze widened as Marlon Wright folded his arms and *dared tell Bobby Zena*: "Get it yourself!"

And – after a dire, deadly pause – Bobby Zena *did*.

John Wright and Marlon had suffered no attacks since Millie Zena confronted the culprits 11 weeks ago. This would continue forever.

Chapter 4

"ROBERTA, A MOST *beautiful house* ~"

"You look ill and strange," sighed Mrs Paley, "Come in." She half-embraced Dewy. "Dah! Dirty clothes. *Ridiculous*! Better feed you – time someone did."

"This house!" gaped Dewy.

"My family's, the Westcotts, 1741. That painting's 1860: great-great-*great* grandmother Eliza, husband Matthew."

Roberta walked through the wood-panelled hall, reciting:

"Original house half-broke up, two storms in a week, 1824. Most of the floorboards floated back to shore. These old, very smooth, deep-honey floors are the originals."

In a traditional, surprisingly cluttered kitchen, Roberta turned to Dewy:

"I'm not excellent, OK? Was gonna cancel. You'd better not be devious or ulterior, I'll see it a mile off."

"Roberta!"

"Refreshment?" said Roberta, lifting an earthenware jug. "Cranberry lemonade. Cranberries from the gardens. Stains like lipstick. Sit down. No: there, in the sun, you look cold."

Dewy sat, Roberta didn't. "*So…* the Stephens's, what's up? Is that lemonade not incredible?"

"Mmm, yeah," said Dewy.

"I'll hear what you have to say, but don't ask anything of me. No involvement. And don't expect me to plead anything on your behalf."

"I wouldn't."

"Why are *you* discussing anyone's affairs? Your own are desperate. A trash-act parasite on the Millards for years."

"Oh! I drove all this way to be *torn apart*? I… I can't get things right yet. I'm *trying* to change. That's why I need to ensure Annette Stephens will be secure. As soon as she is, I'll find a direction, learn contemporary dance…"

"You and Annette *aren't together* now?"

"Well… uh…"

"You girls… for *years*, in each other's arms. Never a more loving pair!" Roberta laughed kindly: "You'd kiss and kiss, no self-consciousness, 100 per cent yourselves, that's why no one bothered. Do I look mid-30s or late-30s?"

"Uh?"

"Do I look my age?"

"What is your age?"

"You tell *me*."

"I don't know. You're… a fine-looking woman. Beautiful."

"'Fine-looking'? What am I, a ship?"

Dewy sighed. Mrs Paley opened a refrigerator, took a pallet of eggs and some vegetarian sausages. "Fix you breakfast, I'll put music on, so you don't feel ashamed of your eating noises. I imagine you have that complex. I wish more people did."

"No music please."

"Oh? You like your Mendelssohn, don't you?"

"How did you remem–"

"I'm a socialite, I remember likes and dislikes. Are you warm yet? If so, please remove that Iron Age Barbour?"

Beyond a cliff at the garden's end, the Atlantic, mid-day-gold. Dewy gazed out, in thought. Roberta paused cooking to look at her. Dewy turned.

"You're a sweet thing," said Roberta.

They resumed their thoughts. A minute on, Dewy asked:

"You came the Millards' that time? Was the real reason to see me?"

"Ha! It *was*, and to see Andrea of course. I waited a respectable length of time after the Kapels incident until ~"

"Oh *no*." said Dewy, "Do people *remember*?"

"Yes, though I wonder what really happened."

"I didn't get invited anyplace after."

"Definitely not. Then one day, Alice of all people, said: 'Where's the tramp?'. And Kirsten said: 'We're having a time for Hal's 40th. Dewy could come, but will someone sound her out?' So I called Andrea for a date. She then called you to come get your mail?'

"You *things*!" said Dewy. "You instructed Va- um Andrea to withhold my mail? So you could entice me out to be examined? My phone rang, Andrea saying 'come by, please'. I was so scared she was with Wal, they were about to ask me to move out. I tried to be brave. Andrea was by the cars, but no Waldo. And there you were."

"And there *you* were, little lost lamb," said Mrs Paley, "I thought: 'how can anyone not want *you* around?'"

"I didn't know you knew Andrea well."

"Waldo longer, he and Stephen were at Princeton."

"Stephen. How is he?"

"Stephen Westcott is well. Tell me what happened with Robert Kapels?"

Dewy looked stricken: "Does *everyone* know about it?"

"Yes, but it was three years ago."

"Does everyone know I had scurvy two winters ago?"

"Yes. That's why Jennifer Leigh hired you for her dumb boutique, really to ply you with hot food and drinks, but she had to fire you after four days. Hell knows what you said, but the customer rang an attorney. Jennifer had to fire you to show immediate action taken."

"You remember that?"

"Everyone does. Anyway, Robert Kapels?"

"Does everyone tell everyone everything?"

"Best way to stop people messing up. Advice sucks, lecturing's useless, gossip *works*. When people know everything, you mend your ways."

"That's why men have secret societies and cabals since time began," said Dewy. "Scared of femininity's gift for gossip."

"Oh, we can't be trusted," said Mrs Paley. "We tell what daren't be told. It's healthy. Social hygiene. Secrets happen when something's wrong. We point out what."

She approached with a teapot, cup and saucer: "You freaked Kapels out. I'm told you came onto him aggressively."

"I didn't touch him!" said Dewy.

"He said he was scared."

"*'Scared'*? He's six-four, 300 pounds!!"

"What *did* happen?"

"He approached. I said: 'Robert! How are you?' He said: 'Whatya doing workwise?' As I tried to figure out an answer, he said: 'Whatdya *do* all day?' I said: 'Robert, shut up. Come outside and fuck me in a car?'"

Silence.

"*Dewy*. Robert's a very devout Lutheran."

"I wasn't serious! I didn't persist! I stopped immediately, ashamed, half the room stopped talking to watch, crowded hall, the Campbells, you know? 'Back away from it, Bobby! Get away from *her*.' I was dying, heading for the door."

Dewy looked wretched. "Can we *not* discuss me, Roberta? Please not? I've come to discuss… a different thing."

Mrs Paley put a plate of sausages, fried tomatoes, scrambled eggs and toast before Dewy, who gasped "Thank-you!" and started eating.

"Wait for cutlery?" snapped Mrs Paley, crossing to get

some. As she handed knife and fork to Dewy, her phone rang. She returned after 10 minutes, saying nothing. Dewy sensed she was being waited for to leave.

"I'm sorry, Roberta. I rambled and failed to address what I wanted your advice on. May I quickly?"

"Sure. Outside?"

They walked past Japanese maples to a copper pagoda.

"Annette has to be looked after," said Dewy. "Married's the answer. Now she has the best opportunity. You met Annie? She and Annette have the purest love I ever saw."

"Why are you telling *me* this?"

"I need to discuss it with people I trust. You and Clifton. Perfect triangle, you detached, Clifton family, me the most involved. I want no more from you. I'd say if I did."

"Come to the port, we'll lend you a car," said Roberta. "Yours – is it Wal's? – is in a bad state. It's been taken for a service. Someone'll drive it to Andrea and Waldo's tomorrow. And don't *dare* treat our car like that."

They surveyed black tupelo and hickory trees that leaned from a century's sea-gales. "So beautiful here," sighed Dewy. "Butterflies! Viceroys, see 'em?"

Her phone rang. "*It's Clifton!* Mind if I take this?"

A minute on, Dewy bounded to Mrs Paley, who looked out to sea.

"He'll meet me tomorrow!" said Dewy. "We'll see his parents, try persuade them to approve Annette's marriage."

They paused on a stone bridge over a full, slow stream. "Clifton goes back to war Monday," said Dewy. He may not be mentally fit for a family crisis, especially one where he's being asked to challenge them. Should I not involve him? But he *is* worried if Annette's OK. He didn't think she was."

"Involve him if he's concerned in his own right. He probably is – has he been up at Joanna and Bob's while on leave?"

"No, New York. He's driving up now, on the 95, just past New London –"

"*What?!* Invite him here! He can take you back, save us lending you a car."

Dewy rang Clifton then ran across lawns to Mrs Paley.

"He says thank-you, he'll be here soon."

"Good. Let's watch the ocean."

Sunlight was strong. The ocean glistened. Mrs Paley's phone rang. She excused herself and walked away, returning 20 minutes later. Dewy sprang up from lying on the grass:

"Roberta, thank-you for inviting me here and letting me talk. I don't get to talk to anyone, I..."

She threw her arms round Mrs Paley and kissed her cheek.

"Get off!" said Roberta Paley, pushing Dewy. "I will *not* be mauled. *Get off!*"

"Please hug me?" said Dewy.

"Step back."

"Can I hug you?"

"*Stop it!* Don't go *weird* like this, Samantha. Step back!! *Step back!*"

"I'm sorry," Dewy retreated, blushing. "I-I don't know what~"

"Don't *ever* do that again! I'll stub you out. Trying to help Annette Stephens? Then *grow up*, or no one will respect *her*."

They entered a sea-sheltered part of the grounds, to a stone bridge, centuries old, imported from France in 1860. A waterfall poured onto a lake. Mrs Paley's ease – natural, or in this moment maybe not – returned.

"You didn't answer: 'Mid or late-30s?'"

"You've a 16 year-old daughter," said Dewy. "Therefore... later 30s?"

"What, exactly?"

"38?"

"Pregnant at 22? Last year at Wellesley?"

"Uh… 39? You can't be 40."

"I'm 43."

"Woah! You can*not*… You look 36. What's wrong?"

"A 'fine-looking' 36 is *not 35*."

Mrs Paley took a call: "OK, have Mr Stephens walk through the rose garden, please. He'll see us at the bridge."

A minute on, a man approached, powerful and relaxed in a navy suit, white shirt open two buttons. Slightly shy, smallest of the Stephens men at five eleven, Joanna's height, Clifton was handsome and well-built with cropped, pale hair. Many said he resembled a buff Paul Newman. His blue eyes often implied the fun of life was never far. But at present they suggested: *I'm glad to see you, but can't easily speak.*

"Good afternoon, Mrs Paley! Hey, Dewy! How are you both?"

"Clifton, I told Mrs Paley Annette wants to marry. I'm sorry."

Roberta tutted: "Dewy, let Mr Stephens arrive and *relax* before slinging this?"

Walking to the house, Dewy unleashed all information about Annette's situation, including an incident that transfixed Clifton. He said she must relate it to his father.

"Above all," Dewy pleaded: "Annie lets Annette *be*. She'll never pester or influence Annette, she allows Annette's mind to roam. Which it must. People thought her dumb, now she's a *doctor*. Anyone annoyed with her or trying to change her is cruel, but people *do*. With Annie around, no one will."

On the drive north, Dewy asked how Clifton was, and his circumstances.

"I'm good, they're… not so good," he said, and fell silent.

After playing an album called "Young Americans", Clifton said:

"It's a… bad situation. When pacifism has no power

and diplomacy's ignored, pressure builds until only force can displace the situation. Of course the world must stop an immoral, murdering tyrant, but it's never simple as that. A tangle arises of opportunists, vested interests, ethnic clashes. We've no longer a comfortable conscience we're simply fighting a Hitler."

"Are you still on a carrier?"

"Yah, Jack's on another, the Harry S. Trumans joined us last year. It's added to the strangeness, me and Jack always half a world apart, now a few miles. He's a First Officer, the glowing apple, I'm the low-down sea-rescue pilot with nothing to do, helping out deck-support. No one sleeps. Missiles launched at night, flash so bright the S Trumans light up a split second. *Boom*, billowing smoke, a white dot arcs high. I don't know a thing going on. People who watch TV do. I sense it's horrific. You know I went the Catskills five days just then?"

"No?"

"First time in 20 years, a place I cherish. Was gonna buy paints and sleep, did neither. Rented a forest cabin by a lake. On my own."

"Not all it's cracked up to be, is it?"

"Ha! When I get back tonight, Mom'll be: 'Where were you all last week!!?'"

Clifton and Dewy fell quiet. An album "Remain In Light" played. Sunset left, Atlantic darker by the minute right.

Clifton turned down a song "The Overload": "I've seen... You'll... be there, won't you, Dewy? For Annette, and Annie?"

"Of course, Clift," said Dewy, waking from reverie. "I hope it happens for them. I-I want it to be special, and your family to feel that also. If that's to happen, your mom and dad need to be convinced it's *right*. So far, they only have my word for it, and I'm trash."

"They don't think you are."

"They do."

"Well, *you* know you're not, I know you're not."

"I am, Clifton."

"Superficially, to some, maybe. But you're not, and in your core you're not. I've learned a lot about humans, Dewy. You are not trash. Nobody is."

THE SERVICED, CLEANED BMW was delivered to the Millards' next day by one of the Paleys' staff. Dewy drove straight to the Stephens's.

Robert III and Clifton were finishing lunch on the west terrace. Dewy arrived unannounced, breathless: "Sir, I'd like to talk to you?"

"What about?" said Robert Stephens.

"Annette."

"We did. Subject's closed."

"Sir?" said Clifton. "I'd like to discuss this also?"

Robert frowned. Warm big rain plapped, start of a shower. "Brought the weather, Dewy," he said, gathering the Wall Street Journal. Clifton picked up plates, Dewy wine glasses and a bottle which, with restraint, she didn't swig from.

In a sitting room, Robert sat in a burnished leather chair. Clifton took a sofa, sat upright, hands on thighs. Dewy blurted: "Sir, please consider the marriage of Annette to Annie, and give her your approval? It is *right* and ~"

"Dewy, sit down?" said Robert Stephens.

Dewy's gaze never left him as she slowly sat on the sofa edge, far end to Clifton, who looked to her.

"Dewy, tell Dad the story?" he said softly. "Dad's more Navy than anyone, understands water better than anyone."

"You're equally Navy, son. We're equal."

"Thank-you, sir," said Clifton. "I... I appreciate that."

Robert Stephens faced Dewy:

"What is it?"

Dewy cleared her throat and began: "Imagine, sir, a 16-ounce glass, four-fifths full of water poured in a building with dysfunctional plumbing, in a district with chalk deposits, chlorination and microscopic silt?"

"Trust *you* to ask a question like that," sighed Robert Stephens. "Yup, OK, visualising."

"The water surface gets membranous," said Dewy. "Like an ultra-thin jelly. My question: how easy would it be to: lift the glass, walk 10 paces, place it on a metre-wide, slightly shaky, wood table on a wood floor, with people watching – one of them a domineering stranger – and *not* break the water surface tension?"

Mr Stephens repeated parts of the question under his breath then replied: "Keeping surface tension unbroken... through the process you describe is... beyond most people's ability."

"Could you do it, sir?" said Dewy.

"Mmm." He bit the side of his lip. "Per*haps*... If the variables were right, table not wobbling, but, you say 'slightly shaky'. Factoring the membrane's fragility too, I guess I'd *most likely not* be able to. Therefore, no. Where's this heading?"

"One more question then I'll tell you."

"Go on?"

"The stranger rudely commands that you lower the glass to the table. The stranger is smug, taller, privileged, more educated than you and glaring from a yard away. You weren't forewarned about the person. Can you still put the glass on a possibly shaky table without water-surface breaking?"

"No." said Clifton and his father together.

"How would you describe a person who *could* do it?"

"Steady of hand and nerve," said Robert Stephens.

"Would you employ that person?"

"Yes."

"Would you be proud to have that person in your family?"

"If he didn't boast about the incident, certainly."

"Annie McClure carried that glass and placed it down as described, sir. The woman your daughter wants to marry. The woman Annette would like to have join your family."

A pause.

"I'd like that too, sir," said Clifton.

ONE SATURDAY ANNIE woke to hear Annette yell her name, run upstairs, burst into the bedroom, Morris leaping and dancing around her. They flung themselves on the bed, Annette waving a hand-written letter.

"Can you read this, hon?"

With Annette's help, Annie slowly read out:

Annette,

Your father +I are happy you're in a partnership you feel stable + lasting. We hope that's the case for many years. If you +Annie plan to marry we support this.

Best to you both,
Mom.

Chapter 5

SEPTEMBER BROUGHT INTENSIVE farm-work. Annie worked 10 hours a day in all weathers, or in glasshouses bigger than football pitches tore brussels sprouts from stalks, picked and bagged handfuls of green beans, radishes, baby carrots, watercress. Outdoors, she unearthed leeks, cabbages, parsnips.

Potato-picking in dry weather was best, comfortably kneeling, five minutes' rest after each row, awaiting the tractor's return, pay by the day, £65, not per basket, like other crops, where Annie worked hard to earn £60, 10 hours.

Annette drove her home each day to a bath, toast, tea and a long, full body rub. Annette would walk Morris, cook his dinner, go upstairs to sleep an hour with Annie in her arms. Early evening they'd drive to Asda. After candlelit dinner, jazz played on quiet radio while Annette read "Frankenstein" to Annie. They were astonished the book was written by a 17-year-old with the sophistication, wit and power of a great writer three times her age. Annette's smartphone gave pictures of Mary Shelley, her mother Mary Wollstonecraft, father William Godwin, lover Percy Bysshe Shelley. They read all Wikipedia entries relating to Mary Shelley. Annie showed little reaction, but remembered everything. Evenings later she said: "After Frankenstein, shall we read her auld man's book 'Caleb Williams'?"

In bed they'd wait until Morris snored, then carefully

rise, tread silently downstairs to make love on the sofa, where Annie might later come down to sleep if Morris's snores kept waking her.

Annie felt like a well being filled with knowledge and deeper thoughts, discoveries, dreams.

Annette felt protected, securely loved while experiencing the sexual awakening of her life. Each time she saw Annie, desire churned in her. She'd urgently reach to tug Annie to her, kiss her mouth, snuffle into her hair, sniff an ear, plaster Annie's face with kisses. At least once a day this led to immediate undressing and a hot journey to shared orgasm. Sex felt incredible when sudden.

Annette's joy was completed by Annie's mutual love for Morris, who often sought Annie, to see how she was, and what she was doing. Annette liked how Annie didn't mind or notice Morris half-standing on her thighs on the sofa, blocking half her face with the side of his own as he stood in thought. She loved how Annie knew exactly when Morris wanted to play tug-of-war, would made one of his toys dance until he dived to try wrestling it from her. She loved how Annie knew when Morris felt anti-social, curled up, paws folded beneath, looking away.

Uncertainty came. The tenancy was ending. They must find somewhere new. Money was short. Annie again tried to give Annette her £900 savings, repayment for the America trip. Annette declined. "Then this 900's for somewhere for us to live," said Annie. But 900 wasn't enough.

Annette had no cashcards she knew of, nor seen her usual one since America. It was probably still there. Unsure of her account details or what money she had, she e-mailed her father. Ever aghast at Annette's incomprehension of money and banking, he ordered she e-mail her new address to Bank of America and request a card and PIN number sent there. He asked if she urgently needed money. Annette said she and Annie had hundreds of pounds, so no.

Online searches for rentals found run-down flats above shops, or houses converted badly into bedsits. They visited Nu Letz, where a yellow-haired woman blared: "If you've dogs you're reducing what we could be working to possibilise!" A youth with a yellow tie sat smirking. The woman sighed to him: "Gotta put 'no pets', it's ridiculous now, for us, really is."

Outside, Annette held Morris and Annie close. "I'm not violent," she whispered, "but I'd set the Marines on that place."

Must they remain in Farrisford? Annie wondered. Why not Crendlesham, Exeter? But Annette was too elsewhere in her mind to discuss this. In six days' time she must give a lecture in a lecture hall, culmination of her year's work. She wasn't sleeping.

"MUM? IT'S ME, Brandon."

"Bran, It's *one* in the sodding morning."

Danii blindly reached for cigarettes, tumbled out of bed, padded to the kitchen, opened a window, lit up.

"Where are you Mum?"

"Can't hear you." whispered Danii.

Brandon also whispered. "Wanna keep my voice down. Dave and Warr don't know you and me are in touch, y'know? I'll go downstairs. Stay on the line."

"I'm tired, Bran, I wanna go back to ~"

"Now I can't hear *you*."

"I don't want to speak up, I'll wake Jade."

"Is she still fat?"

"What a fucking stupid question. *Grow up!*"

She ended the call, their first in two weeks.

Brandon texted: Mum, please call back? Please please call back? Please? I miss you mum i miss Jade. sorry what I said. Ive no one to talk to. i want to move out. also ive been selected for a importan role i started today.

He waited. Nothing came. Anxious, sad, he went to bed.

Next morning he and eight others sat on plastic chairs around a bare room with clattery blinds drawn. The second of two days' induction as Street Wardens was ready to begin. All nine recruits were excited. Each had returned from another room, where they'd been fitted for uniforms coming soon.

Barry Hill, Deputy Senior Team-Builder Executive Officer for Chekka entered, scratching nervously behind his left ear every 10 seconds. A large ex-manager of a multistorey car-park, his Chekka induction talks were mostly about himself, his experiences and views. After greeting the room, he began:

"Each of you is here because you are definite support officer material within a role of street warden, which is essentially what we're doing."

His 10 recruits – the 10th entering now, late – seemed to listen, though in truth each was lost in prideful happiness to be chosen for an organisation whose **CHEKKA** logo had Working In Association with the Police underneath it.

Everyone grinned at the latecomer Darren Tibley. He grinned: "I was still got measured up for uniform because I was last to get called in to get measured?"

"Don't worry, Darryl!" beamed Barry HIll. "What it is you've missed, I've been channelling the importances of *back-up*? For potentially of situations where a suspected person might be less able to manage themselves, and needs preventavised for the sake of public safety? That's when we activate *back-up!* We got *feet on the ground*, got *vans*, got *trained staff* connected to people with *powers of arrest*."

In yesterday's lunch break, four confessed they'd unsuccessfully applied to join the police, though in truth nine had, Brandon twice. Two went on to admit they'd been turned down as PCSOs too, like Brandon had. He also kept quiet about that but sensed he was by no means the only person too ashamed to admit being wrongly denied "a decent crack of the whip". No matter – he was with Chekka now. They all were. Action at last. The real thing.

Today, in the afternoon coffee break, rather than huddle outside waiting to be re-admitted to the building, Brandon, Tibley and two others, Rocky and Tim, strolled near the Communica building. Communica owned Chekka and other new, public sector projects.

"Serious motors here," said Tim, surveying a car-park of near-identical cars by Communica's beige and smoked-glass regional office. He began pointing out makes of the cars. None was unusual.

Tim's boyish stature, inane talk, gentle manner and glasses made him seem harmless. But when a young woman was seen leaving Communica's office he shrieked: "FUCK, see *that?*" and stopped to watch her. Teeth bared, arms dangling like a gunfighter, he breathed fast: "She's a *fuckin' serious bit*! Been with ones like them, know the sort. Look at it, silly cow, getting in her fuckin' car. Can't drive, most like. Ha-ha! That's why we need driverless cars! HA-*HA!!* So whores what can't drive can get around! HA-HA-HA!"

Feeling more serious-minded, Brandon moved away from the group laughter. Under his breath he repeated Chekka mantras learned from the print-out: *Our role: To sound people out. To watch, listen, ask questions. People like to talk. Encourage them to.* **SMILE***.*

Ask what they're doing.

Ask them why they're doing it. **SMILE***.*

Watch. Ask. Listen.

Brandon sighed with happiness. A new future. New dawn. Everything was going to be OK.

ANNIE DIDN'T WANT to alarm Annette, but they'd 12 days left in the cottage. New accommodation needed fees, a deposit, and another month's rent within four weeks of moving. They'd barely half the money.

September 21st, Annette's phone rang on the patio. Annette, busy indoors, asked Annie to answer it.

"Hello?"

"Annie?" said Dewy. "How are you?"

"OK. Annette's studyin'."

"Are you still in the cottage?"

"Aye."

"How long for?"

"Why?"

"Annette's teaching year's nearly over. The cottage is ~"

"Aye, we gotta move," said Annie.

"Where to?"

Silence.

Annie spoke: "Don't talk to Annette about this, OK? She's got a lot of work. A lecture."

"You're taking care not to worry her?" said Dewy. "I admire you for that."

No answer.

"Where will you both go?" said Dewy.

No answer.

"Annie? Are you and Annette in trouble? About this?"

Silence.

"Are you?" repeated Dewy.

Annie sighed. "Suppose, yeah."

"I'm on my way."

REVEREND IAN HENDERSON liked chance meetings with Father Entreton and sometimes asked him back to St Botolph's for tea. Anglican, eager, 44, he'd three daughters and a secretly bored wife, Emily.

Rev Henderson grasped Father Entreton's openness to new approaches to pastoral care and the importance of any church, any faith, as community bedrock, whose leaders should be present and well-known.

Father Entreton, in turn, realised "Ian and I park our cars in the same garage," but missed the days of the Reverend Frederick Kinson-Stewart (and wife Ruth, even more joyous.) Often inviting rock bands to play hymns instead of the organ, the Kinson-Stewarts' 1970-85 reign was never dull and they were loved. "Holy Fred" retired to missionary-work in South America, where Ruth survives him, running a sloth sanctuary.

Today, a Saturday noon, rained heavily. Father Entreton sheltered under the cloisters near the Farmer's Market. Everywhere he looked, he saw tiny moments of happiness in people, even the group of coatless, square-headed, hard-nuts in polo shirts, grinning, teeth missing, shoulders hunched, running in rain to the King's Arms.

He spotted Tessa England emerge from the Town Hall, golden head bowed against wind and rain, bulky folder under an arm. Someone stopped her to talk. She listened, free hand resting on hip, gaze intent at the talker. The priest admired her ability to not look bored. He hoped, doubtfully, he had this trait too.

"Father!" – a familiar voice. "Lovely to see you! Just back from the hockey club. Come for lunch? Emmy's made something."

Over lasagne and four salads, Ian Henderson discussed the town's need for a youth club, and how St Botolphs' food-bank would now be twice weekly like Our Lady's. They planned an outreach idea to take food to the elderly housebound, be they ex-churchgoers or not, while within congregations, more vigilance was needed towards senior members, and stronger links made with community nurses.

Rain stopped. A sunbeam fell on lemon cake. After

coffee, Father Entreton bade farewell to the family: "I hope you don't mind me pottering around the graves? A beautiful spot, so many flowers and bees, herbs…"

"We've a bird table there!" said a daughter.

"Wonderful! I'll look for that."

An ancient, spreading yew gave out to very old grave-stones bunched together. Father Entreton walked, lost in thoughts, reading inscriptions, feeling sadness for so many young deaths in the 19th century, same as Third World countries today. He rounded a corner to the back of the church. The graveyard sloped far down to a line of hedge then fields. Cows gathered to stare at a man leaning over the hedge to stroke their long furry noses. The priest smiled and changed course to allow the man his privacy.

Peacefulness here made him happy. Drops of rain fell from oaks and beeches. A rook cawed. Father Entreton wandered. The church's ancient bell chimed two. He headed back to the old yew. It sheltered steps from path down to churchyard. He could sit on them.

But when he arrived, the man who'd greeted the cows sat there.

"Billy?" said the priest.

"Ah? Aye, a'right, er…" Nevin looked embarrassed. He uselessly hid his can of Kestrel then – more uselessly – retrieved it, sipped, hid it again.

"Mind if I sit?" said the priest.

"Aye, man, I'll budge up. Wait, don't sit yet."

He unzipped his sports bag, tugged out a jumper, flustered to flatten it over the rest of the step for Father Entreton. "Sit down, fella. Bit cold on the ars… er, backside. I, er, put the jumper, for you, like. I'm not drunk, had two cans. That's all I had."

"You seem OK."

"Took myself out of the hospital, this morning, Father. Time to be off. Sort myself out. Bristol. Today I'm going Bristol."

"Good place. Got a ticket?"

"No, I'll- I'll buy one. Bus to Exeter, then... er..."

"Need help to pay for the tickets?"

"No, no, you're all right."

Nevin stood, fidgeting. He wore a plastic hospital bracelet.

"Going for a walk," he said.

Father Entreton watched him march off, slow to a wander, reading graves. The priest was glad someone else read old graves. He often wondered if anyone did.

He looked at Nevin's opened bag, hospital towel across the top of all contents, whatever these were. Everything the man owned was here, the total of a life. "God, am I doing the right thing?" asked Father Entreton, putting £40 deep into the bag.

Nevin came back into view, further away, still reading gravestones.

"Could he be a good man yet, Lord?" prayed Father Entreton. "See the good in him here. Absorbed in thought, lost in truth. A serenity to him."

The priest got up and surveyed graves too. A few were burials he'd attended. From where he stood, his long-sight spotted:

Peter Boyd-Brown	1908–1989
Arthur John Spillet	1871–1960
Margaret Sheekey	1908–1994

Nevin approached: "Always strikes me, the cemeteries, all names, dates? Nothing else, who the person *was*?"

"I completely agree, Billy. I've often thought that. All these people, gone. What were their truths? If even one fact about them could have been inscribed on their stone? 'He was a soldier.' 'She was a mother of nine.' 'She was a mother of one' 'He was a mad keen cyclist.' 'She saved a life at sea.' 'He loved Farrisford.'"

"Aye, t'would make all the difference," said Nevin.

"Their one truth. Everyone has one. They can tell it to anyone, show it to God when the day comes. Their own, unique statement. Something they're proud of, and those who know them, are proud of them for it."

A long pause. Nevin sipped beer, read a gravestone. "This fella – er… El… Elias? Barton, 1824 to… who was he? What was his – 'truth', y'say? How'll we know?"

Father Entreton reached to Billy Nevin, put a hand on his shoulder. Nevin didn't flinch or look round. Rain pattered full-leaf trees.

"What would your truth be, Billy?" said Father Entreton "The thing you have, to take through your life. Will you find it? Your one brief but big statement?"

They passed through the lych gate. St Botolph's chimed three.

"That hour passed quick," said Father Entreton.

"Thanks for spending an hour with me," said Billy Nevin.

"A pleasure, Billy."

"Thanks, pal." He dropped his bag to briefly, beerily hug Father Entreton, then looked awkward. "I'm off. Billy's away. Bless ya, Father, bless this town."

"And bless you, Billy. I hope you find your truth. The thing that's yours."

"Aye, well, don't hold your bre~"

Nevin stopped. Happiness crossed his unappealing features.

"Did your truth come to you, Billy?" said the priest. "Do you know it?"

"Aye." nodded Billy, smiling. "I *do*."

"*Good!* Is it the 'need to know' about Billy Nevin? His honest truth?"

"Aye!"

"And what is it, Billy? What would be on the stone?"

"He put one past Juventus," said Nevin.

He walked away.

Chapter 6

DEWY ARRIVED ON Saturday night, hugged Annette, said: "Hey, why the plain face?" to Annie and knelt to let Morris leap on her.

"Guess what I have for *you*, Morris!" said Dewy.

"A ball with a bell in it!" cried Annette. "He *loves* those!"

Dewy stood, feet together, mouth an 'o' as she leaned to offer the orange rubber ball to Morris, who stood on hind legs, paws clutching her wrist as his mouth found purchase on the ball. He took it, climbed onto the sofa to settle, then tried ways of chewing into the tiny hole to get at the bell: impossible.

"Bachelor had one of those," smiled Annette. "Do you remember?"

"Uh… vaguely," said Dewy.

"It was buried with him."

Trying to forget Dewy's rude greeting, Annie said: "Want a drink?"

"Yes!" said Dewy. "I have duty-free honey vodka! Join me, please?"

Dewy hoped to stay five nights. "If I'm in the way, I'll go down Plymouth. Dumb to be from New England, not see Plymouth?" Her flight back to Boston was in six days, September 28th.

Dewy gave half her last money on Earth to Annie and Annette: £1500. She dismissed their protests: "It's why I came. Added to your money, Annie, you've a deposit, fees, two months' rent. All you do now is find a place."

Dewy drank, ate peanuts and sifted through Annette's unopened mail from the university. "I didn't know mail came here," said Annette. "Mr Fielding gave me this bag yesterday."

Dewy discovered Annette's contract was renewed for another year pending signature on a letter dated June. A reminder had arrived in August.

"Sign it and take it Monday morning, darling," said Dewy, examining the contract: "Oh, look, same as before? 'Accommodation gratis'. That means you'll still live *here*!" She leafed through junk mail, alumni magazines, leaflets, then tore open a Bank Of America envelope. The account of Annette's trust fund and University salary had $24,589, nearly £19,000.

"Now *that's* not a bad thing?" said Annette. "Did you see this, Booboo?"

At 5am Annie was woken by air blowing upstairs from the open back door. Terrible singing was heard in the garden. When Annie later went down to make Annette's and Morris's breakfasts, Dewy was naked face-down on the sofa, knuckles of right hand bleeding. On a white-washed kitchen wall were blood drops at shoulder-height. The honey-vodka bottle was a third full.

Annie sighed, closed the back door, returned to the sitting room. Morris stood, front paws on the sofa, one on Dewy's shoulder, imploring her to wake.

"Let her sleep, weeman," said Annie, picking Dewy's crumpled wet (booze spillage or urine) sheet up from the floor. Bundling it in the wash, she washed her hands, returned upstairs, kissed Annette sleeping and brought new linen to cover Dewy. She looked at Dewy's flawless white skin, long back, toned buttocks and legs, wide, level shoulders under sleek black hair. She felt sudden sadness. That beautiful, unconscious form was miserable, while she, Annie, had found happiness. Lowering fresh sheet and blanket over Dewy, Annie felt a faint urge to lean down to kiss her shoulder, but easily stopped the urge.

Today was Sunday. Annette's lecture was Tuesday. Annette came downstairs, flustered. Seeing Dewy, her face dropped. "I can't work if she's here. I'll have to go to college instead, tomorrow too?" She would spend the day in Exeter University library.

Dewy woke at 2pm, unwell and alone. She wrapped herself in a blanket and sat on the back garden patio, trying to drink water. Annie returned from Asda. She and Dewy hadn't been alone together since Massachusetts parties – the only times they had. Neither was sure how to get through this.

"Want anythin' to eat?" called Annie from the kitchen, voice sharp.

"No thank-you," said Dewy. A minute on, she washed her face, tugged her dress on, found her coat, clattered open the front door, lied she was to "meet people" and left.

Her choice was Yenton, or a footpath into fields. Dewy took the latter, arriving an hour later in Cressy. Founded, or renamed, by mercenaries from the Battle of Crécy, the village was mostly old terraced houses along a B-road. Country surrounding was blocked by low hills. Landmarks were a petrol station, two pubs and church. Pub-restaurant The Lover's Leap, overlooked a large, dark pond with weeping willows and a working mill, the "leap" two quays a yard apart.

After bog-water fields Dewy's feet were stained to the ankles. She'd forgotten she'd cried in the night, discovering now by touch one side of her hair was glued together. She entered The Lover's Leap. On seeing: **PLEASE 'WAIT TO BE SEATED.** *A member "of staff will be u shortly thank for cooperation.* Dewy left.

Sensing eccentricity no disgrace in the area, she asked at the garage for water to clean her feet. An enormous man with a black eye combed his lip with two teeth then spoke like a toad: "Here's a buckut. Fill ut from the cold tap thurr. I'll come put hot in ut."

Dewy nodded. The man filled a kettle.

Cressy's other pub, The Cock, marked the end of terraced houses and wasn't much bigger than one. Dewy approached, clean-footed, her bright but deep red toenails perfect. Nearing the pub, she heard males up-whimper then bawl with joy. Televised football. Best enter now, all attention on the goal scored.

Dewy stayed five hours. By 8pm the pub was empty but for the garage man and a woman of 90 sleeping against a wall. Dewy had forgotten what six pints of Rattock's and several gins did. Everything seemed dark and blurred as the bottom of a sea. The garage man demanded a ninth game of dominoes.

"Can't," said Dewy.

"Come on!" bossed the man, rapping the table. "Win this 'un, yer've won a bit back?" He'd set a £5 bounty per game. Dewy had lost £40.

She carefully stood. "Mrs um… Allen? Cvould you cpall please a cab?"

"Yeah? Time t'go is ut?" said Mrs Allen at the bar.

"And a other more pint of Rattock's, please?"

An hour later, in the sitting room of the Farrisford cottage, Morris stirred. Annie and Annette heard a car. Annette opened the door to see Dewy sitting on the steep grass, descending by digging her heels into it and pulling herself forward. "I'm can't of the driveway…" *HeEEK!*

Annie and Annette helped her stand. Dewy swigged from one of two wine bottles she'd no recollection buying.

"I tried calling you?" said Annette.

Dewy's boisterous, repeated explanations of how her US phone had no UK network, her British one no credit, made Annette invent a law: *never mention phones to a drunk.*

Dinner plans had been forgotten or ignored by Dewy. Annette and Annie had waited, then dined without her.

Annie was in the kitchen now, washing up. She struggled with her conscience. Her new, sudden happiness owed much to Dewy – the person likely to block Annie's and Annette's partnership, but who had most encouraged and supported it. Annie was grateful to Dewy, but couldn't stand her. Dewy's brief, insincere doses of friendship, when sober, were excruciating, and she was hellish when drinking.

In the sitting room, Annette, very tired, sat across the room from Dewy. Morris, curled in Annette's lap, watched Dewy with one half-shut eye. Annie entered with coffee pot and cups. Dewy sat legs sideways on the sofa, thumb-stroking dirt from her soles, ranting:

"They'll *give* me the damn car, y'know? They *gotta*! Else how can I move out? HowcnImove out? How'll I gonna *move house* with…" ***BURRP!!*** "…*no CAR*, huh?"

She glugged wine. The room watched.

"Needa ask Wal I can *have* the car. But we don't speak. Me an' Wal haven't spoked. *Spoken*. Can't ask Vandrea, because it's *totally* Wal's car. But should kinda be *mine*?"

Annie left, upset. She sat in the kitchen. Dewy reminded her of monsters from her childhood. *Drunken adults up all night, talking shite, all of them still there all next day, never, ever going away.* At least Dewy wasn't on cocaine too, as they'd been. At least Dewy wasn't trying to get into Annie's bed while she slept, like that man had: *bastard, bastard, horrible bastard, telling me never tell anywan…*

Morris pattered in. He devotedly gazed up at her. She picked him up.

Annie wiped tears. She'd not cried for years, except nearly, when Annette bought her a dress. Morris stood on her lap now, paws on her shoulders.

"The repeating," she muttered. "They'd say the same thing 50 times. That's what *she's* doing. It's brought up stuff fae ma past." Morris touched her nose with his. "I'll gi' her a vodka," said Annie. "Knock her oot. Then we can all go tae bed."

She took vodka to the sitting room. Annette was saying: "Wanna store your things at Mom and Dad's? I'm sure it'll be OK."

"Nah-uh," drawled Dewy. "Not asking favours from 'em. All I own'll fit in the trunk, back seat. Honey, I sold… I…" She began to cry.

"You sold some of my family's Audubon prints," said Annette. "I know."

"*What?!*" gasped Dewy.

"You sold them for $6,000 in 2005."

"You *know*?"

"You've told me *hundreds* of times when you're wasted and crying. You even told Aunt Meredith, climbing into her bed, telling her ~"

"No! *Never*!" Dewy looked stricken.

"Don't worry," said Annette. "Aired, forgiven, gone. What possessions *do* you have now? Your books still, I hope?"

"E-bay'd 'em, February," said Dewy quietly.

"Oh, your books! Not the Macduis, I hope? *Please* say you didn't sell ~"

"*Annie*! What is that?" cried Dewy.

"Honey vodka."

"*Ahhh!* Thangyou!"

Dewy drained the cup Annie gave her, held the cup out for a refill: "I'll load up Wal's car – *my* car, realistically –" *HeEEEK!!* "– drive to Seattle! Or Louisiana! Isn't Louisiana one of the most beautiful words? Dance company to dance company, offer my services. Sleep in dance studios, the car gardens, a tent. A *pilgrim* of dance, devote me to dance! And if I could *choreograph…*"

At 5am Annie was woken by the crack of the back door's top bolt, the tough one she'd deliberately shut to stop Dewy getting out like last night. Air blew through the house again. No singing, only rain and, faintly: *hffffrrgghhfff!!*

Annie went downstairs. Dewy sat on a patio wall, crying into her hands. Annie called: "Hello?" Naked and drunk, Dewy turned away, hugging herself. Annie went in to get a sheet, saw vodka and red wine bottles empty.

In heavy rain, Dewy was slowly walked to the house but collapsed to the ground. Annie sighed angrily, put her hands under Dewy's armpits, felt their hairiness on her fingers, dragged her to the sitting room, heaved her onto the sofa and covered her with a blanket. Annie used to do this for her mother, or occasionally her mother's friend Loretta. Loretta got beaten to death by a man called Rangsie when Annie was 10. Everyone heard screams along the walkway, none thought it bad. Violence to women always went on. Violence from women sometimes.

Annie's memory broke out. She'd slept at Jim and Yvonne's for months. They never went to bed, selling through the night, dance music pumping. Money and drugs under the other bed's duvet, the metre-long hard thing a gun.

Annie hated memories and was jittery. She froze as a yell of terror and sadness escaped Dewy, who, asleep now, writhed and spun onto her back: "*Aghh! Tierra negra!*" Dewy sat up, cried: "*Estoy cayendo!!*" and fell backwards, face flickering. Suddenly: "*Tierra negra y un vasto mar de fuego! Aggh!! No, por favor! No!!*"

She fell quiet, limbs twisted, eyelids and brow twitching. Annie looked on, shaken. She did not know Dewy was speaking another language, didn't know Dewy mostly lived with Mexican and Honduran housekeepers until age four, her earliest language Spanish. Annie backed away, climbed the stairs.

"Is Dewy OK?" said Annette.

"Deid to the world. She was in a state."

"Oh dear. But I kinda… … I need to be alone here, to study?"

Annie rubbed her back: "Get her to go tae Plymouth?"

ANNETTE COLLECTED ANNIE from a farm near Balaton at 6pm.

"She gone to Plymouth?" said Annie.

"Eventually," said Annette. "Slept until three."

"Agh, Christ."

Annie made penne with coriander pesto. Annette worried about next day's lecture: "I've sleepwalked through this year. I didn't get deep down. It'll show."

"I bet everyone who gives a talk thinks that, pet."

"Oh, Annie. Sure you wanna come?"

"Of *course*! Hope I don't scream when you come on-stage!"

"It's wonderful you and Booboo are coming. It's at 4pm."

They kissed awhile. Annie said:

"My interview's 11.30. If it *is* one. They said: 'come in, talk recipes'."

"You make the best food in the world."

"I'm not sure. And that notice in the window you read out was…"

"'Cool, creative, kick-ass chef required for our cafe brand.'" recited Annette.

"Hmm," they said together.

"But Farrisford Organics is real respected," said Annette.

AT 5AM, MORRIS stirred, jumped from the bed, waking Annie, and hurtled downstairs to stop by the front door. Annie heard rain and scuffling sounds. She went downstairs, opened the door. Dewy reeled in, unseeing. She fell face-down on the sofa and lay still.

Annette came downstairs. "Is BooBoo OK?" She saw Dewy and groaned.

They removed Dewy's soaking clothes. Laetitia Winter's pale Tory Burch coat had oil marks. Dewy reeked of drink. She couldn't open her eyes. When her dress was peeled off she curled into a shivering ball. Annie fetched a sheet, shook it out. The white sheet floated level in air, slowly sinking onto Dewy. Annie said: "I'll do her a hot water bottle?"

"Oh, yes!" said Annette. "For under her head, not too hot."

"Ah…" groaned Dewy. "Wha-ah? *Annette*?"

"It's OK, you're in England," said Annette. "Morris is here. We've put Uncle Kettle on for a glug-glug."

"Summing's *wrong*," said Dewy, in tears: "Annette? Hug me? Please?"

"Morris is trying to, aren't you BooBoo?"

Morris pressed his face against Dewy's neck, foraged in her hair, sniffing, licking. Dewy smiled faintly and fell asleep.

She slept through Annette's departure to Exeter, slept through Annie cleaning the house and her departure for the interview.

Returning at 1pm, Annie found Dewy still asleep. Morris climbed off from beside her to greet Annie, who carried flowers to the kitchen. She stayed, arranging them, filling three vases. Annie realised she'd prefer to work in the florist than the cafe. The florist's felt gentle and happy. Mrs Clyde the 70-year-old owner said she needed help setting up each morning. The timing was such, Annie could easily do that, work in the cafe and be home by 5pm. Annette had spoken of hiring a student dog-sitter Tuesday to Thursday lunchtimes.

An anguished sleep-sentence of no words from the next room jolted Annie back to the present. She decided she'd wake Dewy and tell her to go to Plymouth. Last night had been so peaceful, believing Dewy gone, only to find out at dawn she had not. No way would tonight be ruined by her. This night was Annette's. After the lecture, Annette, Annie and Morris would go to a country restaurant. They'd return here for a sunset walk. Dewy had better be gone.

Annie placed flowers in the sitting room. Dewy slowly stirred. She eyed Annie. "What you *wearing*?" she croaked. "Blouse like *goulash*. What's that metal twisted thing, a brooch?"

Annie marched upstairs to change into the white blouse and navy cardigan she'd planned to wear to the university, then changed her mind, to defy Dewy. She kept her orange paisley blouse on, put her change of clothes into a bag for later and rang Rashid. After a time, she went downstairs. Dewy sat, wrapped in the sheet, eyes closed, quietly crying,

"Fuck's sake," muttered Annie. She went to the kitchen, poured water, took it to Dewy. "Drink this."

"Annie?" sobbed Dewy. "Pl-please hug me."

Annie nearly laughed. "C'mon, drink this."

Dewy did not outstretch an arm. Annie placed the glass on the floor beside Dewy's mottled feet: "Put that blanket round ye as well, ye're shivering."

Rashid rang, minutes away. Annie said she'd wait up at the main road. She locked the back door, took the tote bag of Morris's essentials and passed through the sitting room, stopping to put Morris's collar and leash on: "C'mon, son, we're going." A fresh tear fell down Dewy's cheek.

"Gonna get yourself thegether?" snapped Annie to Dewy.

"I'll g-go," said Dewy. "Don't worry."

"Do what you like," said Annie, enough inflection to mean *Yes: go*.

"I don't like me," said Dewy in fresh tears. "I d-don't like me and never have."

She hid her face in the sheet. Annie checked her keys, counted cash. Dewy had risen now. She came nearer, shaking. Alcohol fumes strongly billowed as she wept and gasped: "Please don't hate me."

"I don't," said Annie, putting on her jacket.

Dewy tugged Annie's arm: "Y'know, no one ever said 'I love you' to me? Not once. Never in my life."

"Ah, Christ," muttered Annie. "C'mon, Morris!"

"No one, not ever," sobbed Dewy.

Annie moved away, annoyed, but almost sorry for Dewy, who hid her face to cry, half-collapsed, in the sheet, head bowed.

Of course I love you, ya bastard thought Annie: *Ye're better than ye seem. But I'm no' playing this 'please say "I love you"' game. Fuck off.*

Annie opened the door. Dewy said:

"If someone would say 'I love you' to me? J-just *one person*…?"

Annie stepped out. Morris delayed. Annie turned to coax him. A sunbeam through curtain gap lit Dewy's profile. She looked beautiful.

"I'm sorry," she said to Annie. Annie closed the door.

A jabbing annoyance recurred on Annie, the brooch, weighing heavily in the viscose blouse, making lengthening holes. She'd bought it on impulse when buying the blouse in a charity shop. Annie dropped the brooch down a drain as Rashid's car pulled up.

Chapter 7

"NICE, HIM!" SAID Liu. "Real gent. Bit of *all right*, actually. Lovely eyes. Strong hands."

She and Danii watched Azdek and Jade cross the narrow road and walk up the terraced hill.

"He's staying where?" said Liu.

"He's met people through his church, y'know, the mosque."

"So they're going up the detention centre now? To visit the boy? And this Azdek man – he's a dentist?"

"Yeah," yawned Danii. "He was studying to be one. Then stuff happened."

"I didn't know Syrians were dentists and things like that," said Liu. "Mind you, people used to say to my mum they didn't think Chinese were like, *normal* until they met her. Though my mum – believe me – ain't normal. I *know* her."

Tired, Danii moved from the window to slump on the sagging sofa. Liu, 25, hyperactive, was enjoying her adventure, third day now. She didn't care the two-room flat above the salon was dark and shabby, didn't care she slept on the sofa.

She looked out the window and smiled. Huddersfield! A business partner in a salon with the best stylist, plus £150 a week free money renting out her Crendlesham flat! Enough to pay the mortgage, and half a flat rental here.

"Gonna view these two flats in the paper, Dan!" she yelled. "Then come back start cooking." Danii was asleep.

At 9pm Jade, Liu and Danii ate lasagne.

"Nice to have you here, Liu?" said Jade. "I love your cooking. It's nice to –"

"Nice to **WHAT!!?**" yelled Danii. "Have a proper meal? Is *that* what you're gonna say?!" She smashed her cutlery down. "Sorry I can't *fucking cook!!*"

"Dan? Dan!" said Liu, trying to take her arm. Danii stormed to the bedroom and slammed the door.

Jade took a deep breath, sighed, counted: "…three, four, five…" **Bmph!** the door flung open, Danii emerged, raging at Jade: "I've gave up *EVERYTHING FOR YOU!!* Still not enough, is it?! What *MORE* can I do?"

"Mum? It's fine. Go for a cigarette." Jade stood: "Oh, Mum? C'mere?"

She hugged Danii, who stood rigid. Jade said: "I know you're working so hard, Mum, I appreciate it. Sit down and eat, this lasagne's right nice."

They ate. Adele sang from a radio. Danii went for a cigarette.

"She's ever so tired," said Liu. "But she's got *me* now. I'm helping. I love the salon, we're gonna make it *so good*?! I got plans, Dan says yes. Listen, I got her a surprise, right? You, me, her, going to a country hotel and spa, Yorkshire Dales, this weekend, Saturday, Sunday nights, yeah? Special offer from a hair product company. You know Dan *loves* hotels?"

"That'll be brilliant, Liu!"

Danii returned, exhausted.

"What you two grinning at? You making fun of me?"

She sat, face crumpled, beginning to cry. "The pair of you can *piss off!*"

Jade threw her arms around her: "Mum, I love you. We're gonna look after you, me and Liu.

"We love you, Dan," said Liu. "We're three of us now. We'll sort things. Everything's gonna be good. I might even marry a dentist."

Chapter 8

THE EVENING WAS scented and starry. Morris drowsed. He'd been well-fed by hand in his baby-sling at the restaurant.

Annette loved the sitting-room's flowers – columbines, asters and lilies. She opened the back door to let Morris out. He went first to his food bowl, found a dog biscuit and the orange rubber ball there. As he crunched the biscuit, Annette said: "Aww, Annie-mommy left you a treat to come home to?"

"Wasnae me," said Annie. "Must have been *her.*"

"Oh," said Annette. They hadn't thought of Dewy for hours.

"Let's stroll?" said Annette. "It's beautiful out there."

Morris was tired. He curled up on the sofa and watched the front door.

"Won't be long, Booboo," said Annette. "You get some rest."

He got none. Annette's phone beside him rang again and again.

When Annie and Annette returned through the back garden gate, flushed, out of breath, quietly laughing, Morris's silhouette waited at the bright, open back door.

"Booboo, it's *us*," said Annette. "What's up, honeyest? We were gone only 10 minutes."

Morris backed away.

"Oh, darrling, Mommy would never leave you!" She heard the ring of her phone in the sitting room. Annie brought it to her. She noticed 9 MISSED CALLS on the screen, and answered:

"Hi, Mom!"

"*Jesus Christ, thank God!*" howled from the phone. Annette, Annie and Morris glanced to each other. "Oh, *Christ!*" continued Joanna's voice, "Thank God. Thank God!" Annette lowered Morris to the ground and slowly sat, clutching Annie's hand.

"Yah, I'm sitting down, Mom," said Annette, voice strange. She listened then jolted, face tense, like swallowing gin. Teeth bared, she shook her head: "And they called *you*?"

Annette listened more, curled her lip, glanced to Annie.

"She had it registered in m-my name, yeah," said Annette to her mother.

Annie glanced to a bowl where the Stag keys were kept. They were gone.

"What's dad saying back there?" said Annette. "Mom, you *have to calm down*. What's dad trying to say to you?"

Annette's voice curdled to a wail: "*Jesus Christ*, what *IS* this?"

Morris climbed onto her. She hugged him, recovered herself: "Yeah, I'm *OK*, me, Morris and Annie fine. I'll call you back, OK? Mom, I'll call you right back?"

Her body sagged, she turned to Annie.

"Dewy has died."

THE HOUR WOULD never be recalled. All lights on, irrational rushing around, from light rooms to brighter rooms, garden, kitchen, upstairs, garden again. When time and space returned, Annette paced the kitchen cradling Morris. Annie upstairs, lay face down on the bed. Like Annette, she was half-sure Dewy wasn't dead.

Hour after static hour didn't pass. The night was forever, lights always on.

Annette returned her mother's call. In June, Dewy had registered Annette's US address, and c/o Farrisford Campus, on the car documents. English police rang the Stephens's via international directory, saying their daughter's car had crashed with a fatality. For 10 minutes Mr and Mrs Stephens believed they were ringing their dead daughter's phone. While Annette eventually spoke to her mother, police rang the Stephens's landline again, telling Robert Stephens no one else was involved in the crash, the incident a suspected suicide.

At first light Annette hugged and whispering to Morris as police officers came to the door. Annie stayed upstairs, heard the voice tones, Annette's sounding calm. After 15 minutes Annette came upstairs to hug Annie. "The woman officer's making tea. Do you want some?" They went downstairs.

The police asked who Dewy was, whether she'd asked to borrow the car, "whereabouts were you at the time?". They left, saying the crash site was in Danelaw Street, a disused car-park. "She drove it at the side-wall of the old Kwik-Save. Driven over distance in a straight line. Reason to believe not accidental."

Annette and Annie took the number 12 to Farrisford. Annette cried, briefly, for the first time, when the bus stopped at Londis. The playpark stretched away left.

In Farrisford they walked under overcast sky, Morris asleep in his baby-sling after hours consoling his owners.

The car was cordoned off by yellow tape between road cones. Its rear metre and a half were intact, the rest mangled. It had been driven at high speed. Annette, Annie and Morris stood no nearer than the car-park boundary. A dozen people stood a few yards from the car. Three PCSOs stood around the cordon. One read his phone, another gazed at the car, hat off, maybe respectful. The third intrusively watched people looking at the car.

Annie and Annette didn't know why people were

there, didn't know the crash had been on local radio each hour, plus regional TV news. A photo of Dewy had been sourced for TV, maybe through the Tattler.

Two women and a boy entered the car park passing Annette and Annie. They stopped, then walked slower towards the car. One carried flowers. When she reached under the cordon to place them, it was clear what had seemed litter or wreckage from this distance, were bouquets.

"Oh, Dewy," said Annette.

THOUSANDS OF MILES away, early-morning social media spread. In a hundred breakfast rooms, kitchens, home gyms, Wall Street offices, war postings, Rhode Island gardens, Connecticut spa-rooms, Boston townhouses, people froze as news arrived Dewy Durant had crashed a sports car into a wall. When shock subsided, five words were inevitably said:

Same as her mother did.

TESSA ENGLAND RETURNED late night from three days in Parliament to a maniacal welcome from Beezer. The dog-sitter had defrosted a bone. Beezer glunked it into his mouth and ran to the garden. Tessa England greeted Rudyard, gave him a Bonio, sifted through the mail. The local paper had been delivered.

EX–TATTLER GIRL SUICIDE CRASH

Stunned a second, Tessa England muttered "Woman, not girl" and read:

A former reporter for this paper died in her car Tuesday night, an apparent suicide.

American journalist Samantha Durant, 27,

known as "Dewy", was found in wreckage of a car driven at a wall of the disused Kwik-Save in Danelaw Street. Police are not treating the death as suspicious.

"Clearly the car was driven fast over distance straight at the wall," said Chief Superintendent Ruth Prior, who stated Miss Durant was eight times over the alcohol limit.

Residents in neighbouring Storer Street spoke of a "very deep engine" near midnight. Resident Anthony Beck, 48, described: "Loud revving, screech of tyres, very fast car, a bang."

"We thought it was kids," said Mr Beck. "There's been problems in that car-park, joy-riders skidding around."

Mr Beck and his son raised the alarm. "From a distance we made out a crashed car. We didn't think anyone was in it. We reckoned kids had done this. We rang the police in case kids returned to set fire to it."

Tessa England gazed again at the black and white photograph of a younger Dewy from a 2012 magazine. Beneath it, a separate column:

From Tatler to The Tattler... **BY THE EDITOR**

From her first moment in this office Miss Durant certainly made an impression. Working with us this year she was professional at her work, vivacious, outspoken and of striking appearance. (Being always barefoot endeared or perplexed all who met her.)

She worked hard, got involved in local issues and had a real interest in our town, its people and history. Her death has come as a shock.

Searching online for her picture we found articles she wrote in a glamorous career in her native New York, freelancing for Tatler, Vanity Fair and others. Three articles were expeditions to Africa, another to Indonesia, one to Saudi Arabia. She reported on war, poverty and women's rights in these countries. We never knew this, for when "Dewy" was with us, she was all about The Tattler. We shall not forget her.

Tessa England put the paper down. The Tattler mentioned nothing of the night before Dewy's death. She hoped that would stay so. Nothing need be hidden, but needn't be known either.

She took a constituency call, walked outside to the side-door of the double garage, gripped the handle, breathed deeply and opened it.

On the far side was her navy estate car. In the nearer, oil-blacked space lay camp-bed, pillow and sheet unslept on, sleeping bag still rolled up, the two digestive biscuits on a saucer, one with a bite out of it. Tessa gazed sadly at the scene where Dewy spent her last ever night.

She returned to the kitchen, poured wine, watched Beezer and pondered, of all things, how rare a person was who could big-bite a digestive and not break the rest of it.

ANNIE AND MORRIS returned from a walk. Annette hadn't moved from her chair. "Mom called," she murmured. "She's coming over."

"Really?" said Annie.

Annette nodded and fell silent.

Once a day she reminisced in bursts, and did now:

"Dewy was a principal ballet dancer. Ovations, huge bunches of flowers. She smiled, looked wonderful, but stayed up all night, saying 'I'm a fraud. I've wasted everyone's trust.' She quit ballet, but never gave up on dance. She choreographed, for Rhythm Nations, a college festival. One time she devised a piece to Mendelssohn

String Symphony number… 11, I think, set in a country house. It was funny. 16 dancers, they enjoyed it. The audience went wild. Next year she choreographed… um… I forget… it's on YouTube…"

Silence.

Annie couldn't rest from private guilt. She got angrier and angrier with herself. *Why couldn't I say 'I love you'? Why didn't I say it? It wouldn't have killed me! But me not saying it killed HER.*

Annette hadn't slept for 50 hours. Annie took her to bed, tucked her in. She fell asleep instantly, Morris snuggled in with her.

Annie sat in the unlit kitchen gazing out at dark over half the world. Tears fell down her face. She went to a drawer, took scissors and cut off her hair in 30 seconds.

An hour on, she went to the bathroom, dared to see the mirror. A miraculous, passable short back and sides with a pompadour three inches high. Annie tidied the back and sides with downward strokes of a disposable razor.

In the kitchen she put on the light, swept her fallen hair into a bag, stuffed it deep in the flip-top bin, put the light out and sat.

Nothing. No thoughts or feelings. Sight only. Darkness.

Annie switched the light on, carefully wrote *Back Soon xxx* on paper, and left.

The night was half-starry. A full moon hid in clouds. Soon the Yenton estate's dark hill and ridge of amber streetlights loomed. Annie broke into a run. She ran and ran, even passing the Lugworm, glancing back to where the car was the night of the hospital. A cry escaped her.

She ran from Cressy Road Bridge to Market Street, to Bridge Street, to a path through dark open ground to Danelaw Street.

Beyond streetlights, the car-park was purest dark. Annie disappeared into it, fell on her knees, walked on her knees, minute after minute. She gathered speed, her knees tore. The moon burst from clouds when Annie was a yard from the wall. In moonlight she saw where the car had been. A broad, foot-high shape had replaced it. Annie flung herself on it, expecting hardness, but landed on softness of flowers, a hundred bouquets or more.

"*I love you, Dewy*," she wept.

At dawn she lay still amid bunches of flowers and notes like:

To the lovely woman no shoes. We wished we had known you. God bless.

You beutiful woman what was this what happend? V sad.

You were so beautiful and mysterous we thought you were a angel. now you are one.

To the America woman we wont forget We enjoyed watching Esastender's with u God bless from all at 'the fuse'

I cant stop crying. M.D.

To the lovely america'n woman. this is so sad. God bless

From all at the Nor'Gate. We wish this hadnt happened. You were a pleasure to have in our pub. We hope you have found peace now

JOHN WRIGHT SAW the paper and had to sit down. The poor, insane, drunk girl they'd brought home, put to bed, who left in the night… John took her note from a drawer and reread it:

Dear kind men,

Thank-you for looking after me. I'm sorry to take wine and leave but cannot help what I do. Might this £40 partly atone? You were good to me and do not deserve this treatment. I'm sorry.

S.C. Durant.

Durant, the name in the paper. She looked a bit different from the photo, but certainly her. Here Monday night. Died next day.

John sat, distressed. "How will I tell Marlon? He carried her. He'll be shocked." He bit his lip: "How troubled that girl was. Very troubled."

THE NIGHT BEFORE Dewy died, Tessa England had arrived after midnight from a day that overran by hours. She always took cabs to and from Exeter, for evening trains from London, spent immersed in correspondence, were improved by an hourly glass of burgundy.

She liked to be dropped off in Market Street, to walk towards the Grand Hotel, take the cobbled lane near it left, where, five Victorian lamps along, stood her Georgian house, obscured by trees and hedges.

Under the first lamp a shoeless figure in a pale coat lay face-down. For the next 30 minutes Dewy staggered, or was half-dragged, to Tessa England's garage. The exhausted, often rude MP wondered if to call an ambulance. Dewy vomited gushes of liquid between rants about "unhumane" Conservative policies, took flying karate kicks to a steel telecom cupboard, sat on the pavement, burst into tears, begged to be hugged (Tessa England refused) blew her nose in her hair, then vomited bile, meaning no need for a stomach-pump or medical help now, only sleep.

Tessa England had steered her into the garage, fetched a camp-bed and sleeping-bag, returning to find Dewy lying on her side on the ground, unconscious. The MP set up the bed, left water and biscuits, put the light out and left. When Rashid arrived at 6am to take Tessa England to Exeter rail station, Dewy had gone.

Chapter 9

"COME FOR A walk?" said Annie.

Annette looked grave. Annie smoothed her brow. Each saw deep dark circles around the other's eyes.

"Should go out, I guess," said Annette, quietly, lips cracked and dry. "Did I tell you Mom's coming?"

"Aye. I've cleaned and tidied downstairs."

"You shake, my love," said Annette, taking Annie's hands.

Morris emerged from under the covers, shook his ears, stretched down, back end rising up. He leaned to Annie. They touched noses.

Annette held Annie and rubbed her back. She felt spiritually strong, but couldn't leave the bedroom, lethargy mixed with fear at her mother coming, plus the new academic year beginning in 10 days. She'd have to be absent for the crucial first week, if Dewy's funeral was in Massachusetts. The words "Dewy's funeral" always shook Annette a second.

"I wish Mom wasn't coming," she murmured. "Never visited me anyplace before. At least she's bringing Lucille."

"Did she say when?" said Annie.

"This week. That kinda means *today*. It's Friday, right?"

Morris jumped from the bed, paced to the stairs, head tilted. A car was arriving.

"It's them," said Annette, worried. "Stay up here, hon?" said Annette, dressing quickly, "I can handle it."

"I'll come too," gasped Annie.

Holding hands they charged downstairs.

Footsteps outside, a person's shape at the door's opaque glass: "Hello-o?"

"Doesn't sound like her," said Annette. She kissed Annie, breathed in, opened the door.

"*Mrs Paley!!*"

"You poor things. You poor things," said Roberta Paley, entering, embracing Annette, Annie, Morris as one. "You poor things. I like your hair, Annie."

"This is Mrs Paley," said Annette to Morris. "This is Morris, Mrs Paley."

"Hello, beautiful boy," said Mrs Paley, shaking a paw.

She bravely smiled: "Jennifer and I were in Cairo, saw your Mom's tweet. I asked Joanna should we call by? She said you'd like that. Did she say?"

"No," said Annette. "A lovely surprise."

"I hope so," said Mrs Paley. "Remember I don't travel alone…"

They looked out. Jennifer Alberone scowled in dark denim and a lemon trilby. She clacked precariously down the driveway, surveying the cottage: "What a shithole."

Tea was made but gin was drunk.

"Damn long getting here," cawed Jennifer. Her hat lay on the sofa. She put it back on when Morris pawed its long, iridescent feather. "Delayed in Cairo, train from London to wherever. Tight-ass little carriage…"

"You've complained all day," sighed Mrs Paley.

"We haven't stopped in 18 hours!" moaned Jennifer. "At the hotel, you're like: 'let's go find the girls *now*?'"

"You were so often good-tempered in Egypt," said Mrs Paley.

"This ain't Egypt. It's a dump. Shoulda checked into a hotel in Eekster."

"*Ex*eter."

"*Ex*eter, huh? You corrected me the whole time in

*Ex*egypt too."

Mrs Paley removed two thin cucumber slices from her eyes, blinked widely:

"Girls, come to the hotel with us, stay a night? Have a change."

"Come *explain* the hotel," said Jennifer Alberone. "No facilities, no *spa*. It doesn't even have a golf course."

A warm evening at a manor house restaurant preceded a night in the Grand Hotel. Jennifer Alberone retired to the next room. Annette, Annie and Mrs Paley sat around in a big bed, drinking rosehip tea with honey and a dot of rum. They discussed Annette and Annie getting married and made wedding plans. Morris slept peacefully on the centre of the bed under his blanket.

They stayed up all night in room one-eight, where Dewy's case once stood days and nights by Angela Foster's shoes.

In Monday night's drunkenness that case had been flung to the Brate from Bridge Street bridge. Dewy had watched it swept fast left to right into darkness. But the shoes had appeared in the Grand Hotel once more. They lay now in a bin outside, awaiting trash collection.

JENNIFER ALBERONE LEFT for Stratford-upon-Avon in the morning. Mrs Paley, Annette, Annie and Morris returned to the cottage.

Dozing on the sofa, Mrs Paley heard a cab, ran to wake the others. Annette looked pale but prepared.

"Hi, Mom, hello, Mrs Hart."

Joanna greeted Mrs Paley and offered her hand to Annette, who clasped it a second. Lucille blared about the journey. Annie recognised her as the woman who'd twice seen Ella Fitzgerald. Annette was glad to see this old family friend, an innocent buffer against her mother.

The newcomers sat on the sofa, Annette and Mrs

Paley in armchairs, Annie a kitchen chair by Annette. Talk was polite: airports, trains, England. More tea, "Sure you don't want to eat?"

Lucille cackled about Jennifer Alberone going to Stratford.

"She *does* know Shakespeare's not around, right? He doesn't hang out. Do you think she'll go see one of his plays?"

"Too long for her," said Mrs Paley. "She'd heckle. She really would. 'Kill yuhself then, ya little prick! Put the skull down, go shoot yuhself.'"

Morris sneezing had distracted Annette and Joanna Stephens. Mrs Paley thought everyone had heard her. She covered her mouth. "Dear God, that was tactless."

"Well, you're so damn perfect you were due a faux pas," said Lucille.

"Oh, dear," said Mrs Paley, welling up. "Poor Dewy. I'm sorry. What a terrible thing I said."

"Ach, don't worry, darlin'," said Annie. "She'd've liked that. It was her kind of humour."

"What was?" said Joanna Stephens.

"Nothing," said Lucille. "Roberta's first bum note in 20 years, that's all."

Lucille left for the wc. Joanna tried to talk personally to Annette. Mrs Paley noticed and said: "Will you show me the garden, Annie?"

"Aye, come through."

Lucille reappeared from the bathroom, intuited the moment, saw the back door open – "Ah!" – and headed out. Annie returned: "Morris? Wanna come?"

"Go with Annie-mommy, Booboo?" said Annette. "*Yes*, good boy."

Annie and Morris left. The room was quiet. Annette seemed relaxed but unreadable, gazing straight ahead. Joanna looked at the ground. She rolled a taxi receipt between finger and thumb.

They looked at each other. Joanna felt afraid. She knew Annette did not.

"Thanks for coming, Mom."

"Oh. Ah…" Mrs Stephens cleared her throat. "Of course. It's the least I… um… H-how are you?"

A weak smile from Annette. She tried to reply, but a fast sigh came. She tried to speak again: "I'm very… …."

Her face tightened. She stared at the floor. A minute passed. For the first ever time, Joanna didn't accost Annette for being silent. She wouldn't dare, both knew.

Joanna began: "I'm… very sorry. Y-your father is too. So's Clift. And Jack. Bobby's not gotten back to me yet. Many people have been in touch. She… was… was well regarded, really. Misgivings were… not deep, not in the end."

A long pause.

Joanna continued: "This must be unthinkably hard for you. You loved her… very much. She loved you. That I really do know."

A lengthening, stranger pause.

Annette looked insane. She thumped the chair-arm, hard. She bashed it again, and again, beat her thighs with both fists, threw her hands up: "What a *FUCKING STUPID thing she did!!*"

Mrs Stephens stared, trembling.

"*Selfish* thing to do," screamed Annette. "*Vile! VILE!!*"

Silence. Far voices in the garden and birdsong. Joanna Stephens stared at a wall. Annette glared mid-distance.

After a minute, Joanna slowly paced, arms folded in white-trimmed navy suit, white cravat. She drew breath and spoke, voice shakier than ever Annette knew: "Dewy… uh… Y'know,… maybe be proud of her, overall? Um… Your father and I were f-fond of her? Very fond… We didn't always *get* on, but~"

Annette looked at her. Her mother in tears was a shock. Annette was 10 when she saw this last, a horse had to be shot.

Mrs Stephens approached.

"Mom, sit over there, I don't like being stared down at."

Annette had waited all her life to say that.

Joanna crouched instead. Her easy athleticism irked Annette too. She reached for her daughter's hand. Annette refused.

"Mom, I don't want bonding. It's not in me. I've *nothing*. She's *killed* things I had. I don't want words, closure, she's *gone*. I don't *think* about her. Go sit there?"

"Sure," whispered Joanna Stephens, upset. After a time, Annette mumbled:

"It's nice you and Lucille came. I… don't mean to…"

"It's OK," whispered Mrs Stephens from the sofa. "Often it's the case –"

"I don't wanna hear bereavement counsellor stuff, Mom."

Footsteps in kitchen, kettle filled and clicked on, footsteps back to garden.

"How could Dewy dump on us?" muttered Annette. "Couldn't she have not gone someplace *else* and ~"

"Annette?" said Mrs Stephens: "Try… to have something in your heart for her?"

The kettle huffed steadily. Joanna stood, paced, sighed: "Your father and… we're… arranging to have her remains flown back…"

"*I don't care!* I'm not *going* to her fucking funeral!"

"*What?*"

"Semester starts in eight days! I'm giving lectures through October, I've done *two* in my life! I've a freshman module, 10 students. I'm *not* cancelling them for *anything*. It's… *agh*…" She hit the chair: "This whole *her* thing is… *I don't wanna KNOW!* She's *gone*! It's what she *wanted*, so *LET* her fucking go!"

Chapter 10

JOHN TALBOT WALKED home quickly on Saturday evening with shopping bags. A baguette peered from one, *Tattler* the other.

"All right, love?" called John, bustling in.

"Hi, yes thanks. Just out the bath." David appeared at the top of the stairs in a bathrobe, flushed: "I marinated the chicken like you said, it'll be nice. Is everything OK, John?"

John tugged the Tattler from the bag. A tin of pears fell, missing his foot. He kicked it half-hard at the skirting board: "go away, *you*".

"John! That's left a mark."

John held up the paper: "Remember her?"

David squinted: "'Ex-Tattler Girl In...' Oh, dear... Poor thing."

"Do you recognise her?" said John.

"Did we know her?"

"No. But the other night. Do you recognise her?"

John climbed halfway upstairs to show the photograph. David peered.

"Mm. Very beautiful."

"You don't remember her?"

"No. Do you?"

"Yeah." John nodded tensely. "She died Tuesday. Your works do was the night before. She was there, later on. Out of her head."

David followed him into the sitting room. To the

right, he had had set out the circular dining room table with dahlias, candles, fresh fruit and silver service.

"Nice in here," said John, giving David a kiss, though lost in thought at the newspaper story. As he and David hugged, John absently saw an envelope against a candle in the middle of the dining table.

"What's that?" said John. "Is it for me?"

"No. We'll open it after dinner."

"Please tell me what it is? I-I'm frazzled, long day, and… now that girl dying."

John began to cry. He instantly stopped, pulled a dining-chair, sat: "She was a desperate mess. Wish I'd seen that, reached out to her."

"You can't take this on yourself, John. You didn't know her."

"What *is* in that envelope, Davie? I need to know?"

"A copy of the resignation letter I posted to Alpha this morning."

"*YESSS!!*" John jumped, arms in a V. "Well done, mate! *Well done!*" They hugged. They kissed. They hugged. They laughed, John more than David.

"Let's get the wine open," said John.

"Bit early. I think I'll –"

"I'm having one," said John, glancing again to Dewy's photo.

An hour on, John and David snuggled up on the sofa. But as the account of Monday night continued, both sat tensely upright.

In the Grand Hotel ballroom, 200 had attended the launch of Alpha's new cinema and TV adverts. John had been there as David's guest. People gave speeches ("I don't know who he is" David whispered often).

The company's new TV adverts were screened on a wall. Both starred an ex-prisoner and bodyguard from London's east end, Phil Colney, who'd begun acting at 40, won awards for two acclaimed films set in gangland,

Involved and *Ambrose Street* before co-starring, as the love interest's father, in highly successful rom-com *Oops A Daisy*.

Six foot three, 20 stone, an ancient knife-scar from temple to jaw, Colney appeared in the Grand Hotel ballroom before the adverts were shown.

After Alpha employees and guests crammed him for selfies, the first advert – for the Alpha hole-puncher – was screened: Colney bursting into a bright, busy office, saying to camera: "If one thing gets my nut it's hole-punchers coming in here, giving it *that*" – he held one up, clicking it fast, threw it away, moved through the office: "Only one puncher gets respect in *my* manor…"

As he spoke on, close-ups of holes being punched in clean paper gave a satisfying crunch. At the end, Colney's voice: "<u>Alpha</u>. *Give it some holes!*" **Give It Some Holes** onscreen as the crunching sound ended the ad.

After long applause came the advert for staplers. Again the office, Colney holding up a document which slid apart from weak stapling: "In my game you need *serious iron* or you're on the floor…"

A close-up of his boot scrishing fallen paper began a similar tale as before, a gratifying *C-krrlunk!!* as a close-up Alpha stapler bound papers. Finally: Alpha – **Give It Some Iron** and a last *C-krrlunk!!*

"Then more drinks were brought in," said John.

"Giant stapler wheeled in too," said David. "I thought: 'time to go home.'"

"I *know* I said I'd come with, David, but I couldn't get away from Clifford Price, chairman of t' football club." John sighed: "Vincent Price, more like."

"More important than me, obviously?"

"Oh, David? I can't go through this again?"

"I forgive you." David kissed John, who said:

"Suddenly I was on duty. Mr Price – a walrus in a coat – asking why 'Asdas's stopped advertising in the match programmes. I didn't know we did. He thought I'd personally cancelled the advert and must explain. His drunk mate Anthony joined in: 'We're only asking £600 a year. 300 people per game – a year's awareness of Asdas'sz, £2 each."

A giant model stapler was wheeled into the centre of the ballroom, the top a 15-foot slide into foam. Employees shrieked down it. A press flashbulb popped, charts music squalled.

"Then t'footballers came onstage and danced…" said John.

JOHN WRIGHT HAD told Marlon about a lawn by the ballroom terrace. Maybe that's where a five-a-side match would be? But when they'd arrived at the Grand, the call wasn't football, as Marlon hoped, but to model the club's new strip at an Alpha Staplers launch.

In the ballroom, 200 people at long tables, last stages of a banquet, Robert Obogo and Martin Daly drinking at the bar, kit-bags on the floor. Marlon approached: "What we doing?"

After an ovation for Phil Colney's departure, Marlon and John Wright sat, arms folded, in a corner with Wayne Stewart and Paul Cassidy. The stapler foam-slide continued. Shrieky pop music blasted. Obogo, Daly and manager Alan Woods came over, plus 70-year-old club chairman Clifford Price and treasurer Anthony Gallant.

"Sorry t'keep you here, laadz," roared Price. A four course meal and brandies had relaxed this giant in a covert coat. "Long evenin' fr'uz awl," he added.

Robert always laughed quite openly at Mr Price.

"Much ground covered," barked Price. "All good. What's good f'the goose – HA!"

"And for the club finanshially," slurred Anthony Gallant. "Five years' sponsirrship from Alpha in the baag."

Bright, sober, Alan Woods summoned the players: "Right, boys? Dressing-room backstage." The five got up and followed him.

To Earth Wind and Fire's "September", Robert danced onstage in the new Farrisford Town kit to ballroom cheers and a surge of females. The kit, dull blue, had grey chevrons down one side, intensifying into shorts mostly grey. On the shirt, *Alpha Staplers* in lime hi-vis.

Obogo danced happily, ending in a double back-flip. To screaming applause he jogged offstage. Marlon waited in the wings, petrified. "Follow that!" laughed Robert, giving him a gentle shove.

Marlon stepped into lights and noise.

"Dance, man! Give 'em sex!" yelled Obogo. Crowd noise dropped. Marlon woodenly faced the hall. He slightly waved.

"Go to the middle of the stage!" pointed Robert.

18-year-old Paul Cassidy saw the agony. He jogged out to help, passing a football to Marlon, who, too tense, let it roll past him. Obogo ran back on to thunderous reaction, for a minute of ball-tricks, bouncing it knee to shoulder, letting it roll down his back to be heeled up high, kicked knee to shoulder again. The others tamely passed a football around. The song ended, all walked off, a comedian sometimes on late-night television came on and ranted into a microphone about sex. The audience liked him immediately.

Unnoticed, the two adverts were silently projected onto walls non-stop, the only lighting except for onstage. Everyone had moving globs of colour or whiteness spreading over them. Mr Wright was less agitated by the too loud comedian than incessant colours and flashes advancing over his clothes, over Marlon, everywhere. Whenever light filled the far opposite wall, John saw dozens of bare patches under new grey paintwork. Each had the dot of a small hole near the top. "Must have been pictures there," he thought. He tried to remember, but couldn't, despite ballroom memories. His older brothers, gone now, had wedding receptions here in 1958 and '61. Speeches were made where the comedian was now.

His brothers, father and grandfather always spoke of legendary Saturday nights here. 500 people dancing to big bands, then swing and jazz. Rock'n'roll arrived in '55. John had been to one or two 'bops' here while on holiday from Brunel University. Tough boys with big motorcycles and black leather jackets gathered outside. One even rode his bike up and down the steps. A fair-haired girl rode on the back. John never forgot her.

In Summer 1971, northern France, on a grape-picking trip with other teachers, John saw her again. She was outside a cafe with tough, counter-cultural men and wore a pink-orange kaftan. Her hair was very long. John found himself lifting up, as if pulled by a thread. He approached her:

"Excuse me? Are-are you from Farrisford?"

She smiled: "Crendlesham."

The young woman stood, picked up a bag, said "Going for a walk," with easeful command to the men, who glared at John. One, voice his surprisingly high, asked the woman "Where you goin'?" Another other told her: "Don't be long, like? OK?" Their voices were from north-east England.

A minute on, the woman told John of a terrible time with them, heading for India, the girlfriend of one absconded in Athens. "She left a note in my bag: 'Going to Paros to escape these drips, see you there?'" The drive to India stalled because Jill, who'd escaped, was the men's source of income.

John and the woman looked around them. Vineyards and valleys baked in silence. A dusty, blue bus purred through heat haze.

"Shall we get on it?" said John. It would be the most

important question of his life.

"Yes!" said Eleanor, raising her arm to stop the bus.

"NAUGHTY, NAUGHTY, *NAUGHTEEE*!" snarled the comedian: "I'll take your *sweeties* off you, make you do potty-training! *Yess!!* I don't care if you're 35!! Get *ON IT*!!"

Roaring, weepy laughter filled the ballroom. The man bawled:

"Before I go – and it's been great being here, with you fucking weirdos – *I didn't say that, I DIDN'T SAY THAT!* Seriously… before I go? I want you. To think. Of one thing. Just one thing."

The hall fell silent.

"If tonight… is that special, magic night when you and yours bring a little third life into the world… …*remember, guys, it's the BABY HOLE you want* for this, *not the POTTY HOLE*!"

An explosion of hysterics continued, resurged, subsided into loud, long clapping.

"And remember…?" yelled the comedian: "Remember… guys? Guys? She only wants sex tonight because she's been watching *me. True!* Look? Look at her face! Ha-ha! *I'm Matt Yelland, g'niiight*!"

Waving a fist in triumph, he departed, leaving a hallful of bellowing cheers,

Less manic, but loud applause and cheering soon greeted senior executives onstage – Toby Fanshawe, Luke Hill, and Mal Harris with four unknown junior managers from Clellan plc. Trish Hammond, and other Clellan executives weren't present (perhaps it wasn't senior staff's habit to attend small-company events. Steve Lomox was resigning anyway, back to London to rejoin the banking sector.)

Applause as Luke Hill stepped to the microphone.

"Hey. I know you're good," he began. "What we've seen tonight is *solutions* based on *synergy*. Not a word used much now, but I *want* it."

The ballroom settled into a changed mentality. Serious faces watched the stage. "*Synergy*," continued Hill. "What's that word's voice? What does it tweet, suggest, tease? Sexy synergy – who *are* you? Where are you? Can we find you? *Yes we can.* But to do that, you need *energy*... and a *decision*..."

"Right, I'm going," said Robert. "Coming?"

"Better wait til Alan says," whispered Marlon.

The other players rose as one and followed Robert. Marlon turned to John to ask if they might leave too. John was in reverie, remembering Eleanor, Marlon knew.

Leaving the building, Wayne Stewart noticed a woman in a pale coat on the hotel steps, head down, struggling to climb them.

"Is she OK?" he said to Paul Cassidy. Both turned to look at her. Obogo and Daly hadn't noticed, talking and walking. Wayne Stewart put his bag down and jogged up the steps: "All right, miss?"

"Uhh," said Dewy, trying to nod. She fell sideways. Stewart caught her in time. "Thanga, sir," she slurred, continuing upsteps, carrying a pair of shoes.

"Don't get cold feet!" called Wayne Stewart after her.

"She OK?" said Cassidy.

"Boozed out of her head!" said Stewart aghast. They continued walking.

Dewy leant against a doorframe, painstakingly insert-ing one foot, then another into Angela Foster's shoes. Very drunk, she believed by wearing these she was sufficiently in disguise to enter The Grand Hotel. The ballroom's noise, heard along Market Street, had lured her.

Dewy peered into the foyer. Seeing no staff, she re-moved the shoes and entered, carrying them. She'd worn shoes for 12 seconds, first time in as many years, felt crushing, sharply sore and hot, even to Dewy's inebriated state.

She entered the ballroom. Onstage was bright, the rest near-dark, with half-full bottles of wine on deserted dining tables. Dewy swigged from a bottle and watched the stage.

"Alpha is *solutions*," boomed a man, with rising emotion. "Alpha is *pride. Tomorrow's* office is Alpha. *You* are its officers. *Feel it.*"

A long burst of firm applause.

"Thanks, people," said the man. "Thanks. Thanks. Liking the love. *Now…* a word from the guys *who've put Alpha in the rooms* of the country through the ads they birthed for us, the ones we watched tonight. Please welcome, from London's Beck-Hallam-Pym agency: Robin Beck, Toby Hallam, Agnetha Hallam, Baz Thorpe, Johnny Pym!"

Six people walked onstage to cheers.

Ad agency boss Toby Hallam's speech referenced Ed Sheeran, Baudrillard, Wittgenstein, The Jam and Foucault. He tried to act amused when a man in a suit ran onstage, to a huge cheer.

"Yes, Matt?" he said.

"Give it some iiiron!!" screamed Yelland, rousing the crowd with swoops of his arms: "Give it some iron! Give it some iron! Give it some iron!" The chant grew. Rhythmic stomps boomed the hotel foundations.

Dewy's drunkenness partly-abated. "What *is* all this?" In a far opposite corner a huge replica stapler stood half-covered by a sheet. "A horse-blanket!" slurred Dewy. "Do staplers get cold?"

She rose and moved near the front. A jumping, manic crowd bawled: "Give it some *holes!* Give it some *holes!* Give it some *holes!!*" The Alpha Staplers logo on T-shirts, plus the big stapler she'd seen, made Dewy realise whose party this was. In three big, head-back gulps, she finished the bottle of wine, and headed for the stage.

All onstage hugged and received bunches of flowers. Dewy saw six steps up to the stage far left. Climbing them to bright lights, she walked towards Toby Hallam, who talked animatedly at colleagues. Dewy interrupted: "Sirr, that was udterly increhibl!"

"Thanks!" said Toby Hallam. "Always interesting to axiomize with clients, who, as you can see…"

He gestured out to the ballroom, where dozens still applauded the stage.

"Look at them!" said Hallam. "They're *fucking*. This isn't product, it's *belief*. It's actual *and* activated."

"Uh-huh," nodded Dewy, vaguely perceiving people around Hallam watching her.

"Who are you?" said Agnetha Hallam. Dewy thought her attractive, if stoat-like. She leaned forward neatly and kissed her.

"I'm Samantha Fent," she blared. "Bachult, Fent and Fanton, New York? *Don't* call me daddy's girl, I've m'*own* account. I want these Alpha guys to know the *time is now* for the USA."

"It is an ad agency you're with?" said Agnetha Hallam.

"Only Bachult, Fent'n'Fanton, hon?" said Dewy kissing her again. "Madison since '24. I wanna tell the Alpha guys our secret to *three times* more sales *overnight*. Bachult, Fent, Fanton's *secret method*."

"*Three times* as many sales?" yelled Hallam. "Tell 'em! Bring it on! I'll introduce you!" He rushed over to interrupt Luke Hill, Mal Harris and others.

"For real?" Agnetha asked Dewy. "*Three times* sales? How many ads?"

"One! Our trademark: three times *overnight*, one ad."

Again she kissed Agnetha Hallam, who stepped back, saying:

"Are you a bit 'out of it' by any chance?"

"Adrenalin an jeh-lag, flew over this mornig, woont miss this forra world."

"Little miss dedicated!" said Agnetha, last syllable three seconds, voice a cello.

CEO Luke Hill was excited by Hallam's breathless account a US agency had arrived onstage to talk faster potential. Looking towards the beautiful, slightly flushed woman with shoes in her hand, Hill put his arm around Hallam and spoke in the microphone:

"Guys? Guys! Everybody? We're not sending you home without *one more star* with something to share! It's *all* about New York, it's *all* about *now*. Alpha Staplers making news in the US, we must get ready to… everybody?"

"Seize it. Act. Push. Surge." murmured the crowd.

"That was rubbish. *C'mon*, guys! The States is calling. What you gonna do?"

"*Seize it! Act! Push! SURGE!*" roared 200 people.

"That's better! And here, New York on line one, Samantha uh F-font, from one of the, um, Madison Avenue agencies, one that guarantees *three times more sales overnight*. Yes, you heard right, *THREE TIMES* more sales."

These words woke many. Accountants, Sales, Senior staff, shareholders, managers, interns approached the stage, focusing intently. Hallam asked Dewy: "Want me and our guys onstage, or off?"

"Off wiv ya heads!" smiled Dewy.

"You got it!" said Hallam. He led everyone off.

To applause, Dewy went to the microphone, took a deep breath, blinked in the lights, saying: "Poor, mind-robbed whores, good evenin'," with such ease no one noticed the words.

"'My tablets, Juan, hark – where is Gonsalvo?'" she snapped. Lights shone in her eyes. She needed the wc. For a moment she blacked out. A seconds' amnesia later: "A'right! Who wants to know the *secret*? Three times mo' sales overnight, garnteed?"

"Yeaayy!" said a few dozen voices in darkness beyond the stagelights.

"I dint hear ya!" said Dewy "Wanna know?"

"*Yaaayyyyy!*"

"Ah, well, too bad, I'll gonna home. Bye."

"*Aaugh!!* Come on!!" chaffed the crowd.

"Well? D'you wanna *HEAR IT*?"

"*YEAAAAAAYYYYY!!*" bawled the crowd.

"Good! OK!" Dewy placed the shoes on the ground, returned upright by clutching the microphone stand.

"OK, TV ad, peak time. Required: paira shoes, one girl, one product – pretend I have the product in my hand, OK? Let's say I got me an Alpha Stapler! In *fact*, someone throw one up? Who has a stapler? Yeah? Throw it here?"

A woman stepped forward. "Don't lob it, hon, *whack* it," said Dewy.

The woman hurled the stapler fast and straight. Dewy's hand caught it without moving. The ballroom cheered. Laughing, blushing the woman returned to her table.

Dewy held up the stapler. "Okayy, we have product, we've girl, we've shoes, we have voiceover. Ready?"

"Yeaayyyy!!" roared the crowd.

"OK," said Dewy. "Previous ad ends, here's the new one: *ours*!"

All watched as Dewy unhooked the microphone and crouched over a shoe. Polite, intrigued laughter became confused frowns.

"Cue voiceover!" said Dewy: "In this case a li'l song."

She badly, clearly sang:

IF you buy an Alpha Stapler she'll piss in her shoe
But if you all buy THREE she'll shit in the OTHER
ONE!"

Gasps and unrest, people realising, one by one, the woman onstage, hidden mostly by her coat, really was urinating into a shoe.

"Cue media *sensation*," slurred Dewy. "Will she shit in her other shoe next time? Stapler sales crazy, people buy three, five, so she'll shit in the next ad." ***HeEEk!!***

Dewy finished peeing, dropped the microphone, hoisted her underwear, stood, saw everything spin and go dark, like going under anaesthetic. Arms raised, she pirouetted, looking up, whispering: "Goddess, we're all of us lost in a dark wood now, help us, please?" and collapsed.

JOHN WRIGHT LOOKED at Dewy's face again and folded the paper. Her picture tilted forward and disappeared. John knew, with sadness, he'd not see her again. He put on his gardening gloves, went out to the wheelie bin, rearranged rubbish to make a space two feet down and carefully placed the Tattler there so Marlon wouldn't see it. John had unconsciously folded the newspaper inward so Dewy's face wouldn't be touched by kitchen waste.

He made tea, fell into memory.

Houselights coming on, people a panicked herd, hurrying to leave. The girl lay motionless. A staff-member onstage stared at her, chewing his knuckle. John had approached. The hotel manager was angered:

"Seen *her* before. Police can take her as far as I'm concerned."

"We thought perhaps an ambulance?" said John Wright.

"I'm not arguing," said the man: "I don't get paid to argue. Hey, what *you* doing? *Hey!*"

Marlon was gently lifting the woman under her shoulders and backs of her knees. Her head rested against his chest.

John Wright caught up with him descending the steps to Market Street, straight-backed, carrying the woman.

"OK, son?" said John.

Marlon stopped. "Sad, innit?" he said quietly. "She should be happier in her life than this."

John went to get the car. Arriving minutes later, he'd found the woman conscious, eyes dim, looking at Marlon peacefully. John Wright got out to introduce himself. The woman did not want to go to hospital, asked to be left to walk home, but sat on the pavement.

"Where do you live?" John asked: "We'll drop you off?"

She'd mumbled about something called millards. John guessed she didn't quite need medical treatment, but couldn't be left here.

"Come to ours for strong coffee? And we'll work out where you live…?"

Dewy had woken in a dark bungalow. She silently explored, finding herself in a white and pale gold sitting room. A photo showed an older white man and a handsome black boy in late teens. Dewy remembered them, but where she couldn't recall. Being easily lured to a house by two men alarmed her, but the men in the photo were benign. Dewy guessed she'd passed out and they'd looked after her.

She opened a sideboard cupboard. An old bottle of Islay malt was stiff to open. Dewy took gulps from it, pausing between each, so not to retch. She surveyed the cupboard's sticky gathering of faded bottles in a house where no one drank. She sampled dry sherry, Campari, Cinzano, Bols Advocaat and Tia Maria. Energised, she wanted to leave the house now, probably with the sherry. She'd leave a note and money. Reaching for the sherry she saw wine.

She walked to town in blackout, drinking the wine fast. Tessa England found her face-down in Pegasus Lane.

"WE OUGHTA HAVE a meal, I guess," said Annette, speaking at last. "Do Lucille and Roberta go back to the States tomorrow? I can't remember who's doing what."

Annie opened out the dining table, brought kitchen chairs. The front room was now crammed, but the change of arrangement a relief. The pristine 1960s sofa – Dewy's last bed – no longer dominated. Anytime Annie saw its dark green upholstery and lacquered wood frame she turned away.

Mrs Paley returned from walking Morris in the back meadow.

"How about I make dinner tonight?" she said. "When Lucille comes, I'll ask her to drive me to buy things?"

"Sure," said Annette.

"Thanks," said Annie.

"Sorry we're so one-word," said Annette.

"Honeys, you've been through hell."

Lucille Hart and Joanna arrived, Joanna pale in thought, Lucille cheery about how the car was easy to hire. She planned to drive to Plymouth early next day, then Cornwall "for a night near my ancestors".

"Going too, Mom?" said Annette.

"Maybe," said Joanna absently. "You fly tomorrow, Roberta?"

"Tomorrow evening."

"Aw, your last night tonight," said Annette, "Sorry we've not been good hosts."

"I'll not hear nonsense, Annette Stephens," said Mrs Paley, hugging her.

"Dewy's remains'll be flown home Monday," said Joanna, silencing the room.

She seated herself, placed documents and papers on the table and sighed: "Well… I identified her."

Annie and Annette clutched each other. Mrs Paley's eyes brimmed.

"I was asked: 'Want her clothes?'," said Joanna. "But…

they warned me these were… 'not OK'. I said 'no thanks'."

She tapped a padded envelope: "I've her passport, phone, drivers license, ATM card, few hundred British pounds, a plastic bow of some kind, from like a cookies' wrapper? I'll… … m-maybe try clean the banknotes? Put 'em in an account for you someplace, Annette?"

"Give 'em to a charity store," said Annette huskily. "Not a corporate one. She liked Hospiscare."

"I'll look it up," said Joanna.

Lucille entered. "Tea? Coffee?"

"I need a *drink*," said four voices.

THAT NIGHT, WITH wine, "Kind of Blue" softly playing, Annette, Joanna and Roberta planned Dewy's funeral. Robert Stephens had called saying it was a week away, so Annette wouldn't miss college. She still planned not to go.

Annette's total silence unnerved Joanna from saying much, while Roberta was discovering she knew less about Dewy than she'd thought. "OK… timeline of the person's life," she continued. "Achievements, interests, then memories or anecdotes."

After another hour, her notes were:

Debussy when people arrive. Then Hank W.

    Boston, '89, born on an airplane frm Newark, Todd polo player. Lived mostly CA til age8, year at Rosie, then MA, lived w Jeanette & Marshall Durant 1-2 yrs, then Stephens's.

    Didn't ride. Pony-trekking once or twice. Little/no interest in riding but liked horses.

    Ballet.

Annette drank wine and began to talk at midnight. She spoke of Dewy's first months in New York at 21, on inheriting $120,000 from her mother.

"…after she was fired from *that* magazine," she continued: "Dewy was bass-player in a women's rock band for six weeks. It was… *loud.* The singer was a spoken-word artist, the drummer's arms were covered in cuts, the guitarist had been in jail six years. All in late 20s, kinda angry."

"Six weeks sounds enough," said Mrs Paley. "Did she quit?"

"They went on tour and didn't tell her. Dewy'd paid off their van hire-purchase, bought them new amplifiers, given tour funds. They vanished."

"Did the group make it?" said Mrs Paley. "What were they called?"

"Fistulas. Dewy'd had even gotten them their break! She'd danced a couple times naked in body-paint for a band Work Breed Die. Its show began with Dewy dancing to drumming, the band coming on as she went off. One night two girls asked she join their band. She said 'I can't play an instrument.' They said: 'You're in.' They gave her a bass guitar. She had three songs to learn, the rest was drinking.

"Through Dewy they met Work Breed Die, which was signed to a label called Specimen Pool. They ran off to support Work Breed Die on tour *and* got signed to Specimen Pool. All through Dewy, but they ditched her, no goodbye."

"Chrissakes," sighed Joanna. "How much did she spend on these people? 20 grand?"

"Mom, she *gave* you 20 grand, probably what she cost you over the years!"

"Dah-dahh-dah, *hold on*," said Joanna, holding up her palms, "I'm *not* insinuating she should have paid me more money."

"Sounded like it."

"I wasn't. It was incredibly good she gave me $20,000 from her inheritance."

"You hypocrite!" yelled Annette, standing. "You were angry as hell! You wouldn't shut up about the 60 thousand you and Dad paid for her operation!"

"I…"

"*You utterly did!*" Annette paced backwards from the table. She mimicked Joanna: "*'Get onto Todd, Bob, we're not a charity.'*"

Annie and Roberta looked intensely at the tabletop. Joanna Stephens helplessly stared at Annette.

"The *first thing you* SAID when she moved back from Brooklyn," blazed Annette, picking up Morris, who was distressed, "the *first thing* you said, in front of many, at the Hartmans': 'Blew the money, huh? You still owe people', *then you didn't speak to her for a year*. She was *so* cut-up by that!"

Joanna Stephens's mouth trembled. Annette sat at the foot of the stairs so Morris could properly cradle in her arms. She buried her face in him.

After a silence, Mrs Paley said: "She'd a heart operation?"

"Yeah," murmured Annette, red-eyed. "Pulmonary valve stenosis. She was 19. Valvuloplasty wouldn't sort it, so they operated to open the valve."

Silence.

"So many flowers," said Annette, gazing at the middle of the floor. "Seemed half of Smith sent flowers, cards, even anonymous cash. Someone she didn't know knitted her a sweater. She woke, looked around: 'Who's room's this?'. I said: 'Yours'. She said: 'Did the last person die? Is that what all this is?'…"

Annie made tea and scones. Mrs Paley paced the terrace and lawn on the phone to her husband. Alone in the sitting room Joanna Stephens spoke at length on the phone to her staff: dressage, shows, accounts, feed, tuition, the horse dentist, an injury, the individual activities of 17 horses.

Upstairs, Annette pressed a pillow to her ear to stop hearing her mother's work voice.

They reconvened at half past midnight.

"So," said Mrs Paley. "Dewy drank heavily in a band who deserted her. Shall we skip that?"

"She sure drank," nodded Joanna. "And from young. I'd no real idea until the Reverend Sharp called by in '08 to meet our first grandchild, Robert Stephens fifth, and his parents, and ~"

"Ah, your daughter-in-law?" said Mrs Paley. "Is she not a McConnell?"

"She is. Celia. Nice girl, rides well. Six horses, two from us. Her daughter's interested, aged five, couple rosettes already! Robert fifth has the sea-legs, like all the boys... Olivia, their youngest is three, and we've *already* been trekking, and we've been to gymkhana. With luck the next generation of women will run the... er... so, um, where were we?"

"Reverend Sharp," said Mrs Paley quickly, sensing Joanna's disappointment Annette would never run the riding school was years deep, and that Joanna knew she couldn't have that attitude now.

"Samuel and Antonia Sharp visited late morning," said Joanna Stephens, "We all planned the christening of my first grandchild sleeping in Celia's arms, east breakfast room. Tea flowed, cake was fresh. Then Dewy crashed past us towards the adjoining kitchen, white nightdress, red-wine mouth. We watched her open the refrigerator, grab a lettuce, shake mayo over it, dump a whole tub of peanuts on it, sit on the ground, legs apart – *thank God* she was wearing underwear. Then ~"

Annette shot up, chair falling: "*FUCK this!* She was a *mess*! Everything she *did* was dumb!! Then she did the *DUMBEST THING OF ALL!* Good *night*!!"

ANNETTE RELENTED AND flew home for Dewy's funeral. Annie and Morris spent three long evenings upstairs, for the sitting room held morbid associations for Annie. The sofa seemed sentient. Annie rushed past if crossing the room. In Annette's four days away, Annie worked her two hours from 7am setting up at the florists, then only three hours, not five, at Farrisford Organics, so to return to Morris. She didn't like the idea of him, or anyone, alone in that house long.

Annette returned, tired and glad to be back. While Annie made toast and tea, she took out Scientific American and a white booklet placed inside to keep it flat:

Samantha Christa Durant
'Dewy'
12/4/91 – 9/26/19

Annette turned the page. Inside:

Debussy	*"Girl With The Flaxen Hair"*
Hank Williams	*"I'm So Lonesome I Could Cry"*
Address	Reverend Louisa Sharp
Christina Rossetti	*"The Iniquity Of The Fathers Upon The Children"* read by Dr A. Stephens
Peggy Seeger, Isla	
Cameron	*"Freight Train"*
S.C. Durant	*"The Lady's Prayer"* read by Mrs R. Paley
Nico	"Afraid"
Address	Dr A. Stephens

Prayer for the soul of Samantha Christa Durant

The Rolling Stones *"Sweet Virginia"*

Annette fell quiet. Morris stood on hind legs on her lap. Annette's hand cupped his head, thumb-tip stroking a hidden dip between his eyes that only Annette was allowed to touch. The kettle clicked and quietened.

"35 people attended," said Annette. "Her father Todd Durant was not there. He replied to Dad's e-mail and said – I quote –: 'This news is generally on my mind. It's regrettable and disappointing. But Samantha was not part of my life."

She picked Morris up to hug him,: "When I recited part of 'The Iniquity Of The Fathers Upon The Children' I announced the title *very* clearly."

She sat for a time in thought, softly stroking the length of Morris's back.

"The casket was grey," she sighed. "She *hated* grey. What a horrid irony. They brought her… they brought the casket in… during a Hank Williams song."

Annette's voice shook. "She loved that song… a line about a robin, that's the moment everyone looked round, saw her being carried, well, wheeled – the casket was wheeled up the aisle by undertakers. Clift asked about that in his e-mail. He said if he'd been there he'd have done everything to get people to join him in carrying her."

Annette began to cry. "Clift was… was m-most upset about Dewy. He's e-mailed me a lotta times."

She took Annie's hand, held it to her cheek.

"Clift's real cut up. Jack e-mailed too. Haven't heard from Bobby and Celia. Also… the Millards weren't at the funeral! That's *strange*. People mentioned it."

Annie looked at the booklet. "You're there twice? At the end too?"

"Hm," said Annette. She quietly blew her nose, let Morris lick her face. "I was last to speak, after Mrs Paley read out a short poem Dewy wrote at High School years ago. Basically The Lord's Prayer reworked into: 'Our Lady, who might be there…' I can't recall the rest. It was very Dewy. People chuckled. She'd've cringed. Then… suddenly I had to step up there again."

Annette stopped herself crying. "Th-thank God I'd

written down what to say."

"What *did* you say, pet?"

"Um…" Annette wiped her eyes, shook Scientific American until a folded piece of paper fell out. Annette opened it, cleared her throat, read out:

"Dewy cherished how her Mom – the late Marcia Van Der Zee – said to her: 'You came from heaven, landed on Earth with a bump.' As many of us here know, that had a literal meaning, for Dewy was born on an airplane just after it landed. But I hope the heaven part was literal too, and that Dewy's returned there. Maybe her Mom has waited for her, and they're together now. Dewy would have liked that. Goodbye my darling friend. Thank-you for everything you gave me and all the times we had."

Annette shakily slurped tea and cuddled Morris:

"That's all I said. Then… it got a little strange. The Rolling Stones group was played, people clapped along, some came up to the casket, stroked it. I was a distance away, Mom holding my arm, Mrs Paley my other hand, Aunt Meredith to the front of us in profile, I was glad of her, I didn't want to be exposed in case anyone approached me, and…"

She sighed and wiped tears. Morris hugged his face against hers.

"I kept staring at the floor, that's all I could do. I wasn't crying, I… or maybe I was, my vision was blurred, *everything was blurred…*"

CRISP, HANDWRITTEN WEDDING updates arrived twice-weekly from Mrs Paley:

Dears, how about this ~?

My daughter Alex {no longer Alexa} is excited to be a bridesmaid, and has begged (demanded) I ask you please might her friends Dorian and Jennifer be too? {Born male, Dorian is gender neutral. S/he wishes to dress like the other bridesmaids.}

This would bring our bridesmaid quota to six. {My two, Celia Stephens's Olivia & Pattie, plus Alex's two friends. My son Oscar – 11 now – is home from school that weekend to be your page, Annette.

We are busy with dresses. Full-skirted, short-sleeved in white taffeta, red, blue, gold flowers embroidered here and there.

Her enthusiasm was boundless. At the Grand Hotel that night, she'd made notes, rung the US, researched dates, venues, caterers. "I'll stop now," she'd said. "It's rude of me to presume Joanna's role."

"Mom's never planned a wedding," Annette had said. "She doesn't even like them. She'll be relieved if you do it." This proved true.

Mrs Paley sent a copy of the wedding invitation. Annie laughed in disbelief. The parts she easily read were:

Mr and Mrs R Stephens

you to the wedding

of their   Annette

to

Miss Annie McLure

of the late Mr James McClure and Ms Siobhan Bailey

of Ardrossan, Scotland

Annie privately wondered – was it wrong to not try contacting her mother? Seeing Siobhan's name there was strange. Annie hadn't seen her for years. Her mother was mild-tempered, on methadone, also addicted to something called *jellies*. She smoked, dyed her hair and slept at daytime TV.

Annette once asked: "What's your Mom like?" Annie replied: "Black roond the eyes like a panda, blinks once an hour, for an hour." As for her father: "His name was Jim, or John Cameron but he was called Tricey. He died. My birth certificate says the faither's Peter McLure, but I don't know him. My Ma said he was a boy she went with before Tricey. Maybe she said he was the faither because Tricey was on the run or somethin'. It's no' worth looking into. These people were mental. They never changed. A lot of them are gone now."

AS A TRANSATLANTIC flight was too long for Morris, Annie took him to America by ship, leaving November 20th. To miss no more than four college days, Annette would fly 9pm Friday for the Saturday wedding, and return by sea with Annie and Morris, Sunday-Thursday, first-class suite a gift from the Stephens's.

Annette and Annie were married by Louisa Sharp in a white wooden church on a late-fall, bright day in Holyoke, Massachusetts.

Annette arrived at the church in a 1958 white limousine. People stopped on the sidewalk to see an emerging bride with flowers in her hair and the happiest smile in the world, barefoot in a dress of whitest taffeta with embroidered blue, pink, red and gold flowers down one side. Similarly dressed, shod bridesmaids emerged, and a page boy with her train. Next a tall man, father of the bride, and a handsome Central American woman in middle age.

In the church, Jack Stephens, Annie and Morris waited at the altar, Morris with two wedding rings clipped to his collar. The Reverend Sharp spoke warmly to Jack, on leave for the first time in 11 months: "Glad to be here, real pleased to meet Annie and be best man! Alongside a – 'a person who is a dog', as my sister terms our, um, canine friends."

These were the last words Annie could take in, so excited, nervous and constantly surprised by all aspects of her surroundings. Each nervous glance over her shoulder saw a cavernous candlelit church, red-carpeted aisle a deepening mass of richly-dressed people. Facing forwards saw the purple and white robes of Reverend Sharp, a raised altar, golden ornaments, polished dark furnishings, stained glass and – assembling in raised, varnished oaken booths of intricate carvings – a *choir*.

"Annette went to school near here," smiled the Reverend Sharp to Annie: "Some of her old colleagues and friends are in this choir."

A full church organ began, all stood, Annie glanced round a last time, made out someone moving, all in white with flowers, people behind her, *coming here, coming to me.*

"Hello!" Annette was by her side an inch away, crying. "Oh, you look *amazing*!" She peered around Annie: "Oh, Morris! Mommy's *here*. Can you hold him firm, Jack? What's on your collarington, Booboo? Oh, the *wedding rings*." She shook with laughter and turned to Annie. "Honeyy! How are you?"

"Ah'm fine, darlin'. You look beautiful."

"So do *you*. I need a tissue, oh thank-you, Jack."

"Ladies and gentlemen," began Reverend Sharp. "We are gathered here today…"

Eyes brimming with love, smiling broadly Annette looked at Annie throughout. She trembled with excitement, smiled in gasps.

Annie couldn't stop looking at Annette, mesmerised by her beauty and lovingness. She occasionally gazed to Reverend Sharp, in case rude to ignore her. The Reverend stood tall in her robes speaking loud at everyone behind them. Annie turned again to behold Annette, her loveliness, her chest gently rising and falling, her beautiful smile…

…*lawful, wedded wife?*

"I do, aye," said Annie.

… *to be* your *lawful, wedded wife?*

"I *do!*" burst Annette.

Now each will place a ring on the other's finger…

Jack lifted Morris. A deep *Awww* and laughter in the church as Annie carefully unclasped the rings. As she did, Morris reached to kiss her nose. Everyone laughed and *Awww*'d louder.

"With this ring I do thee wed," said Reverend Sharp.

"With this ring I do thee wed," said Annie…

Soon the Reverend's voice rang out:

"I now pronounce you married, you may kiss."

Any coldness or objection here to same-gender marriage – and some had lurked, in blinder hearts – ended now. Never had such beauty and grace of real love been so clear as when Dr and Mrs Stephens-McClure kissed.

NEXT DAY, BACK at the Stephens's, Joanna barked to Annette: "Do *we* pick up Dewy's things, send 'em to you? Maybe you fetch 'em, take them to England with you tonight?"

But her insensitivity to the magic of a marriage weekend wasn't enough to dampen it. That morning, flying from Holyoke in the Cessna, Annie, Annette and Morris flew east to clear morning sunrise in sheer awe. Beneath, all was peacefulness and radiant landscapes, colours rich, bright, waters gold.

"Hm? Well?" said Joanna, pouring hard cereal into an empty bowl.

"I'll think about it?"

"The Millards contacted twice last week, Annette. Her things are waiting to go."

Annette went upstairs, annoyed. Annie, packing cases for home, asked what was wrong.

"Nothing, hon. Oh, we're nearly packed? Shall we go for a drive?"

Sun was bright, all colours shone. Annette wore a

light-blue tunic dress. Annie, a second Alexander McQueen suit, a black one, chosen by Roberta, with high heeled red pumps and crisp white blouse.

They headed for Marblehead. Annie again asked what was wrong. Annette told her about Dewy's possessions.

Two things had affected Annie at the wedding reception. In her brief speech, she'd nervously thanked everyone for coming, thanked Mr and Mrs Stephens, Mrs Paley, the bridesmaids, Jack and Morris, then sat down. She'd planned to add: "I'd also like to pay tribute to an absent friend, who'd have been very welcome here. I'm sure you all remember Samantha Durant. She was a good friend to us." But nerves held Annie back from saying it.

As she sat, glancing up to nod thanks for applause, an empty chair, vacated by a guest, looked back at her.

Through the afternoon, whenever Annie turned, an empty chair somewhere, near or far, was facing her. When the bridal couple led the dance, to Roberta Flack's "When You Smile", and everyone in a wide circle smiled, applauded, Annie saw an empty chair watching too.

The other thing that affected Annie was overhearing someone say the Millards were: "… annoyed about *Dewy*, you know, the girl who… *hmm*, sad business. But she owed Wal *tens of thousands*. She left her affairs a real mess."

Now, a day on, Annie agreed they fetch Dewy's effects.

They drove to Ipswich and headed west. Soon the Mustang turned right into Ipswich Road, a long drive through woods. Annette pulled over a moment to dry her eyes, for she'd begun to cry. "So *strange* being back here," she sniffed. "And she's *gone*."

Before the Millards' a new, narrow lane led into the woods. "The track to the cabin," said Annette. "Let's take it. Her things will be there, Wal can come meet us. So we don't have to sit through a hypocritical house visit, avoiding mentioning they weren't at her funeral."

The Mustang slowly bumped along earthy ground. A minute on, Annette stopped the car.

The cabin had gone.

The lawn was churned earth, a huge orange bulldozer parked on it. The hedge had been ripped at the base and bent flat, showing the wildflowers field, ferns, the lake, the grey patch where the Burrages' trees were razed last year. The site of the cabin was a crater. A builders' crane rose high from it.

Annette reversed the car. The scene slowly receded.

Soon they drove up a lane through forest to a neatly landscaped space by a two-storey house so vast, its size couldn't be assessed. A lean man with side-parted hair and a thin mouth stood at a rosewood porch. He approached.

"Hi, Waldo!" said Annette getting out, nervous.

"Hey, Annette" – half-smile – "Well well! I hear you, uhh… got married?"

The wedding was lightly discussed, Annie introduced: "Hey," said Millard to her, unconcerned. He walked to a nearer garage, opened a mini-door. "Wait." He vanished.

Annette and Annie drew breath, looked around them. Much of the house's roof began 10 feet from the ground, rising steeply either side of latticed windows. All around was woodland but for a long, open, car-port with five of the seven cars, the furthest a 1980 BMW, bodywork newly restored and repainted dull silver, same as the other cars. Annette saw Annie also realising this was the BMW Dewy had used.

A trundling sound, Waldo with a trolley, three boxes stacked, each a cubic metre. Annie and Annette tensed.

"Sad business," said Millard. "Two'll go in the back seat, the third …too high for the trunk." He moved away: "Wait here, I'll get a couple bags, unpack that box, stuff'll fit in the trunk. And I can keep the box." His ergonomic sandals and thin beige socks crunched on pebbles back to the house.

Annette was pale. She stared at the boxes. "These are... *Dewy*?"

She lifted the top box to the ground. It weighed little. She opened it.

Annette and Annie stared down at bubble-wrapped objects, thickly wrapped and taped. They opened the other boxes to the same.

"What *is* this?" Annette frowned. She upended a box into the Mustang's trunk. "Bubble-wrapped lumps. Yeah, she'd lots of this stuff. Couldn't pass a yard-sale and *not* buy a vase, old miner's lamp, a cocoa tin. But these aren't *her*. Where are her *things*? Her clutter... her notebooks... she'd lots of sketchbooks?"

She teetered into Annie's arms.

"What have they done with her *her*?" she sobbed. "The magazines with articles she wrote, essays from school, Mina Loy college dissertation, things she always had. Her *clothes*? She hadn't many, but... *And her photos?...* she collected old pictures of ballet and dance. She'd photos of us growing up. And the two photographs of her mom were the most precious things of all to her. Where *are* they?"

Fighting to end tears as Millard returned, she half-sat in the car, door open, hugging Morris.

"Hey, girls," said Millard. "Cute dog! Hey, fella! Hm, doesn't say hi! Right: you'll probably get two boxes in that car easily enough."

Annie spoke. "Is this all there is?"

She wasn't by nature polite enough for Millard. He stared.

"Yes," he said, gaze hard. He turned to Annette: "Well... sad business, I guess."

"Thank-you for packing everything carefully, Wal." said Annette.

"Heyyy, no probs, mainly Andrea. She has her uses, ha-ha-ha-*ha*. Hey, catch you Christmas maybe? Gonna be around?"

"W-Waldo…?" said Annette. "In the cabin… there weren't… um… *clothes*, or, uh… stuff lying around…?"

"No," snapped Millard. "I mean, *stuff*, yeah. *Hell* yes, all over, mess, junk, clutter, mice running around… We got the hell in, took what mattered, got pest control in, stripped the place. I assure you, nothing of worth left. Shame our cabin had been allowed to… well, never mind, we're upgrading now anyway. Listen? I gotta get *on*, so…"

"Was there really nothing else, sir?"

"There's three boxes here, Annette. I mean, she wasn't exactly… a person of means. She even left… a-a slight debt, but… er…"

"How much?" said Annie.

Millard turned:

"I'm talking to Annette."

"How much were you owed please?" said Annie.

The man stepped toward her, eyes square with anger.

"I don't believe I know you," he said.

"I'm Annie Stephens-McClure. How much was that debt? I want tae pay it."

"Ha! Ha-ha-*ha*! Look, *look*, I think we… *Forget* it, OK? Bad debt, let it go."

"We'd like to pay it, Waldo?" said Annette.

"Look, I'm not short of money, OK?"

"The girl's deid," said Annie, wild-eyed, "And you're putting it about she owed you, but won't let the debt be paid?"

"I will *not* be spoken to like that in ~"

"*Yoo-hooo!*" Footsteps crunching. "Hi, Annette!"

"*Andrea!* Hi!"

Blue-eyed, round-faced Andrea smiled in an oatmeal cardigan and slacks. She carried a laptop computer and greeted Morris:

"So *cute*. He is *SO-O CUTE!* Did I remember right: he's a *he*?"

"Oh, yes," smiled Annette. "Morris is *quite* the man!"

"I often get it *wrong*?" beamed Andrea, "Like: 'How's little lady here?' Then there's, like, this *silence*, and the owner says: 'He's a *boy dog* actually!' and I'm like: 'AHH!' Ha-ha-ha-ha-ha! Hello again, Annie. We met ~"

"Why are you holding that computer, And?" snapped Millard.

"Uh? Um... *well*... it *was*... kinda Dewy's? Wasn't it? I thought.~"

"*Ours*," barked her husband. "Nothing of hers on it now. I reconditioned it to sell."

"Oh. But those..." Andrea's tone changed, darkened even. "Those... *things*," she frowned. "On the desktop?"

"Deleted 'em," said Millard coldly. "*Gone.*"

Annette, aching for anything of Dewy's that wasn't in plastic bubbles, said quietly: "I'd like the computer, Wal, please? I'll pay what you'd sell it for?"

"Take it," said Millard, walking away. "I've stuff to do, cheerio. C'mon, And?" He glanced back to summon his wife again: "*And!*"

"I'll be one minute," said Andrea. She then smiled, closed her eyes, hugged Annette and Morris without quite touching: "You got *married*? Is this right?"

"This is my wife," said Annette.

"Oh, *Annie*, how nice!" said Andrea, stepping to shake Annie's hand and hold it in both her own a moment: "Congratulations! You're happy and right together, I feel it! Hope you enjoyed the wedding?"

She and Annette talked. Annie put the boxes into the car.

Andrea Millard suddenly sighed. "I'm not great with words. But... um..." she took Annette's hand. "It must have been... an awful shock. I'm sorry."

Annette nodded. Andrea said: "I, er, I didn't go to her funeral, I was... hurt and angered by something she... ...but-but I *completely* don't care about that now."

She gazed away, to the woods. "I keep looking in that direction? And the old thought: 'What on *Earth* have we got living in our cabin?' comes into my head, as it did for years. *Then*…"

Her eyes brimmed with tears.

"… then I r-remember she's n-not there now. And it's… it's *real sad.*"

Annette and Morris hugged her. "I miss her," said Andrea, crying softly.

Annie waited a few seconds, exchanged a glance with Annette, cleared her throat, and said: "Er… Andrea? She made ye a bit angry you say? Was it because of a debt?"

"*No*, no, it wasn't that, no."

"We'd like to pay what she owed," said Annette.

"No-o, really, don't worry about *that*. We're not short of money…"

"We want to," said Annie.

"Well I… I guess you want to clear her debts? That's honourable. Of course pay, if you wish to…"

"*Thank-you*," said Annie. "Thank-you very much."

Andrea's estimate of Dewy's debt: 34 months' rent, respray and other repairs to the BMW, "plus she owed me 80 dollars, a personal loan", totalled $14,000.

"And you paid that she had her tonsils out, couple years back?" said Annette.

"Oh, that was a gift," said Andrea. "Poor thing was so ill. I paid for that from my own money, not our joint account, I was happy to."

Annie produced a rolled-up bundle – $1,000 – from her pocket. She'd brought her savings to America, mistakenly thinking contribution to the wedding was required. She gave the bundle to Andrea. "Towards her debt."

Millard returned in wellington boots with a tin of car-wax. "And? Gonna polish the Ram, gonna help? Our guests are leavi~"

"Wal, look!" cried Andrea. "A thousand dollars! Towards Dewy's debt! Isn't that sweet they'll pay it? Help her be more at peace, perhaps, who knows?"

"Lemme see that," said Millard, snatching it. He squeezed the money, near-smiling: "A grand in 20s. Not held one in a *long* time. Quite tactile. Satisfying."

"Have another one, joe," said Annie, prodding a second $1,000 into his hand. "Get yerself a lemonade."

MOONLIGHT FLOODED THE calm Atlantic. Annette walked under slanting windows and stepped out into overarching night. She thought about the wedding and smiled. She thought about her baby and cried.

Dewy's death, deep in her chest, brought a slow-pacing trance again, muttered thoughts and arguments, then mental nothingness.

Dewy's possessions lay in a walk-in closet. Hours before, when America lowered from view, Annette and Annie returned to the suite and opened them.

Few of the 117 items were ordinary. Antique jewellery, paintings, 1920s ceramics, a green enamel teapot, glassware, Clarice Cliff saucers, 1930s promotional ornaments, including bright figurines of children sitting on a train engine advertising a long-gone malt drink, another a woman leaning to kiss the cheek of a cigar-store Indian, ad unknown. In a shoebox lay crepe-wrapped bits of cuckoo clock: "That belongs to Bramble Cootts," said Annette. "Dewy threw something at it when it woke her up one afternoon. She promised to get it fixed. She and Bramble had an affair. Dewy had a lot of affairs at Smith. I was sort of in denial, maybe kinda devastated. But I'm happier than ever in my life now, so it doesn't matter."

A bright oil painting on thick bark was signed David Wojnarowicz. "Dewy loved that. She had something else by him and also by another famous artist, maybe Basquiat?

She left them in a Park Slope house she'd moved into without paying anything or consulting the residents. They threw her out after a month, allowed her back in for 10 minutes to get her things. She was drunk and left half."

Annie tore bubble wrap off a long thin object, blew a sigh of relief: "I was worried *this* had gone." She held up the tray Clifton had painted Dewy on.

"*Oh*, Annie!" Annette's whole body sighed. "I wanted that more than *anything*. I didn't dare say so in case it wasn't here."

Now, hours on, Annette shivered on the private deck and returned indoors. Annie slept, arm around Morris. Annette kissed her hand and his paw then made tea in the kitchenette.

The laptop was next to a dog-treat jar. Annette slowly lifted the screen. The machine had been cleaned to look new, no fingerprints or dust. Annette would maybe donate it – she often saw college Laptop Wanted ads. Dewy would have wanted it given away.

She plugged the machine in to check it. Three software icons on a dark blue screen and a Documents folder, empty. Annette moved the arrow towards the internet icon. She was curious if it worked in this remotest place. Distracted by her knuckle nudging a teaspoon, she double-clicked the wastebasket instead.

Two items were in it, accessed on dates after Dewy died, therefore by the Millards. Were these documents related to why they didn't attend her funeral? Why had Millard said "*Gone*." like that? Annette dragged them to the desktop and opened the first:

SAB Jan-Apr
January 10th

Oh the Millards, the holy Millards. I've spent four nights *in their house*! I'm warm here, very comforta-ble and looked after. I've a cold or flu, not

pneumonia like Vacua worried I had.

Monday night snowed five foot high. Tuesday, the cabin was headache-bright, the world quiet. I couldn't move, missed my girl and was dying.

Footsteps out on the porch.

Door: *bang-bang-bang!* "Dewy?" Vacua.

Bang-bang-bang! "Yoo-hooo!"

Leave me, Andrea, I'm nothing, let me die.

Bang-bang-bang! "Dewy?"

I don't want to hear her inane crap: "Wal's out with the snow-plough! He's real happy – apparently its galphunzer connects to rerouters from the crungler!"

Bang-bang! "Dewy?"

Key in the lock. *"Dewy?"* She's in. Hiking boots echoing, now she's here, kneeling. Her unmysterious face hovers nearer. *"Freezing* in here. Your poor hands!" She tugs off a mitten with her teeth, puts her incredibly thermal bare paw around my hand. Heat radiates through me. I start to cough like a jammed Kalashnikov. I don't feel cold but of course it is cold. Haven't left the mattress since putting out the last of the bird-feed, two, three days ago.

La Vac's puffa-jacket arms pull me up to sitting. My head flops back, she catches it with her mittened other hand.

"Gonna walk you to the house," she says, "You'll stay with us awhile."

Sometimes she's so sweet, like now. I start crying. Vacua hugs me, brief, awkward. She smells of Chanel, her house and not-Annette. She's lifting me, we walk, she steadies me.

The turn-ups of Wal's old corduroys I'm wearing have unravelled in bed. If they're not rolled to the knee they clash with my Laurel Canyon Lover toe-nails. I need to tell Vacua this, but my throat's too dry. {She wouldn't understand anyway. Her "mind" can't process things that matter.}

We trudge through snow, her arm around me. She rants how her half hour walk here cleared a path for us. She's shrill about my feet, not realising, as everyone doesn't, *my feet are not cold in snow*. They feel warm and lovely (though today I'm numb all over) and they get beautifully clean.

Her kitchen's oven-hot, I'm emotional about shit knows what, Vacua switches on a TV, thinking it will normalize me/us. She's someone who puts TVs on then doesn't watch them. The thing blasts and roars. A Millard-bought device, therefore a billion-dollar, sub-bass sound-system. People are sonic booms, the ads nuclear-reactor meltdowns.

Vacua chirps away. Wal's this, he's doing that. I attempt a "Sounds good!" As Inuit have 23 words for snow, I've three "Sounds good!"s. None ever works.

Vacua looms with soup: "Waldo *will* invest in the gym franchise after all! *That'll* be interesting!" – the least convincing use of "interesting" I've ever heard. I hope *he* doesn't come into the kitchen. I can't face him *and* her. It's all so embarrassing. Three years ago, he intuited my desperation, offered me a cabin for six months, I stay years, pay nothing, dance naked and blog how I can't stand him or his witless wife, who now sits by me, holding my hand in her thermo-paw, other hand lifting a spoon to my mouth. I slurp soup. Vacua takes me upstairs, tucks me in bed, sits in a chair, holds my hand til I sleep.

Annette scrolled down pages, stopping at:

January 16th 2019 minus 14 last night, minus 3 all day.

Can't bear not being with Annette. I hug my pillow,

kiss it, place a corner of the pillowcase between my lips and softly draw my lips down it, like I do to A's earlobe. I relive the scents of her hair. I miss her body-warmth, her voice, her hot sleepiness in my arms, her soft kisses to my boo's, her kisses to my hands and fingertips.

I cannot live without her. I wake, then a slab topples inside my chest: *she's not here.* She's on the other side of the ocean. She'll be back in 10 weeks. She's been away 11 days and that short time has killed me.

Truths roll in like big waves: will she stay on in England after her year at Exeter school? Will she come back home to live, or get a new posting? What would I (and she?) do if she went to the University of Kiev? Or Melbourne?

The life we've long-shared is ending. Our love will end, the last love I'll ever have. I don't know why I feel that, but I'm certain. Love is the meaning of life, and my life's meaning is dying. This thing I am – a life – will go through the black hole called No-Love-Again, to emerge as one of the billions whose love lottery ticket was dud. Another wordless, mind-blocked, sad, ex-person, one-fifth alive in a void. Sleep, commute, work, commute. Repeat x 40 years then die, six people at funeral.

It's dark out. This winter's long, the first I've spent alone. Last couple years were at Meredith's, the Stephens's or wherever my darling was. I wish I could call her. She is living in a place called Farrisford in a room above a 200 year old British pub. Most bars are called pubs there.

She said she slept with a guy. "A very nice young fellow," There the discussion kinda stops. That brings her total of guys to four, maybe three. I hope he is gentle and kind. I'm trying not to feel ill with sadness, envy and anger at someone kissing my darling, sleeping with her, holding her, being with her. I'm trying not to fall into a darkest pool. I miss her completely and with pain.

I can never ever feel OK about the idea of someone fucking her. But she's not a child. She's *26* in, like, a week. 26!! Annette in her 20s?? Unreal.

Utter joy when she was home Christmas. She's so beautiful. Her eyes shine, her skin's so glowing. She's so *alive*, enchanted, enchanting, sees beauty everywhere.

We tried to buy gifts in Andover but she was overcome by Christmas lights and window displays: "How lovely! Look, Booboo!" She breaks my heart. We were arm-in-arm as always, I'm trying not to sob because she's innocent. One or two monsters squawked at me for not wearing shoes, but stopped in their tracks to see A with Morris in his baby sling – how beautiful her soul as she looks around in wonderment. The monsters retreated, they knew she is holy, never to be harmed.

Chapter 11

As WINTER DEEPENED, Annie and Annette were busy, cosy, happier. They bought a car and spent Sundays exploring Devon, Somerset and Cornwall. After reading a Philip Larkin poem "Church Going", they looked for old, unlocked churches, and liked to sit in them. They loved wrecked castles, and monuments and pubs of ancient towns.

December 23rd saw the Grand Re-Opening of Market Street, much publicised in shop windows, radio and a Farrisford Tattler supplement. Annie was to help both florist and cafe, which, with other local businesses, were allowed a free, pop-up space for the day along a new concourse across Market Street before the steps of the Grand Hotel.

Annette and Annie had wondered what to do with Dewy's things, and decided, if space was available, to sell any objects that held no meaning or reminder of her. Into a pull-along case they packed china animals, coloured glass vases, trays with old advertisements, small abstract sculptures, an autographed baseball glove and baseball (team unknown), religious icons, coloured ashtrays, a gilt, lacquered wooden Chinese palace in kit form and two dozen paintings by amateurs of varying abilities. They kept one of a pelican so earnestly hopeless Dewy had likely loved it.

The day was sunny, Market Street crowded. At 2pm a trestle-table became available, vacated by an estate agency that had offered only leaflets. By 3pm, 22 of Dewy's items were sold, raising £184 for Hospiscare.

"Oh my God it's *you*!" yelled a voice.

Annette and Millie Zena burst into cries and rushed to hug. A handsome, rough, white youth with Millie politely looked on.

"Morris, this is Millie?" said Annette:

"Oh my, he's in a *baby sling*! This is my half-brother Owen, we're visiting the weekend, staying with my dad, who's also his stepdad, if that makes sense."

Millie smiled at Annie and Annette, sighed happily and smiled again. She began: "How's ~" but for a reason she'll never know, stopped saying "How's Dewy?" She surveyed the stall. "These are nice! Some are... interesting?"

"They were Dewy's," said Annette.

Millie stopped, glanced up:

"*Were?*"

After Annette told her, Millie cried for two minutes in Owen's arms.

"*Jesus!*" she wept. "Stupid thing to do! Why'd she do that? Fucking hell. *Why?*" She blew her nose on crepe paper Annette handed her.

"*Why* did she kill herself?" said Millie, "Why do the best people do that? They *mustn't ever*. They're the ones the world *needs*. So *never* do it."

"A mate of mine said suicide's against karmic law," said Owen's deep, smoker's voice. He seemed embarrassed to contribute and took a step back.

"She done a lot for me that Dewy girl," said Millie. "She said 'find out which college course are local and free'. I did. I'm at college in Manchester now, access course, fashion and fabrics."

Owen excused himself to go and meet friends. "I'll come and find you, O, keep your phone on?" said Millie.

She talked rapidly about her life, a boyfriend: "He's

something else. A grime DJ, a Christian as well? We might split up, but I can't get rid of him over Christmas, that'd be heartless. The thing is, I'm sort of seeing this man at college too?"

She was half-barged aside by two middle aged men in hi-vis anoraks:

"Move this table, please!" barked one. "Or a £90 fine. Public highway."

Annie pulled the table back.

"Still too far out!" droned another man. "That table can't be utilised here? You'll have to pack up. We have a legal duty to ensure ~"

"You from the Council?" said Millie.

"We are representing of the Council," said one. "This is an obstruction."

"How comes you're challenging this 'obstruction'," said Millie, "Barely three foot of a 12-foot pavement, when way down there – see? – by Specsavers, them orange barriers, fencing off cement mixers and whatnot, people are having to step out into the road, that busy corner?"

The two men began to move to the next trestle table, demanding it be moved.

"Hello?" said Millie, following them: "Why are you threatening fines *here* but not against the builders what's left all that stuff? Look! Look at that woman, see? Double babybuggy, stepping into traffic what's having to slow and swerve out while she moves past the orange barriers?"

As Millie, Annie and Annette watched, an elderly couple stepped into the road where the corner pavement was barriered. A cyclist in skintight body-stocking, wrap-around shades and a strange, exoskeletal helmet rounded the corner straight at them. He braked so hard the back of his bike rose up, making him tip-toe to full stretch of mantis-like legs. He screamed abuse at the pair's faces.

A Council man, if he was, returned to Annette and Annie's table: "You were advised to move, but didn't utilitise the advice that was actioned? Therefore ~"

A woman in a 'Market Street 2019' sweatshirt bounded over: "The Indoor Market's now as a pop-up, first-come-first-served to stalls ousted from the pavement. Go there quick!"

Annette pulled the suitcase. Millie and Annie walked with the lightweight folding table. The Indoor Market was festive, busy, dark and cold. A maze of stone-floored lanes led past colourful stalls. There seemed no space for more, save a dark, empty area by double fire-doors in a low corner, furthest from the market entrance and a distance across a lane from other stalls. The nearest sold sombre curtains and heavy drapes.

Annie and Annette were unsure they wanted to continue, but Millie's help and cheerfulness were irresistible, though she said she had to leave once they'd set up. Annette invited her to take an object to remember Dewy by.

Millie paused. "I-I don't think I will?" she said sadly. "She gave to me already. She gave me her *belief*. That changed me. It changed everything."

She hugged Annie then Annette and stroked Morris. "Merry Christmas, I love you pair, you're so cool, and you, Morris."

She left, smiling: "Don't take no crap off of nobody! Specially if they *are* nobodies! You *know* who wouldn't stand for that, God rest her!"

ANNETTE SPOTTED A pet stall, returning only five minutes later. "They were OK," she said. "Maybe a little crazy, or glum. He's called Greg and, uh… his wife stared at me. But…" Annette smiled, held up a thin, blue-striped plastic bag: "We've some organic treats and a new kind of chew."

She put the bag on the table and hugged Morris in his sling. He slurped sleepily. Annette sat on an upturned plastic beer-crate and cradled him.

Over two hours many people passed the stall. They sold three objects, of 40 left. An hour passed of no people then twilight began. Occasionally a customer entered Greg's pet supplies up at the far corner, or a babywear stall next to it. Over to the right, a hardware stallholder started to pack away.

Annie felt the atmosphere strange. Perpetual noise of further, unseen parts of the covered market gave a strange incantatory air. It seemed to be building up to something. She looked down at Dewy's objects. She glanced to Annette, whose face was buried in Morris's chest.

A bizarre noise from outside arose. Men in a crowd, singing, ranting to the pounding beat of a drum. Morris stirred. Annette looked up: "What's that, hon?"

"I think it's a football crowd," said Annie.

It was very near suddenly. "Christ," thought Annie, "Don't come in here."

We love you *FARRISFORD, we do!!*
Love you FARRSFORD, we do!!
Love you FARRSFORD, WE DO!
OHH, FARRISFORD WE LOVE YOU!!

The song was repeated, to drumming, clapping and hard thumps against a steel-panel wall of the market. 200 men sang, bellowed and swore on the other side of it. Morris clung to Annette. A new song erupted:

Let's get drunk! Up the Swain!
Farrisford have won again!
Nana nanaa, Na nanaa, na-naaa!

The song receded. The men were passing. Another song: *Please sing a song for us!!* began far off, fading. A figure in blue and white football scarf appeared at the end of a passageway out to an exit. Annie tensed. "Please can he be the only one?" He was.

"Irr, Greg?" he called, voice echoing in the big, empty-ing market space. The atmosphere and acoustics of this corner of the market seemed lonely and strange now. "A'right Hilda? Two-one!"

"*Yeah?*" said Greg, packing up the colourful pet stall. "Cassidy get one?"

"Got 'em both."

"Agh!" said Greg. He stopped what he did, shook his head, sighed deeply: "That's it then innut? Bye-bye, Paul."

"Why-y?" frowned Hilda, voice echoing.

"They'll *sell him*," said Greg and the scarfed man together: "Argyle's watching him," said Greg. "And the Gas."

"Gibbsy got took off, second-half." said the scarfed man.

"*Again?*" said Greg.

"Ankle. Be out months."

"Agh! Means we ain't got a tall defenderr!"

"The lad they brought on's tall. Did the job."

"Yeah? Who's he?"

"Er… new lad. I'll find out." He stepped a distance away to talk on a phone.

In the new silence a uniformed young man and woman swaggered around the corner to Annie and Annette's right. They saw the stall, exchanged glances and approached. The man broke into a smile.

"Not seen you before! How's it going, what you selling?" His smile dipped as he looked at Dewy's items. "Str*ange*. What *are* these?"

"D'you live locally?" said the woman.

Annie had nodded greeting at the man but felt unable to speak. The two stared at her, awaiting answers. None came. Annette stood.

Silence.

"Marlon Wright," echoed the scarfed man, distantly. "That's his name. He'll do."

"These things actually yours?" said the female officer to Annette. "Bit *quirky*?" She picked up a blue, abstract sculpture. "I mean, what 's the use for this? Is it, like, a ornament?"

"Nice little dog," said the man. "In a sling? Why's that for, what's the sling then? Does he not like being on the ground?"

Annie and Annette looked blank. Morris tried to hug Annette. She slowly sat on the crate and comforted him.

The PCSOs exchanged glances again.

"Not very talkative today, girls? Got authorisation to be here?"

Annie said they'd been directed by the Council from outside. The man stared at her with a smirk, looked away as if she hadn't spoken, picked up one of Dewy's vases, looked at it. His colleague had constantly stared at Annette since the questions about the sling, which remained unanswered.

"Where did you get this stuff *from*, if you don't mind me asking?" said the man.

Annie was angry now, visibly nervous. Both PCSOs focused on this.

"Are you not gonna *answer*?" said the man, hard.

Annette spoke for the first time: "I don't believe we're obliged to, sir."

Her accent made both start. The woman PCSO reddened. "*Excuse me?*" she hissed. "In our country if it's a police matter you *are* oblated to answer? We're asking you for simple *information*."

"May I see your designation card, please?" said Annette. "And yours, sir?"

The pair glared. "As I understand it, continued Annette, remembering everything Dewy explained to her one night in May, 'You are Community Support Officers.'"

"We're *police*," said the man.

"*Police* community officers," said the woman.

"But you're not *police officers*."

"Right, you pair are nicked," said the man.

"On what charge?" said Annette.

"Suspected stolen property."

"If you suspect these stolen," said Annette. "Please contact a police officer?"

"We know our jobs!" snarled the woman, dialling a phone. The man stood arms folded, feet apart, radiating satisfaction. The woman finished her call and joined him: "Back-up's on the way." Both smiled.

"We got all the time in the world," said the man, grinning at Annie, who was petrified. His smile faded. His face changed. It tightened with contempt, his eyes were iron, he spoke through gritted teeth "All this, and for the sake of, *what*, 10 quid's worth of old junk?" He shook his head and bared his teeth: "Silly, silly girls."

Annie glanced in panic to Annette who, with her free hand, drew Annie to her and whispered softly: "*Fuck 'em*".

Blankly, with downturned mouth, the woman examined a green bowl with a deer painted in it. A gleam crossed her face as something occurred to her. She replaced the bowl and said to Annette. "Anything concealed in that sling you're wearing?"

"Yeah, what you got in there?" said the man. "Wouldn't mind a look actually. Why's that dog *shaking* so much? Got drugs in there he might have eaten?"

"I think we should have a quick look, actually," snapped the woman.

A voice:

"I'm *well*, thank-you, Greg, but *Beezer* has *worms*." boomed through the market.

The voice disappeared into the pet stall, "H'lo, Hilda. Anything for worms?"

A long-haired Alsatian ambled down the indoor lane. He stopped and sniffed the air. "Look! A *person*!" said Annette to Morris:

Rudyard wandered over, barged through the PCSOs' legs and delicately met Morris's nose.

"How *beautiful* you are" said Annette, smiling.

A blonde woman in an old tweed jacket peered out

from the pet stall, spotted her dog, strode towards them: "Sorry about that. C'mon, Rudyard!"

"Hello, Mrs England," said Annette nervously. "I-I recognise you. M-my, um, American friend interviewed you... er, the newspaper"

"Oh." said Tessa England. "Oh. I'm..., I-I read what happened to her, I'm most sorry. What is your name?"

"Annette."

"And how are you, Annette?"

"Excuse me?" snapped the male PCSO: "You're interfering with police procedure? Can you take the dog away, make yourself scarce?"

"Is that a dangerous dog, madam?" said the woman PCSO. "Is it a Alsatian, isn't it? Have you got a lead for him?"

Tessa England raised an eyebrow and leaned to Annette. "Is everything OK?"

"*Madam*?" snapped the man: "You're interfering with police. I have asked you –"

"No police here," said the MP. "You're support officers."

"Police *staff*," said both PCSOs at once.

"Where are you stationed?"

"Never mind. Move on, please? You're interf~"

"You've no power to move people on."

"You are *obstructing* a police matter!" shrieked the woman. "Get going or you'll be nicked."

"On what charge?" said Tessa England.

"Er... um, obstruction of the law."

"You're getting on my nerves," snarled the male PCSO. "Get your dog out of here and GO. Move it."

Tessa England peered around him: "Ah! Janice. How are you?"

Four police officers arrived around the table. Three looked gravely at Annie and Annette. Had Tessa England not been there the effect could cause panic or defensive violence in most people. Annette remembered Dewy's words: "It's said: 'If you've done nothing wrong, you've nothing to worry about'. *But what if they think you have? And are treating you like you have?*"

The male PCSO told PC Hudson: "Tableful of knock-off, non-English suspects, not co-operating, old lady here blocking procedure!"

To his shock the police officers burst out laughing. He and the other PCSO exchanged confused, worried glances. Tessa England said: "I think you'll find out who this 'old lady' is soon enough."

Janice Hudson dismissed the PCSOs with a toss of her head. They walked away, blushing. She congratulated Tessa England on her re-election eight days before. "Nine thousand majority, wa'n it?"

"Hmm," said Tessa England.

The UK's Conservative landslide victory bewildered, even made her uneasy. Politics seemed unreal, her own increased majority strange, for she'd done no campaigning – the election had so abruptly called there wasn't time.

Annie stared rigidly past the MP, shaken after the incident just passed. Unaware who Tessa England was, she unleashed a bitter, precise account of what had happened. "When ah think of young people, or vulnerable people, even just shy, or quiet people at the mercy of these fake-power *naebodies* ~"

"We get your point. Thank-you," said Tessa England.

"Never thought I'd sympathise wi' coppers," said Annie to the four police officers. "But see the type of people replacing you on the cheap? Weeds are choking your flowers."

When all departed Annie, Annette and Morris leaned against each other. The market day had ended. Bangs, crashes, rattling trolleys, ratcheting shutters all boomed and echoed. Dewy's last possessions were packed. Annie and Annette waited to ensure Morris had recovered from the PCSOs incident. He still slurped and trembled a little.

Annie approached the double fire-doors, shoved the rusty push-bars. The doors flung opened to a high-up view of darkness dotted with lights in their hundreds, nearly half the town. In the foreground were lights from nearer streets. Far left, Garton Road's floodlights still on, a glimpse of empty, blue-roofed stand.

Air blew in, refreshing all the space. Annette and Morris moved to the doorway, faces lit-up as they neared it. Annette's head rested on Annie's shoulder. Morris leaned up to kiss Annie's cheek.

"Ahh, that's betterr," said a voice behind. They turned to see a swarthy man staring out of the doors, smiling at the view.

"Hi, er, Greg," said Annette. "Hello, er~?"

"Hilda," said Hilda, lit bright by a streetlight off to the right of the doors.

Another stallholder arrived, and another.

Over minutes more market staff came. They wore fur-lined nylon boots and padded anoraks with zipped money belts. All looked out at the lights and big, dark beyond.

"Nice bit of air in," said one.

"Nice view."

"Never seen these doors open."

"Nor me, How long I been here? 12 year?"

"Should open' em every week, let the old air out, new in."

All fell quiet. 14 people watched the lights. Some walked away. Eight remained, six, four, then Annette, Annie and Morris stayed. They watched lights uncountable, all colours and strengths, near, far. Above, stars defied darkness forever.

October 2020

Coronovirus has claimed 152 lives from Farrisford, Crendlesham and the villages. Among them: bus driver (Farrisford – Crendlesham route) Natalie Baciu, Sir John Wyce groundsman Martin Stokes, memoirist Mary Winters and Londis co-proprietor Derek Wallis.

Barbara Wallis has continued to run the shop each day during the pandemic.

Survivors of acute Coronavirus include: Ian Balloch, Jane Townsend, Anthony Gallant, PC Steven Pollard, several from congregations of St Botolph's and Our Lady of the Missions, three "Brate Fliers", Karen Lilly's mother Alice, and Jason Reeve, associate of Tyson Bradley.

Milder cases have included: Bernadette Mitchell, Douglas Fent, Zoe Harris (new partner of Fent), Gareth and Fiona Spillet, Geoff and Pauline Carruthers, Alan Woods, Lisa Tarek, six Farrisford Town players, two Tesco Metro staff, three food-bank volunteers, two patients in the Hazel Ward, dentist Michael Wade, his receptionist Fay Pearce, four indoor market traders, Pip Runcolm and Dale Sheekey.

In March, **Annette**, **Annie** and **Morris** moved out of the cottage, feeling it too connected with events months before to allow healing. They live in a tiny cottage with a long, narrow garden of flowers and trees in Orion Mews, adjacent to Pegasus Lane.

Morris is well and friends with Rudyard. Their companionship in East Lane Park leaves Beezer free to run around with Lucas, Bunny, Archie, Basil, Caroline Vernon, Cindy and the other dogs.

Annette, furloughed, teaches via Zoom and short films on YouTube. Unsure if her contract will be renewed, she's applied for 2021 posts, and shortlisted for ETH Zurich and Georgia Institute of Technology.

But these months have endeared her to Britain She's uncertain whether to leave. This arose while volunteering for Farrisford Organics Cafe.

Closed to the public, **Farrisford Organics Cafe** makes hundreds of meals seven days a week distributed free (donations welcome) at several collection points. The operation expanded fast in April, run free by staff and volunteers, including Annette and 17 members of the public. Because of distancing, potatos are baked in houses, sauces made in St Botolph's Church Hall kitchen, pastries in the closed cafe and so on.

Farrisford Organics is in debt. Annette gave them £5,000 in May. She has a small car and helps drive meals to the villages. Annie can drive now, but too daunted by the Theory Test to make this formal. She works 12 hour days in the cafe kitchen and is reading "Jane Eyre" four pages a day without help.

After a spell in the Hazel Ward for clinical depression, **Beverley Dawes** moved to Bath in November 2019. Employed part-time in a hospital kitchen, she's applied to rejoin the police, but uncertain of being accepted.

Father Entreton and **Father Alan** conduct masses and community link-ups via Zoom. Father Alan devotes every spare hour to the Food Bank. Father Entreton keeps up e-mail and letters with Hazel Ward patients, and takes daily phone calls from them.

In a tiny old church by one of the Otterly to Bramham

Steam Railway's stations, **John and David Talbot** were married one sunny January day. The afternoon was spent on a luxurious, vintage train to-ing an fro-ing through a designated Area of Outstanding Beauty. Best man Jonty's deadpan speech reduced two carriages of guests to hysterics.

Mrs Bennett sent a card: *Best to both.*

Asda has delivered widely through lockdown. David has been employed by them as a van driver while the pandemic lasts. He is busy and happy.

Liu saw what was coming in early February and put her Crendlesham flat at quick-sale. She has enough money to keep **Danii**, **Jade** and herself during long months of salon closure. They all moved to a rented semi-detached house. Celebrity Hair & Nails, Huddersfield, re-opened on June 15th, like hundreds of thousands of businesses that day.

Yusef and Jade are very close. Jade visits him every day and is learning Arabic. Yousef draws a lot. He has twice been disciplined at the Centre and placed in solitary confinement for fighting. Plans for his release are unknown. Yousef was 13 on May 8th.

Azdek is staying with a family he met through his mosque. He is not allowed to work and must report to a goverment centre each week.

Marlon Wright is first-team central defender for Farrisford Town, 10 full games before lockdown. He has kept fit, and feels safe to go running in Farrisford's parks and streets for the first time in four years. He helps John at the Our Lady of the Missions food bank twice a week and thinks of Millie every day.

Millie Zena has not enjoyed lockdown in Manchester, living with a 33-year-old art teacher from her college who still sees his wife. She has no money or interest in studying. "I am going off my fucking head." She has started writing.

Tessa England privately despairs of the present Conservative party. But: "The town's voters have made my bed, therefore…"

The hoax Sherrier's Waterfall meeting about Dewy installed in the Tattler did go ahead. Six turned up to find The Town Hall was at least open for a Pilates class and Farrisford Horticultural Society's AGM. The six, who included **Emily Henderson**, talked in the foyer and didn't really notice lack of a leader. After an hour the meeting moved to the King's Arms. The group meets weekly on Zoom, has the backing of **Gregor Finniston**, and awaits formal publication of the planning application, which they will oppose. No application has yet been received yet. Downfall Developments has either given up, gone bankrupt, or is playing for time

Being sacked from The Tattler made Dewy unable to carry out her plan to arrange a smiliar meeting re the Fetton Vale fracking site. But **Cllr Cara Hanson** organised a persistent local campaign, backed by the Tattler, **Tessa England**, several Devon newspapers, Private Eye, Greenpeace and a petition of 8,000 signatures. What will happen is unclear.

Clellan plc ordered redundancies of 48 **Alpha Staplers** staff. Despite the resulting hardship, all, without exception, feel strangely happy. The office has lain empty since March. Hi-vis reception man **Keith Friar** goes in once a week to water the plants.

Dewy's favourites:

UK: hospiscare.co.uk/donate

USA: The Young Center for Immigrant Children's Rights: theyoungcenter.org/donate

Annie and Annette's favourites:

UK: The Trussell Trust Foodbanks:
trusselltrust.org/make-a-donation

Boston Terrier Rescue:
ukbostonterrierrescue.co.uk/pages/donate

USA: No Kid Hungry: nokidhungry.org/donate

US Boston Terrier rescue:
Americanbostonterrierrescue.org/donate

Support your local newspaper! Corrupt powers and secret planners don't like your paper reporting what they're up to. Please buy it every week!

Thanks to: Heather, Mark, Sophie, Anna, Rose, Gabe, Alison, May, Giles, Brendan & Christina, Ian, Tamar, Paul Salvette, Gwynydd Gosling, Theo, Sonia, Waveney, Phil, JH@9BD, Paul G. In Massachusetts: Ingrid, Mike, Tessa

Thanks also to **INQUEST**

Printed in Poland
by Amazon Fulfillment
Poland Sp. z o.o., Wrocław